MEANT TO BE

MEANT TO BE

MONICA MURPHY

PLAYLIST

"Out Of Love" - Alessia Cara
"Supalonely (Lownley)" - BENEE
"invisible string" - Taylor Swift
"Bye." - Mia Smith
"We Belong Together" - Mariah Carey
"i love you" - Billie Eilish
"Dreams" - Fleetwood Mac
"Lucid Dreams" - Juice WRLD
"HURT ME" - benny mayne
"you broke me first" - Tate McRae
"Walking On A Dream" - Empire of the Sun

Find the rest of the **Meant to Be** playlist here: https://bit.ly/
MTBplaylist

You were you,
    and I was I;
    we were two
    before our time.

I was yours,
    before I knew,
    and you have always
    been mine too.

— - LANG LEAV, *LOVE & MISADVENTURE*

Ava: **Eli, PLEASE call me.**
　　Eli: **...**

Ava: **Eli. I'm sorry about my parents. And what Jake said. And that you guys got in a fight. Please answer me.**

Ava: **Eli!!!**

Ava: **OMG if you don't respond to me right now I will...**

Ava: **I don't know what I'll do. Cry forever? Tell everyone you have a tiny dick? I know that's the LAST thing you want me to say!**

Ava: **Even though it would be a lie.**

Eli: ...

Ava: **Why won't you talk to me?**
Eli: **...**

Ava: **I NEED TO TALK TO YOU RIGHT NOW.**

Ava: **You can't ignore me forever!**

Eli: ...

Ava: **Maybe you can...**

CHAPTER 1

AVA

Can you die from a broken heart? Not asking for a friend.

The street is empty. Eli is long gone. I clutch my phone in my hand so tight, my fingers cramp up. He won't respond to my texts or my calls. He's ghosting me.

Pain radiates from my chest, a constant, throbbing reminder that Eli just destroyed me with a few choice words. He doesn't believe me. Worse, he doesn't trust me. I never told my brother about his parents. I don't know who did. Eli may have hinted at things and flat out told me his mother drank too much, but he never talked about his dad cheating. And why would I tell Jake any of that?

There's no way I ever would.

So who did?

I make my way to the backyard to find my entire family is gone. Glancing toward the kitchen windows, I see they're inside. Waiting for me. My parents and Jake, who's sitting on a barstool at the counter with a glower on his freshly abused face. It serves him right that Eli got a few punches in. I don't even feel bad that it happened, though I suppose I should.

Mom catches my gaze and raises her brows, the look on her face plainly telling me, *get in here.*

If I could turn around and run away, I would. I'd run and run and run until I was out of breath and so, so far, no one could find me again.

But I don't move. I definitely don't go inside. Not yet. Dad says something to Mom, and I can tell they're having a minor argument. About me? I wonder if she told Dad about our little secret. How she knew about Eli and I dating.

My gaze sweeps over the scene of the crime, AKA the spot where Jake and Eli fought. The moonlight catches on something on the ground, making it glint and I kneel down, reaching toward the shiny piece. My fingertips touch cool metal and I grasp it between my fingers.

A gold #1 pendant. Eli's. I feel around for the chain, almost desperately, on my hands and knees, but I don't see it. I wonder if he knows he lost it. I'm sure he'll be upset. He loves this necklace and the fact that his father gave it to him.

But would he want to know I have it? Maybe.

Maybe that'll be my one way to reach out to him. I have something he wants.

Unfortunately, from the way everything just went down, it's not me.

"Ava!" I lift my head to find my mother standing in the open doorway of the kitchen, her expression somber. "Come inside. *Now.*"

Rising to my feet, I clutch the pendant in my palm and march toward my punishment. I hang my head as I enter the kitchen, not wanting to look at any of them. Especially Jake. His anger radiates off of him, all of it aimed straight at me. Mom closes the door but, otherwise, says nothing. Neither does Jake. Or Dad.

It's a very uncomfortable silence full of thick tension that seems to last ten minutes, but is probably more like thirty seconds before my dad can't take it any longer.

"Ava." His tone is firm, yet gentle. He's mad, but he doesn't want to show it. "Tell me what Eli Bennett was doing at our house at this time of night."

Jake snorts. "What do you think—"

"Enough," Dad says, silencing my big brother.

This gives me immense satisfaction. Lifting my head, I meet my father's gaze head on. "We're together. Well...we were." The throb in my chest intensifies and I tell myself to ignore it.

But it pounds in my heart, my blood, my head. I can feel it everywhere, a rattling in my bones that reminds me what Eli said. What he did. How he looked at me with complete disgust. He doesn't want to be with me anymore.

My heart is shattered. A billion tiny jagged pieces lay at Eli's feet, and I don't know if it can ever be put together again without him.

"That still doesn't explain what he was doing at my house this late," Dad says, crossing his arms as he waits for my response. "Did he come over here uninvited?"

"No." I shake my head, my breath shaky when I exhale. "I invited him."

"Ava." Dad's sigh is long and weary. "You know you're not supposed to have a boy here that late."

Do I, though? Have those words ever been specifically said? We've never had a discussion about boys and if they can come over or not. Not that I know of. I slip my hands into my pockets, dropping the pendant inside. "We weren't going to do anything..."

My voice drifts and I remember I'm standing in front of them in a robe with only a pair of panties on underneath. That's all. If the night played out as originally planned, Eli and I were definitely going to do something.

3

And it would've been amazing.

The ache inside me just cuts deeper.

"Give me a break," Jake mutters, and this time it's Mom who says something.

"Jake, go to your room."

I chance a look at my brother as he jumps to his feet, his expression full of unabashed anger. "What do you mean? I should be in on this conversation, too, you know. I deserve to know why Eli is lurking around in our yard late at night. That guy hates me. He probably came here to jump me and beat my ass."

"That's a bunch of crap and you know it," I start, turning all of my frustration on my brother. "Eli came here for me, not you."

"I wouldn't put it past that fucker to pretend to get with you to get at me. Tell us you didn't have sex with him, Ava. Go ahead and deny it. That guy will fuck anything that moves," Jake says, and without hesitation, I lunge toward him, my arm extended and my fingers curled, connecting with Jake's jaw.

"Jesus!" Dad explodes, reaching for me. He wraps his arms around my waist and pulls me off of my brother before I can do any real damage. Mom darts in between Jake and I, her back to me, her hand on Jake's jaw as she assesses the damage.

The throbbing of my heart has stopped, at least. Now my knuckles throb from where they connected with Jake's face.

That was oddly satisfying.

"She freaking *hit* me," Jake says, sounding incredulous as he glares at me. "Please tell me she's gonna get in trouble."

"If you'd stop goading her, then maybe she wouldn't feel the need to punch you," Mom says, her voice icily calm. "Come on. Let's go to your room."

Before he can say anything further, Mom is escorting Jake out of the kitchen, leaving me and Dad alone.

Wincing, I cradle my hand, studying my already reddened knuckles as I lean against the counter. I didn't even think I got that good a hit on him, but maybe I did. I hope he's in pain. He deserves to suffer at least a little bit for what he said about Eli. And me.

"Does it hurt?" Dad asks.

"Yeah." I nod. "I don't know why I did that."

"I know why."

My head jerks up at his quietly spoken words. "Why?" My voice croaks like I have a sore throat.

"When we're hurting, we lash out. And right now, Ava, you're hurting." He opens his arms and I go to him without hesitation, clinging to my father as I cry into his T-shirt. His scent is familiar and comforting and I didn't realize I missed my daddy so much until right now, while my tears drench his shirt and my shoulders shake.

He just holds me and lets me cry, remaining silent. His fingers in my hair while he cradles me close. We stay like this for at least a few minutes, until my trembling eases and the tears start to dry up. Reluctantly, I pull away from him, wiping at my damp face with the sleeve of my robe. A little hiccup escapes me, and I cover my mouth, my gaze lifting to his to find him already watching me, that familiar, patient expression on his handsome face.

"You bottle it all up, like me," he finally says. When I frown, he continues. "When I was your age, I kept all my emotions inside. I didn't let anyone know they bothered me. Affected me. I was like a statue. Made of stone. You're warmer than that, Ava. You're more open than I ever was, but you still keep your emotions buried deep, and when you finally explode, this is the result."

A watery laugh escapes me. "What, me trying to punch my brother in the mouth?"

"That and you crying all over my shirt for the last five minutes." He smiles, but I can't. I'm still hurting, and while my father's love is definitely comforting, it's not enough.

Knowing Eli is upset with me, that he might not love me anymore…it's so painful I can hardly take it.

"I'm sorry I hit Jake," I say with a little sniff.

"Are you sorry you snuck Eli over to our house?"

I drop my head and nod once.

"Your mom and I were going to punish you," he continues. "But maybe you're punishing yourself enough already."

"Punish me," I say, the misery in my voice undeniable. "I deserve it."

"You'll have to apologize to Jake."

That'll be awful.

"I don't want to hear any details, but your mother and I can only assume why you snuck out of the house late at night to meet Eli," he says, and I lift my head, ready to explain myself. Dad shakes his head, silencing me. Which is a total relief. I don't want to say too much by accident, and he definitely doesn't want to hear it. "I don't know how I feel about your choice in boyfriends."

"Don't worry," I say miserably. "From what just happened, I figure Eli and I are through."

"Maybe it's for the best," Dad says gently.

No, I want to scream. Eli *is* the best.

The best one for me.

"You'll be grounded for a week. Go to school, go to practice, then come home. No hanging out with Ellie or your friends," Dad says, and I'm shocked. My parents have *never* grounded me. Like, never in my life. And I haven't given them any reason to either. Until now. Sneaking out to meet my boyfriend, eager to get naked with him in the hot tub. If they knew I've already been naked with him, they'd be so disappointed.

I hang my head in shame.

There are no other friends for me to hang out with but Ellie. Well, Dakota and Lindsey, but I'm sure once they find out I'm with Eli, they'll drop me. Maybe even Ellie too. I kept this from her and I'm not sure why, but I know her feelings will be hurt. I tell her everything. Until now.

And look where it got me.

"That's fine," I say to my feet. "I'm going to bed now. Okay?"

He hugs me again, but it's like I can hardly look at him. I'm grateful Mom didn't come back downstairs and join our conversation. I'm close to breaking as it is. Seeing the sympathy all over her face would destroy me.

I run up the stairs and hide away in my room, locking the door. Like a robot, I walk into the connected bathroom and shed my robe—making sure I leave the #1 pendant on the counter—and panties after I turn on the shower. Stepping under the hot, steaming water, I let it wash away all of my sins. My troubles. My cares.

But it doesn't work. They're all still there long after the water shuts off and my body is dry. Reminding me that I'm alone. No more Eli in my life. No more of his wicked smiles, his funny words, his tender looks and delicious kisses.

It's gone. All gone.

Lying in bed with the lamp still on, I clutch the #1 pendant between my fingers, turning it this way and that, watching the light glint off the gold.

At least I still have a piece of him.

CHAPTER 2

AVA

Tell me what I've heard isn't true.

This is what I wake up to at—I check my phone —10:09 in the morning. A text from Ellie, and I can tell just from those few words that she's upset with me.

With fear gripping my heart, I stare at the text, unsure how I should answer.

Maybe I shouldn't answer at all. I need to think about this first.

I set my phone on the bedside table, the usual desire to scroll through social media first thing in the morning squashed. I have no interest in seeing what people have to say, or endless photos of everyone having a good time last night. I'm guessing a lot of people are talking about me. About Eli.

No thanks.

It was hard to fall asleep. I laid in bed staring at the ceiling for what felt like hours, replaying everything that happened last night. It all started out so good. Going to comfort him after his game and making him laugh despite the loss. Kissing him in the backyard, anticipation racing through my veins at the mere thought of his expression when he first opened my robe.

But it all turned to total shit with Jake showing up. Eli didn't get to see me. And now…

He won't ever get to touch me again.

My phone buzzes again, and I check it. Another text from Ellie.

Are you going to answer me???

Dang it, I forgot the read notification still shows up in iMessage. Nibbling on my lower lip, I contemplate what I should tell her.

I decide to ask what she's talking about first.

What are you referring to?

Ellie: **Rumors are circulating that you're with Eli Bennett.**

Me: **Define with.**

Ellie: **That you two are together. Is it true?**

I wait for a moment, blinking back the tears that threaten to fall. I hate being so emotional. Sadness is such a useless feeling sometimes. All I want to do is wallow in it, and that can't be good.

Me: **It was true.**

There is no hesitation in her response.

Ellie: **What the hell???? And you never told me? Seriously????**

Me: **I didn't know how to tell you. I wasn't telling anyone.**

I don't bother mentioning Mom knew.

Ellie: **OMG we need to get together right now. Want to meet for coffee?**

Relief smacks me hard in the chest. I'm so grateful she's not mad, I almost burst into tears. I would give anything to be able to meet Ellie for coffee but…

Me: **I can't. I'm grounded.**

Ellie: **?????**

She can't believe it because it never happens.

I decide to FaceTime her and get some of this conversation over with. She, of course, answers immediately.

"I think you're going to need to start from the beginning," she tells me.

An exhausted sigh escapes me and I launch into the briefest description ever of my relationship with Eli, leading up to what happened last night at my house. By the time I'm finished, Ellie is watching me with bug eyes and her mouth hanging open. She snaps it shut when she realizes I'm waiting for her to say something.

"Um. Wow."

"I know."

She makes a little face. "You actually had sex with him? How—how was it?"

I burst out laughing. Out of all the details I shared with her—and yes, I was pretty brief, but I still told her everything, that's the only thing she wants to know.

"It was." I hesitate. There are no words to describe what those moments were like between me and Eli. "It was really good."

"And then he just dumps you right there in the middle of your road," she says.

"Yes," I say with a wince. "I still can't believe it happened."

"I can't believe it either." Now she's the one pausing. "I can't believe you kept this from me either."

"I didn't know how to tell you. I was afraid if I said anything to anyone, then you'd all try to convince me to end it," I confess.

"I would've never done that!" She rests her hand against her chest. I can tell she's thinking about it before she says, "Well, maybe I would've."

"Exactly. No one likes Eli. He's such a jerk on social media, everyone at our school hates him," I say.

"He totally brought that on himself you know," Ellie says.

"Oh I definitely know. He does too. I think he likes being the local shit-stirrer," I say. "But there's so much more to him than that. He's sweet and protective. He can say the worst things sometimes, but he can also say the absolute best things."

We're both quiet for a while. My mind goes back to last night and Eli's accusations. How much they hurt me, especially when they're not true. He only said those things because he was hurting too. He lashes out. He acts first and thinks later.

What he said…broke my heart. I'm still hurting.

I want to see him. Talk to him. But he's cut me off.

Completely.

"I'm sorry it ended so badly," Ellie finally says.

"So am I." But I'm not giving up yet. No way. I can't. It's been less than twenty-four hours. He has to still feel something for me. I need to convince him we belong together.

Because we do.

"I wish we could get together for coffee," Ellie says. "And I have to be at work by eleven. But let's try and talk later this afternoon?"

"For sure. Call me when you're done with work," I say.

Once our FaceTime call is over, I open up Snapchat and go to mine and Eli's conversation thread. He's my best friend on Snap. We have the red heart next to each other's names.

Well.

We did.

The red heart is gone. Eli's name isn't even on my friends list. Meaning, he either unadded me or blocked me.

WTF?

I search for his name, but it doesn't come up. He *blocked* me.

Seriously. What an asshole.

Now the tears flow, steady and strong. I just let them out, burying my face in my pillow and sobbing into it. I cry like this for a while, my arms wrapped tightly around the pillow. Like I want to strangle it.

Kind of like how I want to strangle Eli.

He must be really mad at me to block me. Of course, not so long ago I blocked him. Only because I was so sick of his obnoxious stories about my brother, about his team, his school and ours. He used to brag all the time.

He still does. But somehow, it went from obnoxious to endearing.

There's a knock on my door, and before I can even say come in, my mother walks into the room, her blonde hair pulled into a high ponytail, wearing my high school colors, which are the same colors as Beck's youth league football team.

"We're leaving in half an hour," she announces when she stops at the foot of my bed.

I barely lift my face away from the pillow to peek at her. "Where are we going?"

"Beck's game."

I sink my face into the pillow. "I don't wanna go."

"Too bad. You have to. Your dad doesn't want to leave you alone in the house." She smacks my leg lightly. "Get up, girly, and get ready."

"Are you saying Dad doesn't trust me to be alone in the house?" I sit up and push my hair out of my face, dread making my stomach roil.

"More like, he doesn't trust Eli Bennett." She raises her brows.

I snort. "Don't worry. He's not going to come over. He's

through with me. Blocked me on Snap and everything." My lower lip trembles and I press down hard on it. I don't want to cry anymore. Especially not right now, in front of Mom.

"Maybe that's a good thing?" she asks, making a little face.

I laugh bitterly. "You sound like Dad."

"We do hang out together a lot, so that's not a surprise." She tilts her head, giving me a look. A look that says, get up and get ready. "Now come on, get dressed and come downstairs so you can have something to eat before we leave."

"I'm not hungry," I say with a groan. The thought of food grosses me out. I'd probably throw up if I ate anything. I feel sick over the breakup.

I still can't believe we actually broke up.

"Then at least get out of bed and get some clothes on. Your father is already tense over everything that happened last night," Mom says. "You don't want to make him angrier."

"Is he really angry with me?" Dread fills me. There is nothing worse than making my parents mad. They give us the "we're so disappointed in you" speech and that is the absolute worst. I hate all of this.

"I don't know if angry is the right word, but he's definitely not happy with you or your brother," Mom says.

"Does Jake have to go today?" God, I really hope not.

Mom shakes her head. "He had to go clean the bleachers at the high school. He's already there."

The bleachers at our stadium are the worst. The janitors do their best to keep up, but it's an impossible job. There is so much garbage beneath those bleachers, it would take hours. Days. Months, even, to clean them all. Sometimes, the coaches make the football players who got in trouble clean them. It's a really sucky job.

"I'm sure Jake will blame me for that," I say, throwing back my duvet cover and sheets and climbing out of bed.

"If he does, tell him he needs to take a good, long look at

himself in the mirror. He was terrible last night," Mom says, sounding irritable. "You weren't much better, hitting your brother like you did."

"He made me mad." At least my dad understood why I did it. Doesn't make it right, though.

"That's not a good enough reason. If that was the case, Jake would haul off and hit you all of the time," Mom says, making complete sense.

I straighten my bed as best I can before I go to my closet to pick out clothes to wear. "Daddy says I have to apologize to him."

"As well you should."

"Jake should apologize to me, too."

"What? For watching out for his sister, who happens to be seeing a boy who hates him?" I turn just in time to see Mom's brows shoot up.

I blow out a frustrated breath. "It's not like that. Eli wasn't with me to get at Jake."

She says nothing, which tells me she's on Jake's side with this one.

So frustrating. It's like no one listens to me. No one takes the time to try and understand what Eli and I shared. They don't care. Now I'm left alone, completely heartbroken. My relationship ruined and on top of everything else, I'm grounded.

I don't like disappointing my parents, but I don't think they're actually listening to me either. They've already made up their minds about Eli.

They're against him. Against our relationship.

But I don't care.

If they continue to feel that way and Eli and I do end up getting back together, their disapproval isn't going to stop me from seeing him. Eli and I belong together. It doesn't matter what my family thinks.

"I need to get ready." My tone is snotty. I am giving myself major Autumn vibes right now. She would use the same tone with Mom when she still lived at home. "Can you leave please, so I can get dressed?"

Mom turns and marches out of my room, slamming the door behind her. I jump at the sound, sinking my teeth into my lower lip. Great, now she's mad at me too. I sort of want to cry all over again.

But I don't. Instead, I tell myself to stop being sad. Easier said than done, but if I have to be out in public, I have to look normal. Like nothing's bothering me. If I seem broken, and someone sends me a sympathetic look, then I'll break even more.

Even though my entire world just collapsed last night. No big deal.

* * *

I'M SITTING at the top of the stands at the very high school Eli attends. Talk about a stab in the heart. If I'd known the league game would be here, I would've fought harder to get out of coming. I might've even offered to clean the bleachers at our school with Jake, and that's one of the worst jobs on the planet.

Instead, I'm sitting here surrounded by all things purple and gold, staring at the field where Eli plays. Where he practices every day. This is his school, his home away from home, and it's like I can feel him surround me, wrapping all around me. His essence is here on that football field, in the very air that I'm breathing, and it's killing me slowly.

No one would know it, though. My expression is forced indifference. Mom isn't talking to me much. Still mad for the way I treated her earlier, which I suppose I deserve. Dad was so focused on Beck and the upcoming game as we drove here, he was oblivious to the tension between Mom and me.

And here I was, worried over him being angry with me.

Once we got to the school, Dad escorted my brother over to his team and stayed. He's basically one of their coaches, though he has no official title. Leaving Mom and I alone. We went into the bleachers, me choosing to sit at the top, Mom sitting one bench below.

Halfway through Beck's game, I spot Wyatt Cahill walking in front of the stands, accompanied by his parents. I sit up straighter, grateful to spot a familiar face.

"Why's Wyatt here?" I ask Mom.

"His little brother plays for the senior team. He's in the eighth grade," Mom says, turning to look at me. "You finally over your little pouting session?"

I send her an irritated look before I train my gaze on Wyatt. I will him to look up at the stands. To see me. I want to talk to him. To hear what people are saying. If they're saying anything about me.

Thankfully, he finally glances up to scan the crowd, and our gazes meet. He smiles. I smile in return, though it feels foreign.

He says something to his mom before he starts running up the steps, heading straight for me.

"Can I talk to Wyatt for a little bit?" I ask Mom, praying she doesn't deny me.

"I suppose," she says reluctantly. "But I'm not budging."

"That's fine." I hate that she feels like she has to supervise my every move. It's clear my parents don't trust me.

I need to earn their trust back, but I'm not going to do anything to please them that in turn risks my relationship with Eli. He means *everything* to me. I refuse to give up on him. On us.

No matter how my parents might feel.

16

"Hey." Wyatt stands on one of the benches below mine so he's eye level, a friendly smile on his face. "Can I sit with you?" His question is for me.

"Sure." I pat the empty spot beside me. Mom is sitting directly in front of me, meaning she'll be able to hear every single thing we say, which means I'm going to have to be covert with this conversation.

"How are you?" he asks, once he settles in beside me, though not too close. "I thought I would see you at Sorrento's last night."

"Yeah. No." I shake my head. "I never go to his house parties. You should know this by now."

"True." He chuckles. "Jake keeps you under lock and key from us. Not sure how you managed to find a boyfriend, considering how closely your brother watches over you."

"About that." One of the team moms calls my mother's name before she comes bounding up the steps, sitting right next to her and pulling her into a quick hug, both of them laughing and chattering away.

I couldn't have made that happen more perfectly if I tried. Mom won't be paying any attention to me.

"About what?" Wyatt asks, after I haven't said anything else.

"Have you heard any—rumors about me?" I send him a pointed look.

He frowns. "Like what?"

"Like me being with…" I lower my voice to the barest whisper. "Eli Bennett."

His frown deepens. "Who the hell is saying that?"

"I don't know. That's why I'm asking you." I assume his strong reaction is based on the fact that I'm referring to Eli—and that Wyatt doesn't like him at all.

"I haven't heard anything," he says, glancing around before his gaze settles on the field, and the giant black

17

mustang painted in the center. He makes a face. "I really hate that prick."

"Everyone does," I murmur. Except me.

"We all have our reasons, especially since he gives them to us. He is an endless shit talker." He glances at me quickly, then does a double take. "Wait a minute. Is the rumor you're asking about actually—true?"

I tilt my head, picking at the artful tear in the right knee of my jeans. I pluck at the white thread again and again, unsure of how I should answer. "Maybe we were a thing. But we're not anymore."

"No shit," he breathes, sounding mildly horrified. I can't look at him. His reaction is exactly what I was afraid of. I'm sure everyone will feel the same way Wyatt does. Shock and horror. "Are you for real right now, Ava?"

I grab hold of his arm for a second, sending him a meaningful look. "Shh, don't talk so loud. But—yes. We were together. Briefly."

Too brief.

His eyes are wide as he slowly shakes his head. "That is some crazy shit."

"I know."

"Does Jake know? He's going to freaking lose it when he—"

"He knows," I interrupt. "It all fell apart last night at my house. They got into a fight."

"Your brother and Eli?" Wyatt says.

I nod. "Yes." I'm tempted to give him more details, but I've probably already said too much. "We ended it."

"You ended it," he clarifies.

I don't correct him. I'm too ashamed of the fact that Eli dumped me. That he doesn't believe me.

That hurts more than I want to admit.

"You didn't see any mention of our names together on social media?" I ask Wyatt.

"No, not at all. I was at Tony's most of the night, after the game, so I guess I wasn't on my phone much. I saw your brother leave with Hannah, which surprised me. I thought they'd stay the night." His cheeks turn ruddy because the only reason any couple stays the night at Tony's is to hook up.

"I don't know why Jake came home when he did," I say, my voice bitter. "I just wanted to make sure you haven't heard anything. And that Jake hasn't said anything to you."

"I haven't seen him since the party."

"Right." I chew on my thumbnail, watching the boys out on the field. Beck is smashing into the mini Mustangs with a vengeance. This rivalry is bred from elementary school on, I swear. "I just don't want people to talk about us."

"If no one really knows about it, then why would they be talking?" Wyatt asks.

I don't have an answer for that. I also don't admit that I ran over to the Mustang side after the game and tried to cheer Eli up over their loss. Why broadcast it to Wyatt if he doesn't know? Maybe no one saw us after all. That would make things so much easier.

My phone buzzes in the back pocket of my jeans, and I grab it to see it's Ellie calling me. I decide to answer.

"Where are you?" she asks.

"At Beck's football game. They're playing against the Mustangs, so we're at their high school."

Ellie sucks in a breath. "Get out of here."

"I'm not lying." I glance over at Wyatt, who's watching me, but immediately looks away when he gets caught. "Wyatt's sitting with me, so he's making the game tolerable."

"Well, I wanted to ask if you're going to the dance tonight," Ellie says. "You are the homecoming princess of the junior class, you know. Are your parents going to still keep you at home or what?"

I go completely still. Oh shit. The homecoming dance. How could I forget? Am I grounded from that too? I sort of have to be there.

"Um, I don't know." I send a cautious look in my mother's direction, who's not paying attention to me at all. "I could ask."

"You really should. Call me when you get home and let me know if you're going or not." She pauses. "I really want you there. It won't be any fun without you."

Please. I'm the mopey girl, sad over a breakup. I won't be any fun.

"I'll call you when I get home. I promise." I end the call and smile at Wyatt. "Sorry about that."

"No problem," he says, smiling in return before he glances down for a moment. "You, ah, want to hang out after the game?"

I make a sad face. "I can't. I, uh, have to go home with my family." I don't want to admit I'm grounded.

"I'll see you at the dance later then," Wyatt says casually, his gaze locked on mine.

"Yeah," I say with a little laugh. "I'll see you at the dance."

"Maybe we could hang out there," he says, and I see all the hope filling his dark eyes.

Oh boy. I decide to change the subject.

"Why'd you come to today's game?" I ask him, my voice light. Like I don't have a care in the world.

"My brother really wanted me to come watch his game. It's an important one to him, considering who they're playing," Wyatt explains. "Just like it's an important one for us. I haven't been to any of his games yet this season, so I had to show up."

"You're a good big brother." I reach over and pat his knee, keeping it completely platonic.

Though it's pretty obvious that if I told Wyatt I was interested in him, he'd admit the same. He likes me. And while it's flattering, and yes, he would probably make a great boyfriend, he isn't the boy I want. Not even close.

The boy I want doesn't want me.

And that is absolutely devastating.

CHAPTER 3

ELI

I stay in bed all damn morning, because it's all I can manage to do. No one's home. Mom is still gone for the weekend, getting drunk by the beach. A weekend wasted. I was supposed to go with Ava to her homecoming dance tonight. Could've shown everybody at that lousy school the prettiest girl in the junior class—hell the entire school—chose me as her date. Chose me as her boyfriend. After the dance, I would've brought her back to my house, got her naked. Done all the dirty things I've been thinking about doing to her all night long.

But then she and the rest of her family had to go and ruin everything.

If I could smother myself with my pillow I would; I'm so pissed off and miserable. Girls suck. Their overprotective douchebag brothers do too.

Finally giving up on sleep, I eventually reach over and blindly grab my phone to look at the time.

It's freaking past noon. Can't remember the last time I slept that long.

I check my notifications and I'm immediately bored.

Same thing, different day. I see I have a Snap from Jackson Rivers and I open it, curious. We don't communicate over Snap. Like ever.

He's sent me someone else's story. A name I don't recognize. It's video of a game in the middle of the day. At my high school. It's the youth league football, I can tell. The camera pans across the crowd in the stands, before zooming in on a couple sitting at the very top of the bleachers. They're engrossed in conversation. I'd recognize that blonde hair anywhere.

Ava.

And she's with that motherfucker Wyatt.

Anger simmers in my gut as they continue to talk, their heads bent close to each other's. At one point, Ava reaches over and pats Wyatt's knee.

What the fuck?

There's a little message on the video at the end.

Who predicted this couple to happen? Yours truly.

Jackson sent his own message to me as well.

Did you see this?? I thought she was your girl.

Look at how fast she moved on. I'm sure her parents would give their stamp of approval for that boring asshole. And how the hell do I answer Jackson?

I decide to be honest.

She was. Not anymore.

Jackson: **That was fast. You broke it off?**

Me: **Yep. Pretty girls are poison.**

Jackson: **Finally you see the light. Welcome to the club.**

Me: **What club?**

Jackson: **The fuck girls club.**

I have to make a joke with that. Seriously, he just set it up perfectly.

Me: **I am always down to fuck a girl, son. Been a member of that club for years.**

He sends me a string of laughing face emojis as his reply.

There. That sounded like the normal me. Carefree, will fuck anything Eli. I need to keep up the persona.

Even though I feel like I'm slowly dying inside.

I don't cry. I don't like feeling sad. I mask sadness with anger. Anger is a proactive emotion. It propels you to do something versus sadness, which just leaves you a broken heap on the floor. Or in your bed.

Or a ghost wandering the halls of your house. Which is what I'm currently doing.

I force myself to eat something but it tastes like cardboard. I take a shower and consider jerking off, but I'm not in the mood. That's when I know something's seriously wrong. And yeah, there is definitely something wrong. A girl broke my heart. She lied to me. Told her brother all of my family secrets like they were meaningless. Like she didn't care.

That's what makes me the maddest. She didn't care about me. Did she ever? How'd I fall for that? Was it her beautiful green eyes? The sweet way she responded to me when I touched her? The way she kissed me? The taste of her lips? How she argued with me almost every single time we were together, to the point I wanted to make her angry because mad Ava turns me on? I could go on and on.

I scrub my hands over my face before I glare at my reflection in the mirror, annoyed with my train of thoughts. I should forget her. Forget everything that happened between us.

But I can't.

It's steamy in the bathroom and the towel I had wrapped around my waist drops to the floor, heaping at my ankles. I kick it out of the way and take a step back, checking myself out in the mirror because...

Why the hell not?

My face is a mess thanks to Jake Callahan. A gash on my forehead, a nasty bruise on my cheek. The worst is the swollen corner of my mouth. When his fist connected there, my teeth cut into my flesh.

I look like hell.

Feel like it too.

Pushing past my fucked-up face, I check the rest of myself out. I work hard on this body and it shows. I look good, minus my beat-up face. I've got a decent sized dick. I'm almost eighteen and in my prime. I look like a fucking catch.

But maybe that's another problem. Looks can be deceiving. I'm not the catch everyone thinks I am. I'm broken and fucked up. I have a shitty family and sometimes I feel like there's no hope for me. My attitude is for shit, and I know it, yet I don't do anything to stop myself from being who I am.

I'm just me. Take it or leave it. And I suppose Ava chose to leave it.

Fuck her.

Jesus, fuck me too, if I'm being real right now.

I'm about to exit the bathroom when I notice something. More like a lack of something.

Where's my necklace? My #1 pendant?

Once I return to my bedroom, I search around for it, but it's nowhere. The necklace must've broke during the fight with Jake 'the asshole' Callahan last night.

Damn it. I loved that necklace. Figures Jake would tear it off my neck. I bet it's lying discarded in a bush in their backyard. Maybe Jake found it later and tossed it in the trash.

Asshole.

Brenden texted me earlier asking if we could get together and I decide to invite a bunch of my friends over to hang out. I mean, why not? Mom's gone and I have the house to myself. We can drink and smoke in the backyard and there's no one I need to hide it from. I have some vodka in the house and, of course, a stash of wine bottles, but none of us want to drink that shit. Jackson promises to bring the beer, and Cory—yes, I invited his pathetic ass, so what—says he'll bring some whiskey and Coke.

I don't even need the Coke. I'll drink that whiskey straight. Fuck it.

I'm gonna get fucked up.

They arrive at my house within the hour, Brenden and Jackson and Cory and a few others. They bring along their favorite party favors—blunts and booze and snacks. We congregate outside by the pool, though it's cooler today. If anyone's jumping in the water, it's either because someone dared them to, or they get so drunk they don't care how cold it is.

That'll probably end up being me later tonight. Too drunk to care.

"What the hell happened to your face?" Jackson asks me, after we've all settled in at the table with the giant blue umbrella.

I send him a death glare. "It ran into someone's fist."

"You've been fighting a lot," Brenden says, sounding like he's my dad.

"You included," Jackson reminds him, which makes Brenden seal his lips shut.

"I got into a fight with Callahan last night," I say, deciding I may as well lay it all out.

"No shit?" Jackson lifts his brows. "Who won?"

"It was a tie." And I lost the girl, so I guess I'm the silent loser.

"Uh huh." Jackson smiles. Tips his beer bottle to his lips and takes a loud swallow.

Smug fucker.

I need to change the subject.

"You break up with Kayla?" I ask Brenden.

Brenden takes a hit off the blunt before he passes it to me, tilting his head back and exhaling a stream of smoke. "Nope."

"What? You chicken motherfucker." I lean over and slap his arm, making him glare at me as he rubs the spot where I hit him. "You said you were going to do it. When I left the party last night, you told me you were about to let her down easy."

"Yeah well." His cheeks turn crimson and he looks down at his lap, where I swear to God, it looks like he's twiddling his thumbs. "We, uh, never got around to talking much last night."

"They fucked," Cory adds, who I guess is eavesdropping on our conversation.

"No shit," I mumble with the blunt between my lips.

"Big mistake," Jackson mutters at the same time.

Brenden glares at the both of us. "What, is it so impossible to think a girl would want to have sex with me?"

I pluck the blunt from my mouth. "I never said that," I start and Jackson just laughs.

"It has nothing to do with your sex appeal and everything to do with the fact that you just had sex with a complete psycho," Jackson explains, his tone dead serious. "That chick is toxic. She's trying to change your entire life. And now that you've come inside her? Forget it. You're dunzo."

I send Brenden a sympathetic look, but say nothing. Pretty sure the only other time he had sex was with some chick our junior year who was a sophomore. A transfer student who showed up halfway through the year. He befriended her, not to get in her panties—that's more my shitty style—but because he's an actual nice person. Things happened and they eventually did it.

Then she transferred out again. And he was devastated. That girl was the only distraction he ever had from his undying lust for Kayla.

27

"They don't change just because you have sex with them," I tell Brenden, my voice low. Jackson and Cory are having their own conversation about girls and sex. I'm sure Cory has zero experience there. A few other guys wander into my backyard and Jackson gets up to greet them like he's the host of this party. Which is fine by me. I'm not in the mood. "She'll still be the same person she was before you dipped your wick in her wax."

Brenden makes a face. "Dipped my wick in her wax? Where do you come up with this shit?"

I shrug. "What can I say? I should be a songwriter."

"Sure. You're a regular fucking poet." Brenden grabs the whiskey bottle Cory left on the table and takes a swig straight from it, instead of being a classy motherfucker and pouring himself a glass. He wipes his mouth with the back of his hand before he says, "It wasn't even that good. She just sort of...laid there the whole time. Didn't do much. Said a bunch of stuff that felt fake."

"Lots of moaning and groaning and acting like she's gonna come any second?" I ask.

Brenden nods, looking as miserable as I feel. Damn, is this shit catchy or what? "Yeah. I was into her at first, but I realized what she was saying sounded really—fake, you know? Kind of turned me off. She wanted me to go down on her afterward, but I was over it."

These are all horrible signs. He's not into this chick. Not anymore. I would've gone down on Ava for hours if she would've let me. Didn't matter when or where. I'd lick that pretty pussy until she was about fifty orgasms in, begging and squirming, desperate to get away from my demon mouth. I was that horny for her all the damn time.

Reaching down, I subtly adjust my junk in my jeans, so it doesn't press against the seam. I'm *still* horny for her. Not like I can just shut off my feelings for her in less than twenty-four hours. I'm not that cold.

"We should invite some girls over," Cory suggests to us, and Brenden and I both immediately shake our heads no.

"Kayla will kill me," Brenden says morosely.

Cory looks to me, his expression hopeful. "You're always up for having girls over." He bursts out laughing, slapping the edge of the table. "Ha! Get it? Up for? Because your dick is always hard for random chicks?"

If I could kick him in the face, I would. But I don't. There's no need to cause a scene at my own damn house. I've done enough fighting. My face and body still ache from where Jake got his few punches in last night.

I hope he's in traumatic pain. I hope his dick is limp for life, too.

"He's still mourning the loss of his secret hottie," Jackson says, as he approaches our table.

I send him an angry glare, and Jackson immediately clamps his lips shut.

"What secret hottie?" Brenden asks.

"It's nothing," I tell him with a faint smile, my heart literally aching once the words leave my mouth. I called her nothing. She treated me like I meant nothing. That's how it felt last night.

I am so melodramatic right now, it's pathetic.

"Yeah, what secret hottie?" Cory pipes up.

See what Jackson started? How am I supposed to explain myself out of this one?

"Ah, he was chasing after Ava Callahan just to piss her brother off, and it worked. That fucker was steaming mad. Am I right, Bennett?" Jackson sends me a pointed look, silently asking me to play along.

"Yeah. Totally." I laugh, but it sounds so goddamn fake, I stop. "Just having a little fun."

"She *is* a hottie," Cory says, making Jackson laugh.

"Right? Completely fuckable. I bet she'd be a fun ride." Jackson's eyes are dancing when they meet mine. He knows he's riling me up. I send him a death glare in return, but it doesn't seem to faze him.

"Getting it on with the freshly crowned homecoming queen, what could be better?" Cory asks, with a giant grin right before he takes a swig of beer.

I take another huge hit off the blunt, holding the smoke in my lungs for as long as I can stand it before I exhale. I set the blunt in an ashtray we only bring out for special occasions such as this and lean back in my chair. "She was the princess," I say, my voice deceptively calm.

Cory frowns. "What?"

"Ava was the homecoming princess, not the queen," I remind him.

"Oh." He shrugs. "Who gives a shit?"

I do, I want to say. *I give a shit.*

Because I *do* give a shit, even though she clearly doesn't. All that crying and carrying on last night was a dog and pony show. She was just upset over getting caught. I'm used to this sort of thing. My mother acts this way at least once a week.

"I wouldn't mind fucking her with the crown still on her head," Jackson says, that devil's grin on his face making me think he's really enjoying this. Torturing my ass. Describing exactly what I did to Ava the night she won. "Maybe have her on her knees sucking my dick, wearing nothing but that little sash they give them?"

I clench my hands into fists but otherwise, say nothing.

"Maybe she doesn't have a problem with sharing. You know, sharing is caring." Jackson turns all of his attention on me, grinning like a loon. "Would you share that hot little piece with me?"

I lunge from my chair like a madman, and the next thing I

know, I'm standing directly in front of Jackson, my fingers curled around the collar of his sweatshirt, yanking his face into mine. That cocky smile fades, and his eyes go wide. "Shut the fuck up before I make you eat my fist," I growl at him.

Jackson just tips his head back and laughs, the asshole. "Give it up. You've got mad feelings for her, even though you don't want to admit it. She wasn't just some casual piece to get with to make her stupid brother mad."

"What the hell are you two talking about?" Brenden asks, appearing thoroughly confused. Cory's eyes are wide as he watches us. The other guys have stopped talking as well. We are pure entertainment for them right now.

Without a word, I shove Jackson away from me before I stalk back toward the house, slamming the door behind me. The door opens seconds later, and I hear Jackson calling my name, so I turn around in the living room and wait for him to come to me.

"I was just giving you shit," he says, as he comes to a halt a few feet away. "No harm, no foul, right?"

"Fuck you," I spit out, not even trying to hide my hostility. "Why'd you even bring her up?"

"You were sitting there like a little pussy, completely miserable because of whatever that bitch did to you last night, and I don't like it. Now she's with that Wyatt fucker, like you never mattered in the first place." He points at me, his expression fierce. "This is what they do, man. This is how they act."

"Who?"

"Women! Girls! *Bitches!* Whatever you want to call them. This is the way they operate almost every single time. They don't care about us. They just use us. And when they're done, they dispose of us like one of those raggedy, black smudged makeup wipes they use on their faces at night. Straight to the trash. Gone and forgotten." Jackson's face is red, he's so heated.

I just stare at him for a long, quiet moment, slowly shaking my head. "Who the hell did such a number on you?"

"Every female in my life, that's who. Fuck them," he mutters, just before he strides past me and exits my house.

Damn. And I thought I had issues.

CHAPTER 4

AVA

I'm not usually one to beg but...

"Please, please, *please*," I say, stressing the last word and stretching it out. "I'm the homecoming princess, Mom! I have to go to the dance!"

"You don't have to go anywhere," Mom says irritably, as she moves about the kitchen. She's prepping for dinner and barely looking at me. Jake and Dad holed up in his study when Jake came home, and they haven't left it since. I feel like Mom's barely tolerating me and Dad and Jake don't even want to look at me. I am on everyone's bad side in this house right now, and it sucks.

I realize begging and whining isn't going to work on Mom, so I decide to change tactics. "Just—let me go tonight. That's it. That's all I'll ask for. My one duty to the school before I'm grounded forever."

She sends me a look, like she doesn't believe me. "You're not grounded forever. Your dad said a week. If it would've been up to me? I'd given you two."

Those last words she mumbles under her breath. And thank God it wasn't up to her.

"I'm grounded for a week, and that's fine. I deserve it. I probably deserve more. I broke yours and Dad's trust, and it's going to take a while for me to earn it back. I know this," I explain.

Mom turns to face me, crossing her arms and leaning against the kitchen counter. "Funny you bring this up. Your brother wants to go to the dance too."

Ooh, this can work in my favor. "I'm sure he does."

She watches me for a while, her lips pursed. She's thinking, and that's always a good sign. "I'm a complete pushover."

"No, you're not," I say, my tone completely innocent.

"Yes, I definitely am," she says with a sigh. "I'll let you both go, as long as your father agrees. But there's one condition."

"What is it?" I ask.

"You and Jake have to go together."

I completely deflate. "But he'll want to take Hannah."

"Oh, he can take her. The two of you can go pick Hannah up," Mom suggests brightly. "Together."

"He's still mad at me." And I'm still mad at him.

"Well, this will be a great way for you two to get over your differences. And if you can't manage that tonight, then maybe you should stay home after all." Mom smiles, looking very pleased with herself.

"Okay, fine. I can handle this," I say softly, more to myself than her. "You'll really let us go?"

She nods. "You really want to go? I figured you'd be miserable after what happened last night."

I'm completely miserable. But I'd rather distract myself with the dance than stay home and cry into my pillow. I've done that enough already today. If I go to the dance, I can make my appearance as homecoming princess, and possibly see what's being said about Eli and me.

More than anything, I need a distraction.

Jake chooses that exact moment to enter the kitchen, coming to an abrupt halt when he spots me. "Can I talk to you, Mom? Privately?"

"We're all in this together. You can talk to me here," she says sweetly.

My brother doesn't even look in my direction. "Dad says I can go to the dance, but I have to take Ava."

"That's right."

"What if I don't want to?"

"Then you can't go," Mom says evenly, her gaze shifting to me. "You two are a package deal tonight."

"I'm sorry I hit you," I tell him, deciding to get it over with. "Even though you made me mad."

His jaw locks. Mom covers her mouth, like she might laugh. "That was a bit of a backhanded apology, don't you think?"

I shrug. Don't bother saying anything else.

"Hannah will be devastated if I don't take her to the dance," Jake says.

"You can take her. Your sister is going to tag along. And when the dance is over, I expect you two to come straight home. When is the dance over?"

"Ten," I tell Mom.

Jake glances over at me with annoyance. What? Did he want me to lie?

"Then I want you home by ten-thirty at the absolute latest. You call or text us if something happens." She smiles. "I hope you two can work out your differences on the drive to the school."

"Yeah," I say.

Good luck with that.

* * *

35

I KNOW some high schools make their homecoming dance a big deal, but ours isn't one of them. There's no need for the girls to wear a fancy dress or the boys to wear nice pants and a tie. It's causal, it's fun and yes, I'm wearing my tiara and sash because this is the last time I get the chance to, and yes, I'm even wearing a dress. Though it's a simple one. Sleeveless black that hits about mid-thigh. I found a gold chain for Eli's lost pendant and now I'm wearing it, safely tucked beneath the high neckline of my dress.

It might burn his ass to know I'm wearing it, but too bad. I'm not going to give up on him—on us yet.

Jake sends me a text fifteen minutes before we're supposed to leave.

Meet me at my truck at 6:45.

I'm sure if things were normal, Jake would be taking Hannah out to dinner first. They'd go to the dance, but bail out early and do God knows what.

If I were still with Eli, we'd do much of the same. Everyone would talk about Eli's arrival, he'd jump all over the dance floor and act like a fool, making me laugh. Then we could leave and go back to his house and do...

Whatever we want.

My heart aches at the lost opportunity. At the loss of Eli. I hate this. I hate that he's blocked me—because yes, he also blocked my phone number and unfollowed me on Instagram. It's like he wants nothing to do with me. He's erased me from his life, like we were never together.

Like I never existed.

Ellie's meeting me at the dance. Lindsey and Dakota tried to get me to come over and get ready with them, but I knew Mom wouldn't let me, so I told them I couldn't. Going to this dance will either be the distraction I desperately need...

Or a huge mistake.

I'm outside waiting by Jake's truck when he approaches

with a blank expression on his face. Again, he won't look at me. I wonder how difficult that is, not making eye contact with someone? He's been doing it for the past twenty-four hours and I'm impressed he's kept it up this long.

Impressed and hurt, because come on. I'm his sister. I wasn't with Eli to get at Jake. He has to know that.

Jake rounds the front of his truck and climbs into the driver's seat. I get into the passenger seat. He starts the engine. Backs out of the driveway. Starts down the road.

We don't say a word to each other.

I mess around on my phone for a little bit, but I can't concentrate. The tension between us is like a living, breathing thing in the close confines of his truck, and when I can't take it anymore, I break first.

"Are you going to be mad at me forever?"

He remains quiet for what feels like an eternity before he says, "Maybe."

"We never did this to get at you."

"That's what you keep saying. God knows what Eli's plan was," Jake mutters.

"His plan had nothing to do with you, and everything to do with me." I poke my thumb against my chest, making contact with the pendant beneath my dress. "You were basically begging him to start a fight with you, considering all the shitty things you said. You do realize this."

"Right. Sure." His snarky response makes me curl my fingers into fists. "That asshole was begging for a reason to throw punches."

"You definitely gave him a reason. And now he hates me," I say.

"He sure dumped your ass fast," he says with a smirk.

If I could smack that smirk off his stupid smug face, I so would. "Because he thinks I told you about his family."

"His fucked-up parents are nothing new, you know," Jake says. "I heard that rumor a while ago."

"From who?" I ask, my mind racing with the possibilities.

"It doesn't matter," he says with an indifferent shrug.

"It totally matters. That's the entire reason Eli dumped me," I tell him, annoyed.

"It's a secret," he says. "Can't reveal my sources."

"Please." I roll my eyes. "Stop acting like you're trying to protect someone and tell me who said it."

"You might not want to know," he says cryptically.

"Oh, now I definitely want to know." Especially since he's acting so shady.

He says nothing for a while and I say nothing either. I just wait. My temper rising with every second that passes. "You know, I'm not that sorry I hit you," I tell him, after he still hasn't revealed anything.

Jake actually has the nerve to laugh. The jerk. "No shit. I don't regret fucking up your boyfriend's face either."

"He's not my boyfriend anymore," I say bitterly.

"Thank God," he mutters.

"Just tell me who told you that stuff about Eli."

He glances over at me quickly, his mouth set in a firm line, his eyes dark and mysterious, until he finally blurts it out. "It was Cami."

My mouth falls open. "You're telling me Eli opened up to her and confessed all of his messy family secrets? And now you're trying to actually *protect* her?"

Why does everyone do this kind of thing for Cami? Protect her all the time? She's not a nice person.

At all.

"It didn't go down like that. She happened to be over at his house once, and was waiting outside for him when his mom walked out and spotted her. Eli's mom came at her, ranting and raving and calling Cami one of her husband's sluts," Jake explains.

"Oh God." That sounds awful.

"Yeah, so Eli had to step in and break things up between them. I guess he tried to explain to his mom that Cami was actually there for him, but his mom didn't believe him. Cami told me she was really drunk. And borderline violent," Jake continues.

This doesn't surprise me at all. She doesn't sound like a pleasant person, and that's an understatement. I also don't think she cares much about what Eli's doing, which I think is why he acts the way he does.

Careless. Rude. Reckless. Mean. Crude.

He doesn't give a shit because no one else does either.

Except me. I care. Probably too much.

"Why would Cami tell you all of this, when she knows how angry Eli makes you?" I ask, curious. Eli is supposedly the main reason Jake and Cami broke up one of the—two? Three?—times they were together. Cami spilling her guts and giving him all of these details is surprising.

"When she tried to get back with me recently, she confessed everything one night. Figured I could use it against him someday." Another smirk appears on my brother's face. "Guess it finally worked."

Anger simmers in my belly. I can't believe this happened because of stupid Cami. She ruins everything. She's in the middle of everyone's business, always making a mess of people's lives.

It still hurts Eli would be so quick to believe I'd rat him out like that. Did he have so little faith in me? Did I not matter to him at all?

It feels like it.

Though I guess everyone in his life has let him down at

one point or another. Maybe he expects it and is almost—used to it. Deep down, maybe he always believed eventually I would betray him too.

"When you said that to him, it took everything out of him," I tell Jake. "And he believes I'm the one who told you. Not Cami. Not anyone else. Me. That's why he ended it."

"Listen, do you want me to be real with you right now?" He quickly glances over at me.

No, I want to tell him. Absolutely not. Please keep your opinions to yourself.

My answer is a shrug.

"You're better off without him, Ava. That guy isn't good for you. He's crazy. He's a total fuckin' wild card and you never know what you're gonna get. I can't stand by and let you be with that guy, knowing everything I know about him," Jake explains. "I know you're pissed at me. I'm still pissed at you, too. But someday, you're going to thank me for getting that guy out of your life. I know you will."

I just stare at him in shock. He firmly believes every word he's saying. He did me a favor. He *saved* me from Eli.

No. He drove the boy I love out of my life, and now I'm alone.

"I love him," I whisper. "Maybe you don't understand what that's like, being in love, though maybe you do with Hannah." My voice raises as Jake comes to a stop at the light in the middle of town. "I'm in love with Eli Bennett, and nothing is going to change my mind about him. I will do whatever it takes to get him to talk to me, to listen to me. I will tell him what you told me, and I will make him see I didn't do this. What happened isn't my fault."

"You can't tell him shit," Jake mutters, glaring at me. "This is between me and you."

"I'm telling him," I say firmly. "You can be mad at me for years over this, but I'm telling him the truth."

"Such bullshit. I knew I shouldn't have said anything."

"I love how loyal you are to me," I throw at him.

"I just fucking love how loyal you are to me!" The words explode out of Jake's mouth, making me rear back so I can get away from him. "I'm your brother. Our dad is my coach. You cheer for our team. Yet you're fucking around with our biggest rival's quarterback? What the fuck is wrong with you, Ava? He's nothing special! He's all talk and no action! Stop being such a follower and quit falling for his bullshit!"

I blink at him, shocked by Jake's outburst. Why does this all have to be about the rivalry? Last night's game was the last time they ever have to play against each other again. The rivalry is done. Dead. Jake needs to move on.

So does Eli.

"Pretty sure he's over you anyway," Jake continues with a sneer on his face. "I saw on his IG story earlier that he's having a party at his place with all of his fellow loser bros, and there are a bunch of chicks there too."

"Stop talking," I tell him, irritated. "Just—I don't want to hear it." And I can't look at his story, thanks to getting blocked. Can't ask Jake to look at it either. I'm sure he'll offer up a running commentary during the entire thing, every word a slam against Eli and his friends.

"Truth hurts, right, baby sister? Lizzo doesn't lie." The light turns green, and Jake turns onto the street that leads to Hannah's apartment building.

His smugness makes me want to choke him. I don't normally have such violent thoughts toward my brother, but his nonchalance about this entire situation is maddening. My world has just collapsed, and he's treating it like a big joke. Instead of being sympathetic, he's hitting me with, "I told you so," platitudes.

We say nothing else as we drive to Hannah's. Once we pull into her building's parking lot, I switch to the backseat of the truck while Jake goes to Hannah's door to pick her up. And once she's in the car, I talk to her, acting like nothing is going on.

But deep down, I'm quietly seething. How dare my brother dismiss my feelings for Eli so easily?

How fucking dare he?

CHAPTER 5

ELI

Goddamn, there's a girl grinding her ass on my junk.

With my vision blurred, thanks to all the weed and whiskey I've consumed the past few hours, I lean the chair back, so it's only on two legs, trying to get away from her swiveling backside. Music is playing, the beat throbbing, it's so damn loud. We're still in the backyard, and it's way past quiet hours in the neighborhood, but no one's said anything yet. I figure we're home free. The lots are pretty big here, and I've had giant parties before, somehow never disturbing the neighbors.

Thank God.

The girl turns and I shake my head a little, getting the hair out of my eyes. It's Josie Price. She's smiling at me, the look on her face hungry, her eyes glowing as she stares at me. "Girl, you need to leave before something bad happens."

She comes for me, throwing one long leg over my thighs, before she settles in, straddling my lap and resting her arms on my shoulders. "That's exactly what I'm hoping for."

I guess those were the wrong words to say. This girl is

dying for someone to fuck her raw, and I assume I'm her target tonight.

Shit, I've been her target for a while. And I'm so damn drunk, I might not be able to control myself.

"You need to go," I tell her, trying my best to hold back the burp that wants to escape.

But I can't. Out it comes and she makes a disgusted face, but otherwise does nothing. "I'm not going anywhere."

"I'm a taken man." God, I sound drunk as hell.

Maybe because I am drunk as hell.

Her eyebrows shoot up. "By who? I don't see anyone around here staking their claim on you."

"She doesn't go to our school." A hiccup slips past my lips, and I blink Josie back into focus. "She's beautiful."

A scowl forms on Josie's face. "Who is she?"

"You don't know her."

"I'm sure I do."

"Nah. Doubt it." I lean in close, my mouth right at her ear. "Her pussy feels like heaven. Tastes like it too."

This would drive a normal girl to run away from me, pissed off I'd bring up another girl's pussy.

Not Josie.

"I'll let you taste mine right now if you're interested," she purrs.

Nope. Don't want to taste that.

"I'm gonna pass," I say, as I lean back in my chair once more, trying to get away from her.

She mock pouts. "That's a shame. I think we'd make a perfect couple."

"Really." I take her in. Like, I really look at her. She's pretty, I can't lie. Long dark hair. Glossy red lips. Very nice tits, can't lie about that either. She's been into me since forever, and I've always pushed her aside. Not sure why.

Definitely can't jump on it now.

44

"Really," Josie says with a firm nod as she leans in, her face in mine. Those glossy lips coming closer. "If you'd let me, I'd rock your world."

I burst out laughing. "I think it's the other way around, sweetheart."

"Oh I know you'll rock my world, Eli. Like I told you, I'd give you a taste of what you could have. Right now." She takes that moment to slowly grind her pussy right on top of my jean-covered dick. Pretty sure she's not wearing any panties either. "And I'd taste you right back."

Something Ava and I never did. Her giving me a blow job. It is the stuff of my fantasies, especially because it didn't happen between us.

"You offering up a free BJ?" This isn't the first time Josie's done this. Probably won't be the last.

Why doesn't Josie go hit up some other guy? She's hot. Nice enough. Why is she always chasing after me?

She nods slowly as she gyrates her hips. "Let's go up to your room."

It hasn't even been twenty-four hours since Ava and I split up. There is no fucking way I can go through with this. It doesn't matter how drunk I am. "Gonna have to take a rain check."

"*What?*" Those pouty lips turn into a frown. "You're a fucking tease, you know that?"

Josie hops off my lap and yanks her dress down, glaring at me. I can only watch her with amusement in return.

"I don't mean to tease you."

"Well, you do. I don't know how many times I've thrown myself at you, yet you always turn me down," Josie says.

"Stop doing it then. I don't deserve your attention." And that's the damn truth.

She stalks off in a huff, steam practically pouring from her ears, and I shake my head. Laugh. Hiccup. Burp again.

45

I'm fucked up.

Glancing around, the party is still in full swing. There are people in the kitchen. There are probably people in the bedrooms, random hookups happening behind closed doors. Brenden is sitting at the table nearby, locked in an intense conversation with Kayla, the bitch. She doesn't look happy. Neither does he.

He should've already broken up with her.

Kayla suddenly leaps to her feet and storms off.

"Kayla!" Brenden calls as he stands, glancing over at me. I send him a look. One that says, *don't do it.*

But the bastard doesn't listen to me, or decipher my look, because he goes chasing after her, straight into the house.

Great. Those two will probably fight and eventually fuck in one of the bedrooms.

No one talks to me. We're at my house and not one motherfucker is saying a word to me. How's that for friends? How's that for people trying to get to know me better? Granted, most of my friends here are currently talking to girls, so I suppose I can't blame them. Even Cory is talking to some chick—wait a minute, is that Josie he's with?

Yep. Now she's gyrating and grinding on his junk. And the look on Cory's face is one that should be documented. He appears stunned. And happier than a pig in shit.

I yank my phone out of my back pocket and open up Instagram, then unblock Ava so I can see her profile. I'm an idiot for overreacting like I did. I blocked her ass everywhere. I didn't want her to have access to me. More like I didn't want to see her. I click on her story to find an image of her posing with her friend, Ellie. She's in a simple black dress that clings to her in all the right places, plus she's wearing her homecoming royalty sash and the tiara. The caption below it says, "Homecoming dance!"

It's freakin' painful to witness her like that. Smiling and

looking normal. Posing with her friend. Her life is just fine, when mine is falling apart. I zoom in on her face, and while she's smiling, I can also see sadness in her green gaze.

That makes me feel a little more satisfied.

I start looking through other IG stories, oblivious to what's going on around me. I follow a lot of people who go to Ava's school, so I'm seeing a lot of footage from tonight's dance preparations and arrivals. There's even video of Ava and motherfuckin' Wyatt dancing together. At least it's not a slow dance. And the guy can't dance for shit.

Seeing them together burns my gut. Burns my ass. Is that what Ava really wants? I doubt it. No one else can make her feel like I do. I remember what she looked like in my bed, her naked body flushed, her eyes sparkling when she curled her finger around my necklace and tugged me down for a kiss. I remember the way she tasted, the sounds she made when I made her feel good.

When I made her come.

Groaning, I slide out of IG and go into my text messages, not giving a damn. I'm weak. Weak like Brenden is with Kayla. He should break up with her, yet he's probably boning her right now.

I should cut off all contact with Ava, but here I am, texting her.

Hope you have fun at your stupid dance with that asshole who probably wouldn't know where your clit is, even if you drew him a map with a giant lit-up arrow pointing to it.

I send the text before I can overthink it. The moment I hear the swoosh noise indicating it's gone, I have mad regret. I shouldn't talk to her. I should leave her alone. She lied to me. She blabbed all my business to her asshole brother and then that asshole threw it in my face. Made me look and feel like a fool. In front of their parents, no less.

I hate him.

Ava doesn't respond. I'm sure she's too busy trying to help Wyatt find her love button.

Another groan leaves me. I can't even believe I thought the words love button. I know my Ava. She's not fucking around with that guy. Not when only last night she was ready to jump me in her hot tub. My girl doesn't move that fast. Even though I blocked her on social media. Even though I told her we were through.

Even though I said all sorts of things I shouldn't have…

I rise to my feet and make my way across the patio and into the house, passing by people who call my name, though I don't stop for them. I stagger through the kitchen then head down the hall that leads to the bedrooms. Throwing open my bedroom door, I find my good friend Brenden, sitting on the edge of the mattress, his jeans bunched around his ankles and Kayla kneeling in front of him. I don't need to see it all to know that she's got her lips wrapped around the tip of his dick.

"God damnit, couldn't you have at least got a blow job in the spare bedroom?" I yell at Brenden.

Kayla jumps to her feet with a guilty expression on her face, swiping at her mouth with shaky fingers. Brenden stands and yanks his jeans up, wincing when he stuffs his semi-erect cock back inside. "Sorry," he mutters, his gaze focused on the floor. "The other room was taken."

"At least you didn't fuck on my bed." I see the covers are all messed up. Can't remember if I made it today or not. For all I know, they—or someone else—already fucked there.

Great.

"You shouldn't just barge into rooms unannounced," Kayla says with a sneer.

"Uh, this is my bedroom so you can go fuck the hell off," I tell her, as I enter the room fully. "Now get out."

Kayla turns to Brenden. "Are you really going to let him talk to me like that?"

He shrugs. "Well, he is right. It is his bedroom."

Her mouth drops open. I cross my arms, watching her. Wobble over a little to the left before I right myself. Brenden finishes buttoning up his jeans, looking put out.

Probably pissed I interrupted his BJ, but that's on him.

"You're an asshole," Kayla says directly to me.

"Right back at you," I tell her, earning a huff from her before she storms out.

She pauses in the hallway, glancing over her shoulder. "Are you coming?" she asks Brenden.

"Unfortunately no, thanks to me," I say, just before I crack up.

Brenden glares at me for a moment before he exhales loudly. "Give me a minute, okay baby?"

"Don't you baby me," she whisper-hisses before she leaves the room.

"Damn it." He rubs the back of his neck, turning toward me. "Sorry about that."

"I don't think I'd care if it was anyone else who had their lips wrapped around your dick. But that chick?" I point at my empty doorway. "I can't stand her."

"I should break up with her, huh." He doesn't even ask it like a question. This dude *knows* he should get rid of her.

"She's toxic as fuck. But if she gives good head, maybe she's a keeper," I tell him with a shrug.

"I need to go talk to her. I'm sure she's pissed. She's always pissed." He sends me a look. "You crashing or what? Want me to get rid of people?"

"Yes. All of them. Thank you. I'm definitely gonna crash. I can barely keep my eyes open," I tell him, as I yank my hoodie off and throw it on the floor, then promptly trip over it as I head for my bed.

I need sleep.

"No problem. I'll have Jackson help me round everyone up and out of here."

Once Brenden's gone, I stumble around my room like an idiot. Shedding the rest of my clothes. Tripping over more shit on the floor before I collapse onto the bed. I lean over the mattress and grab my phone out of my jeans' pocket to see if I have any notifications.

Nothing.

I hate my life. I hate that I pushed the only good thing out of it. I always just act and not think. So what if she told her brother about my parents? Pretty sure lots of people know we're a mess. It doesn't matter anyway.

All that matters is I pushed Ava away. I want to pull her back in.

Opening up our texts, I send her another one.

I'm a stupid fucker who knows exactly where your clit is, and how much you like it when I touch it. Don't ever forget that. And don't give Wyatt the map. Or your heart. That belongs to me.

* * *

"OH MY GOD! ELI!"

That's what I wake up to on a fine Sunday morn—oops, it's past one o'clock—afternoon. I crack my eyes open, wincing at the pain in my head. I smoked too much smoke and drank too much drink and now I am paying the price.

Like hallucinating my mother's screeching coming from downstairs.

Rubbing a hand over my face, I turn over on my side, so I'm facing the wall, letting my eyes fall back closed. The pounding in my head is real. It's intense and it's awful. Swear to God, I hear shitty Muffin Top barking her head off. The sound of my mother's feet stomping in the hallway at a breakneck speed. My bedroom door slamming open. The sickening scent of my mother's perfume.

"What the hell, Eli! You had a *party* here? Just how many people were in my house last night?"

I roll back over so I'm facing her. The look on her face—she would kill me with it if she could. I close my eyes so I don't have to see her. God, why did she even bother coming back? "Maybe."

"And you weren't courteous enough to clean up after yourselves?"

Cracking my eyes back open, I see that she's standing there waiting for an answer, her hands resting on her hips.

"I thought you weren't coming back until later tonight." More like I thought I had plenty of time.

She looks around my bedroom, her nose crinkled in disgust. "This place is a pigsty. My entire house looks like a pigsty, and it's all your fault." She marches over to my bed and drags the blanket off of me, then takes a step back. "Get up."

"Give me a minute." Glad I wasn't naked under the blanket.

"Get. Up." Mom kicks out her foot and nudges my calf with her toes. She has high heeled sandals on and I swear the pointy heel scrapes against my skin and leaves a mark. "And start cleaning the house. Tackle the kitchen first. Now."

I glare at her. She glares at me in return. I don't say a word. Neither does she.

Finally, she stomps out of my room, Muffin chasing after her down the hall. I had no idea the stupid dog followed her to my room, but didn't actually come inside. The little bitch is scared of me.

Good.

Sitting up, I hold my head in my hands, leaning over so I

can rest my elbows on my knees. I close my eyes and try to ignore the roiling in my stomach. I don't feel good. I need pain reliever. And food. I'm hungry, but I'm also nauseated.

Getting drunk and high immediately after a big breakup isn't the smartest move I've ever made.

Speaking of my breakup…

I grab my phone and check my notifications.

There's a text from Ava.

My heart pounding, I open and read it.

I haven't forgotten.

That's all it says.

What the fuck is she talking about?

I toss my phone onto the bed and get up and stretch. Then go to the bathroom and piss. Scrub a hand through my hair and glare at my reflection before I brush my teeth. I can hear Mom banging around downstairs, throwing stuff away while she curses up a storm. So glad she's home. Can't wait to help her.

I change into fresh clothes and collapse on the bed once more, re-reading what I sent her last night. Focusing on the last things I said.

I'm a stupid fucker who knows exactly where your clit is, and how much you like it when I touch it. Don't ever forget that. And don't give Wyatt the map. Or your heart. That belongs to me.

Now her response makes more sense. She hasn't forgotten that I own her heart.

Good.

She owns mine too.

CHAPTER 6

AVA

I wake up Sunday full of hope. Seeing Eli's text after the dance last night sent my heart into complete overdrive. It wouldn't stop pounding. I pondered over what to say to him for what felt like hours.

Of course, it was a typical Eli text. Talking about my clit and how Wyatt would never find it.

I wouldn't let him anyway so no worries there.

Then the second text where he basically claimed me—sometimes that rubs me the wrong way. Last night? I was all about it.

This morning, I'm still about it.

Once I got home and calmed down last night, I finally came up with a simple response. Something true. I haven't forgotten anything. I am still his if he'll still be mine. I can't shut off my feelings like a faucet. I'm not a complete psycho.

The dance was fun at first, but that was me faking it. Faking smiles, faking laughter, faking having fun while dancing with Wyatt. My issues with my brother aren't resolved. Nothing is. I'm half a person who feels like a piece of myself is missing. I'm hollow inside.

Wyatt kept wanting to dance with me and I danced a few songs with him, before I finally begged off and Ellie took over. They danced and danced while I sat alone at a table, watching everyone have fun. Dakota and Lindsey were dancing with guys from the football team. Jake and Hannah snuck off somewhere. Cami and Diego made a big entrance, causing the room to ripple with gossip. Jocelyn, Diego's very recent, very long-term ex, didn't bother making an appearance.

Word on the street is she's pregnant. I really hope that's not the case.

Marty and his new boyfriend showed up about halfway through the night, and they sat with me for a while. But I was such a sad sack, they took off, so they could go dance, and I couldn't blame them. I wouldn't want to be around me either.

They make a cute couple.

The drive home was uneventful. I know Jake resented me telling Mom when the dance got out. He didn't have much time to be with Hannah before we had to head back to the house. He didn't talk to me the entire ride, and I didn't either. It was only then that I checked my phone and spotted the texts from Eli.

Talk about giving me hope. And now I sit here, waiting.

Because he still hasn't responded. And it's killing me. Where is he? What's going on? I have no idea how long everyone stayed at his house and partied. Maybe he's still sleeping it off. He looked really drunk in one story I watched.

I scroll through all the Instagram stories, hoping to catch a glimpse of Eli. There are a lot of photos and videos from last night, both from our dance and the party at Eli's house. There's a video of Wyatt and I dancing, which I hope Eli didn't see. We look awkward anyway, though there's a caption on the video that says: *I predict this is the new couple of the year.*

Um no.

There's a story on Snapchat that makes me sit up in bed and re-watch it. There's something happening in the background and I bring my phone up closer, squinting at it. Eli is sitting in a chair all by himself. And this gorgeous girl, wearing a really short dress, is literally grinding her butt against his crotch.

He's watching her shifting ass with an amazed expression on his stupidly handsome face like he's in a trance. Raised eyebrows, lips slightly parted, gaze locked on her swiveling hips. Perhaps he likes what he sees?

My heart cracks. Like, my chest literally hurts. I press my palm against it, as if that could put my heart back together, but it's no use. The pain radiates, streaming through my blood, into my bones, and I close my eyes for a moment, trying to catch my breath.

The pain mixes with anger too. It's a powerful surge of emotion that leaves me shaking.

I want to kill Eli Bennett with my bare hands.

Rage filling me, I exit out of the story and go to my text messages, my fingers flying as I type out my message to Eli.

Too busy with that girl you were with last night to respond to me? I hope she fu—

Pausing, I backspace on every single word I just wrote, until there's nothing. Just a blinking cursor. I can't respond to him. Not like this. Not right now. Not while I'm so freaking angry. Is he really with that girl?

Maybe not.

Should I care?

Absolutely. He ended it with me less than two days ago and sent me texts last night that basically said he still wants me. Then he gets a lap dance from some girl who probably ended up in his bed. Or maybe with her lips wrapped around his...

No. I can't even imagine it. Let alone think the words.

God. Eli Bennett is beyond infuriating.

"Ava! Breakfast is ready!" my mom calls from downstairs.

With a sigh, I grab a velvet scrunchie from my bedside table, twisting my hair into a messy bun, before I exit my room and head down the stairs. Dad and Beck are already sitting at the table. Jake is grabbing a glass of orange juice from the refrigerator. Mom is currently piling a bunch of French toast slices on a platter.

Hmm. My favorite breakfast. This feels like a setup. At the very least, vaguely suspicious.

"Sit, sit," Mom commands when she sees me standing there, contemplating if I should stay or go. "I made your favorites."

"I see that," I say, as I go to the table and settle into my usual seat. "Why?"

"Can't I make my daughter her favorite breakfast?" Mom asks, as she brings over a plate with freshly cooked bacon piled on it to the table.

"You sleep well?" Dad asks me, his gaze glued to his phone.

"You want coffee, Ava?" Mom asks.

"Sure," I tell her before I glance over at my father. He's watching me now, and I see wariness in his expression. He's probably still upset with me. I suppose I can't blame him. All illusions of his sweet baby girl are shattered, thanks to me sneaking the rival bad boy into our backyard. "And yes, I slept great. Like a baby."

All lies. I tossed and turned last night, wishing Eli would respond to me, yet he never did. Why not? No way could he have been with that girl.

Could he?

My entire body burns just thinking about him being with someone else.

Jake eventually sits, and so does Mom, bringing my coffee and the platter of French toast with her. We all dig in, passing the French toast around. All of us grabbing some bacon. No one's talking. The only sound in the room is silverware against plates and chewing.

I feel on edge. Like they're going to spring something on me halfway through the meal. Do they know something I don't? Am I somehow going to end up in more trouble than I originally thought? God, Eli didn't take any...compromising photos of me, did he? And then release them onto social media so anyone could see them? Including my parents?

Okay, my imagination is running wild. Taking a deep, calming breath, I reach for my coffee and sip from the cup, my gaze latching onto Jake's to find he's already watching me.

"Your so-called boyfriend has already moved on," he says snidely.

These are the first words he's said to me since we sat at the table.

"Jake." Dad's voice is firm. "Stop."

"What? It's true." The faintest smirk curls his lips. "I saw it on Snapchat. Some girl was giving him a lap dance, and it looked like he was enjoying it."

My heart drops, and my appetite disappears. I push the plate away from me, crossing my arms. "Are you purposely being a dick or does it just come naturally to you?"

"Ava!" Mom sends me one of those *don't you dare* looks, but currently, it has zero effect on me.

"At least I'm not the dick who chases after randos at a party and calls it nursing my broken heart," Jake says, just before he takes a bite of bacon.

I'm so glad he can eat. That he can feel completely normal

while I'm sitting here trying my best not to fall apart. And when I say fall apart, I don't mean cry and carry on. I mean get pissed and scream at him.

Yeah. Right now I'm mad as hell.

"Aren't you going to tell him to stop?" I ask my parents, pointing at Jake, who leans back in his chair with a smirk on his face. The same expression he had when he told me about Eli's party last night. "He's purposely trying to make me mad by saying awful things about Eli."

"Please. Have some respect for the family and don't say his name at the table," Jake says, earning a dark glare from Dad, though he says nothing.

"Ignore him," Mom says, waving her hand at Jake as if she's easily dismissing his behavior.

"I can't. He's sitting right there, bullshit just pouring out of his mouth." I glare at Jake, but he won't even look at me.

Again.

Ugh.

Big brothers are the freaking worst.

"Ava, please. Language," Dad says.

"I'm so sick of this." I rise from my chair and storm off, ignoring their calls. Dad says my name, his tone sharp. Mom asks me to come back. Beck asks what's wrong with me.

Jake just laughs.

I go to my room and grab my phone to see if I have a reply from Eli yet. I purposely left it in my room, so I could get away from it during breakfast. Get away from the incessant need to keep checking it for a notification from Eli.

Nothing. There's nothing.

Slamming my phone onto the table, I crawl into bed and pull my comforter over my body until it's even covering my head. I just let loose and cry into my pillow, silently cursing all boys, especially one in particular. I cry myself to sleep, grateful no one knocks on my door or asks if I'm okay. I'd rather be alone. With my thoughts.

With my sadness.

* * *

MONDAY MORNING and I'm exiting my car when the warning bell rings. I pick up my pace as I stride through the parking lot, though I know I'm wasting my time. I'm definitely going to be late to class. And I never get to school this late, but my motivation was zero this morning when the alarm went off.

Yesterday I did nothing but lie in bed. Waiting for Eli to respond to my text, which he never did. I still can't believe it. He sends me those texts and then…nothing.

Really? So rude.

So typical.

My being late to school sets the tone for the rest of the day. I'm running late to everything. I fail a surprise pop quiz in math. My English teacher assigns a five-page essay on the latest book I was supposed to read—guess what, I didn't—and it's due Thursday. Every single teacher I have dumped mega homework on us. By the time school is finished and I'm at the cheer room getting ready for practice, my nerves are frayed. I change quickly into my practice clothes and decide to have a snack before we start. Dakota and Lindsey aren't here yet, so I sit by myself on the floor, munching on Cheez-its when Brandy walks in, her gaze searching, before it lands on me.

And stays.

"I heard a rumor about you," she says as she slowly approaches me.

I go completely still. Brandy hates the Mustangs with everything she's got. She went to this high school too back in the day, so she can't stand our rival team. Like sometimes she's worse than us students.

Okay fine, most of the time she is.

"What did you hear?" I ask carefully, setting the snack bag of crackers aside.

She kneels down in front of me, her voice lowering. "Actually, it wasn't a rumor. It was something I saw with my own two eyes."

I blink at her, but remain quiet.

"You know what I saw, don't you?" She tilts her head.

"I can take a guess," I say slowly.

"Damn it, Ava! Really?" She settles in beside me and now we're both leaning against the wall. She reaches for my crackers and takes a few, tossing them in her mouth.

"You never told me what you saw," I say innocently.

She sends me a pointed look. "I don't want to say it out loud, considering who's in this room and they're probably all trying to listen."

I look around, spotting Cami and Baylee watching us with speculative gazes. They quickly avert their eyes when I catch them.

"Yeah. Them," Brandy says when she sees who I'm staring at. "They'll tear you apart over this, especially you-know-who."

Cami. Who dated Eli. And my brother. Supposedly at the same time.

Closing my eyes, I exhale raggedly. "I have terrible taste in men."

"Yeah, you do," Brandy readily agrees with a little laugh. "Are you two really a thing or what?"

"We're more in the *or what* territory right now." I hesitate for only a moment before I decide to confess. I really like Brandy. And she knows how to keep a secret. I probably shouldn't be talking like this with my coach, but screw it. "Jake found out about us."

"Oh man. I bet that was bad."

"Whatever you're thinking, it was worse," I tell her, making her laugh. But she's not laughing at me. I can tell her laugh is one of sympathy. She's feeling for me.

And I appreciate that. I'd rather laugh at the absurdity of it all. It's either that or I fall apart crying yet again.

Considering I've been on the verge of tears since late Friday night, I'll gladly take this distraction.

"You can't keep it up with that kid," she says, her voice dead serious. "He's insane."

"You've heard the stories?"

"Honey, I've heard every single one. You kids think you move through this school and that the adults are oblivious to what's going on. More like you guys are oblivious." She leans in close. "I know all."

That's terrifying.

"Most of us do," she continues. "And we hear what's happening at the other schools too. Crazy shit. Things I'm not even allowed to tell you."

Okay. That's ominous.

"So yeah. I know all about Eli Bennett and what a troublemaker he is. All the stories he's made trash-talking your brother and the rest of the football team. The car accidents and the girls and the fights and that one time when he got caught on campus with a wax pen." She clamps her lips shut and shakes her head once. "Wasn't supposed to reveal that one. Forget I said that. And the teachers threatening to flunk him if he doesn't get his act together. Yep, I have heard every single story there is out there about Eli Bennett."

"You didn't hear about the two of us together until Friday," I tell her, feeling pretty proud of our secret keeping abilities.

"And I'm assuming you two are already done."

I look away from her, not wanting to believe it. "Maybe. Maybe not."

"He's bad news, Ava. But sometimes, we like bad news. We think we can turn it into good. Most of the time, it's already a lost cause." Brandy pats my shoulder before she rises to her feet. "You should give Wyatt a chance. He's a sweet guy—he's good. I bet he'd make the perfect boyfriend."

He doesn't make my heart race like Eli. He doesn't make me feel like I could burst into flames from just a look. Like Eli. Wyatt is nice. He's cute. He's smart. Brandy isn't wrong. He'd make a great boyfriend.

Not for me though.

Never for me.

CHAPTER 7

ELI

*S*hit goes wrong for me all the time, swear to God. Sometimes, I can blame myself. I know I get myself into sketchy situations, and it's usually because of my big mouth. Other times, it's the idiots *in* my life who fuck things over for me.

Like my parents.

I spent the majority of my Sunday afternoon cleaning up the house and backyard after the party. Mom followed me everywhere I went to ensure I 'tidied it up to her satisfaction', direct quote, nagging my ass the entire time. Once that torture was over, I was expected to go to dinner with my father. He wouldn't stop telling me what a disappointment I was, until I got so pissed off, I told him to go to hell. He asked me very calmly to hand over my phone. So reluctantly, I did.

And now I have no way to communicate with anyone. Specifically, my blonde heartless beauty, who I never responded to in the first place. Which is fine, you know? I keep making Ava sweat, when that girl has made me sweat on a regular basis throughout our relationship.

Now, our relationship is probably a pile of ashes after a

raging fire. We were an inferno, we burned hot and bright, and now we're out. No smoldering. No coals. It's just…

Gone.

I tend to get a little poetic when I think about that girl and our crazy relationship. It's just the romantic in me, I guess.

It's Monday, and my school is a cesspool of gossip. My party is all the talk. So is the homecoming dance at the other high school. The dance I should've been at. And there's another topic of conversation too.

"I tried to keep it down, but word on campus is you were banging Ava Callahan," Jackson tells me at lunch.

I send him an annoyed look before I tear into a bag of Dorito's. "Don't even bring up her name."

"Oh. Let me rephrase that then." Jackson leans across the picnic table we're sitting at and stares deep into my eyes. "People are saying you fucked she-who-shall-not-be-named just to get revenge on her brother."

"Let them talk. They'd still say that, even if they knew the truth." I stare into the open bag of Dorito's, remembering Ava and I sharing some in my room that one night when I told her I loved her.

Shit.

"And what's the truth?" Jackson asks, his voice full of mocking innocence.

That I love her? That having sex with her was unlike any other experience I've ever had? Can't admit that. I'll look like a complete pussy. He already knows I've still got a boner for her. Look at how he said all that shit about her Saturday and I almost beat his face in.

Besides, *do* I still love her? Was what happened between us love to begin with?

"The truth is, I had a relationship with Ava, and right

now, we're taking a break," I explain, before I stuff a couple of chips in my mouth and start eating.

"You're taking a break? Get outta here. That's the kiss of death for a relationship dude, and you know it." Jackson shakes his head, a little smile curling his lips. He's enjoying this shit. My life has turned into nonstop drama, and Jackson is totally here for it. "I could give you a list of couples we both know who went on a break and eventually broke up. Every single one of them."

We're not on an official break, so I guess I wouldn't put us on that list. "Who cares what we're doing? Besides, I thought no one noticed us hugging on the sidelines except you."

"You thought wrong."

Unease washes over me, but I act like his words don't bother me. "Provide some evidence then."

"Haven't you been on your phone this weekend? So much evidence keeps popping up, I can't track it all."

"I wasn't on my phone much yesterday. I was busy cleaning up after our party. You are all a bunch of messy motherfuckers." Jackson laughs. I glare. "And then I went to dinner with my dad, which was a total fiasco. He called me insubordinate—I don't even know what the hell that means —and that I give my mother endless shit. Gave me a big old lecture, forced me to promise I would do better, I agreed, and that asshole still took my phone away from me. I'm phoneless." Told me if I was such a big man who wouldn't listen to reason, then maybe I could pay for my own phone. The bastard.

Jackson rolls his eyes. "Parents suck," he says, as he starts swiping on his phone, going in and out of apps. He turns his phone in my direction and shows me a story that's been screen recorded with me sitting in the background, getting that lap dance from Josie.

"Are you the one who screen recorded this?" I ask him. It seems like such a girl thing to do.

"Nope."

"Why are you showing it to me? What's it got to do with me and Ava?" I'm irritated just watching it. You can tell by my expression I'm drunk as hell and barely staying upright. Josie is really working it, but for the most part, I look pretty bored. Or ready to pass out.

"I heard Ava saw that video and lost her damn mind," Jackson says.

I shake my head, thoroughly confused. "Where are you hearing this stuff?"

"I have sources," he says ominously. "Now. Then there's this." He shows me a photo. It's taken from a distance, like across the football field, and you can see me and Ava on the sidelines, my arms wrapped tightly around her, her head pressed against my chest. Her comforting me after that colossal loss. My heart fucking aches just looking at it, because we were different then. Before her brother said all that shit and made me come for him.

Well, I could've controlled my impulses, but at that moment, it felt so goddamn right to kick his ass, I went on pure instinct.

"Where did you find this? Who's seen this photo?" I ask.

"Not sure. It was posted on someone's Snap story and then taken down within the hour." Jackson sends me a pointed look. "There are spies everywhere. And there are people watching you and Ava. Very closely, especially now."

We're sitting with a few other friends, including Brenden who's ready to spring away from the table at any given moment the second he sees Kayla enter the quad. God knows where she's at. Jackson and I are sitting at the end of the table, a little distance between us and the rest of the group. I glance around to see if anyone's listening to our conversation, then lower my voice. "Ava and I aren't even together right now. Like I told you—"

"Yeah, yeah you're on a break," Jackson says, waving a hand. "What the hell ever. You guys are so done."

I sit up straighter. "No, we're not."

"You totally are. The fact that you don't have your phone right now? Makes it worse," he says firmly. "You can't even communicate with her. Your ship has sailed. It's over."

"Jackson, shut the fuck up. Go...sing a song for one of your groupies," I mutter. I reach into the chip bag only to come up empty, which pisses me off further. I crumple the bag and toss it right at Jackson's smug face.

"What the hell is wrong with you? You can usually come up with some pretty good shit to say. Right now, you're weak. Like a baby kitten." Jackson grabs the crumpled bag and throws it back at me. I bat it away with my hand before it hits my face. "Grow some balls, man. If anyone asks you about Ava, tell them to fuck the hell right off. And if you still want her, forget this 'we're on a break' bullshit. Go to her and tell her how you feel."

Nope. Can't do it. I might've been weak as a baby kitten when I sent her that text Saturday night, but that was a slip. A drunken mishap when I was overcome with jealousy over seeing her with that Wyatt douche.

If I went to her and told her how I felt, I'd probably push her against the wall and kiss the shit out of her. Maybe even try and feel her up. Slip my fingers inside her panties. Whatever I could get, I would take because I'm greedy like that.

Greedy for her.

My overwhelming feelings for her almost—scare me. I want her so bad, even when she does me wrong. I'll forgive her too easily. I know I will. Maybe I need to be stronger, and focus on myself first.

Yeah. That probably won't happen.

"She has to come to me first," I tell Jackson, who rolls his eyes at me. "I'm not the one who did wrong here. She did."

"Pathetic," Jackson mutters.

"Since when do you want me to get with her? Just a few nights ago, you were saying how all women were evil bitches."

"I said that?" Jackson sounds surprised.

"Something like it, yeah," I say, trying to remember exactly what he said and coming up empty. "Maybe. I don't know. You got all heated."

"I did?"

"Definitely."

"Huh. I was drunk Saturday. And high as fuck." Jackson scratches the side of his head, looking confused. "I've not had the best luck with long-term relationships. I prefer to avoid them."

"I get that." I pick at the wood on the picnic table, wincing when a sliver lodges itself beneath my thumbnail. "I've had shit luck too."

"Even with Ava?"

"Even with her."

And that just fucking sucks.

* * *

I COME HOME AFTER PRACTICE, dirty and tired. Coach ran us ragged throughout most of it, thanks to us losing to the Badgers Friday night. It wasn't that he was pissed. More like he was *disappointed.* He sounded like my dad, giving all of us a lecture at the start of practice about slipping up and making mistakes throughout the night, when he knew we were better than that. We all ended up feeling like shit when the speech was over. Then we went on the field and played even worse.

Sucked.

By the time I'm walking into the house, I'm tense, prepared for Mom to attack me with her usual drunken nonsense. When I told her about Dad taking my phone away last night, she laughed. That's it. I really appreciate her constant support.

Yeah.

Anyway, I'm fully prepared for her to say something awful, but when I enter the kitchen, I find her—making dinner. Something she never does.

Odd.

"Hungry?" she asks, her bright gaze meeting mine. I can tell she's been drinking. There's a half full wineglass on the counter, so there's the first clue. But she's also actually cooking. Looks like spaghetti, which I know is a fairly simple meal, but come on. I can't remember the last time she actually played homemaker and cooked a meal for us. It's usually takeout, frozen foods, or those gourmet meal kits that always taste like absolute trash.

"I am," I say, as I slowly set my duffel on the barstool closest to me. I watch as she buzzes around the kitchen. "What's the occasion?"

"Can't I make dinner for my son?" she chirps, as she goes to the oven and opens the door, peeking in. The delicious scent of garlic wafts out and my stomach growls.

This was my favorite meal when I was little. Spaghetti and garlic bread.

"I guess," I say with a shrug. Ah, still can't help but be a little asshole. Guess it's in my blood. "What's the occasion? Dad finally agree to your alimony demands or what?"

She sends me an irritated look, letting the oven door slam. "No need to be rude about it. Can't I do something nice for you?"

"Okay." I go to the fridge and grab a blue Gatorade out of

it, shutting the door as I twist the lid off and drain half of it in one go. "Seriously. What's up?"

"You think I always have ulterior motives?" She sounds offended.

"Yes," I say without hesitation.

Sighing, she sets the potholders on the counter and rubs her forehead. Then grabs her wineglass and takes a few sips. "I had a conversation with your father today. He told me he took your phone away."

"Yeah, I already told you about that." She blinks at me, and I can see the cogs turning in her brain as she tries to remember. "You laughed at me when I mentioned it."

"I did?" She rests her hand against her chest. She's been drinking, but I guess she's not too drunk, considering she suddenly has a conscience. "I didn't mean it."

"Right." I nod, not believing her. See how she didn't apologize for being awful either. I come by this shit naturally.

"Why didn't you try and explain to me why he took it away?" she asks.

"I figured you would get mad too and agree with him," I say with a shrug.

"You need a phone, Eli." She walks over to the desk that's in the kitchen and reaches into her purse, pulling out a familiar white box. "So I got you one."

I'm shook. Mom went out and bought me a brand new phone? "Really?" I stare at the box she holds out to me, almost afraid to touch it.

"Yes, really," she says with a little laugh. "Your dad and I agreed that what he did was—impulsive."

See? I come by that naturally too.

"He shouldn't have taken it away," she continues. "And once he had it, he realized it was pretty beat up."

"It was," I agree, my fingers itching to grab that new phone.

"Here." She holds it out, closer to me. "It's yours."

I take the box from her and slowly pull off the lid, whistling low when I see the shiny new iPhone. It's the newest model, and I'm so overcome with gratefulness, I reach out and pull Mom into a quick, one-armed hug. "Thank you," I tell her, as I press my face into her hair, breathing in her familiar, comforting scent.

"Y-you're welcome." She sounds shocked. Maybe even a little emotional. It should be no big deal, her giving me a phone, but it feels like one.

This feels like a moment. A peace offering.

I'd be an idiot not to reciprocate.

CHAPTER 8

AVA

"Come on Ava. I was hoping you would go to Sorrento's house tomorrow." Wyatt smiles at me, his gaze steady, his entire demeanor calm. The dude could probably lull me to sleep if I let him.

Wow, that is so not a compliment. Thinking that felt catty and mean.

I smile at him and slowly shake my head. "No way. I never go to Tony's parties."

"It's about time you should, right? And what's the big deal? Jake will be there, so what? Lots of people will be there. Plus, he'll be with Hannah and won't even pay attention to what you're doing," Wyatt says, sounding vaguely annoyed. But not too annoyed.

It's like Wyatt has one emotion, and it's completely balanced. He never gets too mad or too happy. He's very restrained.

I don't know if that's a good thing.

We're at the Thursday night team dinner that the football booster club hosts. They invited the cheer team, and Brandy said we should go. Even though a few of us have a huge history test tomorrow to study for.

Like me.

But anyway.

When dinner was over, my dad and a few of the other coaches gave rousing speeches that had all the boys roaring their approval, as usual. Once we were dismissed, I couldn't get out of there fast enough, but I didn't realize that Wyatt was following right behind me, calling my name to get me to stop.

Lindsey noticed. She smirked at me before grabbing Dakota, and they both took off toward her car. I'm sure they'll be gossiping about me and Wyatt on the drive home. Not sure why no one is gossiping about me and Eli, but I say a quiet thank you to whoever is controlling the constant chatter around here and hope that it remains that way.

Quiet.

I hate gossip. I don't want people talking about me. I live somewhat in the shadows of my older sister and brother, and while sometimes I hate that, in moments like this? When all eyes could be on me and my name on the tip of everyone's tongue? I don't want the attention. Autumn dealt with it a lot in high school, and so does Jake.

"I'm always so tired after the games," I say, which isn't necessarily a lie. But if the right boy was asking right now—ahem, Eli—then I'd be agreeing without hesitation.

"Then it'll be a chance for you to relax and hang out," Wyatt says, his tone actually pretty convincing. I should experience Tony's house parties at least once, right? "Come on." He reaches out and gently socks my arm with his fist. "You should go."

That was a total excuse for him to touch me, which is sweet. If I wasn't so hung up and completely hungover from

73

my previous relationship that I still haven't given up on, I'd be more agreeable. But I'm not, so…

"Bring Ellie," Wyatt says. "She told me she doesn't have to work tomorrow night."

"She did?" Hmm. Does Ellie secretly have the hots for Wyatt? We've really only talked about my issues with Eli this week, which isn't fair. I've dumped all my woes and worries on her and she's never said a single word about what's going on with her love life.

I need to be a better friend.

"Yeah. You two should totally come to the party." He smiles, and it's a pretty sight, I can't deny it. My heart doesn't start racing though. Of course, my heart doesn't belong to him. It belongs to someone else. "It'll be fun."

"Okay," I hear myself say. "We'll go."

Well, that was easy.

"Awesome." He holds his hand out for a high five and I give it to him. At the last second, he grabs hold of my wrist, his fingers loose though he doesn't let go. "Can't wait to hang out with you."

"Yeah." My smile is weak. "Same."

"See ya tomorrow," he says, as he walks away from me.

"See ya," I call after him, unaware someone is standing right next to me until he speaks.

"He's a better choice for you, and you know it."

Gee, love it when you offer up your opinion, big brother.

I glance over at Jake to see he's watching Wyatt head toward his car in the church parking lot where the team dinners are held. "Wyatt is nice."

"He's kind of a prick, but he's way better than the colossal douchebag you chose originally," Jake mutters.

"It's not like Eli and I are over," I tell him.

Jake scoffs. "Could've fooled me."

"What are you talking about?" I turn so I'm facing him, my arms crossed, my entire being feeling cross. As in, I'm super angry. Eli has been surprisingly quiet on social media this week. I'd like to think he's taking some time and thinking about us and what happened.

But that's just me projecting. I have no idea what he's doing or thinking. I haven't heard from him since those two text messages he sent me last weekend. And he never replied to the text I sent him. He hasn't posted on Instagram or Snapchat. Definitely no more trash-talking stories. What's the point? They played the game. His team lost.

That's the end of it.

"I don't see him coming around, trying to win you back," he says, his tone condescending. "Pretty sure he's moved on. Not like he's the type to have a girlfriend."

"What, you two are so close that you know and under-stand his dating habits?" Now it's my turn to scoff. "Give me a break."

"Can't you get it through your thick skull that he is the absolute *last* guy you should go for right now?"

I hold my hand up, practically shoving it in my brother's smug face. "I'm over this conversation. We're done."

"What the fuck, Ava?" Jake yells, as I hurry down the steps and into the parking lot, heading for my car. I'm sick of him being this way. Of constantly tearing Eli down, of not letting me ever get a word in when we're having a so-called conver-sation. We're not conversing, Jake's lecturing and I'm supposed to just sit there and listen.

So over it.

I climb into my car and speed out of the parking lot, past my dad and Jake who are standing where I was only moments ago. I drive and drive, until I'm on the highway, passing by the Starbucks parking lot. Where I spot—

Eli's car in the drive-thru line.

I whip around and head back to Starbucks, pulling into the parking lot a little too fast, making my tires squeal when I hit the brakes. The car is a Dodge Charger, just like Eli's but...

It's not his. His car is red. This one is black.

Frustration fills me and I lean forward, pressing my forehead against the steering wheel and closing my eyes. I'm seeing things. He's everywhere and nowhere. I can't keep this up. Thinking I see him when I don't. Is this even normal? I feel like maybe I'm losing my grip on reality. My thoughts are consumed with him, yet he won't talk to me. It's like what we shared never happened.

A horn blares, startling me, and I lift up, glancing in the rearview mirror to see a car behind me, waiting for me to move. I'm blocking the flow of traffic in this narrow parking lot. Waving my hand in the rearview mirror, I pull into the closest parking spot, throw the car in park and lean back against the seat, exhaling loudly. The other car goes speeding by, and I hear laughter. Boy's laughter.

The sound fills me with sadness. Reminds me of Eli.

God, what doesn't remind me of him?

Pulling my phone out of the center console, I bring up our text message thread and start typing.

You never responded to me. So I guess you don't care. Or you're still mad at me. I never told my brother anything about your family. My brother never knew about us at all until the night before the game, thanks to your IG story. But I'm not mad about that. I'm not mad about anything. I'm just sad.

I hit send, then continue typing.

I'm sad because you gave up on us so easily, and I can't do that. Maybe you can. And if you don't want me in your

life anymore, then tell me. Tell me you don't love me. Tell me you never want to see me again, and I'll leave you alone.

I send that text too, because why not? I have nothing to lose and everything to gain.

But of course, he doesn't respond.

Fighting back tears, I put the car in reverse and back out of the parking spot, then head home, so I can cry myself to sleep.

Yet again.

* * *

I PULL into our circular driveway, hitting the brakes extra hard when I see the familiar car sitting directly in front of me.

My sister's.

Autumn's here?

I hustle my butt out of the car, quickly grabbing my backpack and my cheer practice bag from the trunk. I make my way into the house through the garage, chattering voices greeting me when I open the door. I find Mom, Beck and Autumn sitting at the kitchen table, laughing and talking. The smile on my sister's face is huge when she spots me. She looks happy to be home.

She looks happy in general.

"Ava!" she says brightly. "Get in here!"

I hurry over to the table just as Autumn stands, embracing her fully. She's shorter than me by a few inches and I cling to her like she's my lifeline, closing my eyes against the sudden, stinging tears.

I'm totally overreacting, but I also don't care. I've missed her.

So much.

"Happy to see you too," she says into my hair, before she moves to press a smacking kiss on my cheek.

Reluctantly, I let go of her. "Why are you here?"

Autumn laughs. So does Mom. "I got an unexpected three-day weekend, so I thought I'd come home. This way I can go watch Ash's game Saturday."

She's been with her boyfriend since they were high school seniors. They go to different colleges, live about five hours apart, yet somehow, they can still make it work. They're madly in love, though in the early days of their relationship, they had some struggles.

"Aren't you glad she came home?" Mom asks me as we both settle down in our chairs. She reaches over and rubs Autumn's arm. "We've missed having you around. Soon Jake will leave too—"

"Won't miss him," I interrupt, making Autumn giggle.

"I'll miss him," Beck says as he stands. "I'm going to take a shower. You guys go ahead and have your girl talk. I'm out."

With that, he's gone.

Mom just sighs and shakes her head. "Fine, we *will* have our girl talk. Ava, how was your day?"

"It was whatever," I say with a little shrug.

Autumn sends me a curious look. "What's going on?"

"Oh. Nothing," I say innocently.

"She's had some relationship trouble," Mom says, being purposely vague, and she sends my sister a look, like they might've discussed my situation already.

Great.

"We'll talk about that later," Autumn says firmly, her gaze on me.

We chat about other things. Catch up on family gossip, which isn't much. Autumn tells us about her college classes, and how it's going for her. She's a junior and goes to UC

Santa Barbara. I'm jealous she gets to live by the ocean. I wouldn't mind going there.

But my problem is I have no idea what I want to do with my life. I'm only sixteen. I can barely figure out what I'm going to wear each day. I can't plan my entire future by the time I graduate high school.

Dad and Jake arrive about thirty minutes after I got home and they're all over Autumn. Even Jake, who most of the time acts like he can't stand her, though she hasn't lived with us for over two years. I decide to bow out and go take a shower. I'm tired and I still have homework to do and a test to study for. Tomorrow is going to be a typical, busy Friday with the football game, plus Wyatt wants me to go to Tony's house afterward.

I'm exhausted just thinking about it.

I open the bathroom door, steam billowing out as I enter my bedroom. I stop short when I see who's sitting all cozy on my bed, wrapped up in one of my favorite blankets.

Autumn.

"You stole this out of my room." She pats the blanket.

"I did not."

Wait.

Maybe I did?

"This was one of my favorites." She pets it, raking her fingers over the cozy soft fabric.

"Then why'd you leave it behind?" I make my way over to the dresser, grabbing undies, then a pair of sleep shorts and a T-shirt.

"Ha! See, you did take it. Oh well, I guess I can't blame you."

I slip my panties on under the towel then whip it off, letting it drop to the floor as I tug the tank top over my head. My sister is blatantly watching me, her gaze roving over every inch of my skin in that typical big sister, *I am silently judging you,* way she has.

I love her, but we can get into it when we want, which is often, especially when she still lived here. Yet you better never come for me, because she will cut you before you get a chance to attack. Autumn is extremely overprotective of us all.

"I think your boobs are getting bigger," she tells me, as I'm pulling on my shorts.

"In my dreams," I say, my gaze going to her chest. Hers are huge. Bigger than I'd want. Glad I didn't inherit that gene.

"I actually think so. You've filled out more. You have curves," Autumn continues.

"I appreciate your positive assessment," I tell her half-jokingly as I collapse on my bed right next to her.

"Your skin is really clear too," she says as she turns to face me. "You look good, Ava. Tell me why you're acting all down and out."

"Do you really want to know?" I ask. She can only tolerate so much from me. I feel the same way. After a while, we get tired of hearing the sound of each other's voices. It sounds rotten, but it's true.

But my tale is long, and she'll need to be patient with me while I get it all out.

"Yes, I really want to know," she says firmly.

Sitting up on the bed, I launch into the entire story. I tell her everything. This includes all of the sexual moments I experienced with Eli. If I can't confess all to my sister, who else can I talk to? I know she won't judge.

Well, not too harshly.

By the time I'm wrapping it up, she's sitting up as well, cross-legged with the blanket wrapped around her middle, her mouth hanging open.

"You actually had sex with him," she says when I'm finished.

I roll my eyes. "I mentioned that about ten minutes ago."

"I can't believe you actually had sex. You beat me. I was a senior before I did it with Ash." Her cheeks turn the faintest shade of pink. How cute, my sister still blushes.

"Well, when you know, you know." I shrug.

"Do you regret it?"

I think about her question, pressing my lips together as I go over the memory of what Eli and I have shared. "No. Not at all."

"Perv." Autumn shoves at my shoulder, making me topple over a little. I do the same, shoving her with all of my might, nearly sending her off the bed. Next thing I know, we're doing some strange wrestling, pretzel contortionist type thing that has our legs tangled up, laughing almost uncontrollably as we try to hurt each other.

I finally give in first, with Autumn sprawled on top of me, pressing me into the mattress, her hands pinning my shoulders down. She's little, but she's strong, I'll give her that. Eventually, she rolls over so she's lying beside me, and we're shoulder to shoulder as we both stare at the ceiling.

"If you love him," she says quietly, once the laughter dies down, "You can't just let him go. You need to tell him what really happened."

"I want to." I hesitate for a moment, before I exhale loudly. "Jake will kill me."

"Fuck Jake." Autumn says it with such conviction, my head whips in her direction, and I can feel my eyes widening. "What? I'm serious. You can't let him dictate your life, or who you choose to love. You know how many people lost their damn minds when Asher and I got together? A lot of people. Dad wasn't too thrilled at first either, but he got over it. And if your guy is a good person, Mom and Dad will see that."

"The problem is I don't know if Eli is truly a good person," I admit, my voice small. "When I'm with him, he says all of these...outrageous things. He can be wildly inappropriate one second, and really sweet and thoughtful the next."

"You sound like Mom," Autumn teases. "Wildly inappropriate?"

"He says some of the worst things ever. He does terrible things too," I say. "But when it's just us, and we're all alone, he's..." A wistful sigh escapes me.

"Perfect?" Autumn asks, her voice soft.

"Yes." I nod. "He's perfect. Perfect for me. It's like we're... meant to be."

"Soulmates?"

I make a face. "I hate that term. I don't know if I believe in it."

"Okay, Ms. Jaded." She nudges my side with her pointy elbow.

"Ouch." I scoot away from her. "I miss him."

"Maybe he misses you too."

"He won't answer my texts." I completely forgot to check my phone. I haven't really checked it since I got home.

"What an asshole," Autumn says, as I get up and go to my backpack, unzipping the front pocket with shaky fingers and yanking my phone out.

To see I do have a text message.

From Eli.

We should talk. Tomorrow night. Jackson's having a party at the cabin. Want to meet me there?

My heart starts hammering and my mouth goes dry. I'd love to meet Eli tomorrow night. But I don't even know if I can go to Tony's house after the game. Technically, I'm still grounded. And so is Jake. I'd put money on my dad letting Jake go anyway.

Would Dad let me go? I don't know. He's very overprotective of me.

"Look." I show the phone to my sister, and she reads the response from Eli, then starts scrolling up like the nosy B she is. I tug my phone out of her grip. "What should I do?"

"Go meet him at that party and talk to him," Autumn answers without hesitation.

"But I'm grounded still."

She thinks about it for a moment. Even taps her index finger against her pursed lips like she used to do when we were younger and I would ask her for advice and she actually gave me some. Those were rare moments. Usually she just bit my head off when I'd ask her anything. Even over something as mundane as asking the time.

"Tell Mom and Dad you're going to Tony's. I'll tell Jake he has to keep his mouth shut or I'll let it slip to Mom and Dad about the time he snuck Cami into the house and they had sex in his room while we were all sleeping."

"Oh God." I make a gagging noise. "That's so awful, Autumn."

"What, me threatening to rat our brother out, or the fact that he had sex with Cami Lockhart in our house?"

"The last one. For sure." I make another gagging noise before we start laughing again.

"Listen, I'll get Jake to cover for you," Autumn reassures me. "In fact, I'll go talk to him right now, and then we can have Jake go plead your case to Mom and Dad, and by tomorrow morning, you won't have anything to worry about."

"Yeah, I will. I'll be a nervous wreck thinking about meeting with Eli," I tell her, my entire body starting to shiver just from saying it out loud.

Tomorrow night, I could be in the same room as Eli. The idea both excites and terrifies me.

"You'll be fine. Answer his text. I'll go talk to Jake." She starts to get up, but I grab her hand, keeping her from leaving. "What?" she asks me.

"Thank you," I say, my voice sincere. "For talking to me about this. For the advice. For helping me."

"Little sister, you have this figured out. I barely gave you any advice. You know what you want." She pulls me into a hug, and I cling to her. "Go get it. Go get *him.*"

CHAPTER 9

AVA

*E*llie and I arrive at Jackson's uncle's cabin around eleven. When I say we got to the cabin, I mean we parked about a mile out, there are so many cars here, most of them lining the side of the road. I can hear the people at the party before I actually see them as we walk down the middle of the street, the air so cold we can see our breath. After the game, I hurriedly changed into my favorite jeans that make my butt look good and an oversized, yet cropped, black sweater. Of course, I'm cold. I wish I had a jacket.

That would ruin the entire look I'm going for tonight, so yeah. Screw that.

"There are a lot more people at this party than last time," Ellie says, as she wraps her arms around herself and rubs them. She's looking good tonight too, in form fitting jeans, a really cute, cropped hot pink Champion sweatshirt with black slip on Vans on her feet and giant silver hoops in her ears. I'm digging her *I'm a casual but extra girl* vibe.

"I know. Tons more." My heart deflates the closer we get to the cabin. I hear boys yelling and laughing, encouraging someone to do a shot. Screaming girls. The strum of a guitar.

The sight of flames. They're having a fire again, and I'm sure Jackson is sitting beside it, playing for the girls while they all watch him with adoring gazes, like he's some sort of rock star.

Whatever.

"Jackson has his groupies I see," Ellie says, her tone snarky as we approach the hill where the cabin sits.

Yep, right out front like last time, it's mostly girls sitting in a big circle with Jackson in the center facing the fire and the street. Facing us. We approach the group, me reluctantly following Ellie as she picks up speed. She stops behind the row of girls, directly in Jackson's line of vision and it's like he knows. He's bent over his guitar, his fingers plucking at the strings one by one until he pauses. Lifting his head, his gaze searches, quickly landing on Ellie. And then he smiles. This slow, confident smile that lights up his entire face as he shakes his longish blond hair away from his eyes.

Ellie smiles in return and I watch them, my head swiveling back and forth like I'm at a tennis match I can't keep up with. Wait a minute. Ellie and...Jackson?

Nooooo.

Maybe?

My best friend was easy to convince to go to this party instead of our original plans, and I never questioned it. I didn't explain to Wyatt why I wouldn't be at Tony's, let alone tell him I wasn't going to show up in the first place, and I feel like shit about it. I don't want to lead him on, but I couldn't tell him the truth. That would break his heart, and I can't deal with that right now. I'm nursing a broken heart myself.

I didn't know what Autumn said to Jake last night either, but he played nice earlier this morning, before we left for school, and he told me he talked to our parents, and we weren't grounded any longer. That he would say I'd be at Tony's house tonight. He assured me this with far too much ease, which actually made me uneasy, but Autumn told me not to worry about it. She had me covered.

I'm sure Jake has his suspicions, but I can't think about that right now.

I can't stop looking for Eli either. My gaze is searching, searching, running over every single face I see, my breath lodging in my throat when I see a boy with golden brown hair standing just a few feet to the side of Jackson.

But it's not him.

My heart drops and hopelessness fills me. I think about going in search of something to drink, but I can't ditch Ellie for fear I might never find her again.

"Okay quiet down, quiet down," Jackson says, his voice carrying above the noise. Everyone goes silent, even the chattering girls. "I'm going to sing a song that I just learned. I'll warn you that it's old, and originally, it was sung by a woman. But my grandma showed it to me recently and thought I could do justice to it, so I'm going to try." The girls giggle, and he sends them a look, shutting them up. "Yes, my grandma has cool taste in music, and we talk about it all the time. The seventies were awesome. The song is called "Dreams," and it's by Fleetwood Mac. Let's go."

He starts playing his guitar, and it's this low, hypnotic beat. He starts to sing, his voice soft but clear, and I'm captivated by the words. The story he's weaving. The lyrics speak to me, about what you had and what you lost and how you feel. When he starts in on the chorus, I'm totally into it. Singing about thunder happening with the rain, and players only loving you when they're playing.

I think of Eli. I think of what we had, what we lost, and how careless we were. How careless we still are. Pretty sure I'm going to start my period soon, because I want to cry, just from an old song Jackson's singing. I can feel the tears wanting to form in my eyes, and I mentally banish them away. Without thought, I begin gently swaying to the music as Jackson plays, absorbing the plaintive way he sings the lyrics. Ellie smiles over at me, grabbing my hand as we both move to the beat, and when I look across the crowd, I see a boy standing directly behind Jackson, a beer bottle clutched in one hand, his gaze on me.

Only for me.

My heart drops. It's Eli. I hope he's listening to the lyrics too, though his expression is extra serious. Jackson keeps singing, the song coming to its end and he croons that you'll know, you will know and he's right.

I know.

I love Eli. And he loves me. Why are we wasting our time staring at each other when we could be talking? Touching?

"I have to go," I whisper to Ellie, just as Jackson ends the song with one final strum on the guitar and the crowd breaks into enthusiastic applause. I pull her into a quick hug and say into her ear, "I see Eli."

"Go talk to him," she says, hugging me back before she releases me.

"You'll be okay?" I ask. "I don't want to leave you alone."

"I'm definitely not alone," she says, humor lacing her voice as she glances around. We're surrounded by people, so I guess she's right. "Besides, I'll talk to Jackson when he takes a break."

"Okay." I glance over to see Eli is still standing there, watching me. "I'll find you later."

"Sounds good."

I make my way through the crowd, pushing through clusters of people talking, smiling and apologizing as I walk past them. I don't want to lose him, but now I can't see him, and for all I know, he took off when he realized I'm searching for him. Maybe he changed his mind. Maybe he doesn't want to talk to me anymore. Maybe we're—

"Hey, hey sexy. Where do you think you're going?" Strong fingers wrap around my upper arm, stopping my pursuit, and when I glance up, I almost sag with relief.

Eli. Looking so handsome dressed all in black, I feel a little weak in the knees as I take him in.

"I was coming to find you," I tell him, sounding out of breath.

He doesn't let go of me. I take that as a good sign. "Well, here I am."

We say nothing for a moment, just stare into each other's eyes. His grip on my arm loosens, but he still keeps hold of me. Actually, he tugs me closer, his head dropping, so he can murmur close to my ear, "Let's find somewhere more private."

Saying nothing, I go along with him, sad when he lets go of my arm. Happy all over again when he rests his hand lightly against my lower back, the heat of his touch penetrating my sweater, making me tingle. He greets someone who calls his name. Gives a guy a high five as we walk past him. He is the master of his domain at this party tonight and I watch in silent awe, proud to be with him, standing next to him.

I really have it bad for this boy.

"Don't let go," he says, when he snags my hand before we enter the crowded cabin. "I don't want to lose you."

His words have double meaning, lighting me up inside. I cling to his hand, our fingers intricately tangled as he basically drags me through the cabin to the short hallway that leads to the bedrooms. For some reason, the room we enter is empty, and he pulls me inside, letting go of my hand to close and then lock the door.

Turning, I face him, watching as he leans against the door, contemplating me. I kept my hair in a high ponytail because it would've taken too much time to fix after being that way for the last twenty-four hours. Definitely got rid of the bow though. Slicked on some extra black eyeliner. Glossed up my lips. Was going for a *I don't care, fuck boys'* attitude, but I'm sure I now look like a pitiful beggar who'll do anything to get her man back.

That's how I feel, at least.

"You look hot," he says, after approximately thirty seconds of silence.

My skin warms with his compliment, but I pretend to be offended. "Really Eli? We haven't seen each other in a week, and that's the first thing you say to me?"

I shouldn't be surprised. It's so typical Eli.

He shrugs. "It's the truth. I like the cropped sweater. I can see skin."

I tug on the hem of it, though it's no use. My stomach is exposed, and besides, I wore the sweater just for him. "Thank you."

"Bold move, considering how cold it is outside."

"I was hoping you might warm me up." I press my lips together at the slip. I shouldn't say anything like that. Not yet. It's too early in the conversation.

His eyes gleam. There's no other sign of outward emotion. "I wouldn't mind keeping you toasty, but we need to clear a few things up first."

Of course. I knew he'd want to talk, which is perfect because I do too. There are things I need to tell him, but I'll let him start. "Like what?"

"Like the fact that Jake knew way too much private information about my parents." His expression becomes stone. Up goes that wall he so very carefully erects around his emotions. Around his heart. He gives it easily when he wants to. But he just as easily snatches it away.

"I know how he found out that information." I don't bother telling him what else Jake said. How it's common knowledge that Eli's parents' relationship imploded and everyone knows about it.

"Really? What sort of lie did he come up with?"

I tell myself not to get irritated. Tonight isn't about arguing. It's about working past our differences, so we can move forward. "It was Cami who told him everything."

Eli's brows lower, and he frowns. He looks completely puzzled. "What the hell? How does she know anything?"

"She mentioned it to Jake at the beginning of the school year, like she was trading information with him to get on his good side. My brother's an idiot for thinking that though, considering she was messing around with you when she was with him." Eli starts to say something, but I hold up my hand, silencing him. "Anyway, she showed up at your house and your mom came outside in a drunken rage and called Cami one of your dad's...whores." I wince, hating that I had to bring it up.

Realization dawns. It's written all over his ridiculously handsome face. "Oh. Yeah. I remember that."

"Right. She told Jake. And he threw it in your face when he got his chance." I lower my voice. Take a step closer to him. "It wasn't me. I would never tell Jake private stuff about you or your family. That's like giving him free ammunition."

"Uh huh." The doubt is still there. Has he lost complete faith in me? God, that hurts. Worse than I thought it could.

"It's all Cami's fault." I make a face. That bitch comes up way too often in our relationship. I seriously hate her. And I have to deal with her on an almost daily basis since she's the captain of our cheer team. Talk about torture.

"I don't want to talk about her," Eli says, slowly shaking his head. "I don't want to talk about Jake either."

I'm at a loss, since both of those people are the ones who caused all the trouble in our relationship in the first place.

"I missed you," he says, his voice rough. Like it took a lot for him to admit that.

"Then why didn't you talk to me this week?"

"Shit got—weird. My dad took my phone away Sunday night after we got into an argument. My mom bought me a new one the next day and I was just—kind of taken aback, that she would do something nice for me. Plus, I was busy all week. With school. Football. We won, by the way." He hesitates for a moment before he continues. "I was trying to see what my life was like without you."

"And how was it?" I ask, nervous to hear his answer.

"Fucking awful." He dips his head, the tiniest smile curling his lips. I can't help but smile in return. "I didn't like it."

"I don't like my life without you in it either," I say. "I was grounded all week. My parents were so mad at me for trying to sneak you into the house."

He smiles, scratching his jaw. "You weren't sneaking me into your house. You were sneaking me into the hot tub, so we could mess around."

My smile grows. "True."

"I never got to see what you were wearing under that robe," he says.

"You want to know?" He nods. "Nothing," I whisper, exaggerating only a little bit.

Eli slowly shakes his head. "Uh huh. Sorry I missed that."

"Me too."

His smile fades. "You still went to that dance."

I'm automatically defensive. "I was the homecoming princess."

"You're *my* princess," he says gruffly, going all alpha possessive jerk on me.

Tingles sweep over my skin. This is one of those times I

love it when he does that. "I didn't think you'd ever say that to me again."

"I didn't give up on us that easily," he says.

"You sort of did," I point out, mentally telling myself to shut up. I don't want to convince him we shouldn't be together.

He crosses his arms. "Maybe we should take this slow."

I approach him, my steps careful but sure. He's still leaning against the door, his demeanor casual, but I can tell he's coiled and tense. Ready for whatever I'm going to deliver, whether it's good or bad.

"You want us to take it slow?" I ask, a little laugh escaping me when I stop directly in front of him. He's so close, I can smell him. Feel his body heat radiate toward me. My body leans forward on instinct, like I have no control of myself. "Aren't we passed that?"

"Maybe." He tilts his head to the side. "I just thought maybe it would be smarter if we slowed our roll, you know?"

"Slowed our roll?" I'm frowning. It's like he's talking in a foreign language.

"It means we need to slow down. My dad always used to say it. But fuck that guy." He waves a hand, dismissing his feelings, and I want to ask him why his father took his phone away, but I don't.

"What about the girl giving you a lap dance at your party Saturday night?" I ask. I have to know. Who she was and if she means anything to him. He didn't look disinterested.

"Oh damn, you saw that?" It gives me a sick pleasure to see the obvious discomfort appear on his face. "It was Josie. Josie Price. She's on our cheer team. She's a senior. She's been chasing my dick for a long time."

My stomach drops, and I suddenly feel nauseous. "Oh."

"Yeah, oh. Don't worry about her. Not interested. She was

trying, but I told her about you." His expression turns sheepish.

I'm shocked. "You told her about me?"

"Yeah. Uh. I told her I had a girl. I might've said some other stuff. I can't remember." He doesn't say anything else, and I cling to those words. Cling to the fact that even though he was mad at me and he had some girl grinding her butt on his crotch, he mentioned me to her. She was trying her damnedest to get him to focus on her, and he talked about me.

"What about Wyatt?" he asks when I still haven't said anything.

"What about him?"

"That douchebag was all over you at the dance." His voice is full of disgust.

"He was not." Talk about exaggerating.

"Was fucking too. I saw footage."

"You're completely overreacting." I pause. "Is that why you sent that text?"

"What text?"

"Um, hold on." I grab my phone out of the back pocket of my jeans and find the text, then read it out loud to him. "'Hope you have fun at your stupid dance with that asshole who probably wouldn't know where your clit is, even if you drew him a map with a giant lit-up arrow pointing to it.'"

"I said that?" He doesn't seem embarrassed. If anything, he's totally amused. "That's funny."

"You didn't go back and read your texts to me?" I read them over and over again, driving myself crazy with his words.

"Like I said, my dad took my phone away and I sort of... yeah. Didn't go back to our messages when I got the new phone because I didn't want to make myself miserable," he admits, then blows out a long breath.

Aww poor Eli. Doesn't want to torture himself by yearning for me. I hope I tore his heart into tiny little pieces while he mourned the loss of me.

"You also said this." I pause for only a moment before I launch into the next text message from him. "'I'm a stupid fucker who knows exactly where your clit is, and how much you like it when I touch it. Don't ever forget that. And don't give Wyatt the map. Or your heart. That belongs to me.'" When I'm done, I lift my head to find him watching me with this dazed look on his face, his lips parted, his gaze locking with mine. "Did you mean it?"

"Meant every fucking word," he says without hesitation. "And you do like it when I touch your clit."

"Eli."

"It's true. Baby, what we had was real, and when we were together, we were the best. You can't deny it," he says with that cocksure confidence he loves to throw around. To make everyone believe he's the big man on campus. Larger than life. Arrogant as hell.

It's a lie. A cover. Deep down, in his rawest form, he's heartbreakingly vulnerable. His heart, his soul, they bleed. His emotions spill all over the place, but he gathers them back up and locks them away. He can pretend all he wants with me right now, but I've seen the real Eli. And I want more of that Eli. Not this one.

"We don't have to talk about us in the past tense." I reach out and rest my fingers on his exposed forearm, my fingertips sizzling when I make contact. His skin is hot, and the connection between us is instant. Electrifying. As usual. "We can still be the best. Together."

He drops his arms to his sides, and I immediately miss the connection. My hand hovers there, in between us, and he grabs it, pulling me into him. I have no choice but to go to him, resting my hands on his chest, my fingers curling into the fabric of his sweatshirt. A bone deep yearning fills me at being so close to him again. I wish I could pull his sweatshirt off. Run my hands all over his naked skin. Being with him again makes me feel needy.

Greedy.

"I start kissing you right now, I won't be able to stop," he says, his voice serious. Determined.

Yesssss, I want to shout. But I remain outwardly calm. Collected. I stand up a little straighter, thrusting my chest out. His gaze drops there, but only for a second before he lifts those gorgeous hazel eyes to mine. "Then don't stop," I say. Basically daring him.

My Eli can't turn down a dare.

He doesn't say a word, though I see something flicker in his gaze. His hand goes to my cheek, his thumb softly stroking my skin. I close my eyes, his touch filling me with relief that leaves me weak. I sense him moving closer, his head dipping, his intake of breath. I part my lips. Hold my breath. He tilts my head up with his hand, guiding me, and I follow.

In this very moment, filled with anticipation and so much need, I'd follow him off a cliff if he led me there.

His lips brush mine. Warm. Soft. Feather light. Too light. A sigh escapes me, and I swear I feel him smile as he kisses me again. And again. No tongue. Just damp lips connecting, making me shiver.

"You think your brother's gonna bust through the door at any second and break us up again?" he asks, his lips moving against mine as he speaks.

I give his chest a little shove and step away, trying to catch my breath, my mood spoiled. "Don't ruin a good moment."

"Every moment is good between us, princess. You should know this by now. Angry. Happy. Whatever. We're good together." He sneaks his arm around my waist and hauls me back into him. I rest my hands on his chest once more, absorbing his warmth. His strength. He is rock hard. Made of solid muscle.

"Let's go outside," I tell him, tilting my head back when he leans in and drops another kiss on my lips. Yes, I'd rather mess around with him on that single bed sitting in the corner of the tiny bedroom we're in, but then again, that's kind of gross. And I shouldn't give in to him so quickly anyway. I need to make him chase me a little bit. Make him work for it.

Work for me.

"You want to go outside?" He kisses me for real this time, stealing my breath, my thoughts, everything I've got. His tongue sweeps my mouth, circles around mine, and it's like I forgot the power his kisses have over me.

Because they do. Have so much power, it's overwhelming. I'm lost. Lost in the sensation of his tongue caressing mine. The heat of his body seeping into mine. He has so much power over me. So much. He doesn't even know how desperate I am to hold onto him.

"Yes," I say, once I break the kiss, breathless and more than a little mussed. Must be from the way Eli dragged his fingers through my pulled back hair. I'm sure I look crazy. "Let's go listen to Jackson."

"I can croon a few songs in your ear if you want me to." He grins. Reaches for the back of my head and tugs the elastic band out of my hair completely, making it fall past my shoulders. He's frowning as he rakes his fingers through it. "You got a weird lump in your hair."

"I've had it up all day." I try running my fingers through the back of it to make it look better, but it's pointless.

"Wish you showed up here in your uniform. That always gets me, seeing you like that." He nuzzles my cheek with his nose, whispering in my ear, "Maybe you could come over to my house one night, wearing that uniform and nothing else under the skirt."

"Eli," I whisper in protest, just before he kisses me again. Not that I'm really protesting his idea. It actually sounds kind of fun.

"Ava," he whispers back, his hands starting to wander.

And that's my cue to pull away and grab that wandering hand, shifting him away from the door. "Let's go," I tell him, just before I open it and march out of the room. He follows after me, squeezing my hand and I know...

I have never felt more triumphant than in this moment. He's mine again.

Mine.

CHAPTER 10

ELI

*W*as I too easy on her? Maybe. Was she too easy on me? Probably.

But earlier when we were outside, I caught her watching me with those big green eyes, her body swaying to the music as she stood next to her best friend. Jackson was singing that song and I absorbed the lyrics completely, the words hitting me like a smack upside the head. Players only loving you when you're playing, or some shit like that. Got me right in the feels, I can't lie. Reminded me that everyone thinks I'm that guy. The player. The one who'll fuck you and leave you. The one who struts around like he doesn't have a care in the world. Laughing and acting stupid and drinking and smoking another blunt and hey, you wanna get loaded? You wanna get fucked? Oh, you want to get punched in the fucking face? I can manage that too.

I can't blame everyone for thinking that's who I am. That's how I portray myself. It's how I want people to see me. Acting that way makes me feel strong. Tough. Above it all—above my problems.

The only one who knows I'm more than that is this girl.

Ava. The one who's tugging me through the house after I so thoroughly kissed her. Her hair is a fuckin' mess and I kissed all the gloss off her lips—I can still feel a little bit of it on mine, sticky and sweet—and her eyeliner is smudged. Gives her an edgy look, which is not typical Ava. But every time she moves, I catch a glimpse of her flat stomach and her belly button, the sight of her bare skin making me want to trace it all with my tongue, so…yeah.

I can't worry about if I did the right thing or not. Or if I forgave too easily. She's here. I believe what she said about Cami. Wouldn't put it past her to confess all my secrets to that asshole Jake. Why is she so drawn to that guy? Why is anyone drawn to him?

Fuck him. He's the last person I want to think about right now.

Instead, I focus on Ava. The way her ass looks in those jeans makes me a little crazy. I want her. I'm in love with her. I'm not going to stop chasing after her. As long as she wants to hold my hand, I'll keep her.

Forever if she'll let me.

We walk through the crowd of people in the tiny living room, a few of them giving us odd glances when they see we're holding hands, but I say nothing. Neither does Ava. This is my crowd that's here tonight, and I'm sure the moment we leave this room, they're all gonna talk.

Let 'em.

Her people are all over at Tony Sorrento's house, doing their traditional drink and drug and fuck party they have after every home game. I'm sure she was invited. Maybe her little friend Wyatt thought he had a chance with her tonight. Well, fuck that. I still can't believe she agreed to meet me here. But she did.

She glances over her shoulder when we walk outside, her gaze catching mine as a smile curls her perfect lips. I take a couple of extra steps, so I'm standing right beside her, and we're both poised on the edge of the porch, ready to go down the steps, but I stop her.

"You want your hair tie back?" I ask, holding it out to her.

She lets go of my hand and takes it, twisting her hair into this messy, sloppy ass bun that sticks out everywhere. "How do I look?"

"Fucking magical." She could be wearing a paper sack and look like hell and I'd still say that.

Ava grins. "Let's go. I can hear your friend playing his guitar."

We walk down the steps together, side by side, our strides in sync. Once we hit the ground, I take her hand again, lacing our fingers and leading her toward the circle of people around the fire. It's still crackling, though the flames aren't as high, and we stand on the fringe, Ava leaning over to whisper something in my ear. I bend my knees a little so she can reach it.

"Ellie is sitting right next to him!" she whisper-squeals like girls do, her tone downright giddy.

I check out Jackson to see that yep, Ava's best friend is sitting beside him, snuggled up to his side. He's strumming his guitar, but he's not playing a song. He's talking to her. I can see his lips move, and her lips move in response. They're having a total conversation while he's surrounded by at least fifty other girls, all of them ready to cream their panties over his next tune.

And he's not paying attention to any of them. Just Ellie.

"Is he a good guy? Your friend?" Ava asks me.

I contemplate her question. "He's a good friend. Not sure how he is as a date. Or a boyfriend." Bitter about women that's for sure. Should I tell Ava that? "I think he's been burned in the past."

There. That sounds better.

"Ah, he's wounded." She nudges my side. "Kind of like you."

I rest my free hand over my chest, pretending to take offense. "You think I'm wounded?"

"Definitely," she says with a knowing smile. "But that's okay. You're wounded. You're confident. You're sweet. You're dirty. You're even a little mean sometimes. I like all the many sides of you."

Aw damn. She goes and says something like that, and I gotta do something in response. I pull her in close, so she's standing directly in front of me, and I wrap my arms around her middle, giving her a squeeze as I rest my chin on her shoulder. She angles her face toward mine, and it would take nothing for me to lean in and kiss her.

But I don't. Let's keep everyone guessing, though if they're watching closely enough, they'll have us all figured out.

"You think I'm dirty?" I ask her, making her laugh.

I missed that sound. It's light and airy and it makes my heart feel light and airy too. Like I'm going to be all right.

"I say all those things, and that's what sticks with you." She shakes her head, her crazy bun hair brushing against my cheek. "Figures."

"At least I'm consistent."

"You are so consistent." A content sigh escapes her and I nuzzle my face against hers, happy as fuck to have this girl in my arms, in front of my friends.

"Yo, Bennett."

Speaking of friends...

I turn to see Brenden standing next to us, Kayla by his side. She's taking me and Ava in, her eyes wide with shock and disgust, her big, bitchy mouth falling open. God, I hate her. Though even Brenden looks surprised when he sees who I'm with.

"What do you want?" I ask him, feeling like a dick, but not really caring. He was supposed to break up with that chick a week ago, and he still hasn't done it. I assume because she's keeping his ass happy, giving him blow jobs and letting him do her. Considering she lies there and takes it like a dead fish, Brenden has to know there are better prospects out there.

"Nothing, man. Haven't really seen you all night," Brenden says.

"Probably because you've been sneaking around, letting your girlfriend suck you off," I say irritably.

"Eli," Ava chastises, making me feel like shit. She pulls out of my grip and takes a step toward Brenden with a friendly smile. "Hi. I'm Ava."

"Brenden," my friend mumbles, shaking her offered hand.

I can't help but feel proud. Look at my girl, taking the initiative and introducing herself to my friends.

"Oh, you're Eli's best friend. It's so good to meet you. He's told me a lot about you," she says, sounding warm and friendly.

"Nice to meet you too." Kayla clears her throat and Brenden stands at attention, grabbing her hand and acting as if he likes her or some shit. "This is my girlfriend, Kayla."

"Hi," she says, wrapping her other arm around Brenden's arm like she owns his ass, obviously dodging my girl's hand she was about to stretch out.

I sling my arm around Ava's shoulders and tuck her under my arm like I own her too. Thank God she comes willingly.

"Are you two actually—dating?" Kayla asks with sarcastic wonder, if that's even a thing.

"We are," I say without hesitation. Ava rests her hand on my chest as if she's claiming me.

That's kind of hot.

"Watch out," Kayla says to Ava. "That guy you're with is a complete douchebag."

I feel Ava tense up. She's scowling.

Uh oh.

"You don't know him at all, so if I were you, I would watch what you're saying," Ava snaps, sounding ready for trouble.

Damn, I really, really, *really* love this girl.

"It's your funeral," Kayla says snottily.

"It'll be yours if you keep up the insults." Ava walks right out from underneath my arm, heading straight for Kayla. I grab her before she can do any damage.

"Hey, hey little mama. Simmer down," I tell my girl, keeping her in place. She struggles against my hold, and I can admit it.

I'm a little turned on.

"What the hell? You want to fight me? She's perfect for you, Eli," Kayla says with a sneer before she turns her attention to Brenden. "Let's go."

"But I wanted—"

"Come on, Brenden." She takes his hand and they leave us, Brenden sending me one last pleading look over his shoulder before the crowd swallows him up.

"I hate her," Ava says once I let go of her. She turns to face me. "I was kind of shocked by how hostile you were toward her at first, but now I understand why."

"She's a complete bitch. Remember? She's the one who drove a huge wedge between me and Brenden." I touch her cheek, overwhelmed with the need to get her alone. "That was hot by the way, how you wanted to fight her."

"She made me so freaking angry. She doesn't know me. She doesn't even really know you. How could she make all those assumptions about you?" Ava's voice rises, and I can tell she's still heated.

"I don't know." I shrug. "Kayla hates me. Has since day one."

"I hate her too," she says vehemently, glancing around at the crowd, which is gradually thinning. It's cold as a witch's tit out here—fitting since we're transitioning into October in a few days—and people are going home. It's probably getting late.

"Do you need to go home soon?" I ask.

Ava grabs her phone and checks the time, frowning. "Probably." Her gaze lifts to mine. "But I don't want this night to end."

"Me either." Yet again, I yank her back into my arms, and I drop a simple kiss on her lips. "Think people are watching us?"

"Yes." She wraps her arms around my neck, playing with the hair at my nape and making me shiver. "Should we put on a show?"

"Not too nasty of a one." She laughs. "What we do, we do in secret." I kiss her again, absorbing the sweet taste of her lips. There is nothing better in the world than a kiss from this girl.

Nothing.

"I wasn't talking about getting naked in front of everyone, Eli. Jeez." She rolls her eyes and laughs. I'm about to kiss her with full on tongues showing and everything, but Jackson starts singing and she turns her head just as I go in for the kill, leaving me kissing her cheek like a lame ass.

"I always thought he was overrated, but not tonight," she tells me, as we both push our way into the thinning crowd around the fire, so we can watch and listen to my friend sing. I recognize the tune. Can't quite place it, but I know the words. In fact, I start singing along with them and so does Ava, who's laughing.

"He's singing 'Lucid Dreams'!" she says. "But all slow and kind of country sounding."

"It's a fucking great song," I say. "Though it got overplayed fast."

"Whatever, I love it." She's swaying her cute ass to the beat, singing along with everyone else. I watch her, completely entranced. She's having a great time, moving toward a group of girls who smile at her as they all continue singing. She's not acting shy or timid or clinging to me like a class A stalker.

In fact she's having so much fun I'm almost…jealous. That she can have such a great time and it's not all about me. But that's a good thing. She may be the center of my universe, but I want her independent. *Stand up for herself Ava* is my favorite version of this girl.

Well. I'm a real fan of naked Ava, too. Clawing at my back and coming Ava. Gripping my hair while my head's between her legs Ava is also pretty damn fine…

When the song ends, everyone applauds and shouts, and Jackson's grinning as he rises to his feet with the guitar still clutched in his hand. Ava comes back to me with a giant grin on her face, flinging herself at me as she says, "That was so good!"

"You dancing around was pretty good too," I tell her, settling my arms around her waist. "He loves that damn song. You want to hear a funny story?"

"Sure."

"Last year in English, we had to write some freestyle poem as an assignment. Our teacher was like, *write what you feel. Write your pain if you have to. Let me feel it with your words.* So Jackson wrote, word for word, the lyrics to 'Lucid Dreams.' And our teacher made him read it out loud, calling it a masterpiece. We tried really hard not to laugh, but about halfway through, Jackson started cracking up, and we all did too." I shake my head at the memory. "It was so damn funny."

"Did he get in trouble?"

"No. The teacher yelled at us for being disrespectful when Jackson's the one who started laughing first. I even said we were laughing with him, not at him, but he wouldn't hear it." I start laughing all over again. "Poor old Mr. Johnson. He retired after that school year. I blame 'Lucid Dreams.'"

"He probably thought he had a poetic prodigy in his class."

"Yeah, when he really had a plagiarizing asshole who stole from Juice WRLD." I stop laughing. "RIP to that guy. Sucks that he died."

"I know." She makes a little sad face. "I should probably go get Ellie. We need to get home before her parents have a heart attack."

"You're spending the night at her house?" I raise my brows.

"Yeah, that way I don't have to deal with my parents." She presses her lips together, looking guilty.

Leaving me suspicious. "Are your parents cool with us together?" I ask.

"Uh…" Her voice drifts and I'm immediately defensive. "They don't know I'm here with you."

"Where do they think you're at?" I ask her warily. Now I'm flat-out annoyed. I don't want to be her dirty little secret any longer. That shit is beyond tired.

"At Tony's," she confesses, guilt flashing on her pretty face.

Everything good that just happened the past couple of hours blows up in my face. She's lying. Hiding me. I had an issue with that before what happened last Friday night at her house. She promised after homecoming, she'd come clean.

Everyone—meaning her family—would know we're together.

Yet she didn't tell them she came to see me. Is she afraid of their reaction? Is she scared they're going to try and keep us apart? Or is it more convenient to keep our relationship a secret from everyone?

She's putting on a show here. It suddenly all feels fake.

"This won't work," I say, my voice wooden. "If you're going to keep hiding me—hiding *us*—then I can't be with you, Ava. No matter how much I care about you, I refuse to be with a girl who's ashamed to bring me home and introduce me to her family."

Her mouth drops open and her eyes go wide. "I'm not ashamed of you."

"Bullshit. You should've been honest and told your parents you were coming here to see me," I throw out at her. "Maybe you should invite me over tomorrow, so I can hang out with the Callahans for the afternoon. Can you do that? Are you brave enough?"

Her eyes are luminous. Like she might cry at any moment. Seeing her tears would gut me, but damn it, the way she's still hiding me has already left me gutted.

I can't keep going like this.

"That's what I thought," I say when she hasn't responded. "When you're ready to tell everyone who you really want to be with, come see me. If you don't have the guts, then leave me alone."

I turn and walk away from her, my cold- blooded heart threatening to shatter. But that fucker is made of steel, so I know it'll stay intact. Ava calls my name, but I don't turn around. She doesn't chase after me.

Fine. I didn't think she would anyway.

CHAPTER 11

AVA

*T*he back and forth of our relationship is killing me. I knew admitting I hadn't told my parents where I really was would make him angry. But I didn't expect him to get *that* angry.

Or for him to walk away.

I let him go. I didn't even cry. I felt like it, though. I wanted to chase after him and beg him not to go, but he wouldn't listen. I know I have to make things right. With my family. With Eli.

By the time I'm in Ellie's car and we're headed back to her place, I'm in a complete funk.

"So, you and Eli back together?" she asks, her voice lightly teasing.

"Sort of," I mumble, pressing my head against the seat and closing my eyes. "We still need to work out a few details."

"I'm sure you will. You two looked pretty cute earlier, when he was standing behind you with his arms around your waist," Ellie says.

My heart pangs at the too recent memory. Maybe we moved too fast. We should've talked more. I should've been more open about our family situation. How it's still really tense, especially between Jake and me. My parents still aren't one hundred percent happy with me either. I'm making mistakes over and over again, and I don't know how to correct them.

I decide to change the subject.

"Let's forget about Eli and me for a moment and focus on you." I pause. "And Jackson Rivers."

Even in the dark interior of her car, I can tell Ellie is blushing. "It's nothing."

"Oh it's something. Tell me what's going on."

"He's nice."

"Uh huh."

"I love watching him play the guitar. He's got great fingers." A dreamy sigh escapes her as she clutches the steering wheel tight.

"Are you thinking about all the places those great fingers of his could touch you?" I ask. Now I'm the one who's teasing.

But I'm also very serious.

"Oh my God, Ava. Come on."

"Come on what?" I shake my head. "I couldn't have grossed you out. I know you're attracted to him. So what's the problem?"

She's quiet for a moment as she navigates the winding road. A car passes by us going in the opposite direction, its headlights flashing briefly across her face and I see the worry and fear there. All the insecurities she suffers from.

My best friend has always had a problem seeing how great she is.

"I don't think he's attracted to me. I'm not the type of girl he'd go for," she finally says, her voice small.

"That's a bunch of crap, and you know it. You're almost too good for him, if you ask me. You're smart and cute and

funny. You go out of your way to help people. You're interesting and fun to hang out with," I tell her. "I could create a
long list of all of your amazing qualities, but you'll eventually
get embarrassed and tell me to stop. So I'm going to quit now
before it all goes to your head."

She laughs, but it sounds forced. Fake. "I don't have a
chance with a guy like him."

"A guy like him? He's just a guy, Ellie. And I saw the way
he looked at you. You definitely have a chance."

"How did he look at me?" she asks quickly, her gaze
whipping to mine for a brief moment before she refocuses
on the road ahead.

I want to describe the moment I witnessed perfectly. It
looked like something momentous was happening between
them, and he was fully aware of it. And pursuing it. "He
looked at you like he might want to write a song about you," I
finally say.

Ellie makes a face. "No way."

"Yes, he did! I swear!"

"Really?"

I hate how unsure she sounds. Like she can't believe me
when I literally witnessed their flirtation. Everyone by the
fire did, too, if they were paying attention. "Really," I say, my
voice firm. "I think you should go for it."

"But how? What do I do next? What do I say? Send him a
text admitting I have a giant crush on him?" Ellie sighs,
sounding dejected. "He'll be like, that's great. Lots of girls
have giant crushes on me. Next!"

"He will not. I could tell, the way he watched you, he's
interested," I reaffirm. "Maybe just hit him up on Snap. Ask
to start a streak."

"Uh, I already did that," she admits. "We've been
Snapchatting since the last party we went to at the cabin."

Just like I kept secrets from my best friend, she's been

111

holding out on me too. "Get the hell out," I breathe. "You never told me!"

"I didn't want to say anything because it feels like getting my hopes up. I'm always waiting for him to realize that he doesn't really want to talk to me anymore," Ellie admits. "I'm sure he'll ghost me any day now."

"Oh my God, Ellie. You are so negative." I give her shoulder a tiny shove. Nothing too major, so she doesn't wreck. "Are you just sending photos to each other or are you actually talking?" I'm so curious. Maybe there's more going on than she wants to admit, for fear of jinxing it.

"At first, it was just photos. And all of his photos were so hot, I swear he could be a model," Ellie says with a little groan. "Compared to him, I'm so boring."

"You are not," I say irritably because I'm definitely irritated. This girl needs to see her worth, not worry that she's not worthy. "Tell me more about these evolving conversations between you two."

"Right. So after a few days of endless photos back and forth, I finally sent him a photo with me making a goofy face and asking how his day was. And he responded right away telling me it was good, and then he asked me how mine was," she explains.

"Okay." I draw the word out. Sounds fairly mundane.

"And it sort of took off from there. He's told me a lot about himself. About how he used to always move around when he was younger, and how much he hated it. How he loves playing the guitar and football, and how much he likes living here. He's actually very interesting," Ellie says.

"But that's it. You've only talked. Now you see him tonight and nothing else happened?" I ask.

"He hugged me before I left." Another dreamy sigh leaves her. "He's really muscular. And so tall."

"Well, you're kind of short so…" I let my voice drift, grinning when she sends me an annoyed glance. "I'm teasing."

"No, it's true. I'm short. And he's tall. So tall. And broad. I just want to run my fingers through his hair, Ava. Just once. So I know what it feels like." Her voice lowers. "It looks really, really soft."

"Girl, you've got it so bad," I tease her, making her laugh. For real this time.

"True. You've got it bad too. You and Eli are really back together then? I'm happy for you but…how will your parents feel about that?"

I remain quiet as Ellie comes to a stop sign and turns onto the main road that leads back into town, where her house is. "I have to tell my parents Eli and I are back together. He got mad when he found out I lied to them about where I'm at tonight."

"Oh." She's quiet for a moment too. "Doesn't he understand how delicate a situation this is?"

"He doesn't get why I can't just be honest. He believes I'm treating him like a dirty little secret. That's a direct quote." His words and the pain on his face made me feel terrible.

More than anything, his accusations made me feel guilty.

"I mean, you sort of do treat him that way, but you have good reason to. You go to a different school. He shit talked your brother endlessly. They got into a fight. Eli screwed around with Jake's now ex. Their rivalry is pretty well-known around the area. I'm sure your parents don't think the best about him." Ellie makes a face. "You'd think he'd get it."

"But he's right. I can't treat him like my secret any longer. If we're going to be together, really together, then I have to put it out there for the world to see. I have to show him I'm proud to be seen with him," I explain. "That's why he's upset. He thinks I'm ashamed of him, or something."

"You're not, are you?"

"No, not at all," I say, feeling defensive. "I'm in love with him."

"Then I guess he wants you to prove it," Ellie says.

"Yeah, you're right." I stare out the window, watching as the city lights come into view. Grabbing my phone, I send the quickest text to Eli, not expecting an answer.

I'm telling my parents about us tomorrow. I swear I'm not ashamed of you, Eli.

But he does send me a response. And it's only two words. The very ones Ellie just said to me.

Prove it.

* * *

"WE'RE GOING to the Bulldogs game. You're going with us, right?" Mom asks me the next morning when I walk in the door. I spent the night at Ellie's, but she had to be at work at ten, so she dropped me off at the school where I left my car and I drove straight home.

I come to a stop by the kitchen counter, glancing over at the table to see my entire family sitting there. Dad, Autumn, Jake and Beck. In front of them, empty plates with a few scant crumbs. Remnants of their Saturday morning breakfast.

I feel like I missed out.

"Um, sure," I answer hesitantly. It's weird, how they're all staring at me.

Autumn grins. "I'm so glad. We're all going, so we can watch Ash play."

"Doesn't Beck have a game this afternoon?" I meet my little brother's gaze, who shrugs before he returns his attention to his new phone.

"When it's over, we'll head straight for the stadium," Dad says. I inwardly groan. The last thing I want to do is go to another one of Beck's youth league games. "I still have one extra ticket for the game. You want to invite Ellie?"

No. I want to invite Eli. "She's working all day," I say. "She probably can't go."

"Oh, that's too bad. She hasn't been over in a while," Dad says, sending me a meaningful look. I'm sure that's some sort of jab at me, but I'm ignoring it.

"Is Hannah coming with us?" I meet Jake's gaze. He seems shocked I'd talk to him.

"Yeah, she is," he admits.

"Then I definitely have someone I want to invite," I tell Dad. I can feel Mom stiffen next to me. I'm sure she's preparing for my answer. I'm also sure she knows who I'm going to say.

"Who?" Dad says, his brows lowering like he's confused.

I press my lips together, taking a deep breath before I blurt, "Eli."

"Absolutely not," Dad says at the same time Jake says, "Hell no."

Autumn reaches over and slaps Jake's arm. "You can't tell her who she can and cannot invite."

He glares at her, rubbing his arm where she smacked him but, otherwise, says nothing.

"Why not, Daddy?" I ask, my voice shaky.

"I thought you two were broken up," Mom says to me, her voice low.

"We want to make it work." I turn, so I'm facing her. "We've been talking."

"Really?" Mom sounds full of doubt, when I really need her to be on my side.

"Yes, really." I glance over at my father, whose thunderous expression tells me he doesn't approve. "If you get to know him, you'll realize Eli is actually a good guy."

Jake makes a derisive noise, and I send him a dirty look.

"I don't care who they are. No boys are good enough for my daughters," Dad says with a scowl.

"What about Ash?" Autumn asks, as she gets up from her chair and walks over to our father, dropping into his lap. He automatically wraps his arms around her waist, and she loops her arms loosely around his neck. "You approve of him, right?"

Her pointed question and expression make him visibly squirm.

"I've—come to accept him," Dad says haltingly, making Autumn laugh and shake her head.

"Then you have to give Ava's boyfriend a chance," she tells him, and I stand there in wonder, watching as my big sister works our dad over for me. When she still lived at home, she treated me like garbage. All the time. I was a nuisance, a pest. I didn't understand. I was too young and got in all her shit and was too nosey and she basically made my freshman year a living hell.

Now, finally, she's on my side. It's actually pretty amazing.

And heartwarming.

"Let him come with us," Autumn continues, as she plants a noisy kiss on Dad's cheek before she rises to her feet. "Not like he's going to try anything when we're all there together. He'll be on his best behavior."

"Yeah right. You have no idea what this guy is like, Autumn. Trust me, he doesn't know how to be on his best behavior. I don't want him there," Jake says. Always making sure we know how he feels about Eli.

We get it, Jake. We get it.

"We know," Autumn says drolly before she glances over at me and Mom. "You won't know what he's really like unless you actually spend time with him. Don't judge him for what he's done."

"He's done some pretty awful stuff," Dad says.

"Please?" I turn to Mom who offers me a soft smile. "It would mean so much to me—and to Eli—if he could come tonight. Let him prove to you that he's not a bad guy."

Mom sends Dad a knowing look and he returns it, lifting a brow. It's pretty crazy how they can communicate with each other without ever saying a word. "What do you think, Drew? Should we let her invite him?"

Nerves eat at my stomach as I wait for his answer. His expression is like stone. Unreadable. Then there's Jake, who's totally annoyed. Beck could care less. He'd rather play on his phone.

"Just say yes," Autumn tells him, making Dad sigh.

"Fine, yes. He can go."

Jake pushes back his chair, the legs scraping loudly across the wood floor as he jumps to his feet. "Keep that asshole away from me tonight," he mutters, before he exits the kitchen.

Ignoring my brother's outburst, I rush over to Dad and give him a hug, pressing my cheek against his chest. "Thank you for letting him go."

"You better ask him first and make sure he can go," Dad says gruffly, as he gives me a squeeze before he releases me.

"I will." I go back to my mom and hug her too, before I grab my bag and race up the stairs, isolating myself in my room, so I can text Eli in private. I hope he answers. I hope he hasn't blocked me again. He was mad last night, but not totally furious. More like he was disappointed. I keep letting him down. I need to prove that I want to be with him. No sneaking around this time either.

If going to a Fresno State Bulldogs game with my family isn't public enough for him, then I don't know what is.

Picking up my phone, I start typing.

You want to go to the Bulldogs game tonight?

He responds within seconds.

Eli: **With who?**

I decide to FaceTime him. I don't have the patience to type it all out. Plus, I want to see his face.

He answers quickly, and when his face appears on my phone screen, I feel a little giddy. He's clearly still in bed. His hair is a mess and he's shirtless. "Why are you texting me so early?"

"You answered." I shrug, smiling at him. "So, do you want to come with us to the game tonight?"

"Who's us?" He yawns. Scratches his chest. I watch his fingers trail across his bare skin and tingles sweep over me.

"My entire family," I answer.

That gets his attention. "You're serious?"

I nod. "My parents, plus Autumn is here. Jake and Hannah. My little brother, Beck. We're all headed to campus after Beck's football game. Autumn came home for the weekend to spend time with us and with Ash."

"Ash fucking Davis?" Eli sits up, the comforter pooling around his waist. "He's a legend. I always forget they're together."

"They'll probably get married eventually." Pretty sure Autumn's already got her wedding colors picked out and everything.

"Will we get a chance to talk to him?" Eli asks eagerly.

"Maybe. I'm not sure." I pause. "So. Do you want to go with us?"

"Your parents are cool with me going? And Jake?"

"I wouldn't ask if they weren't." I won't mention Jake and how he acted earlier. We'll just steer clear of him this evening. Plus, he'll have Hannah there as a buffer too. Just like I'll be a buffer for Eli.

It should all work out. No problems.

"Yeah, I'll go. That sounds dope as hell." He smiles at me

and I can't help but smile in return. "You've made a complete turnaround, Callahan."

"Hey, you told me to prove it," I say. I lean back against the pile of pillows on my bed, yanking up the very blanket Autumn accused me of stealing so it's wrapped all around me. "Maybe you could come pick me up at my house in a little bit?"

"Uh, sure." He runs a hand through his hair, his biceps bulging with the movement. He has the best arms. He has the best everything. "I need to take a shower first."

"You have a Bulldogs T-shirt?" I ask. "Make sure you wear one. We all do when we go to their games."

"Do you go to them a lot?"

"Yeah, to support Ash. I didn't go to many games last year though. I thought they were kind of boring," I admit.

The expression on his face is nothing less than horrified. "Football *bores* you?"

"I mean...it's not my favorite." I wrinkle my nose.

"That's it. We're done. For sure." My heart drops to my stomach for the quickest second, before he starts laughing, and I realize he's teasing me. "You are such a contradiction, Ava Callahan. You come from football royalty. Your dad and uncle played for the NFL. Your brother will probably play for a pro team too. Your sister is going to marry a guy who might end up a top draft pick, and you're like, 'it's not my favorite.'" He says the last part in a high-pitched voice.

"I do *not* sound like that." I'm vaguely offended.

"You kind of do." He's smiling. His eyes are sparkling. He's enjoying this.

"So what time are you picking me up?" I ask, changing the subject.

"How is this working exactly?"

"Well, my parents have to take Beck to his football game in a few hours. Autumn will probably end up going with

119

them, since she won't be able to see Ash until after the game. I assume Jake will go get Hannah and meet us down there. We can meet everyone down there too. They'll want to tail-gate before the game starts. Dad always brings his mini barbecue and makes beer butt chicken." I make a face.

Eli bursts out laughing. "Sounds delicious."

"I'm sure you'll love it," I drawl. "You want me to text you when they leave?"

"What, they're going to allow their precious baby girl to be picked up by me when you're all alone in the house?" He raises his brows.

"I haven't given them a reason not to trust me." I lift my nose in the air, going for innocent.

But if Eli wants to mess around a little bit, I'd be down.

"Lately you have. But I guess they can easily forgive you." He's got this look on his face, and I'm guessing it might be related to the fact that his parents—his mother, specifically—doesn't seem to trust him at all. Not that he necessarily earns her trust. "I'll hop in the shower and you text me when you're ready for me to come get you," he says.

"Okay. Sounds good."

"See you later, baby."

"Eli," I say, just before he ends the call. "I'm glad you're coming with us."

"I'm fuckin' glad you invited me," he says with a little laugh.

Making me laugh too.

CHAPTER 12

⚜

ELI

I still can't believe Ava actually asked me to join her for a family fun night at a Bulldogs game. This ought to be interesting. Me and Jake sharing the same air, hanging out together? Fucking insane. That guy will probably shoot daggers at me with his eyes the entire night. If I'm lucky, I'll chat up Drew Callahan and get him on my good side. Maybe I'll even get a chance to talk to Asher Davis. That guy is an amazing quarterback. I think his chances to go pro are huge. I'd love to hear what he has to say.

But the best part of this? Being with Ava. Just—sitting next to her and not having to hide the fact that we're together. Like I told her, I don't want to be her dirty little secret any longer. I pretty much announced to all my friends last night that we're together. Hell, I'd strut around everywhere I could with that fine ass girl on my arm. That fine ass girl who just so happens to be mine.

I take a quick shower and jerk off to ease the tension. With what happened last night, I know I won't be able to do much with her this weekend, especially since we'll be with the fam bam. Gotta be on my best behavior. I might be picking her up at her house when no one else is there, but I don't think we're gonna get down and dirty. She's playing shy right now, and that's fine. I'll chase her.

Eventually, I'll catch her.

I dig through my closet looking for a Bulldogs T-shirt, but I don't have one anywhere. When you live close to a university, you tend to pick up one of their shirts eventually, but I guess I lost the one I know I had a long time ago.

I end up in my brother Ryan's room and go through his closet. He took pretty much everything he wanted with him when he went away to college, and none of this stuff left behind means much to him. Lucky for me, I find a Bulldogs T-shirt. It's navy blue versus the typical red, but it has a giant bulldog on the front of it, so that'll work. I tug the shirt on over my head and check myself out in his dresser mirror. I look good. Pretty sure this T-shirt is practically brand new.

I'm about to leave the bedroom when my eyes snag on a picture frame sitting on top of the dresser. Picking it up, I check out the photo. It's of me and Ryan and my parents. We're in Maui. One of the last family vacations we took together during Thanksgiving break. I'm a freshman and Ryan's a senior and I'm pretty sure it was a last-ditch effort between my mom and dad to make things right between them, but it didn't work. I remember them arguing a lot. Mom drinking a lot. Things were tense between them. You can see the strain in my dad's eyes. My mom's tight lips and glassy stare. Even Ryan looks like he'd rather be anywhere but there.

Me? I'm smiling wide and looking like a cheesy motherfucker having the time of his life in Hawaii. I look oblivious to the tension, though I wasn't. It was just easier to pretend none of that was happening.

I remember hooking up with a cute girl who was a year older than me. Sixteen to my fifteen. She taught me to slow down with kissing, use less tongue and not be so eager. I owe that chick a lot.

I don't even remember her name.

I set the frame down, hating the melancholy that washes over me, slowing my steps. Darkening my mood. My family broke apart soon after that photo was taken. I could blame my dad for cheating on my mom, but let's be real. They were both at fault, always playing the blame game.

Now look at us. I'm alone in this giant house. I have no idea where Mom is right now. My father hasn't lived here in a couple of years and I rarely see him. When I do, he yells at me. Ryan is like a ghost. He just up and disappeared. Went away to college and never came back.

Fucking sucks. I miss him.

Once I'm back in my room, I grab my phone and send Ryan a quick text.

You need to call me tomorrow. We have a lot to talk about.

That's all I say. I hope it's enough to scare him. At the very least, concern him. Fill him with curiosity. I'm tired of being treated badly by every important person in my life. I need people to step up.

At least my girl finally did.

My phone dings, and I check it eagerly, ready to see a response from Ryan. But it's not my brother who's texting.

It's Ava.

The coast is clear. My family is gone. You can come over whenever you want.

I feel like her text is loaded with innuendo. Or maybe that's my horny side reminding me that it would be real easy to get Ava naked in her room.

But will she let me?

Guess I'm gonna find out in approximately thirty minutes.

* * *

I MAKE it up to her neighborhood by the lake in what feels like record time, my engine roaring as I floor it, while climbing the mountain highway. Even though summer's long over, the tourists still come out on Saturdays and drive like assholes. Tour-ons is what my dad used to call them instead of morons, though it's not like we've lived up here for decades and have the right to call them that. All the locals do. But the majority of businesses need those tourists to survive, so they shouldn't complain.

Honestly? I can't wait to get the fuck out of here. I didn't grow up here, I have no real ties to this place. Everyone knows my business anyway. Small town vibes kill my big-time dreams on what feels like a daily basis.

By the time I'm pulling into the Callahan driveway, I'm nervous. Which is a foreign sensation because come on. What do I have to be nervous about? The Callahans aren't even here so I have no one to impress. My girl is the only one who's waiting for me in that house. The nerves will really kick in by the time we arrive at the stadium. I'll have to get myself under control and hope I don't make a complete ass out of myself.

Though I've been making an ass out of myself for the last few months and I'm sure every single person we'll be hanging with tonight has witnessed it at one point or another. So fuck it.

I'll just be me.

I jog up to the front door and push the doorbell, the chimes ringing loudly. I shove my hands into the front pockets of my jeans and look around. The neighborhood is quiet. No one's outside. The only sound is a bird calling in the distance and if you really concentrate, I can hear the roar of a boat engine out on the water.

The door suddenly swings open and I turn back around only for my jaw to drop open. Ava's standing in front of me, wearing form fitting dark blue jeans with a rip in the knee and a cropped red T-shirt with the bulldog mascot front and center and "Bulldogs" in giant letters above it. Her hair is perfectly straight and flows past her shoulders and she's smiling at me.

"Goddamn." That's the first thing I say, like an asshole. I scrub a hand over my jaw. "You look hot as fuck."

She laughs and opens the door wider. "Come in."

I follow her inside, tilting my head back to take in the soaring foyer, the giant chandelier light thing hanging above my head. It's not a classic chandelier dripping with crystals. Definitely got a more modern feel about it.

Everything about this house has a modern feel to it.

"This is the first time I've walked inside your house normally," I tell her as she shuts the door.

"You want a tour?" she asks.

"Sure."

Ava escorts me around the house, showing me the many rooms. There are actual wings to this place. There's an entire office and guest suite, along with a giant bathroom that occupies one end of the house. There's a living room and family room and the kitchen is massive. Her parents' bedroom is down here too, in its own wing, and it's freaking huge. She didn't even show me the bathroom, but I can only imagine. And this is just on the first level.

I thought our house was nice. This place is a palace.

"Let's go upstairs," she says, as she grabs onto the railing and starts climbing.

I'm right behind her, eye level with her perfect ass, and I'm tempted to reach out and touch it, but I keep my impulses under control. Those things get me in trouble, and I'm trying to be respectful right now.

Don't want her thinking I only want to maul her.

She points at a closed door. "Jake's room. And no, you're not allowed even a peek inside."

"Not that I give a shit," I tell her, though it's kind of a lie.

I wouldn't mind checking out his bedroom, though I doubt it would tell me much about that motherfucker.

"Autumn's old room," Ava says, pointing to an open door. It's very clean and pretty plain. I assume she's taken everything that matters with her to college. "And Beck's room." She points at another open door, and inside it's messy with all sorts of video game and 49er posters hanging all over the walls. Clearly it belongs to a boy.

"Here's my room," she says, stopping in front of another closed door. "Though you've been here before."

How could I forget the time I crawled up the side of her house and climbed through her window? Yeah, that's a memory etched on my brain. "I have."

She opens the door and walks inside, me trailing after her. The room is cleaner than the last time I was in here. The bed neatly made and no sign of clothes tossed over furniture or a messy desk. The entire room is spotless.

"You've got a giant room," I say as I look around it, spotting the open door that leads to a connecting bathroom.

"Yours is pretty big too," she reminds me.

I clamp my lips together, refusing to make a dirty joke. Why am I always tested like this? "You definitely win this contest."

"I can't help it if my father has money. And not just because he played football either. He comes from a very wealthy family." She smiles at me.

I stare at her for a moment, dumbfounded by her beauty, not giving a shit if she has money. Not even really giving a shit right now that her dad is a famous ex-NFL quarterback and my idol when I was a kid.

How'd I get so lucky to snag this girl and make her mine? I'm a complete fuckup, and she's the golden girl. To everyone else I'm sure we don't make any sense. I saw her years ago sitting in the stands and I thought she was so damn beautiful. A pretty princess with an easy smile and flashing green eyes. Seeing her, making eye contact with her that night, set my heart on fire. I can't explain why. Love at first sight?

I always thought that was a bunch of crap. But maybe not.

Back then, I made an idle promise to myself that one day, she'd belong to me, never thinking it could actually happen.

Yet here I am, standing in her bedroom. The two of us the only ones in this giant house. She's got this particular gleam in her eyes, like maybe she wants to jump me or something.

This is a good sign. A positive sign.

"Are you sure your family isn't coming back here before they head down to the stadium?" I ask, keeping my distance. I don't want to start something we can't finish, especially if we could potentially be interrupted by her parents.

Talk about a nightmare.

"I'm sure. Mom went over what they needed to bring with them about fifty times before they finally left the house," Ava says with a firm nod.

"And what time are we supposed to meet up with them again?"

"Game starts at 7:30, so we should be down there at least two hours before it begins so we can go to the tailgate party and eat." She grins. "Beer butt chicken, remember?"

"How could I forget?" I don't really care about chicken cooked with a beer can in its butt. All I can think about is me. And Ava. Alone in this house.

When I arrived here, it was around one. We have a shit ton of time before we have to leave.

Like…a shit ton.

"Are you sure they're cool with me coming to the game?" I

ask. "You're not—hiding me again here, are you?" I have to make sure. I don't know why it bothers me so much, but I'm tired of feeling like her secret. I want her to admit to the world that we're together.

I need her support now more than ever.

"My family wants you there," she says easily, her expression never faltering. That reassures me. Kind of. "I want you there. You wanted me to prove to you that I want you in my life? Well, here I am. Inviting you to my house. Inviting you to spend time with my entire family at a football game. If that doesn't prove to you how I feel, then I don't know what else will."

We stare at each other for a few tense filled seconds. Not a bad tension, though. More like...sexual tension. Like, my hands are itching to touch her. Explore that sliver of skin exposed by her cropped T-shirt. And she's eyeing me like she wants exactly the same thing.

I go to her bed and sit on the edge of it, spreading my legs a little. "Come here," I tell her with a flick of my head.

She comes to me with slow steps, like she's trying to drag this moment out. Which is fine by me, because I want to savor this too. When she stops in front of me, right in between my legs, I reach for her, settling my hands on her hips, my fingertips grazing the bare skin above her jeans. She watches me with eyes full of hesitancy, and I blink up at her, momentarily confused.

"You okay?" I ask.

She nods.

"What's wrong?"

"Nothing." She shakes her head. Then holds up her hand. "I'm shaking."

Ava's right. Her fingers, her entire hand is gently quaking. I grab hold of it and give it a squeeze, trying to calm her down. "Why?"

"Just nervous, I guess." She shrugs.

"Princess." I tug on her hand and we both fall onto the bed, rearranging ourselves so we're facing each other, our heads on the pile of pillows. Damn, these things are soft. "You have no reason to be nervous. We've done this before, remember? A few times. I have intimate knowledge of your O face."

And it's burned in my memories forever.

"You would say that," she says with a laugh, her cheeks turning the faintest pink. I love it when she blushes. I love it when she does just about anything.

"What are you nervous about?"

"Losing you again." She touches my cheek, her fingers featherlight as they skim over my skin. "Messing up and making you hate me."

"I could never hate you."

"I thought you hated me last week, when you walked away from me." Her lower lip trembles and her eyes get watery.

"Ah, shit. Don't cry." I pull her into me, my hand cupping the back of her head as she buries her face against my chest. "This is supposed to be a hot moment, not a sad moment."

She laughs again, though it also sounds like she's crying. "A hot moment?"

"I planned on getting you naked," I whisper into her hair.

"Really?" Ava tilts her head back so our gazes lock, her eyes a little red. "I didn't think you'd want to."

"Please." I always want to get naked with Ava. "I didn't think *you'd* want to." Now it's my turn to touch her face. I trace the length of her nose. The curve of her lips. "I figured you might want to take this slow."

"I thought the same about you."

I send her a *come on* look. "I'm not a take it slow kind of person. You know this."

"No, you're really not, are you?" She smiles. Her eyes are clear. I don't think she feels like crying anymore. "Did you bring condoms?"

She whispers that last question.

"Maybe." I did. I carry one tucked away in my wallet where it's not obvious. There are more in my car. I'm not stupid.

"If you didn't, we can do—other stuff." She scoots closer to me, and I slip my arm around her waist, sneaking my hand up the back of her shirt so I can touch bare skin.

"What sort of other stuff are you thinking?" I kiss her nose. The corner of her mouth, keeping it gentle. Downright chaste. I'm both eager to get inside her and dying to drive her out of her mind.

Still not sure which side will win, I decide to see where this takes us.

"Oh, I don't know," she says before I kiss her full on the mouth now, my lips lingering. Tugging on her lower lip with both of mine. "What do you want to do?"

"Strip you out of your clothes." Another kiss. This one longer. I swipe my tongue across her upper lip right before I end it. "Kiss you all over your body."

"I might like that." A shiver escapes her when my mouth drifts across her jaw, down her neck.

"Only might?" I keep kissing her neck. She likes it when I do that. "What if I took off your panties with my teeth?"

A laugh escapes her. "You think that's possible?"

"Don't say it like that. You know I love a challenge. I'll prove to you it's possible," I say, right before she kisses me.

And what a kiss it is. Full of tongue and heat, with these soft whimpers coming from the back of her throat. She shifts out of my grip so she can hover over me, her mouth seeking mine again, the next kiss getting sloppy. Dirty.

I reach for her, threading my fingers in the soft hair at the back of her head. I slide them down, streaking across her nape, and when my fingers stumble over a chain, I can tell something is hanging heavy on it, dangling from her neck.

Breaking the kiss, I lean back, trying to take her in, but her mouth chases after mine, reconnecting with an impatient moan. I place my hand on her shoulder and give her a light nudge, making her break the kiss. She lifts away from me, a little scowl on her face. "What's wrong?"

That's when I see it. My #1 pendant hanging from her neck. On a different chain, one that's much more delicate. A mixture of joy and possessiveness floods my veins at seeing my number on her.

I thought it was lost forever.

"Where'd you find this?" I touch the pendant. Curl my index finger around the thin chain.

"It must've broke when you got into the fight with Jake. I found it that night in our yard, after you already left." Her fingers brush against mine as she touches the pendant as well. "I've been wearing it ever since. So I always had a piece of you, even though you left me."

I broke her fucking heart. Just like she broke mine.

"This is mine." I tug on the thin gold chain, pulling her down so our lips are perfectly aligned.

"You want it back?"

"Keep it. You're mine too." I kiss her. Nip at her lower lip with my teeth, making her gasp. "I eventually wanna see you wearing that necklace and nothing else."

"I can make that happen," she says eagerly.

"Oh yeah?" Another kiss. "Prove it," I murmur against her lips.

CHAPTER 13

AVA

*H*is words are just the push I need.

I pull away from his kiss, smiling as I climb off the mattress and stand. Eli rolls over so his head is propped on the pillows and he's watching me with a smirk on his face, his arms bent behind his head.

He looks good lying on my bed, wearing jeans and the Bulldogs T-shirt, white socks on his feet. He must've kicked off his shoes at one point. I didn't even notice.

Reaching for the button on my jeans, I undo it, then slowly slide down the zipper. I thought it might feel awkward, stripping in front of my boyfriend, but from the appreciative gleam I see in his eyes, I realize it's not awkward at all.

I feel empowered. A rush of heat sweeps over me, my body reacting to only a look from him.

Shimmying out of the jeans, I eventually have to bend over and tug them off of each leg, kicking them onto the floor, hoping I don't look too silly. I stand up straight and brush the hair out of my eyes, ready to pull the shirt off over my head when Eli says, "Wait a minute."

My arms drop to my sides. "What?"

"Keep the T-shirt on. And your panties." A wicked smile curves his lips. "Take off the bra though."

"Really?" I wrinkle my nose.

He nods. "Really."

I reach behind me, sneaking my hand beneath my shirt, finding the back snap. I undo it with a flick of my fingers, the bra springing away from me. Quickly I take it off, sliding one strap down my arm, and then the other before I pull the entire thing from under my shirt and let it fall to the floor.

"That was kind of sexy," Eli says.

"It was not," I say with a laugh. I rest my hands on my hips, letting him look his fill. My panties are white and lacy. I was going for the virginal look, though I'm not a virgin anymore, thanks to this boy.

"It was to me." He makes a motion with his finger. "Turn around."

He loves to have me turn around. Always checking me out. Sometimes I feel like I'm some sort of visual plaything to him.

Really I suppose he's just very into watching when it comes to sex.

"Damn woman." He's shaking his head when I face him once more, his gaze locked on my chest. "I can see your nipples poking against the T-shirt."

I can actually feel them tighten when he says that. This boy makes me feel bold. Comfortable—and not in a boring way. I trust him. I trust who I am when I'm with him. And I hope he trusts me too.

"I'm guessing that was part of your plan," I tell him.

"You guessed right," he says with a chuckle, appearing very pleased with himself. "You don't know how good you look right now. I wish I could take a picture."

"Why don't you?" I rest my hands on my hips, thrust out my leg and strike a pose like I'm some sort of supermodel.

Furthest thing from the truth, but I may as well act silly and have a little fun. Eli never seems to mind.

"You'd let me take photos of you like this?" He sounds incredulous.

"Um, as long as you promise to hide them somewhere on your phone." I shrug, acting like it's no big deal, but secretly shocked I'd say such a thing. Am I really doing this? Making this offer? Have I lost my freakin' mind?

"I can put them in the My Eyes Only section on Snapchat," he offers as he grabs his phone from the back pocket of his jeans.

I frown. That's the folder on Snap where you can hide photos with a passcode. I might have a few, but nothing too scandalous. One of me and Ellie the first time we tried weed, both of us clinging to each other and grinning at the camera, Ellie clutching a bong in her hand. Yeah, that's a damaging photo we would never want out in public. "Do you have any other photos in there?"

I'm referring to any nudes a girl might've sent him. I know he's received them before. Probably multiple times from multiple girls.

He slowly shakes his head. "None. You'll be the only one."

"Really?" I find this incredibly hard to believe. I mean, this is Eli Bennett, the player, we're talking about.

"Well, okay. Let me explain. My first two years in high school, that's where I'd stash all the nudes I had. Not just ones sent to me by girls, but also ones that my friends would send me that girls would send them. We all shared and swapped them," he explains.

"That's terrible." I am so glad I never sent nudes to any boy, especially my freshman and sophomore years. Plenty of times a girl's photos would get leaked, and it would turn into a big scandal around campus. Even the vice principal got involved a couple of times. Boys pass them around to each other constantly. I became aware of this pretty early on my freshman year.

Which should make me really wary of letting Eli take any photos now.

But we're older. Eli loves me. I love him. We've already had sex. He wouldn't share my photos with any of his friends. That's just—wrong.

"Yeah, well, eventually I didn't want those photos anymore. Felt kind of sleazy to have them, you know? Not like I used them for anything." I make a face when he says that, and he laughs. "I just stashed them in there for safe-keeping and never looked at them again. So I deleted them all."

"No other girl has sent you nudes recently," I say.

He slowly shakes his head. "Nope."

"I find that hard to believe."

"Baby, they all lost interest in me once Jackson started roaming around campus with his guitar. That guitar gives him major game," Eli says, and we both laugh.

I'm sure what he says about Jackson is true. I've seen the way girls lose their minds over him. The blonde hair, the sparkling blue eyes, and the rock star persona.

But forget Jackson. I want to focus on my boyfriend.

"So how do you want to do this?" I ask Eli. When he frowns, I explain. "Take photos of me."

"Oh. Well." He scratches his jaw as he contemplates me. "I don't want to show your face. That way if anyone does find them, they won't know who you are."

"Okay." I nod, suddenly feeling foolish. This is the craziest suggestion I've ever made in my life. Doubt swamps me. "Um, is this a bad idea?"

"No." He jumps off the bed and comes to me, his hands

back on my hips, his gaze locked with mine as he slips his fingers beneath the waistband of my panties. I want to melt. "It's the fuckin' best idea we've had in a while. Come on, it'll be fun."

"Yeah, you really think so?" I ask, my voice faint. Being with him makes me want to do things. Experimental things that I would never try with anyone else, let alone tell anyone I'm doing.

I trust him. I trust him so much, I'm willing to let him take inappropriate photos of me.

Oh my God, that last part sounded like my mother.

"If you don't want to do this, you don't have to," he says, his voice soft, lifting his hands away from my hips so he can cup my cheeks. He leans in, dropping a soft kiss on my lips and I close my eyes, wanting more. He gives me exactly what I want, our lips connecting again and again until his tongue sweeps into my mouth, sliding against mine in a slow, seductive glide. I lean into him, a shiver stealing over me when his hands sweep over my waist, over my butt. He moans and breaks the kiss, his fingers impatiently tugging on the hem of my shirt and yanking it up.

I raise my arms and let him take it off of me, so now I'm standing in front of him in just my panties. Nothing else.

His eyes turn darker as he drinks me in. "Pretty," he murmurs, curling his fingers into fists. Like he's trying to restrain himself from touching me. "Go lay down on the bed."

I do as he asks, draping myself across my bed, lying on my stomach. I'm not necessarily wearing thong underwear, but they're pretty cheeky and before I can say or do anything, he's already snapping photos. "Hey." I rise up on my elbows, glaring at him from over my shoulder. "You didn't even warn me."

"I think that's the best time to take a photo, don't you think?" He grins and takes another one.

I stick my tongue out at him. "What if I want to take photos of you?"

He looks at me over his phone. "You want me to send you dick pics?"

"No!" Why do boys always think that's what we want to see? Maybe some girls want to but I'm more of a… "I prefer your abs." I would say his thighs too, because they're big and muscular and hairy and I have a not so secret thing for them.

"Oh." He shoves his phone in the back pocket of his jeans and whips off his T-shirt, letting it drop to the floor. "Let's do this."

We mess around for at least a half hour, maybe longer. Laughing and taking stupid photos. Serious ones. He makes me roll over on my side so he can capture the way the lacy waistband of my panties stretches across my hip bone. I take a photo while I'm sitting behind him on the bed, my butt propped up on all the pillows so I'm at the perfect angle to catch his perfect abs and his jeans, which are currently unbuttoned.

It's all very sexy. Like foreplay.

Once we're done and both lying on the bed next to each other, we scroll through our photos, deleting the ones we don't like, stashing them away in our private folder on Snapchat.

"This is my favorite," he says as he stops on one photo. I'm lying on the bed, my back to him, my exposed lower butt cheeks peeking out beneath the white lace. You can only see my lower back, my butt and my thighs. No one would ever know it's actually me. I actually look pretty good. It's an area I don't really see. It's not like I check out my backside every day in the mirror. "I never figured myself for an ass man, but this is…" His voice drifts.

"It's what?" I ask when he remains quiet.

"It makes me want to bite you." He points at one bared ass cheek. "Right there."

His voice is low. Deep. His head lifts. His gaze meets mine. Holds. Sensations swirl within me, tangling together into a knot in my stomach. Between my legs.

I laugh like he's joking, but deep down, I'm fascinated with the idea of him sinking his teeth into my flesh. My skin prickles, and I swear my lacy panties become damp. Oh God, maybe he could move over and push his face right between my...

"Did I shock you silent?" he asks, sounding vaguely amused.

I decide to change the subject a little.

"This one is my favorite." I stop on the photo in my camera roll. It's of the both of us from the waist down. I'm sitting on his lap, my legs draped over his denim clad thighs, and you can see the bulge straining against his jeans. I took it from a downward angle, so again no one would have any idea it's us if it was ever found.

"That's hot," Eli agrees, his voice soft. He shifts a little closer, his knee nudging against my thigh. "This was fun, right?"

"Lots of fun," I say, my voice light, my gaze dropping to his bare chest. "Though I don't understand why I'm basically naked and you're not."

"You're not basically naked." He snaps the elastic of my panties, a little frown on his face. "Well, you kind of are."

"And you still have your jeans on," I remind him.

"I'll take them off." He climbs off the bed and makes quick work of his jeans, slipping out of them in seconds. His collection of wildly colorful boxer briefs is endless. Today's are bright red with aggressive looking snakeheads all over them.

Their eyes and fangs are neon yellow. Also in neon yellow are the words, "snake charmer" scattered all over them.

"Snake charmer?" I ask when he rejoins me on the bed.

"Hell yeah. You wanna see my snake?" He cups his erection and gives it a little shake, making me laugh. "I *know* I can charm your panties off."

"You are unbeliev—" He cuts my words off with his lips, the kiss searing hot and full of tongue. I moan when his hands slide over my breasts, his thumbs brushing against my nipples simultaneously. Sparks cascade all over my skin from his touch, lighting me up. Making me warm.

So warm.

The more his hands roam, the more his lips devour, the harder my heart thunders. Until it's a roar in my ears, in my head. He is all around me, free to touch and kiss me however he wants. No one else around. This giant house all ours for the afternoon. I try my best to focus on the taste of his hot, damp lips. The ache that grows with every stroke of his tongue. He breaks our kiss to slide his mouth down the length of my neck. Pressing sweet, gentle kisses on my skin. Making me shiver.

He licks me and I gasp. I feel him smile against my throat as his lips continue their journey. Along my collarbone. Down my chest. Across my breasts. My breaths grow heavier, and I crack my eyes open to watch my chest rise and fall faster and faster. Eli glances up, our gazes connecting, and heat floods me when he draws my nipple into his mouth.

I close my eyes on a whimper, barely able to stand it. I'm ruined. Ruined for anyone else. His fingers continue the journey his lips started. Gliding across my stomach, his featherlight touch making me shiver. Those same fingers tease at the waistband of my panties and I hold my breath, dying for him to touch me there.

He doesn't disappoint. His fingers brush across the fabric. Press there. Testing me. My entire body is tense, waiting for the moment he touches me where I want him to. His thumb drifts back and forth. Back and forth. Without thought I lift my hips, encouraging him. Wanting more. Needing more. Harder. Faster. All of it.

Eli withdraws before I start to beg and my eyes flash open. I can feel the glower on my face, but he ignores me.

"Let's take these off," he whispers, just before he shifts down and starts tugging on the thin fabric of my panties.

With his teeth.

His mouth teases and torments. Absolute, utter torture. Teeth scrape my flesh, gentle yet sharp. His tongue sneaks out for a long, dirty lick and I spread my legs farther, wanting more of that.

Again, he's a tease. He gives up his original intent and lifts up, resting on his knees between my spread thighs with a frown on his handsome face.

"Can't take them off if you've got your legs spread like that." He runs two fingers along my slit, over the miniscule panties, and frustration nearly chokes me.

I swing my leg over, nearly kicking him in the face, I'm so impatient. I make quick work of removing my panties before I reposition myself. My thighs spread. Eli still kneeling on the bed between them.

His eyes go wide as he stares at the very center of me, his teeth catching his bottom lip for only a moment before he lets it go and breathes out a long, shaky breath.

"Fuck," he whispers reverently. "I missed your pussy so damn much."

"Eli," I say, chastising and encouraging him at the same time. He wants me. He's not scared to say it. Not scared to let all those raw, honest feelings fly out of his mouth.

"You like it when I talk like that," he says, his voice smug. He lifts his head, his eyes meeting mine. "Bet you got wetter when I said it."

I don't look away when I whisper, "Why don't you touch me and find out?"

CHAPTER 14

⧉

ELI

*O*ooh, look at this girl. Getting all daring and shit. With her legs spread before me like she's offering herself up so I can do whatever I want to her.

And I want to do everything to her. My feelings for her are all-consuming. They make me feel desperate.

Even a little shaky.

I can't fuck this up. I can't.

She raises a brow. Her cheeks are flushed and I'm pretty sure there are little dots of sweat along her hairline. I let my gaze drift down the length of her, noting that same rosy flush all over her skin. She always turns rosy when we mess around. I like it.

"Let me check," I say conversationally, like we're talking about the weather versus me slipping my fingers inside her. I touch her there, my fingers encountering nothing but wet, slick heat and I stroke her once. Twice. Brush my thumb across her clit.

She sucks in a breath. Her thighs are trembling. Her entire body is shaking. There are all sorts of ways I could take this. I could go down on her. I could finger her straight into O-Land. I could keep the snake charmer boxer briefs on and grind against her until she falls apart.

Really? I just want to fuck her. We've only done it once. It was great but we have the potential to be even better.

I keep stroking her, my gaze never straying from her pretty face. She closes her eyes, her lips parted and her head tilted back, exposing the long line of her throat. Her nipples are hard, her pussy is glistening and I can't stop touching her, the juicy sounds fucking torture to my ears.

Torture because I'm dying to get inside her.

"I can't wait any longer," I tell her, abruptly pulling my hand away from her and leaping to my feet. I yank my boxers off and grab my jeans, pulling out my wallet and fishing the condom from within.

Ava rises up on her elbows, her eyes hazy as she watches me. "What are you doing?"

"This." I roll the condom on and she watches me, her lips parted in fascination.

I am all about the visual. I put on a show, and I want a show in return. I want to *see* Ava. It's all part of the fantasy. Why do all this with closed curtains and no lights? Let's look at each other and enjoy it. I think my girl is the same way. She's currently watching me like a starving woman and my dick is a giant pepperoni pizza.

Rejoining her on the bed, I'm about to climb on top of her when she rests her hand on my shoulder, stopping me. "Can I be on top?"

Like I'm going to tell her no. "You want to ride me?"

She blushes. Nods. "Yeah. I think so. I might mess up. I don't know what I'm doing."

Her worry makes my heart fucking sing. "You can't mess this up."

The uncertainty in her gaze is obvious. "I totally could. Just—be patient with me."

143

I could be honest and tell her no girl has done that before with me, but I keep my mouth shut. I prefer to act like the one with all the experience. "Let's go, cowgirl."

A laugh escapes her as we rearrange ourselves so now I'm the one lying in the middle of the bed and she carefully climbs on top of me. She rests her hands lightly on my chest, her hips pressed against mine, my condom-wrapped dick nudging against her perfect ass. He's eager to get inside and I tell myself to take my time. I don't want to blow it.

It would be so easy to blow it. As in, blow my wad. I'm that amped up to get inside her.

And she's so damn fine, sitting on me like this. Her hair is a mess, her nipples are hard and she's got her arms pressed against her tits, making them look bigger. She does this thing with her hips, her wet pussy making contact with my skin and I rest my hands on her hips, stilling her.

"Come here," I rasp.

She leans down and I tangle my fingers in her hair when her mouth settles on mine. The kiss is greedy. All tongues and teeth and eager lips. I reach down between us, grabbing my cock and shifting so I can push inside her. She rises up, I position myself, and slowly, she lowers herself on my dick. I watch, my gaze glued to where our bodies are connected, a groan tearing from my throat when she finally takes me all the way in.

There is no more talking. I can barely form words, I'm so damn fascinated with this girl who's riding me like an expert. Like she's done this dozens of times. Maybe I don't know any better. Maybe it's just that good because the girl I love, the girl I'm completely fascinated with, is fucking me like she never wants to be with anyone else.

Just me.

She's a natural, squeezing her inner walls around my cock every single time she shifts down, and it feels good enough to make my eyes cross. I'm going to come too soon if I don't calm down. I try to think of other things. What if her brother was in the next room over? Such an asshole. Hate that guy. Wouldn't it be great if he could hear me give it to his sister? Wouldn't it burn his ass?

Yeah, that train of thought didn't work. Now I'm even hotter. Even closer to the edge.

Blindly reaching out, I grab hold of Ava's hips, keeping her still. She stops moving, her brows lowered as she studies me, confusion written all over her pretty flushed face. "Wh-what's wrong?" She's panting. Out of breath. Her entire body is slicked with a fine sheen of sweat.

So is mine.

"Nothing." I swallow hard, hating that I have to admit I'm close to losing control. "Let's just—slow down."

"But it feels so good." She rocks against me. Slow and easy, a little moan falling from her lips and damn it, she's not helping.

I give up. Give in. Let her use me. Closing my eyes, I loosen my grip on her hips and she starts moving once more, falling forward with her hands on my shoulders and her face in mine. I open my eyes to find her right there, her mouth open, her eyes unfocused. A choked breath escapes her and I can tell.

She's close.

Holding her in place, I start giving it to her. Sliding in and out of her at a rapid pace. Her eyes fall shut. She leans her head back. I can't stop staring at her as I grip her ass. She moves with me, and unable to stop myself, I slide my other hand down, feeling where our bodies are connected, overwhelmed with the sensation. I then shift my fingers up, touching her clit, circling it and she gasps.

"Oh God."

Within seconds, I send her straight over the edge. She's

coming, her inner walls milking me, squeezing in this rhythmic motion that wrings my orgasm right out of me. I groan her name, my entire body shuddering and when it's all over, we collapse, lying side by side, in a heap of sticky, sweaty limbs all tangled up in each other.

"Dang," she whispers once she's caught her breath.

I laugh. "I made you say wow once. Now it's dang?"

"Mmm, yes." She squirms against me, her hands sinking into my hair as she cracks open her eyes and smiles. "That was amazing."

"Hold that thought," I tell her, thrusting my finger in her face before I climb out of bed and run into her bathroom, disposing the condom in the trash—wrapped it in toilet paper first, so hopefully, no one finds it—before I dash back into her bedroom and practically fly onto the bed. "What made it so amazing?"

Yes, I want a play by play on the action from her point of view. I can't help it.

She's laughing as she stretches, her naked body rubbing against mine and making me realize I could be down for a round two if she's up for it. "I have no idea what you were thinking, but being on top was just as good as I imagined. It was like I had complete control over the situation and I felt so—full of you."

Ava ducks her head against my chest, hiding her face. I skim my hand over her back, drawing lazy circles on her bare skin.

"Sometimes, you're shy and other times, you act like this." I streak my fingers across her flat belly when she rolls over on her back. "I like it."

"You like me like this?" She smiles up at me.

"Naked after we just fucked? Hell yes, I do." I lean down and drop a kiss on her lips. Rest my hand on her tit. Give it a squeeze. Toy with her nipple.

"Do you always have to be so crude?" she asks, her voice soft.

"Want me to call it making love?" I raise my brows.

She makes a face. "Ew, no. I prefer to say we're having sex."

"And I prefer to say we fucked." I drift my fingers back and forth across her stomach, like I'm trying to put her in a trance. From the dreamy way she's looking at me, I think it's working. "It doesn't change how I feel about you, Ava."

"And how do you feel about me?"

I dip my head, my mouth hovering above hers. "I'm in love with you." I kiss her. "I love you." Another kiss. "I want to fuck you again."

"Really?" She sounds so hopeful.

"Really about me loving you? Or about us fucking again?" My hand goes lower. Touches her between her thighs. She's wet and sticky. Her thighs part. A sigh falls from her lips.

"Both. I just—" She hesitates for only a moment. "I thought I lost you, and I was so devastated. I still can't believe that you're here. In my room. Right now."

"I'm here. It's real. This is happening." I remove my hand from her pussy and set my fingers on her lips. "Taste."

Ava sucks my fingers between her lips, and I can't help but groan. This girl is so fucking sexy, I just can't. Always eager to do whatever I want, whenever I want her.

I am the luckiest motherfucker I know.

* * *

AFTER I WENT to my car and grabbed a couple more condoms, we did it one more time and then Ava said we had to get ready to leave. It was close to four and we needed to make it to the tailgate party on time. I took a quick shower and tried to get her to come in it with me, but she refused.

147

Then she took a quick shower, straightened her hair in less than five minutes and we put back on our game night clothes.

"That T-shirt should be outlawed," I tell her as I shake my head. Her stomach on full display for all the Bulldogs' fans to see? No thanks.

She laughs. "You sound like my dad."

I scowl at her. There's no reply for that. Sounding like her dad isn't high on my list of things I want, that's for damn sure.

"I'm bringing a sweatshirt." She holds it up. Looks like a navy blue Badgers one, blech. "I'll be covered up once the sun goes down."

"Thank God," I mutter, as we both start walking down the stairs.

She goes through this elaborate ritual of setting the house alarm and making sure all the locks are locked. Twice. Once we're settled in my car, I start the engine, the speakers blasting the song I was last listening to from one of my Spotify playlists.

I immediately reach over and turn it down. Only a little though. "Sorry."

Ava appears amused. "Wouldn't figure you were a Cardi B. fan."

I shrug. "I like this song."

"You would," she says. It's WAP by Cardi B. and Megan Thee Stallion, and it's dirty as hell. "Are you listening to a playlist you made?"

Unease slips down my spine. "Uh, yeah."

"Can I look at your playlist? I want to see if we have any songs that we have in common." She smiles at me.

"Sure." I open my phone and hand it over, shifting the car into drive and pulling out of her driveway.

She sucks in a breath and I know what she's just read.

"Wait a minute. This playlist is called 'Songs that make me think of Ava'?"

"Uh huh." Shit. I hope she's not offended.

"The song WAP makes you think of me?" My girl sounds fuckin' horrified.

"Babe. You've got a wet ass pussy. There's nothing wrong with that," I tease her.

Ava slaps my arm, but she's smiling. "Gross!"

"Look at you, sitting here telling me it's gross when not thirty minutes ago I was buried deep in that wet ass pussy and you were moaning my name," I say, as I turn onto the main road that leads us to the highway.

It was a good afternoon. Taking all the time I want with my girl. Touching her everywhere. Driving her out of her mind with my fingers and my mouth. Filling her up and making her come. No one else around so she can be as loud as she wants. And she's pretty loud.

Never figured Ava Callahan would be a screamer.

"Stop." She shoves me again, her cheeks are on fire, and I can't help but think she's the cutest thing ever. "You'll have to restrain yourself around my parents."

"You really think so?" Damn. I know I have to be on my best behavior, but I was also going to be myself. I don't want to act phony in front of them. They need to see the real deal. The real me.

"You definitely can't go around singing the lyrics to WAP," she mumbles.

I pull over to the side of the road and put the car in park. I reach over to caress her cheek, my gaze locked with hers as I say, "I won't do anything to embarrass you."

Her smile is tremulous. "I know you won't. I trust you."

"You should. I love you more than anything else in this world." I stroke her face. Trace her bottom lip. "I'm going to make your parents like me. I promise."

The smile on her face grows. Becomes more confident. "You will. I know it."

We drive the rest of the way to the Bulldog stadium talking about nothing and everything. Our conversation flows easily, and I'm lazy with satisfaction.

Two orgasms will do that to you.

It didn't even dawn on me that she never said she loved me back until we're pulling into the parking lot, Ava flashing the VIP parking pass her dad must've given her before they left, to the lot attendant.

And now, I can't help but feel unsure about her.

About everything.

CHAPTER 15

AVA

I'm nervous. I can't lie. We're walking through the parking lot where they have the tailgate party at Fresno State, and when I spot my parents' SUV up ahead, my stomach twists into knots. My palms are sweating, and I'm sure Eli can feel it, since he's currently holding my hand.

Or maybe his hands are sweating too and making mine feel sweaty. I don't know. We're both worked up, I'm sure.

"Tell me Jake's not going to try and throw a punch," Eli says through clenched teeth, his gaze locked up ahead. Where the majority of my family is hanging out.

Dad's monitoring his chicken. Mom's opening up bowls of food she brought, setting them on the table. Autumn is dropping forks in a cup. Hannah is hanging all over Jake. Beck is digging into a giant bag of barbecue chips.

It all looks so normal, but there will be tension. I know it.

I don't want Eli to worry about my brother. That'll only make him even more uncomfortable.

"Jake won't throw a punch," I say, giving Eli's hand a squeeze. "He wouldn't be that stupid."

"He punches me, I'm punching him back." Eli's posture is rigid, as is his jaw. He looks furious.

It's kind of sexy.

"He will not punch you. No one will," I reassure my boyfriend, rising up on tiptoe so I can press a quick kiss to his cheek. "You're going to be fine. I promise."

He smiles down at me, but it's strained. I hate that he's so tense.

I'm tense too.

We slow our pace as we approach them, and Mom notices us first, putting on her polite smile as she comes to greet us. "Ava. So glad you're finally here." I let go of Eli's hand when she pulls me into a hug, murmuring close to my ear, "You're late. We were about to give up on waiting for you and eat."

"Sorry," I say as we pull away from each other. I grab Eli's hand once more, dragging him over to my mother. "Mom, this is Eli. My boyfriend."

"Hi Eli," Mom says with a smile.

"Nice to meet you, Mrs. Callahan," Eli says, a shocked expression on his face when she yanks him into her arms and gives him a quick hug.

"I'm a hugger, sorry," she says, her face relaxing when she releases him. Which tells me Eli's not giving off bad ju-ju vibes, thank God. Mom has this thing about people's aura. Claims she can tell when someone's a terrible person within three seconds of meeting them.

Whatever.

"Well, let's eat. We're all starving, and your father's butt chicken is ready," Mom says with a smile as she heads for the table where the spread is. We all like making fun of the beer butt chicken. It drives Dad crazy, which is why we do it.

We follow after her, me taking Eli's hand once more, trying to present us as a united front. Jake is watching us with a blatant sneer on his face. Hannah catches my gaze, her eyes full of sympathy and I smile at her.

I don't blame her for Jake's bad behavior. That's one hundred percent on him.

Autumn appears in front of us, seemingly out of nowhere, wearing a giant smile and her attention solely on Eli. "Who's your friend, Ava?"

"Eli, this is my sister, Autumn," I say, shocked when my sister pulls him into a quick hug too.

Eli has to bend over to hug her, considering how short she is. Pretty much like our mom. "It's so great to meet you," Autumn says.

"You too." He looks shellshocked. Like he came fully prepared for war and confronted peace instead.

Well. From the female Callahans at least. He hasn't talked to my dad yet. I'm sure Jake won't even look at him.

"This is my brother, Beck." I point at Beck who's sitting in a chair, concentrating on his phone. He lifts his head when he hears his name mentioned, offering a wave to Eli. "Hey." He pauses, his gaze narrowing. "I remember you."

"You do?" Eli asks, ambling over to him. "From when?"

"Over the summer. At the camp. You're the one with the big mouth."

Everyone laughs. Even Jake. Even Eli. "You're not wrong," Eli tells him. "I've heard of you too. You're the one who's an excellent defensive lineman."

Beck's eyes go wide. "You've heard of me?"

"Hell yeah. Everyone knows who Beck Callahan is." Eli glances in my direction to find me watching him, and he winks.

I always thought winking was kind of cheesy. But when Eli does it, I can't help but feel all warm and fuzzy inside.

Or maybe that's from him being so kind to my little brother.

Mom gets us all lined up, so we can start serving ourselves food. There's red potato salad with rosemary and dill. A green salad. Chips and salsa are both still set out, though most of it is gone. Probably thanks to me and Eli being a little later than usual.

Dad still hasn't talked to Eli, still too busy working on his chicken, but he's at the end of the table serving everyone their portion. I'm in front of Eli, so I'm the one who talks to Dad first.

"You made it." He smiles at me as he sets a slab of chicken on my plate.

"Sorry we were late."

"Yes, sorry, sir," Eli adds.

Oh, he sounds so nervous. I almost want to reach out and set my hand on his arm in the hopes I could calm him.

But I'm guessing no one will calm him. Not even me. Not when he has to face my father for the first time, knowing what we just did in my parents' house.

My cheeks go warm just at the thought.

"I'm just glad you both made it." Dad glances over at Eli, a stern expression on his face. "Nice to see you again, Eli."

"You too, sir."

"You can call me Drew."

Eli visibly relaxes while I snap my mouth shut. Did my dad say Eli can call him by his first name? I think he made Ash call him coach for years. But of course, Ash was conditioned to call him that considering my dad was actually his coach. "Thank you for inviting me to the game. It's been a while since I've gone to one here."

"Have you seen Ash play before?"

"On TV, yeah," Eli answers. "And I played against him my sophomore year when he was a senior."

"You were a QB on the varsity team when you were a

sophomore?" Dad sounds impressed. More impressed than I was when Eli mentioned that little fact.

Of course, I was trying to grind on his thigh at that particular moment, so I had other things on my mind.

"Yes, I was. Our senior QB was benched for the rest of the season because of an injury," Eli explains. "Coach Weston had faith in me that I could do it."

"I vaguely remember that," Dad says, his gaze sharp and only for Eli. Sizing him up. "I know you guys lost."

Eli laughs. "We did. But it was an honor to have my ass handed to me by Ash Davis."

Dad laughs along with him, plopping two giant pieces of chicken on Eli's plate. "Well, wait until the game tonight. Ash is a pleasure to watch. I hope you pay attention. You might learn a thing or two. Ash is an excellent quarterback. I told Jake the same thing—that he needs to watch Ash carefully."

Eli stands even straighter. "I won't take my eyes off him."

"Good." Dad nods. I study them, relieved that they had a decent conversation, and my father didn't give Eli too much grief. Actually, he gave him no grief, which surprises me. "You going to stand here all night or go eat?"

Eli laughs. "Sorry. Thank you again for dinner."

We sit next to each other in fold out chairs my parents brought, as far away as we can get from where Jake and Hannah are sitting. Autumn is sitting with them. I'm sure she's interrogating Hannah, and I'm grateful she's not over here doing the same thing to my boyfriend. Beck is with my parents, and my dad is sitting on the side closest to Jake.

Meaning we're sort of, but not really alone.

"Your dad was cool," Eli says just before he shoves a forkful of chicken in his mouth. His eyes light up as he keeps chewing. "Damn, this butt chicken slaps."

"Everyone in my family was nice to you." I glance over my shoulder to glare briefly at my brother. "Except for Jake."

"I'll need to work on him, though it's going to take a while." Eli keeps shoveling food in his mouth. He always acts hungry. I don't know where it all goes, since he doesn't have an ounce of fat on him.

"Are you ever going to apologize to him?" I ask.

He makes a face like I asked him if he'd jump off a cliff for me. "Hell no. He's talked shit on me too."

"Not as publicly as you have," I point out.

"Yeah, but that was part of my schtick." He flashes me that arrogant smirk, and I didn't realize until I saw it, just how much I missed seeing that cocky smile on his handsome face.

"I don't think he appreciated your schtick," I say dryly.

"He'll eventually get over it. They beat our asses, after all. They do every year. They'll probably go on and win league." Eli makes another face and shakes his head. "We'll make playoffs and maybe we'll get a chance to play them again."

"You better hope not," I say with a sly smile. "Because we'll beat you again too."

"So disloyal." Eli shakes his head, though I know he doesn't mean it. "Your sister seems nice."

"I thought you already knew Autumn," I say.

"I knew *of* her. I don't actually know her. Like, I'd never met her before." He contemplates me for a moment, his gaze trailing all over my face. "You guys don't look that much alike, you know."

"We both have the same green eyes like our mom," I point out.

"True." A wicked smile curls his lips and he lowers his voice. "You're prettier than your sister."

"Stop it." I'm smiling too, though. I don't think anyone has ever told me I'm prettier than Autumn. She was always the most popular one. The prettier one. The more active one. The one who was going to make a difference in the world, while I was just...Ava.

"Hey, it's true. You're gorgeous." His eyes turn a shade darker as he continues to watch me, and I want to squirm in my chair. I recognize that look. It's the same one he gets right before he kisses me. "Never knew I could be so gone over a blonde."

"Blondes have more fun," I tell him with as much seriousness as I can muster.

"I'll say." He shakes his head, making me laugh. "Jake looks just like your dad."

"He acts like my uncle Owen, though," I say.

"Now there's the one I want to meet. That guy is cool as fuck. I was a Drew Callahan fan when I was young, but I straight up idolized Owen Maguire. He was a badass on the field. Always causing trouble. Talking shit. Getting fined." He glances around after all those bad words slip out of his mouth. "Hope no one heard me say that."

I shake my head but say nothing. Mom's admitted she had a terrible mouth when she was young. Dad too. I guess it just runs in the family.

"What's it like, being surrounded by pro football players all the time?" Eli asks.

"I don't know anything else," I say with a shrug. "It's been that way my entire life."

"Even Asher Davis is a part of the family," Eli says with a shake of his head.

"We'll probably see Ash after the game, and you can meet him," I say, my voice low. "I'm sure he'll come see my parents and Autumn."

"No shit? That would be amazing."

We keep eating, Autumn calling out to Eli every once in a while, asking him a personal question, which he always answers vaguely. At one point, Jake tells her to knock it off, and Autumn glares at him.

"I'm just trying to get to know your significant others,"

157

she says with a little sniff. She's been giving Hannah the third degree too.

"Well you should freakin' ease up a little," Jake mutters at Autumn, who looks ready to fight him.

I feel her pain.

"Jake," Dad says in warning.

It takes everything I've got to hide the smile that wants to spread across my face. I love it when my brother gets called out for his shit.

"We need to pack this up soon so we can head into the stadium," Mom announces a few minutes later, rising to her feet. "I hope everyone enjoyed dinner."

Dad gets all the compliments for his beer butt chicken, but I'm the one who goes to Mom and tells her how much I love her potato salad.

"If you told me twenty years ago I'd be making potato salad for a tailgate party with my family, I would've laughed in your face," she says, shaking her head as she grabs a trash bag and shakes it out before dumping dirty plates inside.

I start to help her, putting lids on the salad bowls and tossing miscellaneous trash in the bag. "Why do you say that?"

"My life before I met your father…I couldn't imagine having a family. Let alone wanting one," Mom explains with a little sigh. She turns to look at me, really look at me, and I stop what I'm doing, wondering what she's about to say. "Your father changed my life for the better. I was young, and I *never* believed in love. I didn't believe in any of it. I thought it was all a crock of shit being fed to me my entire life." The words are bitter, and it's like she's spitting them out.

"What made you change your mind?" I'm so curious. They don't talk much about their past. About those first moments when they met. It's shrouded in mystery, with snippets revealed here and there.

"Your dad. I saw what his family life was like. He had all the money in the world, and he was still miserable. I had nothing and was completely miserable too. But at least I had my brother, who loved me unconditionally. I realized your father had no one, and I wanted to be that someone." Mom's gaze is gentle as it settles on me. "I saw the same thing in Ash, and honey, I see the same thing in Eli. He feels like he has no one but you. I see it in the way he looks at you. I saw it in the way he grabbed onto your father's attention when he gave it. That boy is starved. And not just for food or attention from a pretty girl."

I let Mom's words sink in, wishing I could deny them.

Knowing that she's right.

"Our community is small, and I've heard the rumors about his parents before. It was an asshole move, what your brother said to him that night." My mouth drops open in shock. "What? It's true. It was a low blow, and what Jake said devastated that boy. Jake knew where to hit him where it hurts. We're smug in the fact that we love each other. We take care of each other. You have your entire family who loves you, no matter what. And it looks like you have a handsome boy who loves you too. He watches you with stars in his eyes," Mom says, making me blush.

"I love him too," I confess.

"Just make sure he's not here because of something else."

I frown. "What do you mean?"

"I don't doubt that he cares about you, but he might be a little starstruck too, if you know what I mean." She glances to her left, and I follow, seeing Eli talking excitedly to my father as he helps Dad clean up his chicken mess.

"He's not using me to get close to Dad," I say weakly.

"I hope not," Mom says, her tone ominous.

Her words, her tone, they stick with me long after we finish cleaning up, and we're headed to the stadium.

CHAPTER 16

AVA

*J*t's cold out and the game seems to go on forever. Early October around here is full of warm days and cool nights. At home, it's even cooler. But we're currently about an hour away from home and about three thousand feet lower in elevation, which makes a difference.

I slipped on my sweatshirt once the sun went down, and there was a look of total relief on Eli's face when he saw what was on the front of my sweatshirt.

"I thought it was a Badgers hoodie," he says.

I glance down at the red letters spelling out Bulldogs on the front. "Navy is their color too."

"I guess I forgot." He shrugs. Returns his attention to the field.

Where it's been all night.

I never thought I could say I was jealous over a football team, but I am. Football has always been a part of my life, since the day I was born. When your father is a famous NFL player, you know this, but it doesn't hit you until you're older. It's just a part of your life. Something you can't change, so you have to live with it.

How I dealt with it? By ignoring that part of our life for the most part. Until recently. Until now. Cheering for our high school team? I have to care. Dating a boy who loves the game? Thrusts me right into it, kicking and screaming.

Eli is literally sitting on the edge of his seat, his gaze locked on the players out on the field. "You think he's gonna throw it?" he asks no one in particular, referring to Ash. The Bulldogs are leading, but their time is almost up with the ball. And there's still enough time on the clock for the opposing team to score and get ahead.

"No way," Jake answers with finality, surprising me he'd respond to Eli in the first place. "If he makes a mistake, they could intercept it."

"He'll throw it," Dad says with that easy confidence he has. Like he can read players' minds without knowing them at all. It's an eerie, sixth sense trick of his, and he's always used it to his advantage.

Ash does indeed throw the ball. And one of his receivers catches it with ease, speeding up as he runs it into the end zone. The entire stadium erupts in cheers, and every member of my family rises to their feet, including Eli.

Excluding me. And when I realize they're all standing, I jump to my feet too, yelling and clapping, trying to look enthusiastic. But I'm tired. Dead on my feet.

I just want to go home.

"Did you see that?" Eli asks me once we're back in our seats. His entire body is practically vibrating. He's so excited by that last play, and his expression is downright boyish. Staring at him in this moment, I feel like I know exactly what he looked like when he was eight. I've always thought he has a bit of a baby face, though it's more man than boy now. And there was nothing boyish about the way he treated me and the things we did earlier. "What a fuckin' play."

161

I nudge him in the ribs and whisper, "Not so many f-bombs."

He makes a face, waving a hand and dismissing my words. "Baby, we've been dropping f-bombs all night. Your dad included."

I wouldn't know, considering my father is sitting on the other side of Eli, with Jake on the other side of our dad, and they've been putting their heads together and chatting about the game the entire night. Autumn is sitting next to me, but she's barely talking to me either. She's too wrapped up in every single thing Ash does on the field.

By the time the game's over, it's past ten, I'm totally exhausted and we still have to wait for Ash to come around so we can all congratulate him on his game. Pretty sure Autumn is going home with him afterward, and I wonder what that's like, realizing our parents know exactly why she's leaving with her boyfriend because she's headed straight home to eagerly get naked with him. Do our parents care? Does that freak them out? Does Autumn care? Is she afraid to feel their judgement?

It's kind of a trip to consider. Yet something that doesn't seem to faze my sister in the least.

Well, she is almost four years older than me, and way more mature. I'm still practically a juvenile compared to her, while she's a full-blown adult.

God, even in my thoughts I sound young. Immature. With no knowledge whatsoever. Maybe I'm just tired. And over being at this game. A little bent out of shape over my boyfriend seeming to have more fun with my father than he is with me tonight.

This is what I wanted, right? For my boyfriend to receive my parents' approval. It's important to me, having them like him. I know it's important to him too. I should be happy. Thrilled that they've seemed to embrace him so easily, especially after what happened last weekend. My father was ready to banish him forever, and now he's acting like Eli is one of his long-lost sons. Even Jake has begrudgingly spoken to him throughout the game tonight, though always with reluctance and a heavy dose of attitude.

I sort of hate what Mom said earlier. I know she's just watching out for me, but now she's put all sorts of doubt in my head. Doubt I don't want to focus on.

But I can't help but focus on it. It's all I can think about.

We wait around after the game finishes for what feels like forever, until finally Autumn returns to us, bringing Ash with her. He slings his arm around her shoulders and pulls her in close, dropping a kiss on her forehead. She beams up at him, her hand resting on his chest, and I can just tell. Despite the fact they've been together for three years, that they started out as a high school romance, they're still madly in love. It makes me want what they have.

With Eli.

But can we stick?

"It's good to see you guys," Ash says in greeting to us, and we all take turns giving him a hug. He embraces me close, and I can't help but think he smells amazing.

Not better than my boyfriend though.

"Who's the guy?" Ash asks me, his voice a low rumble.

"That's my boyfriend." I wave Eli over and he approaches, trying his best to look cool. Like he's not completely starstruck by Ash. Which is funny considering how comfortable he is around my dad, and he's a way bigger star than Ash. "Eli Bennett, this is Asher Davis."

They shake hands, Eli with a giant smile on his face. "So great to actually meet you. I played against you my sophomore year when you were a senior, and you kicked our asses."

"Really?" Ash laughs. "Who do you play for?"

"The Mustangs."

"Oh." Ash takes a step back, assessing him before his gaze cuts to mine. "What the hell, Ava? Dating the enemy?"

"I know, right?" Jake slaps Ash's shoulder, like they're bros in this situation. Ash glares at him before returning his attention to me.

"You must really like this guy if you're willing to date a Mustang," Ash drawls.

Eli stiffens, his expression turning to stone. "We try not to let that rivalry bullshit divide us."

Ha! It's been the biggest problem with our relationship from the get go. But maybe Eli is changing. I know I've tried to let it go. Maybe he has too. The high school rivalry bullshit as Eli called it is dumb. We shouldn't let that get in the way of what we have.

Easier said than done, but hey. We're trying.

"Props to you, man. You've got balls." Ash holds out his hand and Eli takes it, the two of them performing some ritualistic bro shake that I have no idea where they learned it. Or how they knew they should do it.

Boys are so weird sometimes.

The relief on Eli's face is obvious. The anger on Jake's is almost comical. He didn't expect Ash to be so accepting of my boyfriend.

Of course, Ash isn't some petty jerk like my brother, so thank God for that.

We all talk for a while, Ash patiently answering all of Eli's questions. Jake and Hannah bail, Jake claiming he has to get her home before it gets too late.

I know for a fact her mom works nights at one of the local hotels, so that's a lie. But I keep my mouth shut.

Eventually, Ash and Autumn leave too, Autumn going back to his apartment to stay the night. Mom and Dad hug her and Ash before they turn their attention on us.

"You're riding home in our car, right Ava?" Mom asks.

Oh. I figured Eli could take me home. "I sort of planned on going home with Eli."

"Let's leave," Beck says, sounding tired. When the kid is done for the night, he's absolutely done. There's no convincing him otherwise.

"It doesn't make sense for Eli to drive all the way to our house and then turn around and go back to his," Mom explains.

She's got us there. I turn to look at Eli, who's frowning a little. "I don't mind driving her home."

"You should probably get back home," Dad says, his voice firm. "It's late. You won't even get there until close to midnight."

"Yeah." Eli blinks, turning his attention to me. The look on his face says it all. He doesn't want to go home. No one cares about him there anyway. "You cool with that?"

"Sure. Of course." Not really. But what am I supposed to do? Tell my parents no, when they obviously want me to ride home with them?

"Perfect. We'll let you two say goodbye. Meet us at the car," Dad says, his gaze shifting to Eli. "Glad you were able to come to the game with us tonight."

"Thank you so much, sir." Eli approaches my parents and shakes their hands again. "And Mrs. Callahan. I appreciate the invite. I've had a great time."

"You're very welcome," Mom says, smiling broadly at him. I think he might've won her over.

Eli high fives Beck, who is so over this night, I'm surprised he hasn't dropped to the ground, already asleep.

Dad's expression is stern. Not too sure about him yet. He's very overprotective of us. Especially me and Autumn. "Don't take too long with your goodbyes," he says, his gaze and words for me.

"I won't." I send him a smile, one that hopefully says move along.

We don't need an audience.

Once they start walking away, I turn to face Eli, a shocked breath leaving me when he suddenly pulls me into his arms and plants a kiss on my lips. "I thought I'd have more time with you."

"Didn't we have enough time together earlier?" I ask, tilting my head up to smile up at him. "Did you have fun?"

"Yeah, I had a great time." He leans in and drops a kiss on my forehead. "Sorry if you thought I was ignoring you."

"I didn't," I say with a sigh. No way can I admit that I actually was. I don't want to put a damper on his good time tonight. "I know you were having fun with my father."

"He's not so bad. I'll get him to warm up to me," Eli says with that easy confidence I know is a bit of a front. When he talks like that, it's because he's feeling insecure and trying to hide it.

"My dad will grow to love you," I tell him, voice firm. "I know it."

"If you say so," he says with a tired smile. "Hey, wasn't it cool when Ash put Jake in his place?"

"Yes." I laugh. "Their relationship has always been tinged with animosity."

"Isn't that how everyone's relationship with Jake is? Maybe not Hannah though. For some reason, she tolerates his ass." Eli shakes his head.

"She's good for him. He needs her to calm him down." I rise up on tiptoe and brush my mouth against his. "I hate leaving you right now."

"I'll be fine," he assures me, before delivering another kiss. We're standing in the parking lot, the last stragglers still exiting the stadium and heading for their vehicles, but I don't care who sees me. I love being in Eli's arms. Feeling his mouth on mine. Knowing that he loves me. Knowing that he belongs to me.

There's nothing better.

CHAPTER 17

AVA

I'm at cheer practice chatting with Dakota and Lindsey before we start stretching when Cami and Baylee make their approach. I try to ignore them at first, focusing on Lindsey telling a funny story about a kid who almost blew up his backpack by accident in her AP Chemistry class, but when Cami clears her throat extra loud, I finally turn to her.

"Can I help you?" The hostility in my voice rings loud and clear. I should probably respect my cheer captain, but it's so damn hard when I know so many horrible things about her.

Horrible things she's done and said.

"So is it true?" Cami crosses her arms. Baylee copies her. Even their snotty expressions match.

God, they're annoying.

"Is what true?" I ask, when she doesn't further explain herself.

"That you're actually going out with Eli Bennett?" Cami raises a single, skinny brow. Looks like she's been playing with the tweezers too much, yet again.

Baylee thrusts her phone in my face. There's a photo of

me and Eli standing together with his arm around me inside Bulldog stadium, right before the kickoff. I look pretty cute if I do say so myself. That cropped t-shirt/jean combo totally worked. And I like the possessive way Eli's hand is resting on my hip. Like he's staking his claim.

"Did you actually screenshot this off my story?" I ask Baylee before I glance over at Lindsey and Dakota.

They're wide-eyed and dead silent, watching all of this unfold in complete fascination.

"Yes. I did," Baylee admits without shame as she drops her arm to her side, not embarrassed in the least that she's completely tracking me. "I had to document this and send it to Cami. I couldn't believe my eyes when I saw it. You and *Eli?*"

"Picking up my sloppy seconds, hmm?" Cami says, smirking at me.

Rage flows through my veins and I curl my hands into fists. Tell myself to keep it together. She's not worth the aggravation. "You were barely with him."

"Long enough to know what he tastes like." Cami takes a step closer, lowering her voice to a whisper. *"Everywhere."*

I see black. Red. Without thinking I swing, my fist making solid connection with Cami's jaw. She squeals and drops to the ground, clutching her face and writhing around on the grass. I stand above her, breathing hard, quickly coming back to reality, realizing far too late what I've done.

Oh. Shit.

"What the hell is going on here?" Brandy appears out of nowhere, making her way toward us. The entire team is circled around us, Baylee mingling with the rest of them, like she had no part in this.

It feels like I'm moving in slow motion when I swing my body in Brandy's direction. "I, uh…"

"She fucking hit me!" Cami shrieks, leaping to her feet.

Still cradling the side of her face with one hand and pointing at me with the other. "I want this bitch *gone.*"

"Now Cami—" Brandy starts, but Cami won't hear it.

"No. No way. You can't defend her. She fucking hit me—"

"Language," Brandy interrupts.

Cami snaps her jaw shut, then winces like it hurt. I hope it did.

Oops. I shouldn't think like that. I'm about to get in some major trouble. I know it. I don't even really remember actually hitting her. It's like it happened while I was in a blind rage, and I blocked the moment from my memory.

Taking a breath, Cami restarts. "Ava hit me in the face, coach. With her fist. And no matter what you say or how much you want to defend her, that's wrong. It's grounds for getting her ass—butt—kicked off the team."

"She provoked me," I say, my voice calm.

"What, like I *asked* you to hit me?" Cami taunts.

I'm about to lunge for her again, but Dakota and Lindsey each grab hold of my arms and keep me back.

"What exactly did she say?" Brandy asks me.

I don't want to repeat it. I'll get mad all over again.

"Just some silly stuff about her boyfriend," Cami answers for me, waving her hand dismissively. "I can't help it if I dated him first."

Oh, that sets me on fire all over again, and I'm jerking against Dakota and Lindsey's surprisingly strong hands, wishing I could yank all that long hair out of Cami's head.

"Everyone, go stretch. Now. Baylee, please lead them," Brandy commands. The other girls take off to the practice area, the sound of nervous, high pitch whispering going on between them. Brandy turns and faces me and Cami once more. "Can we try and work this out, just between us?"

"No. Freaking. Way," Cami says through clenched teeth, glaring at me with narrowed eyes. She looks really evil right now. The worst feeling washes over me, making me sick to my stomach. It feels like I might've fallen into her trap. Like maybe she set me up, knowing I'd lose my mind over her rude comments. "I'm going to the office. I want the health aide to document this."

"I am the health aide, you idiot," Brandy says, making me crack up. Brandy sends me a look, essentially shutting me up before she continues. "You've only gone to this school for almost four years. Didn't you realize this?" she asks Cami.

"I forgot, okay?" Cami shrugs. "Then *you* can take photos of me and all the damage Ava did to my face. I want this in my file, and I want it documented that Ava Callahan did this to me. It's assault! I have witnesses!"

"Who saw it?" Brandy looks around, all of the girls returning their attention to stretching and not watching us, which is really what they've been doing.

"Everyone! Even her little friends. They'll vouch for me. They have to," Cami says, pointing at Dakota and Lindsey, who are both doing their best to not look over at us. I'm sure their ears are burning.

With a sigh, I decide to go ahead and confess. "It's true. She said something rude, and I hit her."

Brandy's mouth drops open and she rests her hands on her hips. I can see the disappointment in her body language, the way she's watching me. The utter disbelief in her eyes. "Are you freaking serious right now? What the hell, Ava?"

"I don't know! She made me mad." I throw my hands up in the air.

"Not a good enough excuse," Brandy starts, but Cami cuts her off.

"There's *no* excuse. I'm sick of her crap. I want her off the team!" Cami yells.

"Come on, settle down. Despite you always thinking

you're in charge, that's not your decision," Brandy says to Cami. "Let me look at your face."

I wait for them while Brandy closely examines Cami's jaw, the spot where I punched her. Did I really hit her that hard? No. Her skin has a small red mark, but it isn't swollen or cut up or anything. I bet she won't even bruise.

But she's going to make a huge deal out of this. She'll do her best to get me into lots of trouble, and I deserve it. I just might've fucked up my high school cheer career completely, thanks to my impulses.

And I'm not an impulsive person. Not by a long shot.

Brandy sends Cami over to the rest of the girls to continue leading practice before she turns to me. "Ava."

The sadness in her voice just about breaks me.

"I know," I say miserably. She doesn't need to say anything else. I'm screwed.

"You actually hit her?" Brandy shakes her head. "You've got some balls, I'll say that. No one messes with Cami. Most of the teachers leave her alone so they don't have to deal with her wrath."

"She's a horrible human being," I spit out bitterly.

"Doesn't matter what you think of her, or how horrible she acts in your presence. You can't put your hands on another student. You definitely can't physically harm your teammate during practice." A long, ragged sigh escapes her. "You know with this incident, I'm going to have to suspend you from the team."

Tears start flowing down my cheeks, and I briefly close my eyes. I have no one to blame for this but myself. I ruined my cheer season. It'll disappoint the girls who count on me, which is all of them, but especially my stunt team.

"For how long?" I ask, wiping away the tears, but they keep on coming.

"At least a week. I'll have to talk to the athletic director about proper protocol with situations like this." She makes a wincing face, as if she knows what she says next will hurt. "You'll have to go speak with Adney in her office tomorrow morning."

The vice principal's office. Great. I've never gone there before in my life, with the exception of when I needed something from her in regards to leadership. I'm supposed to be a good kid, not a bad kid who gets busted for fighting.

"Okay," I say, ducking my head.

"This suspension could last longer. You might even get kicked off the team. I'd hate to lose you. You're one of the strongest bases we have, and it's only your first year. You're a natural, just like your sister." I glance up just in time to see the disappointment written all over my coach's face. "I'd hate to see you go."

"I'm so sorry," I say, my voice cracking.

"Can you apologize to Cami? See if that'll get her to ease up?" Brandy asks gently.

"Absolutely not." She pretty much asked for me to punch her.

A ragged sigh leaves her. "Being stubborn is what got you into trouble in the first place." Brandy shakes her head, and my heart sinks. "I'm going to have to ask you to leave. You're done for the day. Most likely for the week. Gather up your things and expect to see Mrs. Adney during first period tomorrow."

"Okay." I nod once and stalk over to where my backpack and Hydro Flask sit on the ground, scooping them both up and walking away as fast as I can. I hear Cami start to call my name. Brandy immediately tells her to stop.

But she doesn't tell me to stop. She lets me go. I suppose she has to. After all, I just punched Cami in the face.

Holy shit, I actually *punched* Cami Lockhart in the *face!*

I wander through campus, making my way to the school parking lot. Clouds are rolling in, and when I glance up at the sky, I see they're gathered to the north, dark and ominous looking. It'll probably rain.

The weather reflects my mood. I'm mad. At both Cami and myself. More myself, because I couldn't control my emotions, and she totally baited me. Did she expect me to hit her? Probably not. But did she say that knowing how upset it would make me?

Most definitely.

I stomp my way toward my car, grateful no one is around to ask questions. Everyone's either gone for the day or at practice for whatever sport they participate in. Once I toss my backpack behind the passenger seat, I start the engine and tear out of there, enjoying the squeal of my tires when I turn out of the parking lot and onto the road.

It's when I'm driving past the town limits sign, heading south, that I semi-realize where I'm going. Definitely not home. I don't bother calling or texting Ellie to see what she's up to. She's currently at work. I suppose I could've stopped by the Juicery and bought a smoothie, but again, Ellie would've wanted answers as to why I was there.

And I don't feel like dealing with that. With her. With everyone.

Except for one person.

Instead, I drive with purpose down the highway, like I'm trying to outrun the thunderous clouds chasing after me. They keep pace with my speeding car, almost like they really are following me, and by the time I turn into the school parking lot, fat drops of rain splatter on my windshield.

I drive slow through the lot, until I'm close to the stadium, and pull into an empty spot that's right next to Eli's gleaming red Charger. I shut off the engine and squint into the distance, spotting the football team out on the field, still practicing. *Screw it*, I think as I climb out of the car, grabbing the extra hoodie I keep in my trunk and slipping it on before I make my way over to the stands.

As I approach the field, I spot Eli first. He's getting ready to throw the ball, his arm cocked and poised, the ball gripped in his hand. He's wearing a black T-shirt and athletic shorts, and he's got this wide, stretchy headband in his hair that all the boys love to wear. I can see why, since it keeps their hair out of their face, and honestly, he should look ridiculous, but guess what?

He doesn't. He looks frickin' fine as hell. My heart lurches when I take him in, and I stumble a little bit. Almost trip and fall.

Talk about making an entrance.

I discreetly settle in on the bottom bench of the stands, yanking my hood up to cover my head when I feel the rain start to actually fall. I will sit out here for the next two hours watching him if that's what it takes to talk to him. To have him put his arms around me and tell me everything's going to be all right.

I need that right now. I need him.

It takes him about five minutes to notice me. He's concentrating on throwing that ball, his expression intense, his brows lowered. He throws it again and again, and when he's knocked to the ground by one of his own players playing defense, I jump to my feet with a gasp, hoping he's not hurt.

Eli gets back up with no obvious issues. He even yells, "Can't take me down, motherfucker!" to the guy who just tackled him.

Typical Eli. I can't help but smile.

When he finally does notice me, his eyes go wide and he

rests his hands on his hips, studying me. I offer up a little wave, my heart rate starts to increase as he makes his way over to me.

"Are you really here? Or are you a figment of my imagination?" he calls to me.

I stand, anxious for him to get closer. "I'm really here."

He jogs toward me and yanks me into his arms. I cling to him, resting my cheek against his chest. I can feel his hammering heart, smell his woodsy scent. He's damp from the rain and he feels like heaven and I swear to God, I will be so mad at myself if I start crying.

"Not that I'm unhappy to see you, but what are you doing here? I thought you had practice." He runs his hands up and down my back, as if he can sense I need comfort.

"It's a long story," I say, my voice muffled by his T-shirt.

He slips his fingers around the side of my neck, pulling me away slightly so he can look into my eyes. "You all right?"

His voice is low and his eyes are full of concern. I can feel my lower lip tremble, and I bite down on it. Hard. "Not really."

"Practice is almost over—"

"Bennett! Get your ass back on the field!" a booming voice yells. I assume it's his coach.

Eli swiftly glances over his shoulder, before returning his attention to me. "Practice is almost over. Just—give me fifteen minutes. Don't sit out in the rain. Go to your car and wait for me. Where are you parked?"

"Right next to your car," I tell him with a faint smile. The relief I feel at being in his presence is absolutely staggering.

"Go wait for me where it's dry. I'll join you as soon as I can. Okay?" I nod, and he dips down to lightly press my mouth with his. "See ya in a few."

He turns and jogs back across the field. I stay where he left me, too captivated by the easy way he moves. He claims football doesn't consume him, but I don't know. He's a natural athlete. He's really good at what he does. Maybe not as good as Jake, but he's definitely a solid A-tier quarterback.

And I'm the lucky girl who gets to say that #1 QB belongs to me.

CHAPTER 18

❦

ELI

"*W*ho's the skirt?" Coach Weston asks me when I return to the sideline.

I wipe the rain from my face, then wipe my hand on the side of my shorts. "That's my girlfriend, coach."

I can't believe he called her a skirt. Who the fuck says that? What era is he from anyway? Sounds like something out of the eighties. Or maybe even older.

I don't know. Before 2000 is all history to me.

"You actually have a girlfriend, Bennett?" Coach's eyebrows shoot up toward his non-existent hairline.

"He's fucking Jake Callahan's sister," one of my asshole teammates yells.

Glancing behind me, I scan their faces, searching for the one dumbass who said that. They all look equally innocent— or equally guilty.

Annoying fucks.

"Is this true? You're dating Callahan's sister?" Coach hesitates for only a moment, his eyes buggin' out. "Drew Callahan's *daughter?*"

He sounds downright flabbergasted.

"Yeah," I say irritably. "I am. Is that a problem?"

"Hell no, son. You might want to try to get some intel? Find out their secrets? Get a gander at their playbooks somehow?" Coach asks hopefully.

There is no way in hell I'd even contemplate doing something like that. It would put my relationship with Ava—hell with her entire family—in jeopardy.

Nope. No can do.

I make a hissing sound, like I'm full of disappointment. "Afraid I can't help you there, coach."

"Damn. It was worth a shot." He shakes his head. "You're playing with fire, dating that girl. She's the enemy."

I am so fuckin' tired of all this rivalry, enemy talk. It's bullshit.

"I'm in love with her," I say firmly. "So no. She's not the enemy." I turn to face the rest of my team, letting my irritation show. "Let's play, pussies!"

"But it's raining!" one of them whines.

"Get over it! Let's go!"

"Yeah, get out there! Now!" Coach says, backing me up.

I appreciate that, but I'm still annoyed he called Ava the enemy. I'm tired of the drama. Tired of the us versus them mentality. I sound kind of like a wimp, but damn. That girl, my supposed rival, is my world. I'm in love with her. Sometimes, I worry I love her more than she loves me. Isn't that the way it happens in a relationship? There's always one who loves harder than the other? I saw it with my parents. Mom had a perpetual boner for Dad, and he seemed only about fifty percent into her most of the time, if that.

Thinking back on it, seeing that sucked. Mom always sucking up to him. She used to talk in this simpering baby voice that grated on my nerves. He always seemed to respond to it too. As if he actually liked it.

179

Thank God, Ava doesn't treat me like that. Talk to me like that. She's real. As real as they get.

And I am real ready for this practice to be over so I can talk to her. Find out why she's here. She should be at cheer practice. It's difficult for us to see each other during the week. We're both always so damn busy. There's no normal reason for her to be here during this time of day.

I need to find out what's going on.

* * *

TWENTY MINUTES later and I'm heading toward the parking lot, satisfaction seeping through me when I see her car parked right next to mine. That sleek BMW is one fine ass vehicle, and my fingers are itching to drive it. Especially in the rain. I bet I could make the tires squeal like a mother on the wet roads.

"Why is she here anyway?" Brenden asks curiously. He's walking beside me, Jackson on the other side.

"I don't know. I didn't ask," I say. "But I'm about to find out."

"Something's up," Jackson says.

"What makes you say that?" I ask, sending Jackson a skeptical look. I never thought of him being particularly perceptive, but maybe he is.

"I saw her face when she first showed up. She looked kind of upset," Jackson says with a shrug.

She did. She also clung to me when I hugged her, and her throat sounded thick with tears. I hope nothing bad happened. I hope her brother didn't do anything stupid. Or her parents said she couldn't see me anymore.

Panic grips me in a chokehold, and I mentally tell myself to calm down. I hope to hell that's not the case. I refuse to let anyone's shit get between us ever again.

"Maybe cheer practice let out early," I say, though I know deep down that's not the case. She bailed and came to see me.

But why?

"I'll see you guys later," I tell Brenden and Jackson as I break away from them, heading straight for Ava's car. She's sitting in the driver's seat, her head bent over her phone, I assume. She's still got the light gray hood over her head, and I catch only a glimpse of her bright blonde hair, peeking out from under the hood. Her lips are pursed and just seeing her makes my heart swell full to bursting.

I round the front of her car and go to the passenger side door, knocking lightly on the window. She startles and jerks her head in my direction, rolling her eyes at herself when she spots me. She hits the unlock button and I open the door, slipping inside the sleek, leather scented interior.

A hint of her perfume lingers inside the car as well. Or maybe that's just her. She smells fucking delicious. Makes me want to eat her whole.

But that's not what this is about right now. I need to focus on my girl's needs and make sure she's okay.

"You're wet," she says, reaching out to brush rain drops from my cheek with a soft sweep of her finger.

Again, I'm tempted to make an inappropriate joke. Statement. Whatever. I am tested on a daily basis, swear to God.

"It's starting to rain harder." I point at the windshield. "See?"

We both look just in time to see a few of the girls from the cheer team walking by the front of her car. Including Josie Price. She does a doubletake when she spots me, her mouth forming an O as she blinks at me sitting in Ava's car. She nudges one of the girls walking beside her, blatantly telling her to check me out, and they both swivel their heads in my direction.

Busted. But really? I don't give a shit.

181

"Isn't that the girl who was giving you a lap dance at your house?" Ava asks, her voice steely.

Uh oh. She sounds pissed.

"Yeah," I say warily.

Without warning, Ava grabs me by the front of my hoodie. Yanks me close to her. Presses her mouth to mine and kisses the hell out of me. I pop my eyes open to find her eyes are open too and she's glaring at Josie as she continues kissing me.

Damn. My girl is fired up.

When Ava finally breaks the kiss, Josie is walking away with an expression on her face like she just smelled stinky shit. Her friends trail after her, their mouths flapping.

I'm assuming Ava and I will be the topic of their discussion for the rest of the night.

I rub my mouth with the back of my hand, staring at this furious version of Ava sitting next to me with a glower on her pretty face. My Disney princess is rockin' the villain look. "Don't think she'll be giving me lap dances anymore."

"She better not," Ava spits out.

"Whoa, easy there, tiger. What's got you so twisted up?" Reaching out, I push her hood down so I can touch her hair.

A ragged exhalation leaves her before she says, "I think I got kicked off the cheer team today."

My fingers still in her hair at hearing what she said. "What do you mean?"

She turns her head so her gaze meets mine. "I got in trouble. Brandy asked me to leave practice."

"Why did you get in trouble?"

Ava shrugs. Looks away. "It's all Cami's fault," she mumbles.

"What did Cami do?"

Now Ava looks downright pained. "She said something shitty to me and I—I hit her."

Shock courses through me, rendering me still and silent. All I can do is sit there and gape at her like a dying fish. My lips parting and then closing because I can't come up with anything to say.

And I've always got something to say.

"What?" she asks after a few silent seconds. "Why aren't you saying anything?"

"Are you fucking kidding me?" The words push out of me forcefully, like it took everything I had to say that.

Holy fuck. Ava actually *hit* Cami?

"No. I wish I wasn't." She curls her fingers into a fist and punches the edge of her steering wheel with so much force I lean away from her a little bit. "I hate her, Eli. I hate her so damn much. Maybe it's a good thing I'm going to get kicked off the team. I'm tired of dealing with her digging comments and her shitty dirty looks. She's a horrible human being."

"Babe." I reach out and rest my hand on top of her thigh and feel her trembling beneath my touch. Like she's shaking with rage. "Tell me what happened. From the beginning."

She explains it all. How she was talking with her friends when Cami approached with that psycho bitch Baylee, and she started in on her about dating me. Then said something rudely intimate about me, which sent Ava into a tailspin, where she effectively shut Cami up by socking her in the face.

Unbelievable. My girl is an absolute badass.

"...so I understand why Brandy had to send me home. I couldn't be there with Cami. I just hit her. My coach is going to make an example of me, and my moment as a cheerleader at school is officially over," she finishes with a sigh.

I give her knee a squeeze. "Are you going to miss it?"

She nods, looking glum. "I won't miss the Cami and Baylee drama, but yeah. I'll miss it. I like going to the games.

Doing stunts. Cheer is hard work, though I know the majority of you guys don't believe it."

"Nah, that's not true. Don't lump me in with everyone else. I know you and your team work hard," I say. She turns her head toward me, her expression flat out pitiful. "You look really fucking sad right now, and that breaks my heart."

"It's just that I don't usually get in trouble," she whispers, glancing down at where my hand is covering her knee. "I'm scared to go to the vice principal's office tomorrow. I'm afraid of what Adney might say. Then my parents are going to find out and they're going to be so pissed at me. And disappointed. God, I hate it when they use that line on me. I always feel so guilty."

I make a dismissive noise, though I'm not trying to dismiss what she's saying. "My parents are in a constant state of disappointment when it comes to me. I've been to the principal and vice principal's office so many times, it's like they have a chair with my name on it. Trust me, you'll be fine."

"What I did was really bad," she murmurs, her voice shaky.

"More like badass." Her head jerks up, wide eyes meeting mine. "You got in a fight with Cami over me. She's always giving everyone endless shit, and you shut her up with a slug to the face. If that's not badass, I don't know what is."

"You're just trying to make me feel better."

I turn in my seat so I'm facing her. "I'm trying to tell you that what you did was fucking awesome. Cami deserves worse. She is the daughter of Satan."

Ava giggles. "She's terrible."

"Evil," I say.

"Rude." Another giggle from Ava.

"Yeah." I nod enthusiastically. "You did everyone at your school a favor. Wait until the rumors spread, because you know that's already happening. They'll probably consider you a hero tomorrow. People are going to approach you, some you won't even know, and they'll offer up their thanks for putting that bitch in her place."

Ava laughs, and hearing the sound fills me with relief. I don't want her sad over this. Cami isn't worth her worry and tears. "I don't know if that's going to happen."

I put on my best skeptical expression. "Come on. They'll bow at your feet."

Her laughter slowly dies, though the sparkle in her eyes doesn't. "Thank you for making me feel better."

Leaning in close to her, I cup the back of her head, drawing her mouth to mine. "There's nothing else I'd rather do," I tell her.

Just before I kiss her.

CHAPTER 19

AVA

*E*li takes me to that little Mexican restaurant we went
to a while ago. The place with the delicious tacos. I
let him drive my car and even though he, at first, took
corners like a maniac, I eventually got him to calm down and
drive like a civilized human being.

That, and all the rain slowed him down too. It's really
coming down. So hard, Eli makes me stay in the car while he
dashes out through it, running to the takeout window, so he
can place our order. I grab my phone and text my mom,
letting her know I met up with Eli for dinner and that I'll be
home later.

Mom: **Drive safe! It's supposed to rain the rest of the
night.**

Me: **I will. Love you.**

Mom: **Love you too. Be home by ten.**

Me: **Ten? That's so early!**

Mom: **It's a school night.**

Me: **You've let me stay out later before.**

Mom: **Not when it's raining like crazy. I want you
home by ten. Not a minute later.**

"Ugh." I say the word out loud, though there's no one around to hear me. I should feel guilty for keeping my run in with Cami out of the conversation, but how am I supposed to bring that up via text? It won't go over well in person either.

In other words, I'm screwed.

Glancing over my shoulder, I check to see what Eli's doing. He's sitting at one of the tables that are under the overhang by the takeout window, messing around on his phone. He's got this intense look on his face, his messy hair tumbling over his forehead, and an ache forms deep inside me.

We don't have a lot of time tonight. And I'm desperate to feel his hands on me.

Ten minutes later and he's ducking back into my car, carrying a fragrant to-go bag. "I'm starving," he says as he rips into the paper bag, pulling out foil wrapped tacos and handing them to me. "This is yours."

"Thank you." I undo the foil and inhale deeply. The taco meat smells spicy and delicious, and without hesitation, I grab one and take a big bite. "Oh my God, this is so good," I tell him, my mouth full.

He immediately appears in pain. "Babe. The last time you went on about those tacos, all I could think about was how much I wanted to eat your taco."

"Eli," I choke out as I start to laugh. "Seriously?"

He nods. Grabs a taco and shoves almost half of it in his mouth. "You make sexy sounds when you eat," he says after he swallows.

Grabbing the edge of the shredded paper bag, I peek inside to see a smaller paper bag at the bottom. I pull it out and open it up to discover warm tortilla chips. "You went all out tonight," I tease him as I pop a bit of a broken chip in my mouth. "Did you get salsa?"

"Of course," he scoffs, as if I asked the craziest question ever.

We arrange the chips and salsa on the dashboard so we can both reach for them, and then continue eating our tacos. We both have our water bottles with us too, so we have something to drink. It's cozy in here. An impromptu dinner for two. And the steady hum of the rain hitting the roof of my car is kind of...nice.

"I'm glad I came to your practice," I tell him after I finish my first taco.

He's already halfway through his second. "I am too."

"Thank you for dinner." I wave a hand at the chips and salsa. "My parents would kill me if they saw this."

He hesitates in his eating, his gaze meeting mine. "Why?"

"They don't want me to eat in this car."

"Whoops." He laughs, swiping a chip out of the bag and dunking it in the salsa. "Guess it'll be our secret."

"Just don't drop anything," I say.

"I'm too hungry to let anything drop." He grabs his last taco and starts devouring that too. "What else is going on with you?"

I tell him about the past few days. We talk every night, but last night he was exhausted and wasn't much for conversation, so I let him go to bed. There's not a lot going on anyway.

If I'm no longer on the cheer team, they'll be even less going on for me.

"How about you?" I ask when I'm finished. "How was your day?"

He grabs his water bottle and takes a drink. "I got an email from the offensive coach at Fresno State this afternoon."

My mouth drops open. "What? Are you serious?"

"Yeah. I guess they watched my film. He asked if I was considering applying to Fresno State."

"Are you?"

Eli shrugs. "I don't know. I kind of wanted to get the fuck out of here."

My appetite disappears, just like that. "Where do you want to go?"

"I don't know. I kind of want to be like Ryan. He up and left and never comes home. Like ever." He shakes his head. "I still haven't heard from that asshole, and I texted him Saturday."

"I'm sorry," I say, my heart hurting for him. His broken relationship with his older brother hurts far more than he likes to show. He'd prefer to be angry about it.

"Fresno State is a great school," I tell him. "And they have an excellent football program. Ash loves it."

"Yeah, after talking with him, I wonder if he said something." Eli glances over at me. "Did you hear him say anything about that? Or did your sister mention it?"

"No." I shake my head. "We met them for lunch Sunday before Autumn left for Santa Barbara, and they didn't mention you at all."

"Ouch. So offended." He clutches his heart, but he's grinning so I know he's teasing. "I might consider applying there. Shit, I don't know what I want to do. My grades aren't total shit, but they're not the best. I took the SAT last year. Once. Maybe I should take it again."

"What was your score?" I ask. I took the pre-SAT last year and bombed it like the biggest bomber ever.

"I don't know. Around 1300 I think?"

I gape at him. "That's...really good."

Like, very impressive.

"Is it?" He doesn't seem concerned in the least.

"Um, yes," I say. "Are you a secret genius?"

"I told you, I don't get the best grades. But they're not complete shit." He shrugs and looks vaguely uncomfortable.

"Do you not understand your classes? Or is it more you just don't care about them?" I ask.

He smiles. "The last one. Definitely."

"Eli." I shove at his shoulder, quietly marveling at the rock hard muscle beneath my fingertips. "You're going to graduate this year. You should totally care."

"Eh. I have no idea what I want to be, or what I want to do. When I was younger, I wanted to be a professional athlete, but let's get real." He sends me a pointed look. "I don't have a shot in hell."

"You don't know that," I say, my voice quiet.

"I do. I know that. I'm not as talented as your brother. As much as it pains me to admit. I don't even come close to your dad. He's a god. Ash is going to end up being a god too. I can just tell." The faraway look on Eli's face tells me he's wishing he could still be a potential god too, but he's trying to be a realist.

My family is full of people who've made it. Who've done something. My parents are firm believers in never squashing our dreams, no matter what they are. When Autumn announced last summer she wanted to be a heart surgeon, my parents immediately supported her.

Of course, we're lucky. They have money, and they can help us with our education. I know Eli's parents do well, but they don't come close to what my dad is worth. Hardly anyone does. Maybe his parents can't afford to pay for college? Or they don't want to help him at all?

It could also be that his parents are so wrapped up in their own bullshit, they don't pay attention to what's going on in his life. And they're not offering him any guidance whatsoever.

That makes me sad.

"You don't think you have the potential?" I ask him.

His gaze locks with mine. "Let's be real, baby. I'm a show-boater quarterback at best. A mediocre one at worst. There is nothing special about my game play."

He's magnetic on the field. Even when he's losing. All that swagger and confidence. How can he call himself mediocre? I'm about to protest when he changes the subject, sending me one of those smoldering looks of his.

"You wanna get out of here?" He reaches over and grabs the last couple of chips, dunking them in salsa before he shoves them in his mouth.

"Where do you want to go?"

"I don't know. The lake?"

"And do what? Dance around in the rain?" Yuck, no. Plus, it'll be way colder up there. Just like I'm sure it's way colder at my house.

"No, more like mess around in the backseat." He glances toward the backseat for emphasis.

"I have to be home by ten," I tell him with a wince. "My mom is worried about me driving late at night because of the weather."

"Maybe we should just go back to my house then," he suggests. "That won't be as long a drive."

"What about your mom?" I ask, trying to ignore the dread that fills me just thinking about her. I don't want to get in the middle of their family squabbles. I want to support Eli, but I also don't want his mom coming for me, like she did Cami.

Ugh. Cami. Just thinking her name makes me angry.

"What about my mom? What's she going to do when we show up at the house? Stop you from coming inside?" He instantly becomes heated. "Fuck that."

"Don't get mad." His mother is such a touchy subject, I regret bringing her up. "Is she home right now?"

"Yeah, probably. She might be at her friend's house

though. She's been going there a lot lately. I don't know. She's never really around." His tone is dismissive. "We can drive back to the school and I'll get my car, and then you can follow me over."

"Okay," I agree, though I'm uneasy. I remember what Jake told me. When Cami went to Eli's house and his mom came out, calling her a whore or whatever. I don't want to make her angry or make her think I'm something I'm not.

I want his mother to like me.

"Okay? Cool." He starts the car and tears out of the parking lot, making me gasp. He immediately slows down, his expression contrite as he quickly glances over at me. "Sorry if I yelled at you. It wasn't you at all. Talking about my mom always makes me feel…"

"Awful?" I add for him.

"Yeah. That." He's quiet for a moment as he drives, and all I can hear is the swish of the water on the road hitting the tires, the faintly squeaky slide of the wipers on the windshield. "If she's there, I want you to meet her. More like, I want her to meet you. I want her to know that I've got a girlfriend, and that she means everything to me."

The sincerity in his tone gets me. I can't help it. I am such a sucker for this boy. "That's so sweet."

"It's the truth." He settles his big hand on my knee again, then slowly runs it up to my thigh. "Remember the last time I drove your car and you had that dress on?"

"Yes," I admit quietly, wishing I had it on once more. There is no better feeling in the world than Eli's warm hands pressing into my bare flesh.

"And how I kept brushing my fingers against the front of your panties?" He's saying all of this completely nonchalant, his gaze focused on the road ahead.

All while I'm sitting in my seat feeling a little flushed. A lot hot. "Yes."

"I also asked if you'd ever be down to give me a BJ while I'm driving." Another quick look from Eli. I'm sure he's checking me for a reaction. "Remember?"

"I'm not giving you a blow job when the weather's like this," I tell him sternly.

He chuckles. "I like it when you get all bossy on me. It's sexy as fuck."

"Uh huh." I cross my arms. "I'm sure you just love it when I deprive you of blow jobs."

"I'd rather get a blow job from you when we're all alone. So I can concentrate on what you're doing."

"Oh my God." I cover my face with my hands. I may be feeling freer when it comes to sex and Eli, but he still has this way of embarrassing me with a few choice words.

"You know I'm all about the visual. I like the idea of watching you wrap your lips around the head of my dick." He reaches between his legs and readjusts what I assume is his growing erection. "I need to stop. I'm getting myself all worked up just talking about it."

I can't help but laugh. "You're crazy."

He shoots a grin in my direction. "You don't even know the half of it."

CHAPTER 20

ELI

*W*e're about to walk inside my house when I grab Ava's hand and give it a squeeze. I can tell she's nervous. Her fingers are a little shaky and she clings to me like she does when she's feeling needy.

Honestly? I'm a little worried too. Mom's home. Her car is in the garage, and the lights are on in the family room. The last time I had a girl over and she caught us, she lost her mind on Cami. Not that Cami didn't deserve someone losing their mind on her. That bitch gets away with everything.

That night? It was unwarranted. Mom mistook her for one of Dad's secret girlfriends and went apeshit. It was a bad scene. I can't believe Cami admitted that story to Jake. And that Jake held onto that information long enough to blab it in front of pretty much his entire family. Making me look like a complete jackass.

I still hate that guy. I'll make an effort to be nice though, if that's what makes Ava happy. I'm all about that.

Ava grabs hold of my arm with her free hand, stopping me from reaching for the door handle. "Are you sure she'll be okay with me just showing up with you unannounced?"

"She won't mind," I reassure her, but deep down, I have no idea how my mother will react. I never know what her mood is going to be like.

"If you say so," Ava says, but she sounds unsure. With good reason.

I'm feeling unsure too.

We enter the house and make our way to the family room. The moment the door opens, Muffin starts barking, the little shit. As we get closer to the family room, I can see Mom sitting on the couch, curled up with a blanket and a glass of wine on the end table beside her. The TV is on, and she's watching that bitchy show with real estate agents set in Los Angeles. Swear to God, she watches that show repeatedly.

Muffin spots us and hops off the couch, making her way toward us, her long claws clacking on the bare floors.

"Oh, look at her!" Ava lets go of my hand to crouch down and greet Muffin with a sweet crooning voice I've never heard her use before. "Aren't you the cutest thing? Look at you. You're so sweet!"

Muffin is yipping and hopping up and down, trying to rest her paws on Ava's knees. Once she's successful, she barks again. Then licks the side of Ava's face.

Gross.

But Ava doesn't seem to mind. She's laughing and petting the dog nonstop, and I can't believe how nice Muffin is being to her. Of course, Ava is being equally nice to Muffin, so maybe that's the secret.

"Eli, is that you?" Mom calls.

"No, it's a stranger coming to steal all of your valuables," I say to her, pausing only for a moment. "Yeah Mom, of course it's me."

"Well, you don't sound like yourself. I thought I heard a

female's voice. And Muffin isn't barking like crazy like she usually does when she sees you."

"I brought someone with me, that's why," I say.

Ava glances up at me before she rises to her full height once more, grabbing my hand so I can lead her into the family room.

Mom grabs the TV remote and pauses her show, a giant, beautiful blonde woman filling the screen with a bitchy expression, her glossy red lips parted as if she's ready to blast someone with a string of mean words. "You brought someone with you?"

"Yeah." Nerves are suddenly dancing in my stomach, but I try my best to play it cool. "This is Ava."

"Oh." Mom leaps from the couch, running her hands over her clothes like that's going to magically eliminate the wrinkles. "You brought home a *girl*. I wish you would've warned me." She rakes her fingers through her hair, trying to smooth it out, but it's still a little messy.

But at least she appears more presentable than usual.

"Hi," Ava says with a little wave.

"Hello," Mom says, plastering on a pleasant smile. It wavers at the corners, and I'm worried she's going to say something horrible when she turns her gaze onto me. "Are you seeing this girl, Eli?"

"She's my girlfriend," I say, my voice stiff, as if I'm talking to a stranger. Sometimes, when it comes to my mom, I feel like I am.

"Oh, she's your *girlfriend*." Mom smiles, and it actually looks genuine. "It's so nice to meet you, Ava."

"Nice to meet you too." Ava glances down at Muffin, who's furiously sniffing her shoes. "And your dog."

"Muffin seems to like you." Mom laughs, though it sounds as if she's a little on edge. Normal mother behavior, which is almost reassuring.

But then again, it's not. Not at all. When she has too much to drink, Mom can pop off with the shittiest remarks ever. She knows how to sling a good insult when she wants to.

Meaning, I've learned from a master.

"I like her too." Ava kneels again, letting Muffin hop all around her, trying to lick her face. She laughs and I glance over at Mom to find her watching them with warmth in her eyes.

Mom lifts her gaze to mine, the warmth remaining in her gaze and she smiles at me, mouthing, *I like her.*

I mouth back, *I like her too.*

"I'm gonna show Ava my room," I say after a few minutes of idle chitchat about my sworn enemy of the house. Muffin. Who knew Ava would get attached to that stupid ass dog so quickly? "I just wanted to introduce you two first."

"It was very nice meeting you, Ava." Mom approaches us, stands before us awkwardly for a moment before she pulls my girlfriend in for a quick hug. "I hope Eli brings you around more often."

"I would love that," Ava says, a little flustered as she steps out of my mother's arms. She flashes me a quick look before returning her attention to my mother. "It was nice meeting you too."

We start to walk away when Mom calls out, "Oh Eli. I forgot to tell you."

I pause and glance over my shoulder. Ava remains beside me as well. "What?"

"Your brother called the house." Yeah, we still have a land-line. Mom refuses to get rid of it. "He mentioned to me that you won't quit texting and calling him. He asked if one of us was in jail."

Ha. Ha. Not funny, motherfucker. God, my brother is annoying. "I'd quit if he called or texted me back," I say between clenched teeth. Annoyance flashes through me. Leave it to Ryan to make me sound like a pest.

"He said he'd try and call here tomorrow late afternoon." Mom makes a little face. "Though you'll probably be at practice."

"If he calls here first, tell him to call back at eight. I'll make sure my ass is in this house at eight o'clock," I say.

Mom scowls. I'm sure it's because I said *ass* in front of Ava. If she only knew. "I'll let him know, but Eli…you shouldn't harass your brother so much. He's hard at work at college. He has to concentrate on his studies."

Making excuses for him. Figures. I refuse to get into this right now. "Just tell him to call back, okay? And come on, Mom. You can be really busy and still make time to call your family, right?"

Before she can answer, I grab Ava's hand and lead her through my house. My steps are fast and furious, and Ava's having to run to keep up with me, until she finally jerks her hand out of mine and falls behind.

"Are you okay?" she calls softly.

"Yeah, I'm just…" My voice drifts and I stop in front of my closed door, leaning my shoulder against it, watching Ava as she approaches. "Irritated. With my brother. He's been ignoring me."

"For how long?" she asks when she stops directly in front of me.

"Oh, almost three years." I sound like I'm joking, but I'm not. "Come on." I open the door to my room and she follows me inside.

"Are you being serious? He's ignored you for the last *three* years?" Ava asks as she glances around my room before her gaze lands on my bed. Wonder if she's remembering what went down the last time she was in my bed.

That was a good time.

"I'm kind of exaggerating, but kind of not. Since he went away to college, he doesn't really talk to any of us. And he hasn't come home. Not once."

"Not even for Christmas?" Her eyes widen the slightest bit. "You do celebrate Christmas, right?"

"Yeah, we do." I send her a confused look. "Why wouldn't we?"

"I don't know. Some people don't." She shrugs.

"Well, we do." The last couple of years, Christmas hasn't been so great, but I won't bother telling her that. "And no, he doesn't come around for any holidays. None of them. It's like we don't exist anymore."

"That's terrible." The sad expression on Ava's face says it all.

She feels for me. My pain is her pain. I've never had someone like that before. Someone who feels for me. Someone who's on my side and no one else's. Mom's torn between the three men in her life: me, Ryan and my dad. Even though my dad shits all over her still, she cares about him. She wants to make him happy.

Dad is selfish. He only cares about himself, and how we all make him look. It's all about the image for him, and currently, our family image is tarnished beyond repair.

Ryan? He's a runner. An avoider. He can't even manage to send me a text. But he'll call the house and tell Mom I'm a pain in his ass. Like I'm bugging him when I'm just trying to get some support from my big brother.

But this girl? Standing in the middle of my bedroom, looking at me like I'm the only thing that matters to her? She supports me no matter what I do or what I say.

She's just...there. For me.

That shit is mind blowing. Like, I'm a complete idiot most of the time. I say and do the craziest things. I don't think, I just do. That's how I've lived my life. I've never cared about, you know, doing right. Watching out for myself. If it's my time, it's my time. That's what I used to say after I nearly got into a car accident, or that one time when I jumped off the cliffs at the lake and almost broke my fucking neck.

Now, I don't want to be so reckless. Life is fucking precious, and I want to spend every day of it with Ava, if I can. I want to make amends with my family. I want to do well in school so I can get out of here and go to a good college.

Still don't know what I want to do with the rest of my life, though. I guess that'll come. Eventually.

I'm just living in the moment right now.

"He's going through his own shit," I finally say, making excuses, as usual, for my brother. "I don't blame him. I think I'd run too if I was in his shoes."

"Are you going to do that after you graduate?" Her question is casual, but I see the fear in her gaze. The worry in her features. "Leave and never come back?"

If she would've asked me that question a couple months ago, I would've said yes with no hesitation. I can't take it here anymore. I want out. No one cares about me anyway, and I feel the same exact way.

Ava has changed me, though. She's given me a connection when I've felt untethered for the last few years. When no one seems to care what you're doing or where you're at, you don't really care either. You smash through life, causing chaos and destruction wherever you go.

I still have chaotic tendencies. I'm still too impulsive. But I'm trying to control myself better. All I can do is take it one day at a time.

"You've actually got me considering going to Fresno State, so no. I'm not going to leave and never come back," I tell her.

She blinks and the fear disappears from her gaze. Just like

that. It's just that easy. "We've only been together for a little while."

"I feel like I've been waiting for you my entire life," I say, my voice low. Serious. I take a step toward her.

Ava rolls her eyes. "Come on."

"I mean it." I stop directly in front of her, but I don't touch her yet. Didn't Ava tell me once there's something to be said about anticipation? How good it can feel? Or maybe I heard that somewhere else. I don't know, but before Ava, with other girls, I rushed everything. I just wanted to get to the good stuff, and I never wanted to linger.

Now, I want to linger. Savor. Revel in it. Revel in *her*.

"I've been dealing with a lot of shit these last few years, most of it brought on by my family. Or myself," I start, reaching out to touch her face. I skim my fingers along her cheek, pleased when her eyelids flutter and her lips part. Every touch from me makes her body respond, no matter what. "I try to act tough, because it's easier that way. No one can hurt me. My family does it on a daily basis, but if I talk shit and put on a front and beat the fuck out of guys who cross me, who cares? I've got this, right?"

"You don't have to do that with me." She slowly shakes her head, her imploring gaze locking with mine. "You don't have to suffer alone."

"I know. Since I've met you, I'm starting to realize that." I cradle her face with both hands, my hold light, as if she's a fragile and precious thing. To me, she is. "I'm not perfect. I've fucked up. I'll probably continue to fuck up, but I love you. I love you more than anyone else, and I will do my damnedest to make sure I never hurt you."

A tremulous smile curls her perfect lips and I lean in, gently pressing my mouth to hers. "I can't guarantee I won't hurt you again. I probably will."

"I love you, too. And I don't want some perfect, fake

version of you. I want you just the way you are," she whispers, just before I rest my mouth on hers again.

We stand in the middle of my room kissing, Muffin scratching at the door and whining, like she knows I've got the best fuckin' girl in my room and I'm keeping her to myself. It's true. She is the best girl.

And I'm definitely keeping her all to myself.

CHAPTER 21

AVA

"*I* cannot believe you're in my office this morning. I also can't believe what I heard you did to Cami Lockhart yesterday at cheer practice," Mrs. Adney says with a long, disappointed sigh as she leans back in her chair.

I wish I could hang my head and avoid her gaze, but that's cowardly. I need to face her head on. "I can't believe it either."

"Why'd you do it? What in the world possessed you to actually slug Cami in the face?" Mrs. Adney shakes her head. "If that had happened during school hours, you would've been automatically suspended for three days."

"Really?" My heart feels like it just lurched in my chest. Like it's trying to dislodge itself and take off running. "Are you going to suspend me?"

She sends me a hard look, her lips tight, her eyes narrowed. "I should. Cami wants me to. She showed up first thing at my office. Her parents want me to as well. They'd already left multiple phone messages by the time I actually got around to calling them. Have you told your parents about this yet?"

I assumed she'd already told them yesterday, figuring

Brandy had contacted her and let her know. But when I arrived at home last night after being with Eli, completely on edge and prepared to defend myself, my parents acted like everything was normal.

So I did too. I never mentioned it.

Slowly, I shake my head.

"Well, they're gonna find out. I'm contacting them as soon as our little meeting is over." She sighs again, rocking back and forth in her chair, contemplating me. I really like Mrs. Adney. She enforces tough love like no other, yet all the students respect her. She doesn't yell just for the sake of yelling. Her discipline is necessary, and deep down the majority of us know it. The good kids love her, the bad kids love her—for the most part—and we all bask in her compliments and glowing words when she offers them.

But when she's looking at you like she's currently looking at me? I can't help but feel like slime on the bottom of someone's shoe. The lowest of the low.

"I'm sure they'll be mad at me," I offer up, not sure of what I should say.

"Look." She leans forward, her chair squeaking extra loud, making me wince. "Cami Lockhart is—difficult. I get it. But I have to draw the line on physical violence."

"I understand."

"Good. I'm sure you know that you're suspended from the team."

"Okay." I expected that, thanks to what my coach said. "For how long?"

"Two weeks minimum. Maybe longer. Maybe for the rest of the season." She levels me with a look and I want to crumble. Instead, I sit up straighter, fully prepared to take my punishment. "Your position on the team is currently under consideration."

"If Cami had her way, I'd never come back," I say, my heart twisting at the thought of actually never going back.

My heart twists at being on the team too. Dealing with Cami in the aftermath doesn't sound pleasant either.

"You're damn right. You probably shouldn't be on the team. We do not condone that sort of behavior on campus. So with that…" She pauses, most likely for effect. "You'll have to do Saturday school. For two weeks."

"Oh God." I take a deep, trembling breath, surprised that's my punishment. I thought it would be a lot worse. Did I hear her right? "Two weeks?"

"Yes. If this had happened last year, you definitely would've been suspended. No question. But the laws change frequently in our state, and this recent change is to your advantage." The stern expression on her face tells me I should consider myself lucky this is it. "I explained to them the situation, and the Lockharts are not pleased. They've already expressed their feelings in regards to this matter, but there's nothing else I can do about it. The law is the law. Now get out of here."

"Thank you," I say with a jerky nod as I rise to my feet. "I'm sorry."

"Don't tell me you're sorry. Apologize to Cami Lockhart," she says as I open her office door.

Fat chance that'll ever happen, I think as I make my way out of the maze that is the administration and staff offices. I walk through the door that leads to the lobby and spot a few students sitting slumped in the waiting area chairs with dark expressions on their faces. I'm sure they're anticipating their punishment as well.

Great. Now I'm a bad kid. A bad kid who can't cheer. Who'll have to report to Saturday school for the next two weekends. My parents are going to be so pissed.

My phone buzzes in my backpack and I go to the

zippered pocket where I keep it and pull it out to find a text from Eli.

What happened?

I type out a quick response.

Suspended from cheer team for two weeks. Maybe longer. Saturday school twice.

Eli: **That's not bad.**

Me: **I know. Could've been worse.**

Eli: **Chin up babe. Now you can come watch my games.** 😉

Oh. I didn't even think of that.

Me: **You're right! OMG!**

Eli: **I can always find a positive in a negative.**

Me: **Yeah you can.🖤 I have to go to class. TTYL**

Eli: **Love you.**

Me: **Love you too.**

* * *

"So what happened with Adney?" Ellie asks me once we're seated at our usual picnic table in the quad at lunch. We have classes together, but I didn't really have a chance to explain to her everything that happened, so I give her the quick rundown.

Marty is sitting with us since his boyfriend Thomas had to do something with band during lunch so he was free. He makes all the right sympathetic noises as I talk, and actually rests his hand against his chest when I tell him I punched Cami Lockhart. "No flippin' way."

I nod. "I don't even know what came over me. It's like I can't explain it. One second, I'm standing there thinking about how much I hate her and the next, she's on the ground thanks to me socking her right in the face."

Marty grins. "Holy shit, I love it! Bitch got what she deserved. Wish I'd been there to see it."

"I'm not one to condone violence but…" I'm about to explain myself further but Ellie starts talking instead.

"She's a nightmare, let's be real. Plus that overbearing mother of hers, *God.* I was in volleyball with her during middle school and let me tell you, you'd think her mom was running the team, not the coaches. And when Cami didn't get her way? Forget it. She turned into a complete lunatic. Both of them did," Ellie says, her tone bitter.

"I never saw her mom around much, but it always feels like Cami is right there. In front of my face, taunting me nonstop." I shake my head. "She's the worst. Seriously. I sort of feel bad for hitting her, though."

"You shouldn't," Marty says firmly. "She's been a school-yard bully since kindergarten. And a complete judgmental bitch. It's about time someone knocked her to the ground."

They both laugh and I do too, but I still feel uneasy. Haven't heard from either of my parents yet, so that's part of the problem. They're going to be so angry with me. I just know it. Cami was Jake's girlfriend at one point. Well, at a few different points. I'm sure Mom and Dad will be incredibly disappointed in my behavior.

"Hey, Ava!"

I glance over my shoulder to see Hannah approaching our table with a wide smile on her face. "Can I sit with you guys?"

"Of course," I say, though before I even got my answer out Hannah was already scooting in next to Marty. They give each other a hug since they're such good friends.

"Where's Sophie?" Marty asks her.

"With Tony," Hannah says with an eyeroll before she starts laughing. "Though I shouldn't act like that. I'm always with Jake."

"True that," Marty says with a pointed look. I know sometimes he feels abandoned by his best friends Hannah and Sophie since they got boyfriends. He's confessed as much to Ellie, who told me. But I also know once he got with Thomas, he's sort of glad he wasn't hanging out with his best friends so much. I bet not having them around forced him to be a little more open. And a lot more social.

"Where is Jake anyway?" I ask his girlfriend. Sometimes he goes off campus to eat lunch with his bros, but most of the time I see him with his girlfriend.

"He had to go meet with his dad. *Your* dad," Hannah corrects at the last second. "Something to do with football. Of course."

"My dad is on campus?" My voice comes out way squeakier than I expected and I clear my throat, hating how dorky I sound.

"I guess so," Hannah says with a shrug before she glances around, then leans in across the table. The rest of us do the same, fully expecting Hannah to share some major gossip. "So is it true?"

"Is what true?" I ask, even though I know what she's asking.

"That you punched Cami during cheer practice yesterday?" Hannah's brows shoot up.

Here come the rumors. "Yes, it's true," I say with a little sigh.

"Oh my God!" Hannah holds up her hand over the table. "High five!"

I slap my palm against hers, marveling at how my socking Cami has turned into some sort of hero moment. Who knew that many people hate her so much?

Me. I should've known.

"Tell me allll about it," Hannah says eagerly.

So I launch into the story all over again, and everyone listens intently, like it's the first time I've told it. More people join our table as I continue talking, and when I'm finished, I'm rewarded with a round of applause and words of encouragement.

This is freaking surreal.

"Seriously," Marty says, reaching out and settling his hand on my arm. "Thank you for standing up to her. Not enough people do. This is why she gets away with so much. It's almost like we've all become so used to her, her bad behavior doesn't faze us anymore."

"Well, it should. And unlucky for her, she said the wrong thing to me at the wrong time," I tell him. "I can't stand her and her big mouth. She shouldn't be allowed to say such awful things."

"She's the worst," Hannah agrees, and others have something to say about Cami too. We spend the rest of the lunch period listening to people voice their complaints about Cami. The girl has terrorized people on this campus for the past three years, and they're all over it.

The animosity toward Cami is much worse than I thought. I believed I was the only one going through my own personal hell with her. Turns out, we all are.

When lunch is over, I'm headed to my class when Jocelyn, the ex-girlfriend of Diego, who happens to be my brother's best friend, calls my name.

"Can I talk to you?" she asks, her words hesitant and her expression full of uncertainty.

"Of course." I wait for her to approach, stepping off to the side so other students can walk past us.

"I know what happened between you and Cami." She breaks out into a smile. "And this may sound evil, but when I heard what you did? I couldn't stop laughing."

With that statement, she actually starts laughing.

I let her, because if there's anyone who deserves to punch Cami in the face, it's Jocelyn. Diego was cheating on Jocelyn with Cami for a long time, and it caused a lot of problems between them. And between Diego and Jake, since Cami is his ex. It turned into a big disaster, Diego and Jocelyn broke up over Cami, and then that other major rumor started across campus after homecoming.

That Jocelyn was pregnant.

Hannah confirmed to me that the rumor came straight out of Jocelyn's mouth. Not that I'm going to ask her about it now. It's none of my business.

Though I can't help but be extremely curious.

"Did you get in trouble?" Jocelyn asks once she's finished laughing.

"Yeah." I nod. "I'm off the cheer team for a couple of weeks and I have to do Saturday school."

"Was it worth it?"

"Considering I don't know what's going on with cheer, or whether I'll be let back on the team or not, I don't know. That part sucks. I'm going to miss cheer." I shrug. "But going to Saturday school two weeks in a row isn't so bad."

"If I ever got my hands on her, I don't know if she'd survive," Jocelyn says, her expression darkening. "That bitch ruined my life."

"I'm sorry you and Diego broke up," I offer. If you ask me, she should be pissed at Diego. He's the cheater in this situation. Not that Cami is an innocent party, but come on. Diego knew what he was doing, and he did it anyway.

"So am I," Jocelyn says bitterly. "Especially since...you know." She sends me a pointed look.

"I know what?"

"That I'm...pregnant." She presses her lips together, like she can't believe she said that.

Or maybe she can't believe she's actually pregnant.

"Is it...true?" I ask, my voice lowering.

A sigh leaves her and I swear her eyes mist up. "Yes. It's true."

"Oh Jocelyn." My heart breaks for her. Not because she's pregnant—though that's traumatic enough—but because she's alone. Diego is with Cami. Even if Diego wanted to get back together with Jocelyn, she'd probably turn him down. He did her so wrong.

"It's okay." She stands up straighter, sniffing. "My family has been really supportive. I'll switch to online school after winter break. It'll work out. My mom said she would help watch the baby while I go to college."

Her words are optimistic, but I hear the sadness there too. She's so young. So is Diego. And I feel so bad. I don't know what I would do if I was in her position.

Unable to help myself, I reach for Jocelyn, pulling her into a hug. She clings to me for a moment, and I squeeze her tight. "You're so strong," I murmur as we start to pull away from each other. "You're going to be fine."

"I think so too. It's hard though. This entire breakup has been such an emotional rollercoaster. I still miss him." Jocelyn seems to shake herself out of her funk with a quick toss of her head, her long black hair falling down her back. "Forget him. I just wanted to thank you for doing all of us a service and taking out Cami. What you did was huge."

"It really wasn't," I say, but Jocelyn laughs.

"Don't act all modest. No one has dared to ever cross her before. Not really." Reaching out, Jocelyn gently pats my shoulder. "I need to go to class. I hope you get back on the cheer team."

"Thank you," I tell her, turning and watching her as she walks away. She's the hero in this situation. Rising above it and taking care of herself—and her future baby.

I can't believe she's actually pregnant. And Diego is strutting around campus acting like his life hasn't changed one bit.

Not sure how my brother can still be such close friends with him. Diego did him dirty too, getting together with Cami...

Frowning, I head for my class. I didn't mean to become some sort of leading advocate for the anti-Cami campaign, but somehow, that's what I ended up being. And it's freaking weird, though I've always fought for the little guy, so I guess it fits.

Crap, I figured I was going to get into major trouble and be grounded yet again. Still haven't heard from my parents, so the potential is there, but even if I do, I'm kind of thinking hitting Cami and getting kicked off the cheer team was worth it.

Standing up for yourself usually is.

CHAPTER 22

AVA

*M*e: **I'm meeting up with Eli after his practice.**

Mom: **Oh no you're not. You need to come home so we can talk.**

Me: **It's Wednesday. I don't have practice.**

Mom: **I heard you don't have practice for the next two weeks AT LEAST.**

Oh shit. When Mom uses all caps, you know you're in for it.

Me: **I can explain.**

Mom: **You don't have to. Mrs. Adney filled us both in.**

Dread sinks my stomach to my toes. Mom and Dad know what's up. I can't believe I didn't get a call or text sooner.

My phone lights up with a call from Mom and I reluctantly answer it.

"Were you never going to mention that you got called into Mrs. Adney's office this morning?" Mom hesitates for only a second before she continues. "Because you punched Cami Lockhart in the jaw?"

"Like I said, I can explain," I start, but she cuts me off.

"I'm sure you can. I'm sure you have a perfectly valid excuse. But you can't go around hitting people, Ava Elizabeth Callahan. I don't know where you learned to be so—violent, but let me tell you something. I. Don't. Like. It." Mom punctuates those last four words with enough force they're like bullets shooting out of her mouth.

Heh. Talk about violent.

"You wouldn't believe the things she's said and done to me over the last few months, Mom. She's like, the worst human being on the planet," I say, though I don't really get into the details. Especially about the last thing she said in regards to Eli.

I get mad all over again just thinking about it.

"Where are you right now?" Mom asks.

Dude, she pretty much ignored everything I just said. So annoying.

"I'm sitting in my car in the parking lot. School just let out." I was going to hang out with Ellie at Starbucks and we were going to do our homework together while sipping on PSLs until football practice was over. I may as well take advantage of my free time and spend it with Eli.

"What are your plans for the rest of the day?"

"I was going to do homework with Ellie at Starbucks."

"Really." Mom sounds like she doesn't believe me.

And I'm immediately offended.

"Yes, really," I huff.

"Oh. I figured you were only wanting to spend time with Eli," Mom says.

"He has football practice, remember? I was planning on seeing him after though. Unless I'm grounded again," I say, sounding like a bratty teenager.

Ooh, guess what? I never give my parents trouble, but I guess I'm feeling kind of bratty.

Mom sighs. "I don't know. Should you be grounded?"

"Mom, come on. Cami sucks. You didn't particularly like her, I know it."

"Jake could've done so much better," Mom mutters.

"Right. And he did. He's with Hannah now, and Diego has to deal with Cami. Who is a terrible human being as you well know, and says terrible things to me all the time. She says terrible things to *everyone* at this school. I actually had all sorts of people congratulate me today for hitting her. How messed up is that?"

"It's pretty messed up," Mom agrees before she sighs. "Fine, you're right. I suppose she's a terrible human. I'm sure she said something that warranted a reaction, but hitting her, Ava? It's so unlike you. Violence is never the answer."

Tell that to Jake, is what I really want to say, but I keep my mouth shut.

"I know, I know. I guess I just hit my max level with her," I admit.

"What are you, a video game?" Mom laughs and I start to relax. Maybe I'm not going to get in trouble after all. "Fine. I suppose your punishment from school is punishment enough. How long until you're back on the cheer team?"

"I don't know. Maybe I don't want to go back. Not if Cami's there," I say, hating how sad those words make me feel. I do want to go back. But maybe not this year. Let Cami have her moments of glory as the cheer captain for the rest of the season. Then she'll graduate and be gone, and I can come back without ever having to deal with her again.

But would Brandy take me back? I don't know. I might've blown my chance with her forever. I need to go talk to her.

"You shouldn't let that girl determine what you can and cannot do," Mom says, her voice firm.

"It's not that. It's more like, do I want to subject myself to her horrible behavior every day until cheer season is over? Don't forget, she's the team captain," I remind her. "After everything that happened, she'll do her best to make my life miserable, and she'll succeed."

"It's your choice. I'll stand by you, whatever you want to do," Mom says.

"Thank you."

"You know what's so funny?"

"What?"

"You are like, the perfect combo of me and your father, with a hint of your Uncle Owen mixed in. You know he punched your dad in the face when he was only fourteen," she says.

"Yeah, yeah, I've heard the story," I say with a little laugh.

"Right. And I wasn't the best behaved when I was your age either. I was actually…terrible." She laughs too. "I didn't get in trouble for causing fights though. More like I was the cause for fights."

"Yeah well, did you ever have to deal with a girl who claims she had sex with your boyfriend?" The moment the words leave me, I close my eyes and bang the back of my head against the driver's seat.

Shit. I sort of forgot myself just now.

As in, I forgot I was talking to my *mother.*

She's quiet for a moment, which makes me nervous.

"Ava. Are you and Eli having sex?"

"Uhhh…"

"And if you are, is he at least using protection?" Before I can answer, she drops a bomb. "Maybe you should get on the pill."

"Mom!" I cover my eyes with my hand, even though no one can see me. "I can't believe you're asking me this."

"You're sixteen years old with a serious boyfriend who's a year older than you. I am not stupid," Mom says.

This is the problem when you have parents who don't forget what they did in their teen years. They ask you about your sex life and act like they've done everything you're currently doing so you can't trick them.

Sometimes I wonder if it's all a front. Did my uncle really punch Dad in the face? Did my parents really meet under unusual circumstances? Mom has even confessed she used to smoke, too. So gross!

"Maybe I should get on the pill?" How did this conversation swing so wildly from one subject to the other?

"I can make an appointment for you with your doctor," she says, like it's no big deal. "Do you want me to go with you?"

"Um, okay. But don't tell Dad about this." It's embarrassing to know your dad knows you're having sex. Heck, it's embarrassing when your mom suspects it too.

"Honey, he's the one who suggested it to me in the first place. Don't forget, he was once a teenage boy himself," she says. "Be home by ten."

Great. Dad is way more perceptive than I thought.

"Mom, wait! Can I come home by eleven? I'll have my homework done, so I won't have to worry about it," I say, using my best pleading tone.

"Ten-thirty and no later. There's school tomorrow, and it's getting extra cold at night. I don't want you driving on those roads. They could ice up. Love you."

We end the call and I drop my phone into the center console, staring off into the distance. That was a lot easier than I thought it would be. My mom isn't totally mad at me for hitting Cami, which is a miracle. Then she goes and offers to get me on birth control, which is just…shocking.

Though being on the pill would make things a lot easier. I wouldn't have to worry about a condom breaking, and me possibly getting pregnant. I don't want to go through what Jocelyn just experienced. Though I would still want Eli to use a condom. He's been with a few girls in his not so distant past. I don't want to catch a STD.

Huh. Life is weird.

A few minutes later I'm at Starbucks, sitting at a table for two with Ellie, the both of us waiting for the PSLs we just ordered. While it's cloudy and windy outside, it's warm and cozy indoors, and there's some folksy music playing on the speakers. We've just cracked open our notebooks and text-books, and I'm tapping my mechanical pencil against the wire binding of my notebook, thinking about Eli and what we might do tonight.

As in, will we have sex? I want to. I've been craving it since the weekend, but we couldn't mess around last night. Not after he just introduced me to his mother—who was very polite and pleasant—and with Muffin scratching at his door. I eventually made him let her inside and she sniffed around his room everywhere, like she's never been in there before.

I bet she hasn't. He hates that sweet little dog.

Even if we wanted to have sex, there's nowhere for us to go tonight either. I honestly don't want to do it in the back of my car, or his. I really wish one of us had a SUV.

"Hey." Ellie nudges me with her elbow. "Your drink is ready. They just called your name."

"Oh." I glance over at the counter. "You want me to grab yours too?"

"Sure. I'll keep watch over our stuff," she says.

You can't leave your table unattended for too long at our local Starbucks. There aren't many tables inside since it's pretty small, so it's a struggle to find one in the first place. And once you do have a table, a lot of people don't want to let them go. They'll sit there for hours, their drinks long gone and not giving a crap if someone else wants it.

The after-school rush always brings lots of people

through Starbucks and the majority of the other tables have students sitting at them. Once I grab our drinks, we dive into our homework, discussing the test we have coming up in our environmental science class when the door flies open and a gust of wind blows in.

Cami and Baylee enter the building, and I swear to God, the entire place goes silent. All you can hear is the hiss of the espresso machines and the sweet folksy music still playing. Cami scans the room, I'm sure she's looking for an audience, and when her gaze lands on me, the disgusted expression on her face makes her look downright evil.

I lift my chin, mentally preparing myself for battle. I hear Ellie mutter "oh shit" but otherwise, she says nothing.

I can't blame her. I don't expect her to rush to my defense or call Cami out on her shit. This is my fight.

And everyone is watching.

"Check it out, B. It's not happy hour, it's bitch hour at Starbucks," Cami says gleefully, making Baylee laugh.

That was a pitiful attempt at a so-called funny insult. I keep my expression impassive, steeling myself for the next slam she'll throw my way.

"What are you doing here?" Cami asks me, sending a withering stare in Ellie's direction when she lifts her head.

Ellie ducks back down, staring at her textbook.

"What does it look like?" I toss back at her, already sick of her shit. I hold up my cup of coffee to clue her in.

"You have a lot of nerve, showing your face around town when everyone knows what you did to me," Cami says, taking a step closer to our table. I'm surprised she would. I was hoping she'd think I might hit her again.

"Actually, it's surprising that you're the one who's showing *your* face around town, considering everyone is congratulating me on putting you in your place," I say coolly.

Her cheeks immediately turn bright red and she casts her

glare about the room. Everyone is blatantly watching us. Even the baristas behind the counter are paying attention to our little conversation. "Such bullshit," she spits out.

"It's true. Just because you think you rule our school doesn't mean people actually like you. No one does." I grab my drink and take a sip from it, waiting for her reply.

She gapes at me like a dying fish, opening and closing her mouth as if she's trying to come up with something to say. She treats everyone like complete trash, yet expects us all to fall in line and actually like her? She's delusional. The only one who seems to tolerate her is Baylee, and they've been extra chummy only recently. Oh, and then there are the occasional boyfriends Cami acquires.

They never last long either. I'm sure there are already bets placed on how long she and Diego will be together.

I don't understand her. Worse, I don't get why she acts the way she does. She can't seem to keep friends for very long. I always find that a total red flag.

"You're never getting back on the cheer team," she finally says.

"Good." I fix my gaze on hers. "I don't want to deal with you anymore anyway."

"Same!" She glares at Baylee, who seems to snap to attention. "Let's go."

"But I wanted a coffee," Baylee whines.

"We'll go to the Starbucks in Vons," Cami says, referring to the supermarket down the road. "Besides, there's too much trash here."

With that, they turn around and walk out.

My entire body seems to sag with relief once they're gone. Everyone around us resumes their conversations too, as if those two never walked in here in the first place. "God, I hate her," I tell Ellie.

"I don't know how you were able to stand up to her like that. She's so intimidating," Ellie says.

"She's a person, just like all of us." Truthfully, I'm not sure where I got the courage to talk to Cami like that either. I feel pretty powerful right now, knowing that I drove her out of the Starbucks. Knowing that I gave just as good as I got— maybe even better.

She can't hurt me. I refuse to let her. Caving in to her demands gets a person nowhere. The only way she'll back down is if you stand up to her, and even then, she'll still fight to the bitter end.

Well, so will I. I refuse to let her boss me around any longer. Being captain of the cheer team gives her an inflated sense of authority, and while I know Brandy does her best to control that, she doesn't see and hear everything Cami does. I don't know if I want to deal with her shitty attitude anymore.

If quitting the cheer team in order to protect myself from Cami is the right thing to do, then I'll do it. Though I'll miss everyone else.

Terribly.

CHAPTER 23

ELI

I'm headed to the locker room to change for practice when my phone rings. I answer without checking who it is, fully expecting to hear Ava's sweet voice on the other end. We have plans after practice. I feel bad that she's suspended from cheer, but we're also going to take advantage of the situation. Spending more time with Ava is always my goal.

But it's not Ava who's calling.

"What's up, little bro?"

It's Ryan.

I come to a complete stop, leaning against the nearby fence. "I almost didn't recognize your voice, it's been so fuckin' long since I've heard it."

Ryan blows out an irritated breath. Probably wasn't the right thing to say to him at the very beginning of our conversation, but I give zero fucks right now. "Glad to hear your voice too."

"It's been a long time," I say, my voice tight. Hope he can tell that I'm mad at him.

"I know. That's all on me."

"Right." I want to say more, but what? That I expect an apology. An explanation. Something so I can make sense of his complete abandonment of me and our parents. Maybe he's chatting it up with our dad all the time, I don't know, but it feels like once our parents split up, Ryan split up with us as well. Took off, never to be heard from again.

"I hear you guys are doing good this season," he says, trying to get me where it used to matter the most.

Football.

"Where'd you hear that?" I ask, fully prepared for him to say Dad told him.

"I check up on you guys. There's this thing called the internet. You've heard of it, right?" he asks with a low chuckle.

Relief trickles through me. I'd be super pissed to find out Ryan and Dad were still in constant contact. It's been a secret fear of mine. Dad acts like he barely has time for me. If it was because he's spending it with Ryan, I'd feel like absolute shit.

I know I'm a disappointment to Dad already. I feel like we all are.

"We've had a good season," I say, my voice tight. "Still didn't beat those damn Badgers, though."

Ryan laughs. "Hate those fuckers."

"Same, though I'm actually dating one."

His laughter dies. "What do you mean?"

"My girlfriend goes to their school. She's on their cheer team," I explain.

"Get the hell out of here."

"I'm serious. Ava's gorgeous. Sweet as hell." And all mine. "You'd know this if you'd come around sometime." I'm all about the verbal jabs right now. Ryan deserves every single one of them.

"Yeah, about that." He pauses for only a moment, but it feels like it drags on forever. I say nothing to fill the silence. This conversation is all on him, and he knows it. "I'm coming home this weekend to see you guys."

"What?" I choke out. I can hardly believe it. "Are you serious?"

"Yeah. I'll be there Friday. I want to watch you play. Is it a home game?"

"It is."

"Perfect. I'm gonna go. And I was hoping all of us could go out to dinner Saturday night," he says.

"Who's all of us?"

"You, me, Mom and Dad."

I burst out laughing. I can't help it. Ryan is living in a dream world. I guess this is what happens when you go away to college in another state and pretend your family no longer exists. "They hate each other, bro. Like, seriously. Mom would rather eat gravel than have a meal with Dad."

"I already talked to them both. They're willing to have dinner together for the sake of our family," he says, sounding utterly sincere.

"Please tell me it's a restaurant so neither one of them can do or say something they'll regret," I say.

"It is," Ryan says reassuringly. "I already made a reservation. Are you and your girlfriend pretty serious?"

I'm hesitant. Sharing how I feel about Ava with Ryan leaves me vulnerable. We had a decent relationship before he up and left us all, but he would also give me endless shit. I felt like he never took me seriously. Like I was one giant joke to be made fun of.

"You being quiet is answer enough," Ryan says.

Now it's my turn to blow out a ragged breath. "We're serious."

"You should ask her to go with us Saturday."

Now that is just flat out crazy talk. I do not want Ava to witness my family of four all together. It'll turn into a complete shitshow and fast. "I don't think that's a good idea."

"Come on. Has she met our parents yet?"

"She actually met Mom last night."

"If she can handle Mom, she can handle the rest of us. Mom's worse than Dad," Ryan says, chuckling again.

His comment irritates me, and I don't know why. Yeah, it's true. Mom is more prone to act like a lunatic, especially when she's drunk, but come on. Dad is just as bad. He's going through a midlife crisis that makes him want to fuck every woman he sees.

It's embarrassing. The both of them are. I don't want Ava exposed to that. What if she thinks less of me when she sees all of us in action?

I can't risk it.

"I think it's best if it's just the four of us," I tell Ryan, my voice firm.

"Whatever you say. I'll call the restaurant back and make the reservation for five, just in case you change your mind," he says.

"Don't even bother," I start, but he cuts me off.

"Hey, I have to go. My break's over. But I'll see you Friday night. Look for me in the stands. Okay?"

He ends the call before I can say anything else, and I kick the fence as hard as possible, just because I can. A group of girls—they all look like freshman, I don't recognize any of them—all squeal and run away from me. Just to freak them out even more, I yell at them, a loud *HEY* that makes their feet move even faster.

"What the hell, Bennett? Have you lost your damn mind or what?" someone calls to me from behind.

I turn to see Jackson walking toward me, moving with that easy way of his, like he's got all the time in the world.

Thank Jesus he doesn't move that slow on the field, or he'd be kicked off the team. "More like 'or what,'" I tell him as he approaches.

Once he's right next to me, I fall into step with him, the both of us headed for practice. With the call from my brother, I'm close to being late, which I never am, and which Jackson almost always is.

"What's got you so pissed off?" Jackson asks as we both duck our heads against the gusty wind. "That cute girlfriend of yours giving you trouble again?"

"Hell no. She's perfect." I try to focus on the fact that I'm seeing her again tonight, instead of being pissed at my brother. After plenty of consideration, I've figured out a plan on how we can both get naked for hours with no one bugging us. My car trunk is filled with a couple of pillows and a shit ton of blankets. It's all part of my plan. "My brother called me."

Jackson frowns. "You two don't get along?"

"More like Ryan has been avoiding me for the past three years," I tell him.

"Damn. What happened? He fall off the face of the earth?" Jackson asks.

"He went away to college in Oregon. My parents announced they were getting a divorce. I think Ryan's chosen to stay away because shit isn't right." No one else really knows this besides Brenden, Ava, Cami (fuck me sideways, that sucks so bad) and now Jackson.

Though Ava did mention that there are rumors about my family. Our community is spread out all over this mountain, but there aren't very many people around here, and they all fuckin' talk. And according to Ava, supposedly they've been talking about my parents.

Sucks.

"I heard your parents were divorcing a while ago." He

sends me a sympathetic look. "Sorry, man. My parents are divorced too."

"I don't even care if they're getting a divorce. It should've been finalized over a year ago, but nope. It's the way they act toward each other and me that I hate. It's like they've both gone crazy. Dragging each other through court, like they're trying to prove some sort of fucked up point. I don't get it." I shake my head. "And my brother acts like he doesn't give a damn about any of us. He frustrates the shit out of me."

"Maybe his staying away is the only way he can deal with it," Jackson suggests.

"Yeah well, the least he can do is send me a text once a week or something. Once a month, even. Hell, I'd be happy with just birthday and Christmas cards. But it's like he cut off all communication with us. The dude fucking ghosted his own family." I shake my head. "It's going to take me a while to forgive him."

"He's your brother," Jackson says. "You'll forgive him."

He says it so easily, and I wish I felt that way. Automatically forgiving.

But I'm wary. After everything I've been through these last few years, I don't trust hardly anyone. When it comes to Ryan, my walls are up. And it's going to take him a while to tear them back down.

* * *

ONCE PRACTICE IS OVER, I take a shower and get ready to see Ava. Not everyone on my team takes showers after practice. Most of the time, I don't either. I'm in too much of a hurry to get home, so I just grab my stuff and leave and take one there. At least the water is guaranteed to be hot the entire time. Plus, I can take my time in my own shower. In the locker room, we're all hustling to get out of there.

But tonight, I gotta look good. I need to smell good too. Ava doesn't want me showing up all smelly and gross.

When I'm finished, I leave school and head up the hill to pick her up. During the entire drive, I can't stop thinking about my brother, and how he called me like we talked only yesterday. Such a bunch of bullshit. I wonder what it's like, to move through life pretending that everything's cool when it's really not?

Huh. I should know. I do the same thing.

Despite my anger and resentment, deep down, I'm glad he's coming to watch my game. He's never seen me play since he graduated high school.

My only fear is he'll bring Mom or Dad with him. Or worse, both. So they can get in an argument in the stands for everyone to see? No thanks. I do my best to keep my family business private, yet it still gets out and everyone talks about us behind closed doors.

By the time I arrive at the Starbucks where I'm picking her up, it's starting to rain. I see her through the giant window, sitting at a table all by herself, her head bent over her notebook as she writes furiously across it. I park directly in front of that window and just watch her for a while, the sight of her easing the tension running through me. My shoulders relax. My heart rate settles. I don't even have to talk to her and she already calms my frayed nerves.

That girl works magic on me, swear to God.

Her pencil comes to a stop on her notebook, and she lifts her head, as if she can sense she's being watched. It's already dark outside. I'm sure she can't tell it's me sitting in the parking lot, staring at her. But she's got a sixth sense or whatever the hell you call it, and she knows.

She knows I'm outside.

My phone rings, the Bluetooth on my car picking it up and I lean forward, hitting the screen to answer the call.

"Are you here?"

"Yeah."

"Why didn't you text me to let me know?"

"I like watching you," I say, which is the damn truth.

She's quiet for a moment. "That's a little creepy."

"Not like I'm stalking you. I just like—watching you. You look cute in there. Like a good girl working on her homework." That's exactly what she is.

But she's the good girl who likes to do bad things. With me.

Talk about a lucky bastard.

"I didn't think you liked good girls," she says, her voice low and teasing.

"Oh I love good girls. Specifically, one good girl," I say, watching as a slow smile curls her perfect lips. "Now get your pretty ass out here so we can leave. I have a surprise for you."

"A surprise?" She sounds excited. She looks it too, from the way she's hurriedly gathering up her things and shoving them in her backpack. "What is it?"

"If I tell you, then it's not a surprise," I tease her.

She rises to her feet, the phone still clutched to her ear. "I'm starving."

"Good. I am too. Let's grab a pizza."

"A pizza?" She wrinkles her nose. "Too many carbs."

"Trust me. You'll need the carbs to keep up your strength. What I have planned tonight, we'll be burning them off long after dinner." My voice is full of promise.

"You are so bad." She exits the coffeeshop, pushing through the door and heading straight for my car. "What sort of plans do you have?"

I unlock the doors and she slides in, a little windblown despite the brief seconds she was outside. I end the call and smile at her. "Naked plans."

She sets her phone into the cup holder in my center console, nestled right next to mine. "I love naked plans."

"Me too." Leaning over, I kiss her, taking it deep right away. I'm not holding back tonight. I feel like I've been full of pent up energy since what happened between us Saturday, and I'm impatient with wanting her. Plus, I'm still pissed and frustrated over my brother's relaxed attitude when he called.

And when I'm pissed, I need to let off some steam. Getting aggressive on the field only helped a little bit. I need something more.

"Where do you want to get pizza?" she murmurs against my lips. "I have to be home by ten-thirty."

"That sucks."

"Better than last night's curfew," she says as she pulls away and settles into the passenger seat. "She's worried about ice on the roads."

"Your mom?"

Ava nods.

"Let's get a pizza from Round Table," I suggest.

Ava's already busy looking up the number on her phone. She really must be starving. "I'll call it in."

"Maybe we should go grab it, eat it real quick, and then we'll come back by here to get your car. You can follow me up," I say.

She frowns. "Follow you up where?"

"I can't tell you, remember? It's a surprise."

"If you want to take me to that cabin again, I'm going to pass. It's cold and drafty in there." She mock shivers for emphasis.

"There goes my surprise." My girl is too damn smart. "And really, it's not that bad. Besides, you should see my trunk. It's full of blankets and pillows for us. And I can make a fire." Reaching out, I lift her hair away from her neck, tracing the soft skin there.

Ava leans into my hand, her eyes falling at half-mast as I continue touching her. "With what firewood?"

"Jackson assured me there's firewood inside the cabin. Plus some old newspapers to help light it." I don't remember seeing anything like that the last time I was there, but maybe this abandoned cabin has turned into the hookup place for Jackson and his friends.

Which, honestly, is kind of gross, but I will take advantage of it when I have to, and tonight, I have to.

More like I *need* to.

"I don't know," she says, eyeing me warily. "Are you just using me for sex?"

"Fuck yeah," I tell her without hesitation, making her laugh. "You know it's more than that, babe. Come on."

She studies me with a solemn expression, her eyes downright luminous thanks to the lights from the businesses I'm parked in front of casting across her gorgeous face. "Did you have a good day?"

I shrug then look away from her so I can stare out the driver's side window. Most of the time, I like it when she's perceptive. Makes me feel like we're completely attuned to each other.

Other times, like now, I don't want her to know what I'm hiding. What I'm thinking. How annoyed I still am at Ryan. I don't want to burden her with my problems. Besides, the only one who has a problem with this is me. If I was normal, I would be fuckin' excited to finally see my brother after all these years.

Instead, I feel nothing but dread. Resentment. Worry over how this is all going to turn out. Cautious.

Yeah. Cautious as fuck. I'm balls to the wall with everything else in my life, but not when it comes to my family.

"I'll tell you about my day over pizza," I finally say to her with a quick nod. "Call it in. And make it an extra-large. I'm fucking dying of hunger."

Laughing, she leans over the center console, her phone still clutched in her hand. "I love you," she murmurs before she kisses me.

I savor the sweet sound of those words falling from her perfect lips far more than she'll ever know.

CHAPTER 24

AVA

We go to Round Table and eat inside, instead of taking the pizza to go. Hardly anyone is in there anyway, and we both know a few of the people working tonight. One guy is someone who was on Eli's football team last year, and he takes one look at me, swings his gaze back to Eli and starts hooting like some sort of demented owl.

"Oooh, damn so it's actually true? You're going out with Ava Callahan?" he asks, his eyes nearly bugging out of his head.

Eli leans over the counter, his voice lowering, his expression sincere. "I'm only using her for sex."

The guy keeps hooting and laughing, sending me wary glances. I glare at him but cozy up next to Eli. Go ahead. Let him say he's only using me for sex. We know the truth. We love each other.

Oh, and we're using each other for sex.

The pizza is delicious. Piping hot and cheesy, with crisp pepperoni and yummy olives and mushrooms. I'd wanted onions, but Eli was totally against it.

"No onion breath when I kiss you," he said when I was trying to order, and I went along with him.

I suppose I can't blame him.

Once we're done eating, Eli drives us back over to the Starbucks parking lot so I can get my car. I'm supposed to follow him to the cabin—he was a little disappointed I figured out his surprise, but he quickly got over it—and while I'm reluctant to go there, I guess I should take my opportunities when they arrive. As in, there's nowhere else Eli and I can go to be completely alone tonight, so the cabin will have to do.

As we get closer to the lake, the rain becomes heavier. To the point that my windshield wipers are working extra hard and it's still hard for me to see. Plus it's so dark out here. I live on the opposite side of the lake, where the majority of the homes are filled with people who live here year-round. The cabin and the old resort are on the more touristy side of the lake, where a bunch of other resorts and summer residences are located.

By the time we finally make it to the cabin, it's close to eight and the rain isn't letting up. I run out of my car and go to Eli, who's opened up his car's trunk. He shoves a bunch of blankets in my arms. "Wait for me on the porch."

I do as he says, trying to avoid the puddles forming on the ground before I run up the porch steps and stand just beneath the narrow overhang. At least the rain isn't falling on me any longer. I watch as Eli grabs a couple more blankets and two pillows, then shuts the trunk, pretty much jumping over all the puddles like a showoff and bounding up the porch steps, making the entire thing rattle with the force.

"Hold on." He's got a key in his hand and he sticks it in the deadbolt above the handle, turns it and the door swings open with an eerie creak. "Ladies first."

I slowly walk inside, stumbling forward a little when Eli pushes himself in behind me and slams the door, turning the lock with a low click. It's dark inside until Eli hits the light switch, illuminating the cabin in an almost sickly, yellow glow. The light fixture is so old, I swear I can hear it buzzing. I watch as Eli drops what he's carrying on the old couch before he shrugs out of his soaked sweatshirt, leaving him standing there in a T-shirt and his damp jeans. He scrubs his hand over his head, sending raindrops scattering everywhere.

"I'm going to start the fire so we can warm this place up," he says, glancing around the room until he spots a bundle of firewood sitting near the fireplace, a stack of old newspapers right next to it.

"Sounds good," I say, as I shrug out of my hoodie as well, grabbing his off the floor and taking them both over to the small kitchen table. I drape each sweatshirt over a chair so they can dry before reentering the living room, where Eli already has a fire started.

"That was easy," I tell him, impressed when he grabs an old fireplace poker sitting in a stand on the brick hearth and prods at the burning paper.

"Of course, the paper will burn. The real trick is if I can get the wood to start up." He pokes at it a few more times, resting on his haunches as he watches the flames rise. They cast an orangish glow on his face and I watch him, wondering how I got so lucky to get such a gorgeous boy to fall in love with me.

Because he is. Gorgeous. Every time I see him, I swear he gets better looking, and I find myself falling onto the edge of the couch, just sitting there watching him as he keeps his eye on the fire.

"I think we're good," he says, glancing over at me and

doing a double take. "You okay? You look like you're about to drool."

I'm tempted to grab the closest pillow and toss it at his smug face. "Can't I look at you without you making a rude comment?"

"No," he says with a quick grin. "You're the one who called me creepy when I was watching you."

"Fine." I lift my chin. "I guess we're even."

Shaking his head, he laughs. "Grab some of those blankets. Let's lay them out on the floor. Hold on, I think there's something we can use in the closet."

He leaps to his feet and heads for the hall closet, opening the door and uttering, "a ha" when he finds whatever it is he's looking for. He returns to the living room with two sleeping bags under each arm.

"We'll lay these out on the floor first, to give us some cushion."

I help him undo and unzip the sleeping bags before we spread them both out on the floor right in front of the fireplace, making sure they overlap each other at least halfway. Then we grab the slightly damp blankets and lay them all out too. I toss the pillows right next to each other, then step back and admire our work.

"It looks cozy," I murmur, touched that he would want to do this for me.

For us.

Eli walks over to the wall and hits the light switch again, the room going dark save for the growing flames in the fireplace. He stops directly behind me, resting his hands on my shoulders and giving them a gentle squeeze. "That was the plan."

Who knew the loud, brash, crude Eli Bennett could be romantic?

"We have two hours," I tell him, sucking in a breath when his arms slip around my waist, pulling me closer to him. "It's around eight right now, and it'll take me at least a half hour to get home, especially with the weather."

"Shh." He pushes my hair away from my neck and presses his mouth right at the spot where my pulse beats. And it is now jumping, thanks to that first touch of his warm, damp lips. "Don't worry about anything else," he murmurs against my skin, making me tremble. "I've got you."

I go quiet, wanting only to concentrate on what Eli is doing to me. I can hear the crackle of the fire, the steady rhythm of the rain pounding on the roof. The glide of his fingers across my stomach when he slips his hand beneath my shirt. The sound of his lips on my skin when he kisses my neck once again. My knees go weak and I lean into him, closing my eyes when he rests both of his hands on my stomach, his fingers splayed, as if he wants to touch every little piece of me that he can.

"You are so fucking beautiful," he whispers, right before he gently sinks his teeth into my earlobe. A shiver steals over me and I suck in a breath when his tongue licks at the sensitive spot just behind my ear.

He's trying to drive me crazy. And it's working.

I concentrate on the sound of my breathing. It becomes more accelerated when his hands skim upwards, his fingers brushing against my bra, his palms coming up to cover my breasts. My bra is lace and thin. I wore it in hopes of Eli discovering it, and the low growl of approval that he makes when he strums his thumbs back and forth across my nipples fills me with satisfaction.

He definitely likes it.

His touch leaves me needy. I try to turn so I can face him, but he won't let me. Instead, he continues to touch me, driving me out of my mind. I lean my head back on his shoulder, cracking my eyes open so I can watch his hands shift and move beneath my shirt. An impatient noise leaves him and within seconds, the shirt is gone, and I'm standing there in my jeans and shoes and black lace bra.

"So pretty." He cups my breasts once more, my nipples poking the fabric. "You wear this kind of stuff just for me?"

I part my lips to speak, but no sound comes out, so I nod furiously instead.

"I definitely like it, but let's take it off." He reaches behind me, and with a flick of his fingers, the snap comes free, and he slowly tugs the bra off, the backs of his knuckles rubbing my nipples. No doubt on purpose.

He's a tease. He knows how to drive me out of my mind with lust. I watch his big hands touch me. His long fingers drift across my skin. A whimper leaves me when he presses his damp mouth to the side of my neck, his hands still moving. Wandering.

"I want to make this last," he whispers. "But I don't know if I can."

I move against him, restless with need. "Take your shirt off. I want to feel you."

He pulls away from me and shrugs out of his shirt before he returns to his position, his hot, hard chest pressing against me. Reaching up, I wind my arms around the back of his neck, my fingers playing with the soft hair at his nape as I slowly arch my back. A choked sound comes from the back of his throat and I know he's watching me. He likes what he sees. I already understand what he enjoys. What arouses him. He wants me to touch him. He wants me to put on a show.

I lower my arms and move my hands so they're directly behind me, my fingers brushing over the snap of his jeans. I undo it. Lower the zipper, slip my fingers between the spread denim and touch the front of his boxer briefs. I'm sure they've got a wild print on them, and I can't wait to see them.

But right now, I want to feel him.

"Jesus," he whispers when I close my fingers around his erection. His hold on me loosens and when I realize it, I take advantage, turning so I can face him. I curl my hands around the waistband of his jeans and start yanking them down, smiling up at him when I see the flames printed on his boxers.

"What are you doing?" he asks, though he must know what I'm doing. It's pretty damn obvious.

"Take off your jeans," I tell him, and he does what I ask, kicking off his shoes and his jeans, so that he's standing in front of me in those flame boxer briefs and nothing else.

"This was supposed to be all about you," he starts and I shake my head, sneaking my fingers beneath his boxers, encountering velvety hot, hard flesh. I keep my gaze trained on his face, savoring the pure pleasure taking over his features. "Oh fuck, Ava. What are you doing to me?"

Laughing, I withdraw my fingers from his boxers and drop to my knees in front of him, raking my nails down the front of his thick thighs. He's got the best thighs. They bulge with muscle, and I can't help myself when I lean in and press my mouth to his warm, firm flesh, everything inside of me going liquid when I think of those times I pretty much got off while rubbing myself on his thigh.

"Ava." His voice is stern. His fingers tangle in my hair, yanking a little, and I glance up to find him scowling at me. "Are you trying to make me come in my shorts?"

I burst out laughing. "No."

"Well, you're about to. It's not every night I've got a blonde princess on her knees in front of me, her tits shining like gold thanks to the firelight and her mouth on my fucking leg," he says, his voice tight. Like it takes everything out of him to say that.

"That wasn't my plan," I tell him with a smug smile, running my fingers lightly along his length. It jerks beneath my touch. "Actually, I wanted you to come in my mouth."

His mouth pops open, and his eyes go dark. "Fuck me, woman. Let's make it happen."

CHAPTER 25

ELI

*T*hank God I didn't forget condoms.

Or those blankets.

The pillows came in handy too.

Like when Ava gave me that fucking unbelievable blow job earlier. My beautiful girl on her knees in front of me, naked, save for her skimpy panties and her lips wrapped tight around my dick, her eyes never really leaving mine the entire time. She had her knees on top of that pillow, and I bet that made everything a lot more comfortable. And when she started to lick and suck my cock like I was her favorite ice cream treat? Fuck it, I shot off like an amateur, and she sucked me dry like a pro.

Or when I had her stretched out across the blankets, completely naked and totally restless. Her head propped up by both pillows as I went down on her, so she was at the perfect angle to watch.

Listen. I love to watch. Ava on her knees like that sucking my dick? Top tier fantasy material come to life right there. Ava lying on a pile of blankets while I go down on her wet pussy, my hands keeping her thighs spread wide while she whimpers and moans with every lick of my tongue?

More fantasy material.

Now, we've both got our heads on the pillows, our breaths fast, our skin sticky with sweat. That fireplace is raging like crazy and it's making the tiny living room hot as hell. Or maybe it's all the friction our bodies are creating as we continue to rub against each other.

I don't know. I'm not complaining.

"What time is it?" Ava asks, a few minutes after she came all over my mouth, panting like she's still so overwhelmed.

Satisfaction washes over me as I reach across her and grab my phone from where I left it, on the end table by the couch.

"A little before nine." I set the phone down and resettle myself next to her, yanking her into my arms.

She comes willingly, her hands running over my chest, sliding down until she's got one hand curled around my hard dick. I think she's grown attached to it. "We still have almost an hour."

"Mmm hmm." I kiss her. Drown in her. Slide my tongue against hers, thrusting deep, mimicking what I want to do when I'm inside her. The blow job was amazing. Eating her pussy got me all horny again.

Now I'm dying to fuck her.

"You brought a condom?" she asks.

"Babe, I brought three."

She laughs. "I don't think we'll use all three."

"Don't say shit like that. I take it as a challenge, remember?" I grab one of the condoms resting by my phone and tear the wrapper off, rising up on my knees so I can roll it on. My dick kind of hurts, it's so damn hard and eager, and I grip the base, my gaze going to hers as I slowly start stroking.

Her eyes fall to where my hand is moving, her lips parting

a little. Her tongue sneaking out to lick at the corner of her mouth. She is always hungry for my dick. Does that sound crude? Kind of awful?

Well it's fucking true.

And I'm hungry for her. All the damn time. I'd feast on her perfect pussy every single day if I could. Not that I can. Not like her parents would be down for me moving into her bedroom. I would if I could though. I'd love nothing more than to sleep with my girl. Fall asleep with her wrapped all around me. Wake up in the morning with her cute ass snug against my junk. I'd fuck her nice and slow from behind first thing, reach around and touch her clit. She'd arch her back and make those sexy little noises—

"You're wasting quality time touching yourself when you could be touching me."

Her snappy voice makes my eyes fly open and I glance down at myself. I was sitting here jerking myself while she's within touching distance. Fucking distance.

What the hell is wrong with me?

"Though it's kind of hot, watching you do that," she admits, sinking her teeth into her lower lip, her eyes big and her cheeks flushed.

I really love that flush she gets every time we're together like this.

"Hotter if I wasn't wearing a condom," I tell her as I move so I'm hovering above her, one hand planted by the side of her head, my other hand still wrapped tight around the base of my cock. "We should do that next time."

A gasp escapes her when I brush my dick against her clit. "Do what?"

"Touch ourselves in front of each other." I do it again, dragging my head back and forth through her soaked folds. I keep this up, I'll lose it and come too quick, but it feels so damn good, I don't want to stop. "What do you think?"

"I don't know." She lifts her hips, as if that's going to make just the tip slip in but I withhold myself from her. "What are you doing?"

"Say you'll do it for me, or you don't get the dick." I laugh at myself, shaking my head. It is so much fun being with her. Seriously, who knew it could be this good?

"Eli." She pouts.

"Say it, Ava. Say, 'yes Eli, I'll touch my juicy pussy in front of you until I squirt all over my fingers.'" I'm grinning.

She's groaning. And not because she's hot for it either. "That is so disgusting."

"No, it's so damn hot. I would give up a lot of shit to watch you finger yourself until you come." Ah fuck, it's so true. Just saying those words out loud has my dick jerking in anticipation.

"Only if I can watch you at the same time," she says, her eyes falling closed when I reward her for what she just offered.

I slide inside her. Just a little bit. Just enough so she can feel me. And hell, I can feel her too. Hot and tight and wet. She's too tempting. I ease in a little more, not for her but for me. I cannot resist her.

Ever.

"Deal. We'll get off for each other. Sounds fucking fun as hell." I slide all the way, as far as I can, until I'm fully inside her and I hold myself there, my eyes tightly closed as I breathe in deep, trying to calm myself.

She wraps her legs around my hips and I sink even further. A groan leaves me and I start to move. She moves too. Slow for only about a second, before we start picking up tempo. Until we're fucking like eager rabbits, me pounding into her willing body again and again, our damp skin making a slapping noise with my every thrust. I've lost all control. I don't even know what I'm doing anymore. Nothing's calculated or planned. I just fuck like an animal, with no thought, no care. I'm just feeling. Doing.

Savoring.

I crack my eyes open to find hers are open too, and she's watching me, her body jolting with my thrusts, her tits jiggling. Leaning down, I kiss her. It's a dirty, sloppy connection of lips, with zero finesse and plenty of tongue and she's moaning. I swallow every sound, drinking from her lips like I'm dying of thirst and when she goes tense beneath me and her inner walls start milking my dick, I know she's coming.

And I am too, right after her, the sound of her name falling from my lips as the orgasm washes over me. I'm a stuttering, shuddering mess, and when it's over, I collapse on top of her, trying my best to not let my entire weight press down on her, but she wraps her arms around me and holds me there.

Like she wants to absorb me.

"Oh my God," she whispers against my cheek, right before she kisses it. "Does sex just keep getting better every time we do it? Because I don't know if my heart can take it."

"It's only ever been this good with you," I tell her.

She makes a scoffing noise. Like she doesn't believe me. I lift up a little so I can stare into her beautiful green eyes. "It's true. Maybe it's because I love you so damn much."

Her eyes go soft, and her lips curl. "I love you too."

I bend down and kiss her because I have to. After coming like that, making those sorts of declarations, the moment calls for a sweet, tender kiss. I love this girl, just like I said.

So damn much.

* * *

I GOT RID of the condom in the bathroom and came back to find Ava wrapped up in a pile of blankets, looking sexy as

245

hell with only her bare shoulders showing, the flames bathing her smooth skin in golden light. Her hair shines extra bright too and I come to a stop for a moment, staring at my princess. My girl who fights for what she wants. My girl who is currently wearing the #1 pendant around her neck and nothing else.

Meaning she's branded as mine and no one else's.

She turns toward me with a smile on her face. "There you are. I missed you."

"I think I've been gone for all of two minutes." I join her on the floor, slipping beneath the covers and reaching for my phone at the same time. It's only nine-fifteen. We still have forty-five minutes so I'm going to enjoy this time with Ava. I want to talk to her about what happened to me. Ryan's call. What it means. I need to get it all out.

But first, I want to know what happened with her.

"Was it bad today?" I ask, reaching around her shoulders and tugging on the ends of her messy hair. "Dealing with all the Cami fallout?"

"It wasn't so bad. Better than I thought it would be." She shrugs. "Like I told you, the vice principal gave me two Saturday schools. Plus I'm off the team for two weeks."

"Are you upset about that? Two weeks is a long time." I'd fuckin' lose it if I got kicked off the football team for two weeks.

"I'm sad, yet I'm not. At least it gives me two weeks of freedom away from Cami. And two weeks of spending more time with you." She leans her head against me, and I tug her in even closer, tangling my legs with hers. We're propped on the pillows facing the fire, her hand resting on my chest, my fingers drifting down her arm. "I'm liking that part a lot."

"Me too." I pull away slightly so I can kiss her forehead. "But I know you like doing cheer."

"Do I though? My mom and sister convinced me to try

out. It's fun, I've made new friends, but do I really *enjoy* it? Love it? Not with Cami trying to boss me around all the time." She dips her head, her hair falling and covering her pretty face. I reach out and brush it back with my index finger so I can see her. "It's a relief not dealing with her right now. Though I saw her at Starbucks earlier."

"What happened?"

"She tried to insult me, but I threw some crap back in her face and she eventually left." Ava smiles. "I must be pretty powerful if I can drive a person out of Starbucks."

"You're the most powerful girl I know," I tell her sincerely. I wish she knew just how much she affects me. How much she means to me.

Maybe she does know.

Ava rests her hand on my thigh. "My parents weren't that mad either. Well, I got the 'violence isn't the answer' speech, but my mom never really liked Cami in the first place so was she really that upset? I don't think so. I talked to her right after school. Somehow we ended up talking about birth control, too."

Oh shit. "What do you mean?"

"As in, she thinks I should be put on it. The pill I guess?" Her gaze meets mine. "What do you think?"

"I think that would be awesome." Going bareback in Ava's pussy? Talk about a dream come true.

"We're still using condoms," she says, killing my dream, just like that. "You've been with other girls. What if you— give me something? And the pill isn't foolproof."

"How foolproof is it? Ninety eight percent maybe? I could pull out." I'd be down for that too. Whatever she'll let me do, I'll do it.

"I don't know. I'll ask when I go to the doctor." Her gaze lifts to mine. "How many other girls have there been?"

"Uh." I squirm a little bit, because this sort of thing makes me uncomfortable. I've never discussed it with a girl before. I've never had a steady girlfriend so that's why. "Do you really want to know?"

"Yes, I do," she says firmly. "I'm not going to judge you for it. Or ask for names and addresses. I just want to know."

"Two."

She frowns. "That's it?"

"What did you expect? Me to say like twenty?" I laugh uncomfortably. "Would a bigger number make you feel better?"

"No. Absolutely not. I just thought there had been more." Her lips form the faintest smile. "I'm glad it's only two. Now three."

"No one compares to you," I tell her, threading my fingers through her hair.

Ava leans in and kisses me, murmuring against my lips, "Tell me about your day."

So I do. I tell her about my brother calling and acting like it was no big thing. Telling me he's coming home this weekend so he can watch my game.

"But that's great," she says when I'm in the middle of the story. "Aren't you glad he's finally coming to see you?"

"I guess," I say with a shrug, wanting to hang on to my anger for a little while longer. It's my go-to emotion lately. The one that's got me through all this family bullshit the last few years. "I hope he doesn't bring my parents to the game."

"Why not?"

"What if they get into an argument in front of everyone?"

"You won't know if they do. You'll be out on the field," she points out.

"True, but people will talk. I'm tired of rumors and drama. It's all bullshit," I spit out, sounding bitter as hell because yeah, I *am* bitter as hell.

"You're going to deal with that no matter what. Not only

because of who you are, but also who you're with." She laughs. "Me."

"Like I'd leave you because of that. I'll suffer through the drama and rumors when it comes to you." I drop a kiss on her shoulder and she giggles. "But seriously. I don't know how I feel about Ryan showing up, acting like he hasn't been gone for the last few years."

"Maybe he didn't know how else to act. Maybe he's feeling just as awkward and angry as you are about everything," she says. "You should give him a chance, Eli."

"I don't want to," I mutter, sounding like I'm about five years old and the world's biggest grudge holder.

"The least you can do is hear him out. Let him explain himself. And you should tell him how you feel, too. You can't keep it bottled up forever." She hesitates before she continues. "Maybe I can sit with him and watch the game."

"Hell no." This is my immediate response. I can see from the hurt in her gaze that she didn't expect me to react so strongly. "Bring Ellie with you or something."

"That's a great idea. I probably will. But why can't we all sit together? I'd love to get to know your brother. Unless you didn't tell him about me." She sounds sad, and that is the absolute worst sound in the world.

"I told him about you," I admit, and she brightens, her eyes sparkling once more.

"You did?"

I nod. "I said we were serious."

"Are we?" Her voice lowers to a whisper, and that lingering doubt she still has almost does me in.

"I'm not just using you for sex," I crack, making her laugh. "And hell yeah, we're serious. Do you really think I'd be wrapped up in a blanket naked with you in a cold ass cabin in the middle of a rainstorm if I wasn't serious?"

Another shrug from Ava. I think she eats this shit up.

"I'm dead serious about you. I love you." I kiss her. Once. Twice. "I love you so damn much, I think about you all the time. You consume my thoughts. My dreams. When I leave you, I immediately miss you and think about the next time I can see you again."

"I love it when you say stuff like that," she says dreamily.

"I know." I kiss her nose. "I love your pretty face. And your smart brain. Your smart mouth too." She laughs. "I love your body. Your pussy."

"Stop." She puts her hand on my mouth and I lightly bite her finger, making her drop it with an exaggerated scowl.

"But what I really love? Is your heart." I reach between the folds of the blanket to touch her chest, my palm pressed right in between her breasts. "It's big and passionate and gives zero fucks. I love that about you, Ava. You fight for what you want, what you believe in. You tried to kick Kayla's ass because of me."

Ava scowls. "She said mean things about you."

"And now you're beating up Cami because of me."

"She said shitty things about you, too." Her scowl deepens.

I skim my fingers over her face, trying to soothe her. "Don't let any of them get to you like that. Fuck them. Fuck Kayla and her judgy personality. And fuck Cami and her black soul. They can't touch us. Together, we're untouchable."

"I love you, too," she says, her voice trembling, her eyes locked with mine. "I love you so much, it almost—scares me."

"Why would it scare you?" I'm frowning. I don't like to hear her say things like that.

"I'm afraid it's so good between us, something—or someone—is going to come along and snatch it out of our hands."

"Baby, you can't say words like snatch and expect me to keep a straight face," I tell her just before I crack up.

She elbows me in the ribs. "I'm being serious! Aren't you afraid that someone is going to try and destroy us?"

"Like I told you. You and me? We're untouchable." I kiss her again because I can. "Don't worry, babe. We've got this."

I believe that. One hundred percent. Does that make me a fool?

Maybe.

CHAPTER 26

AVA

"You sure you don't mind driving to the game?" I ask as I slide into the passenger seat of Ellie's car.

She slams her car door and glances over at me. "Of course not. I figured you'd want to go home with Eli anyway."

"You're right. I do." I smile, thinking of what we did a few nights ago at the cabin. I couldn't see him last night. He had his team dinner to attend and I had to study for my environmental science test. Cami tried to make some snide remark about me sitting in the stands watching them cheer tonight during lunch, but I blew her off, informing her I wouldn't even be at the game.

She got flustered, called me a bitch and took off. Considering I had witnesses, I made sure and told Brandy that Cami is going around campus insulting me. Trying my best to get her in trouble, I guess, which is dumb, but also oddly satisfying.

"This ought to be interesting, us showing up at this game tonight," Ellie says as she turns onto the main road that leads to the highway. She offered to pick me up at my house, and I wasn't about to turn that down.

"Eli asked if I was going to wear purple and gold." I make a face. "I don't know if I can do it."

"Clearly you're not," Ellie says with a laugh as she glances over at me. I'm wearing jeans and a black sweatshirt. That's about as neutral as I can get. "He didn't give you his jersey to wear?"

I slowly shake my head. "He didn't."

And that was kind of disappointing, but I didn't dwell on it. How can I? At least I'm able to go to his game. Plus, I'll hopefully get to meet his brother tonight too. I have no qualms in approaching him and introducing myself, if I can figure out who he is. I want to meet Ryan.

No matter how reluctant Eli is over it.

He keeps his family somewhat of a secret and I don't understand why. Is he embarrassed? Maybe. Is he ashamed? I suppose I would be if word around town was my mom's a raging alcoholic. I guess a rumor started in gossip mags a long time ago when I wasn't even born yet that my dad was having an affair with the nanny. Crazy. Has anyone ever seen the way my father looks at my mother? He's always looked at her like that. As if she's everything to him. He's still madly in love with her all these years later.

But there are rumors and there are facts, and Eli has told me his mom drinks too much. The rumors are true. And that's embarrassing. I can kind of understand why Ryan stayed away for so long. Maybe he didn't want to deal with it.

Maybe he didn't know how.

"Do you think people would've given you grief for wearing his jersey?" Ellie asks, pulling me from my thoughts.

"I don't know." I shrug. "Why should they care? Don't you think people at our school would be angrier? They'd call me a traitor or something stupid like that," I say irritably.

253

"True."

"Besides, I'm already wearing his number." I pull the pendant out from beneath my hoodie and let it hang there. "I guess that's good enough, right? I don't need a jersey to prove anything."

Ellie glances over at me, then does a doubletake. "Where did you get that?"

"It's Eli's." I rub my fingers against the warm metal, surprised at myself that I never told her about the necklace. "When he and Jake got into a fight in our yard, Jake tore it off. I don't even think he knew that. I found it on the ground after he left. The chain is mine, though. I like wearing it. I feel like I can always keep him close to me this way."

"Aww." Ellie smiles. "That's so romantic."

"And silly." I'm a little embarrassed by what I just confessed; I can't help it.

"Not silly," Ellie says with a firm shake of her head. "You're in love with him."

Giddiness rises inside me, making me grin. "I am. So much."

"You've had sex with him since that first time." She states this as fact.

"Yes, definitely," I say with a wistful sigh.

"And it was good."

"Good doesn't even begin to describe it."

"I forgot to ask you," Ellie says. "But did it hurt the first time?"

"Yes. A little. More like a pinch. I was sore the day after more than when we actually had sex," I explain.

"Hmmm." Ellie says nothing else. And even though she's driving and totally paying attention to the road, I can tell she's lost in thought.

"Are you thinking of someone specific right now, Ellie?"

"What? No." She says that way too quickly.

"You sure about that?" I'm teasing her, because I have a feeling I know exactly who she's thinking about. He's playing in tonight's game too.

She sighs. "It's Jackson."

"I want a complete update. And don't leave out a single detail," I tell her eagerly.

"There's nothing to update! Not really. We're still talking a lot, but he never seems to want to take it to the next level," she says, sounding a little whiny.

"What's the next level?"

"I don't know, actually talking to each other face to face?" Her voice raises, and I can tell she's frustrated. Maybe even a little angry. "We chat all the time on Snap. He shares silly Tik Toks with me and I do the same. We have these long conversations where I feel like I actually know him, but he never asks me to do anything with him. Like, we never go grab coffee or go on an actual date or even just get together and do homework."

I crack up at that one and she sends me a dirty look, silencing me.

"The way he acts makes me suspicious, and I hate it. Is he having long conversations like ours with other girls? Am I just one of many? It feels like that sometimes. Like I'm getting played. He has groupies, for God's sake." She shakes her head. "I can't forget about his fan club. I wonder if I'm the president of his fan club."

"Last time at the party at the cabin, he seemed totally into you," I remind her gently. "Maybe he's just shy."

Ellie bursts out laughing. "If Jackson Rivers is shy, then so is Eli Bennett."

I laugh too, because Eli is the furthest thing from shy. He takes what he wants and never bothers asking for it most of the time. I'm guessing Jackson is similar. "Okay, okay. You're right."

"Right. So maybe I don't mean anything to Jackson. I'm just the girl he talks to when he's lonely. The girl he's embarrassed to be seen with." Her voice is full of pain and my heart breaks for her.

"Aw, Ellie."

"Don't be sympathetic toward me right now, Ava. I might start crying." She shakes her head, her expression tight. "I'd rather be mad."

"What if he tries to talk to you tonight?"

"I'll be polite."

"That's it? You'll be polite? Like, 'how do you do, sir?' type polite?" I'm giggling.

Ellie giggles too. "I don't know! More like, 'don't fucking look at me' type polite," she says viciously.

Now we're both full blown laughing, coming up with a variety of scenarios of how Ellie might act if Jackson talks to her. I'm hoping he does. I'm hoping he gets what's coming to him after the game. I hope Ellie really gives it to him.

And then I hope that Jackson falls madly in love with her when she speaks her mind and kisses her right there on the football field in front of everyone.

Yeah. That's what I really want to see.

* * *

WE'RE SITTING in the stands, an island of two among the sea of purple and gold surrounding us. They don't sit too close because they know we don't go there. Most of them must realize by now that I'm Eli Bennett's girlfriend. I swear I hear the low murmurings of snotty remarks made by some of the girls. They can say whatever they want about me. I truly don't care. And if they don't watch it, I might come for them.

Stupid right? But I do have a reputation now. One that is of me throwing fists at girls who piss me off.

Jeez, who am I?

The second quarter is almost over when a really good looking guy catches my and Ellie's attention. We send each other a quick look before we play it cool, and I'm startled that he's making his approach.

In our direction.

The guy heads up the steps, his gaze finding mine, and I realize he's actually coming for us.

He's familiar. Hair a darker golden brown. Green eyes. Tall and lean yet muscular too. Very, very attractive. Older than me, older than all of us high schoolers in general.

He's got to be Eli's brother.

"You're Eli's girlfriend, aren't you?" he says when he comes to a stop in front of us, standing in the next aisle.

"And you're his brother," I say with a faint smile. "Ryan?"

"That's me. Ava?"

I nod, gesturing toward Ellie. "And this is my friend, Ellie."

"Nice to meet you both." He actually shakes our hands. What a gentleman. And when he smiles, I see Eli. They look very similar. You can definitely tell they're brothers.

But I think Eli's better looking.

"Can I sit with you for a while?" Ryan asks.

"Sure." Ellie scoots over and Ryan settles in between us. Whatever cologne he's wearing smells really good and I'm pretty sure I just caught Ellie discreetly sniffing in his direction.

"Are you having fun here tonight?" I ask him.

"It's kind of weird, coming back to your high school and watching your old football team play," he answers. "I only went here for a year, you know."

"Oh, I didn't realize that," I say.

"We moved here the summer before my senior year. I was kind of pissed about it at first, but I made friends pretty quickly and was accepted by everyone on the football team. Overall, it was a decent senior year. Slightly fucked up at times, but still good," he explains with a little chuckle.

I see he's not afraid to drop f-bombs in front of me. Much like his brother.

"Eli is a great player," Ryan says as his gaze returns to the field. "He has a lot of potential. More than I ever did."

"I think so too." I smile as I watch Eli out on the field, his deep voice ringing out as he makes his calls before they make their play. They're winning tonight, thank God. "He doesn't think he's good enough to play in college."

"Why the hell not?" Ryan sounds outraged, and I appreciate that. It means he cares. "He totally can."

"Do you play for a college team?" Eli has never mentioned it before. Though he doesn't talk much about his brother or his family.

Ryan shrugs. "I played my freshman and sophomore year. Got benched for academic probation my junior year. Now I'm like, third string this year thanks to that. I get zero play time. It's a bye week for us, so that's why I decided to finally come down and see my family."

"What team do you play for?"

"University of Oregon."

Um, holy shit. That's a PAC-12 team. They're kind of a big deal. I let my gaze roam over Ryan again. He's tall and muscular, but he's not as big as you'd think he should be for college ball. Especially at U of O.

"This is it," he says dryly, sending me a sly look. "My last year playing football and I'm not going to see any game time unless we're winning by a landslide and they let all of us losers loose on the field. Sucks. But I have no one to blame but myself so…"

I can only offer him a sympathetic smile. There's nothing else I can say or do to make him feel better. I wonder if their parents realize just how much their split has hurt their children? Eli suffers. It sounds like Ryan suffers too.

"I was sitting with some old friends of mine, but I saw you and had a feeling you were Eli's girl. He told me you're a Badger," Ryan says to me.

Ellie laughs and looks around. "What clued you in?"

"The fact that no one is sitting near you two?" Ryan laughs as well. The buzzer sounds and the boys jog off the field. The first half is officially done. "I'm going to head back over to my friends. It was nice meeting you both."

"Nice meeting you too," I say, Ellie murmuring the same.

Ryan rises to his feet, hesitating for a moment before he asks, "Did Eli tell you about our family dinner tomorrow night?"

I frown. "No."

"Oh. I told him to invite you to come out to dinner with us tomorrow night. We're going to Axis. I made a reservation at seven for five, so you're more than welcome to come with us," he says.

I'm immediately put on guard. And the tiniest bit offended. Why didn't Eli ask me? He never even mentioned it. "That sounds nice."

"Talk to Eli about it." He smiles. Pats my head like I'm his pet. "See you tomorrow hopefully."

And then he's gone.

I say nothing for a while and neither does Ellie, until she looks like she can't stand it any longer.

"Are you mad Eli didn't mention that family dinner invite?"

I shrug. Try to act like it's not bugging me. "Not really. He has his reasons."

"It felt like Ryan mentioned it just to rile you up."

I turn to look at her, my voice going low. "You really think so?"

I felt the same way.

"I don't know." Ellie's got that contemplative look on her face. It's the one she wears when she's really thinking about something. "What he said was vaguely suspect."

"What's suspicious is that Eli never mentioned it," I say, my gaze narrowing. I can sort of understand why he didn't say anything to me. I think he finds his family embarrassing. Maybe he doesn't want to expose me to the toxic dynamics between them. He might think that'll scare me away.

Doesn't he realize by now that nothing will scare me away from him? Well, something pretty freaking major would have to happen to send me running from him.

I'm a little hurt he never said anything though. I sort of get it, but then again, I don't. All I know is…

My boyfriend has some explaining to do.

CHAPTER 27

ELI

*W*e won. I knew we would. The moment the buzzer sounded and the game was over, I ran over to Jackson and slapped the back of his helmet, roaring in his face like a maniac. He tore his helmet off and roared his approval in return, the both of us jumping up and down and bumping chests like a couple of macho dicks.

We're fuckin' ridiculous, but I don't care. I'm riding the win high. We've been on a streak since the Badger game, and I feel invincible. So does the rest of the team. I live for nights like this. Moments like this.

Knowing my girl is up in the stands watching me play makes it even better. With Ryan up there too? I can't help but feel like a god. On top of the world.

"Not bad little brother," Ryan says to me when he spots me on the field and makes his approach.

He knocks me off my pedestal with those four words. Just like that. The motherfucker.

I return his offered high five. "Thanks," I say gruffly.

Ryan pulls me into a quick hug, slapping my back. I

remain stiff, pulling away from him as quickly as possible, no smile on my face, nothin'. I'm mad.

Mad he'd make light of my win. Mad it took him this freakin' long to show his face around here. Mad he doesn't have to deal with any of our family shit on a daily basis while I still do.

Yeah, that's probably what makes me the angriest. The fact that he can walk away from this so easily, while I'm left behind having to pick up the pieces. Having to listen to my mom's rants and my dad's tirades and witness the stupid battles they're always engaged in. Sometimes they put me in the middle of it, using me, trying to claim they want to make things better for me. It's all a bunch of lies. It fucking sucks.

And Ryan fucking sucks too for leaving me.

"Aren't you glad to see me?" he asks when I still haven't said anything. "It's good to see you. You've changed. You're taller."

He tries to ruffle my hair like I'm fucking three, but I duck away from his touch. "Stop treating me like a little kid."

Ryan laughs. "Sorry. Didn't know you were so sensitive."

I ignore his rude comment and turn my back on him, calling out to Brenden when I spot him only a few feet away.

"Good job tonight," I tell him as he walks over to me.

"You too." Brenden grins. "You going to Jackson's later?"

"Fuck yeah." We're actually partying at Jackson's house tonight, versus going to the lake. I'm glad we don't have to drive as far as we usually do, considering Jackson lives in the same neighborhood as me.

His house is almost twice as big as mine. And usually, his dad and stepmom are always home. Not tonight though. They went out of town for the weekend.

Party time.

"Me too. I'll see you there." We slap hands and I watch as he walks over to the stands where Kayla's waiting for him.

Knowing full well Ryan is still behind me, standing there patiently.

Finally I turn back around to find Ryan with his arms crossed and a pissed expression on his face. "If you didn't want me to come to your game, you should've told me."

"I didn't realize I had a choice," I throw back at him.

He drops his arms to the sides. "Look. I know you're mad at me. And I suppose I can't blame you. I left and I didn't come back, but shit, do you blame me? This place is a shithole. Our parents are fucked up. Why would I want to come back?"

"For me!" The words blast out of my mouth with so much force, Ryan takes a step back, like he can't take it. "You bailed. You fucking ghosted me. Ghosted all of us! You left me behind to deal with them all alone!" I slap my hand against my chest, trying to drive my point home.

"I came back for a reason. I'm trying to make amends," he says, his voice calm, his expression completely blank. Looking nothing like the Ryan I used to know. "I'm trying to do right by you. And Mom and Dad."

"Your efforts are a little too late," I mutter before I take off. I need to find Ava. I need to hold her and have her tell me everything's going to be okay.

This is some straight up bullshit.

I stalk toward the stands, ignoring the remaining onlookers who offer me congratulations and tell me good job. I don't say a word, too determined to find Ava. I don't see her pretty little blonde head anywhere, and my chest grows tight.

Did she not show up at all? Of course, she did. I saw her earlier. Couldn't help but see her the entire game whenever I looked in the stands. And no way would she bail on me after the game. She's not that cruel.

Damn, do I have abandonment issues or what?

I finally spot her standing in the middle of a circle of my teammates who are still out on the field, tagging along with her friend, Ellie. They're talking to freaking Jackson.

What the hell? How did I miss her?

"Eli," she says when she spots me. She leaves Ellie and comes running toward me, and I wrap her up in a hug, holding her close. "Congrats. You played amazing tonight."

"Thanks, babe." I kiss her, my lips lingering. I wish I could keep kissing her, but she breaks away first, smiling up at me, her hands resting on my chest. Like she's trying to hold me back. "I'm glad you're here."

"Me too." She frowns, her gaze searching my face. "Are you okay?"

"I'm great. Never better." I smile, but it's more like a baring of teeth. Like I'm a wild fucking beast ready to tear into something, and right now, I sort of feel like one. "We won, so I've got no worries, right?"

"Yeah, you guys won," she says with a nod, a faint smile curling her lips, though I see the worry lingering in her eyes. "Jackson just mentioned he's having a party at his house. He invited Ellie and I to go."

"I bet he wants Ellie at his house," I say, making Ava laugh. "Do you want to go?"

She shrugs. "I want to be wherever you are."

Relief smacks me right in the center of my chest. This is what I need. What I crave. Ava not caring where we're at, as long as we're together. She stands by my side no matter what.

Unlike other people I know and who supposedly love me.

"Let me change and then we'll head out? You want to ride with me?"

She nods. Smiles. Grabs hold of my hand and gives it a squeeze. "Definitely. I came with Ellie so I'll need a ride home, too."

"Do you even need to go home?" I raise a brow. I'm sure I can sneak her into my house. Mom will be sleeping by the time we leave the party, and Muffin will be locked in her room. Ryan will be there too, but fuck that guy. I don't care what he thinks. Or what he sees.

"My parents think I'm staying the night at Ellie's," she says with a coy smile. "So I'm free all night."

"Meaning you're mine all night." I drop a quick kiss on her forehead. "Give me fifteen and I'll be out. Maybe wait with Ellie in her car? I'll come find you and then she can follow me to Jackson's house."

"Sounds perfect." She tilts her head back and smiles. I dip down, kissing her again. Needing more of her, but telling myself I need to be patient.

I'll have her later.

Every which way I can.

* * *

By the time we arrive at Jackson's house, the party is in full swing. There are people spilling out of the front door of the massive house onto the lawn, and it's so cold outside that when I climb out of the car, I can actually see my breath.

I rush to the passenger side and open the door for Ava, pulling her into my arms the second she's standing. I run my hands up and down her back, feeling her shiver. "It's fucking cold out here," I tell her.

"Let's go inside," she says, withdrawing from my embrace and taking my hand, interlocking our fingers together.

I lead her into the house, pushing through the throngs of people that are congregated everywhere. Ava spotted Ellie's car parked alongside the road when we first got here, so she's walking practically on her tiptoes, scanning the crowd and looking for her best friend.

We find Jackson in the kitchen, no Ellie in sight. I can tell Ava's disappointed. She's hoping those two make a connection, and that would be cool and all, but I don't think it's gonna happen. Jackson is just...Jackson. Single and always ready to mingle. Bitter toward women, and I still don't know why he feels like that. He thinks they're all out to screw him over. Some chick had to have done something horrible to him, and now he's scarred for life.

I can relate. My mother is a terror. But I'm grateful I let myself open up to the possibility of Ava. She changed me.

For the better.

"Where's your friend?" Jackson asks Ava after we say our hellos.

She sends him a skeptical look. "I was going to ask you the same question. I think we share a mutual best friend."

Jackson frowns like he doesn't understand her. Honestly? I have no idea what she's talking about either.

"Ellie told me you two talk." She sends Jackson a pointed look. "All. The. Damn. Time."

Uh oh. My girl is feeling feisty.

Jackson's cheeks actually turn ruddy, as if he's embarrassed. Caught. "Yeah. We keep in contact. Ellie's cool."

Ava lets go of my hand and takes a step toward Jackson, her hand out, her index finger pointing. She jabs it dead center in Jackson's chest, and he winces. As if she hurt him.

It takes everything I've got to contain my laughter.

"You can't treat every girl like a groupie, Jackson. It's clear you like Ellie. Make a move," she says, her voice fierce. Like she's giving orders.

He rubs his chest where she just poked him. "We're just friends."

She rolls her eyes and sends him a scathing look. "God, I really hate boys sometimes." She turns to look at me. "Even you frustrate me, you know?"

I frown, surprised at the way she automatically swung her anger straight at me. "What are you talking about?"

"Were you ever going to mention the dinner invite for tomorrow with your family?" She crosses her arms, waiting for my answer.

"That's my cue to get the fuck out of here." Jackson raises his arms and makes his way out of the kitchen.

Anger bubbles up inside of me. This has to be Ryan's fault. I wait until he's gone before I start talking. "You spoke to Ryan?"

"He sat with me and Ellie for a while," she bites out.

Irritation fills me. I can't believe that fucker mentioned tomorrow night's family dinner to her. "You don't want to go."

"How do you know?" she retorts.

"Because I don't want you there, okay? It's going to be a fucking nightmare, and you don't need to witness the Bennett family slinging passive aggressive insults at each other across the dinner table while pretending to make nice over an expensive meal. It's total bullshit," I spit out, annoyed as fuck.

She takes a step back, a disgusted look on her face, and I know I overstepped, but fuck it. I can't lie about this. "You really think I would judge you because of your parents?"

"Fuck yes, *I* judge me because of my parents. Everyone does. This entire community looks down their noses at us, thanks to my stupid parents. What makes you the exception?" I'm yelling now. I've completely lost my temper. And I'm not mad at Ava. No, I'm fucking super pissed at Ryan.

That asshole just ruined my entire night. What's up with older brothers, huh? Why are they such meddling pieces of shit?

Ava lifts her chin, her green eyes blazing. "You're a jerk," she says before she stomps away from me.

267

"Ava! Ava, come on." I start to chase after her, but Jackson magically appears out of nowhere, grabbing my arm and stopping me. I struggle against his hold, but he won't cut me loose. Dude is stronger than he looks. "Let me go, asshole."

"Nah, son. Let her go. She won't go too far. Plus, you should give her some space. You need to cool off and so does she. Come on." He smiles and tilts his head. "I've got a secret stash hidden in my dad's office. Care to partake with me?"

"What do you got?" I ask warily, my gaze scanning the room. Looking for her pretty blonde head. I see it in the near distance, moving with purpose and heading for the living room, just before it gets swallowed up by the crowd.

"A bong full of the finest fucking weed that'll blow your damn mind, plus a fifth of Belvedere."

"My mom loves Belvedere," I say with a reluctant chuckle.

"Well so does my dad. And so do I. You will too. Come on. Let's go to his office and get high and drunk out of our minds," Jackson says with a grin.

I let Jackson lead me through the kitchen and down a short hall that I've never seen before. We spot Cory emerging from a tiny bathroom with a girl, his hair mussed and his lips swollen. He grins at us and waves. We give him the finger in return, and he just laughs.

Good for that loser, getting some bathroom action. At least someone is.

Jackson approaches a closed door and whips a key out of the front pocket of his jeans. He unlocks the door and cracks it open, waving me to go through it. I step sideways to slip through and Jackson does the same, quickly shutting the door behind him and locking it once more.

"I don't want anyone in here with us. My dad said he could give a shit if I wanted to throw a party, as long as I cleaned up afterward and that everyone must stay out of their bedroom and his office. Study. Whatever the fuck he calls it." Jackson cracks himself up. "He keeps all his expensive liquor in here, hides it away in a locked cabinet. Plus, there's a safe in here with all the family jewels and documents or whatever. I don't know. All I cared about was finding the key to the liquor cabinet."

"Did you?" I ask.

Jackson produces a key from the front pocket of his jeans. "Sure the fuck did."

"Is your parents' bedroom door locked? You know someone will sneak in there to use the bed to fuck in," I say, wishing I could be that person.

Pretty sure that's the last thing Ava wants to do tonight.

"Hell yeah, it is. My stepmom has all of her expensive handbags in her giant ass closet. She threatened me with actual death if any of her Chanel bags went missing."

"Your dad's loaded," I say as I check out the cavernous office.

"He's a G," Jackson says with a nod, going to a cabinet and kneeling before it, sticking the skinny key into a slot before he cracks open one of the doors. He withdraws a giant bottle of vodka out of it and stands, holding it out to me. "Here we go."

"Where's the weed?" I don't want to get drunk. Not really. I'd rather get high and forget about my brother and what he did. How he messed everything up tonight just by showing his face and shooting off his mouth.

"Patience, grasshopper," he says, laughing. "My dad used to always say that to me."

Jackson opens the bottle of vodka and takes a long swig straight from the bottle, hissing through his teeth when he's finished. "For that much money, you'd think that shit would be a little smoother."

"It probably is if you weren't chugging it like the town drunk," I say snidely.

Jackson grins and points the bottle at me. "Touché, motherfucker. Okay, let me find my bong."

He goes digging around the office, never once turning on a light. I go to the window and check out the backyard, which is also filled with people. I go to school with most of them, though I see a stray person here and there, and figure they go to the other school. Ava's school.

Shit. Where is Ava anyway? Did she find Ellie? Are they both cursing our asses right now and talking about us? How awful we are? I guess we deserve it. I know I do, and an apology will be in order. I didn't mean to lose it on her like that, but damn. Why did my brother have to say what he said? Asking her to go to dinner with us when I specifically told him I didn't want her to go?

It's like he did that shit on purpose.

And why does Ava pretend like everything's cool with my parents when it's so not? She knows how it is at my house. Between my parents. I've told her enough. She totally knows how I feel.

It is almost like she's disrespecting me. Like she doesn't believe what I say. That's some straight up bullshit right there.

"Hey," I say to Jackson, who's still in search of the stupid bong. I need something to take the edge off. "Hand me over that vodka."

He presses the bottle into my open hand and I take a long drink from it, making a smacking sound when I'm done. "Did you lose the bong or what?"

"Found it." Jackson holds the glass bong above his head like he's holding a trophy. "I purchased some high quality weed a few days ago. Went to a dispensary and did a little shopping."

"You got any edibles?"

Jackson shakes his head. "Already ate 'em. Got high as fuck too."

He laughs. So do I. "Take me on your shopping trip next time. How'd you even get in there?"

We're both seventeen. We can't shop legally in dispensaries yet.

"I have my ways," he says with an evil grin.

We light up the bong and take a few hits. I hold that smoke in so long, it fucking burns my lungs before I'm finally exhaling with a cough. Jackson laughs at me and then does the same exact thing. We take turns drinking from the bottle and taking hits, not really saying anything, just savoring the moment of getting high.

"Your chick is mad at you," Jackson says once we finally give up on the bong.

"Yeah well, that's not my fault. I'm mad at my brother. He fucked everything up in the first place," I mutter.

"You yelled at her."

"She's full of shit."

"Yeah, go tell her that," Jackson says, a gleam in his eye.

He has a point. I can't say that to Ava. She'll want to kick my ass. The crazy thing? I know she's capable. That girl is tough with a capital T.

"I'm going to have to say sorry, aren't I?" I sound miserable. Because I am a miserable son of a bitch, starting unnecessary fights with my girlfriend when none of this is her fault. What the hell was I thinking?

"Yeah, you definitely are," Jackson says, leaning back in his dad's desk chair. "This is why I won't go out with one girl. They get under your skin and make you say and do stupid shit."

"That's not true," I start, but the look Jackson sends me shuts me up.

It's so true. I say and do stupid shit all the time. I did

before Ava, and I still do during Ava. Probably will after Ava as well.

My chest suddenly aches and I rub my hand over it, desperate to ease the pain. I don't like thinking about after Ava. If I have my way, that moment in time will never exist.

It will always be during Ava. With Ava. That's it.

End of story.

"You need to go out and find her," Jackson says, tipping his head toward the closed door. "You need to search through all those people and find your pretty girlfriend and tell her you're sorry. And you have to mean it. If you spot her gorgeous friend, tell her I'm sorry too, okay? Tell her I'm an idiot, and there's no way we can be anything else but friends."

"You go find Ellie and tell her that yourself, you miserable son of a bitch," I bark at him, snatching the bottle from his dad's desk and taking one last gulp. "God damn, that stuff is awful."

"Vodka has no taste."

"My ass. It tastes like it's trying to destroy my taste buds." I make a face.

"You're a pussy."

"So are you." I point a finger at him. "If you had any balls, you'd go find Ellie your damn self and fuck her like you want to."

Jackson straightens up. "I don't want to fuck her."

I can't help but start laughing. "Such a liar. It's all you want. That's why you hide from her and only talk to her on Snapchat or what the fuck ever. Because you know if you looked her in the eyes and heard her sweet voice and saw the way she watches you? All dreamy eyed and shit? You'd take her and keep her for as long as you could."

Jackson is firmly shaking his head, but I see the uncertainty in his gaze. "No way, my friend. Absolutely not. I'm not interested. She's got serious written all over her, and I don't do serious."

"I thought that way too." I rise to my feet a little unsteadily, overcome with booze and smoke. "But then I gave Ava a try and realized I only do serious for her. Give it a shot. You might find out it's not so bad."

Turning, I start for the door, stumbling over my own damn feet as I make my way there. When I'm at the door, I unlock it and crack it open, glancing over my shoulder to find Jackson watching me.

"I gotta go apologize to my girlfriend," I say.

"Good luck, loser," Jackson says with a grin.

"Hey, at least I'm the one who's gonna end up getting good and fucked tonight after all. Unlike you," I say with a laugh.

Jackson gives me the finger.

I slam the door behind me and set out to find Ava.

CHAPTER 28

AVA

*E*li Bennett is the most frustrating human being alive. Like seriously, who does he think he is? Yelling at me like that in the middle of a party in front of other people. In front of Jackson, who watched the entire thing with an amused expression on his too good looking face. Eli can't speak to me that way. Like some pissed off bully who yells at his girlfriend for no apparent reason.

Ugh. If I didn't love him so much, I'd hate him.

But I can't hate him, because I love him.

God, this relationship stuff is frustrating sometimes.

I wander through the crowded rooms in search of Ellie, but she's nowhere to be found. Worry hits me, and I tell myself not to panic, but where could she be? Who is she with? God, I hope she's okay. I hope she's not with some random guy who's trying to drug her drink or whatever. I love Ellie, but sometimes she can be a little naïve. She sees the good in everyone, and not everyone is good.

Like Jackson Rivers. That guy is just a player, and he's playing Ellie. He's not interested. Not really. He'd rather keep her a secret.

And that's horrible. What a dick.

Men suck.

I'm marching through the living room, ready to go out to the front yard when I hear someone call my name. Glancing over my shoulder, I finally see Ellie making her way toward me.

"Oh my God, there you are!" I gasp when she throws herself at me, her arms tight around my middle as she practically squeezes me to death. "Are you okay?"

She pulls away so she can look me in the eyes, her expression grateful. "I've been at this stupid party for the last twenty minutes all by myself, looking for a familiar face. I don't know anyone here!"

"Me either," I mutter, my voice filled with annoyance.

Ellie frowns. "Where's Eli?"

"Last time I saw him, he was with that dick, Jackson. God knows where they are now." I roll my eyes.

"What happened? Why are you calling Jackson a dick?" she asks.

"Because he is one, Ellie. And so is Eli. They're both jerks. I told off Jackson for not making a move on you. Then Eli yelled at me. It was terrible." I shake my head.

Ellie is nothing short of horrified. "Wait a minute. You told off Jackson for not making a move on *me?* Why would you do that?"

"Because he's a chicken shit, and he needs to be called out for it! You deserve better than him, Ellie. Don't settle for the scraps he gives you. You need to find a guy who's totally into you and not afraid to show it," I say.

"At least he's giving me scraps! No other guy out there acts like he might like me. Not a single one. Not at our school, and not at this one either." She scans the room before returning her gaze to me. Now she looks flat out miserable.

"And now you've probably blown my last chance with a guy. A really good looking guy."

"Oh come on. If Jackson blows you off because of something I said, then he wasn't worth it in the first place," I reassure her, reaching out to rub her arm.

She shrugs away from my touch. "Maybe to you. But he's totally worth it to me. He always has been. And if I have to wait a year, two years, however long it takes for Jackson to get his head out of his ass and realize we'd make a great couple, then I'll wait!" Ellie yells.

I stare at my best friend, wondering what happened to her. I take a step closer, try to rest my hand on her shoulder, but she shrugs away from me again. Like she's really angry with me. "Ellie, you don't have to wait for—"

"I *want* to, and that's the difference. I'm not like you, Ava. You snagged Eli's attention and he pursued you with such determination, it's almost scary how fast you two happened. Have you ever stopped and thought he might be using you to get back at Jake in some way?"

My mouth drops open. I've told her everything about my relationship with Eli. And how Jake still believes Eli is just using me to bother him. She knows how much I hate that assumption. "You know that's not true," I say vehemently.

"See, that's the problem. I don't know. And neither do you. Just like you think I'm an idiot for waiting for Jackson to realize his feelings, sometimes I think you're a complete idiot for falling in love with Eli when he's probably just using you." She lowers her voice. "For sex."

"Oh. My. God." I step away from her, annoyed. Offended. Devastated.

"See?" Ellie tosses her hands up in the air. "It hurts, huh? I can't just give up on Jackson, just like you can't give up on Eli. So stop belittling my relationship with Jackson when yours with Eli isn't that great either."

I gape at her, shocked by her outburst, the things she's saying to me. Like she doesn't care if she's hurting my feelings or not.

Though I suppose I didn't care if I was hurting her feelings either, after everything I just said about Jackson.

"At least I have an actual relationship with Eli," I say, knowing the exact moment my words crush her soul by the way her eyelids flicker when I say the words *actual relationship*. God, I'm a total bitch.

Turning, I walk away from her, holding my head up high despite the shitty way I feel. I called Eli a jerk? Well, I'm being a jerk too, stomping all over my best friend's feelings. What is going on tonight? Why are we all acting like this? It feels like a domino effect. Ryan said what he said to me and it started the dominos falling.

I should go back and apologize to Ellie. Tell her I didn't mean it, because I didn't. I so didn't. I can't just pop off and say such shitty things like that to her. I'm a terrible friend.

Horrible.

I glance over my shoulder, looking for her, but she's already gone. I don't even see her.

I lost her.

Grabbing my phone out of the back pocket of my jeans, I send her a quick text.

I'm so sorry. I'm an asshole. Please forgive me.

But ten minutes go by while I'm walking all over this giant house and smiling at people I don't know, and still no response from Ellie. She either doesn't hear or feel her phone, or she's purposely ignoring me. I'm hopeful it's the first one, though I guess I can't blame her if it's the last one either.

Being a jerk to my best friend isn't normal. Eli set me off. Crap, this entire week I've been set off. Angry at everyone. I don't like it.

At all.

"Oh God, what are you doing here?"

The aggravated voice belongs to Cami. This night just keeps getting better and better.

"Don't talk to me," I snap. I'm this close to breaking completely. I don't need to add an argument with Cami to the mix.

"Just let me say one thing." Cami crosses her arms, and I look around for one of her minions, but she's completely alone. I don't even see Baylee anywhere. And why is she at this party anyway? Who invited her?

"Spit it out," I tell her, sounding hostile. I hate this girl so much, I can barely stand looking at her.

"You're really going to quit the team?" She raises a brow.

"If it keeps me away from you, then yes. I am." I cross my arms too. "We don't get along, Cami. That much is clear."

"It's just—" She throws her arms up in the air, clearly frustrated. "We're better with you on the team."

My mouth drops open. I can't believe she just said that. "Are you for real right now?"

"I know we don't get along. I can't stand you. You can't stand me. But your stunt team misses you. You're a great base," she practically chokes out.

It's shocking, hearing her offer me compliments. I feel terrible for what happened—more that I let down the team by getting in trouble. I don't regret hitting Cami at all.

She deserved it.

"I miss them," I tell her. "And I feel bad for disappointing them. But—I can't be on a team with you, Cami. It won't work."

Cami lifts her chin, her expression blank. "Sure. Okay. Whatever. Your social status will drop, especially because you're with Eli Bennett, but that's your choice."

Her remark tempts me to say something horrible in

return, but I keep my mouth shut. Instead, I remain calm as I watch her turn and walk away, relief nearly making me sag. Admitting my feelings about the team—and Cami—was a lot easier than I thought it would be.

Inhaling deeply for strength, I start wandering again, searching for my jerk boyfriend. I spot Eli's best friend Brenden with that bitchy girlfriend of his wrapped all around him, her face in his like she wants him to see only her.

Annoying.

There's a girl standing next to them, and she's watching me with a disgusted look on her face. It takes me a minute, but I eventually put two and two together and realize it's the same girl who kissed Eli the first time I went to the cabin. At that party, when he was sitting on the tree stump and she was sitting on his lap.

Whoops. I guess I won this time around, even though I'm completely pissed at him.

Tearing my gaze away from hers, I turn and run straight into a solid wall of muscle. I throw my hands out, my palms connecting with soft fabric and warm flesh beneath, and when I look up, I find it's my very own boyfriend grinning down at me.

His eyes are cloudy. His smile is lopsided. He looks drunk. Or high.

Possibly both.

"I was hoping I would run into you." He starts laughing at his lame joke.

I take a step back and rest my hands on my hips. "Where have you been?"

His grin fades. "What do you care? You're the one who left me."

"Because you were being rude."

"You came at me kind of aggressively about the dinner thing," he says.

A sigh leaves me, and I shake my head. "Your brother mentions it like I should already know, and he made me feel stupid, okay? And then I got my feelings hurt when I realized you never mentioned it to me. Like you didn't want me to go."

His expression shifts, and his gaze turns almost pleading. "Princess, you gotta understand. My family is…fucked up. Yours is wholesome and perfect and mine is a mess. I don't want you to see them all together. It's going to be shitshow. I promise you. You don't want to be there."

"My family is definitely not wholesome," I say firmly. "But I'm grateful that my parents are still together and love each other."

"Exactly. That's the point I'm trying to make," he says, pointing at me. Yeah, he's definitely had something to drink. And possibly something to smoke too. "That's why you're so great, and I'm such a fucking disaster."

"You're not a disaster." I slowly shake my head. "You're amazing. And I'm not perfect. I make mistakes too. That's all I keep doing tonight."

He frowns. "What are you talking about?"

"I yelled at Jackson. I yelled at you. I got in a fight with Ellie. I'm sure she hates me now," I say miserably.

His gaze turns gentle and he reaches for me, pulling me into his arms and giving me a hug. It's just what I needed. "I'm sorry I yelled at you. It was a dick move. Jackson even said so."

"I'm sorry too," I tell him, resting my hand on his chest. I can feel his heart thundering beneath my palm, and I wonder if he's nervous. Afraid I might tell him off some more. Who knows? It's funny, how we're standing by the entry into the formal dining room, surrounded by all sorts of people, but I don't even notice them.

I only have eyes for Eli.

"Wait a minute," I say, just as Eli is dipping his head to kiss me. "Jackson told you what you did was a dick move?"

He laughs and kisses me quickly. "Yeah, he did. Then he took me to his dad's office and we drank almost an entire bottle of vodka and took a couple of hits off his bong."

"Eli," I chastise, because I can, because I always do.

"Ava," he returns, because deep down, I think he kind of likes it when I talk to him like that.

"Hey." I grab the front of his sweatshirt, yanking his head down so we're face to face. Eye to eye. "I want to go to the dinner tomorrow. I don't care what happens. I want to be there for you."

He grimaces. Scrubs his hand over his face like that might sober him up. Good luck with that. "Are you sure you really want to?"

I nod. "I'm your girlfriend, and I want to support you no matter what. I'm not going to judge. I'm not going to freak out if your dad yells or your mom drinks too much. I promise you that." Reaching up, I touch his cheek, running my thumb over the prickly stubble there. "I love you. Your family won't scare me away."

Eli kisses me. Right in front of everyone, he kisses me with tongue and everything. I'm rising up on my tiptoes and chasing his mouth when he finally breaks away, that giant grin appears on his face once more.

"How'd I get so lucky that you're mine?" he asks, his expression slightly dazed. Like he can't believe I'm here, saying these things.

"I feel the same exact way about you," I say, squeezing him tight.

I'm about to kiss him again when I hear someone screech

281

my name and then a tiny body is hurling itself at me, chanting, "I'm sorry, I'm sorry!" over and over again.

It's Ellie. And oh God, she's actually crying.

"Please don't cry!" I tell her, pulling away from Eli completely, so I can hold my best friend in my arms. "I'm sorry too. I said terrible things to you."

"I said terrible things to you too! I didn't mean it." She sniffs. Hiccups. "I was trying to hurt you."

"Well, you did." I smile at her. Smooth her hair out of her eyes. "And I know I hurt you too."

"Oh you definitely did. You were a total bitch," she says.

"Right back at you." I wipe her tears from her cheeks. "I didn't mean any of it."

Well, I sort of did because I'm worried about Jackson and how he treats Ellie, but it's none of my business. I need to learn to keep my mouth shut and only offer advice when she asks for it.

But that's so tough. I want to watch out for her. I don't want her to get hurt.

"I didn't mean it either. I know you hated it when Jake accused Eli of all that stuff, so I threw it back in your face," Ellie says morosely.

"Hey hey, did I just hear my name get dropped?" Eli cozies up to my side, his gaze all for Ellie. "Girl, why you crying? Jackson ain't worth your tears."

"Oh shut up," she mumbles, slapping his chest and making him laugh. "Is he high?" she asks me.

"As a motherfucker," Eli answers for me, and this time Ellie is the one who's laughing. "Okay. There ya go, that's better. No crying allowed. We're at a party, remember?"

"Is someone actually crying at *my* party?"

I want to roll my eyes so badly when Jackson makes his approach, but I don't. Plus, I see the way Ellie's face brightens, like his appearance just made her day. Week. Month.

Year.

Oh man, she really does like this douchebag.

"Nope," Eli says. "Ellie isn't crying at all. Are you, Ellie?"

"Not at all," Ellie says to my goofy boyfriend with a too wide smile.

"Are we all kissing and making up then?" Jackson glances at me and Eli, before he settles his gaze on Ellie. He's pretty much eye fucking her in front of us, and she's eye fucking him right back. "I'm all for it."

"Don't you dare—" I start, but Eli covers my mouth with his hand, silencing me.

"Let him flirt. This is progress," he whisper-hisses.

I glare at Eli with wide eyes, then lick his fingers. He doesn't react.

He doesn't remove his hand either. For at least another ten seconds.

"I thought there was no kissing on the first date," Ellie teases Jackson, her cheeks flushed, her smile pretty much the widest I've ever seen it.

"This isn't a date. This is a party. There are no rules." He grins. Grabs hold of her hand and yanks her close to him, his arm sneaking around her waist.

And then proceeds to tenderly kiss her lips.

Eli starts making a lot of noise, causing a little scene with his oohs and ahhs. "Holy shit. It's going down tonight!"

I slug his arm, but that has zero effect in silencing him.

Jackson grins.

And Ellie? It appears Jackson's sweet kiss just put stars in her eyes.

He's just made everything ten times worse.

CHAPTER 29

AVA

*E*arlier this morning I went to my first Saturday school for four hours. Talk about torture. But I was able to finish my math homework I was a little behind on, so I call that a win.

After I got out, I drove straight home and then Mom and I went to Fresno to shop for dresses. We found a couple of options for me to wear to the Bennett family dinner tonight, and while Mom wasn't a big fan of me wearing the one I'm currently modeling for Ellie via FaceTime, this is the one I'm definitely going to wear.

But I'm afraid it's a little too scandalous.

"You sure this dress isn't going to be too much?" I take a step back from where my phone is propped on my desk so Ellie can see the entirety of my outfit. "It's kind of short."

"And kind of low cut," Ellie says critically. "Don't you think you'll get cold?"

"Tonight isn't about me getting too cold, Ellie," I tell her. "This is about me looking pretty for Eli."

"Well, if that's your only goal, he's definitely going to like it. Trust me." Her voice is firm.

"Thank you," I tell her, grateful for her honest opinion.

The dress is white with red and blue delicate flowers scattered all over it. The skirt has three ruffled tiers, and the short sleeves also have ruffles, accented with lace. The neckline dips into a low V, but my boobs are small enough that I'm not falling out of the dress.

I think that's what Ellie means by me being able to wear it. Oh, and the dress has a similar V in the back. The waist is elastic so I can just slip it on and go, and I feel so pretty, so grown up in this dress. I want to look like Eli's mature, sweet-natured girlfriend.

Because that's what I am, damn it.

"How are you doing your hair?" Ellie asks.

"I'm going to curl it, but nothing too structured. I have a cardigan that almost matches the red flowers. I can make it out of the house if I wear that dumb sweater. That way my dad won't freak out," I say.

Ellie laughs. "Yeah, your dad is *not* going to approve of that dress."

"With a sweater covering it, he'll be fine."

"Rebel," she teases me.

"Who's the real rebel, hmm? You still haven't told me what happened between you and Jackson last night after Eli and I left the party," I tease her.

We stayed at the party for a long time. Eventually we made our way to the backseat of Eli's car, where we made out for a while. Felt each other up, but our hands were lazy. So were our bodies. Eventually, he fell asleep. So did I. Woke up with a kink in my neck and shook Eli awake so he could drive me home at six in the morning. I snuck into the house to find the house quiet, everyone still asleep, and collapsed into bed. When I woke at ten, it was to my mom coming into my room, startled that I was already home. I played it off by saying Ellie had to work

MONICA MURPHY

early and she brought me home, and thank God, she didn't question me.

I feel guilty about all the sneaking around, but it's the only way I'm able to see Eli. I'm breaking my parents' trust, but I don't know how else to do this. How else to spend time with my boyfriend—alone time.

I'm sure I'm not the first teenager to do this. And I won't be the last.

"Nothing really happened," Ellie says with a sigh. "He didn't kiss me again. We talked. For a long time. Jackson is a talker."

"I bet," I say sarcastically.

"Hey. Don't bash him. I'm sure Eli is a sweet talker too."

"Yeah, but he talked me straight out of my panties pretty fast, unlike Jackson." I cover my mouth to stifle my laughter, but it's difficult.

Ellie laughs too. "Truer words were never spoken."

"Shut up."

"You said it, not me." Her laughter dies. "It almost feels like all this talking is like...foreplay. A build up to the main event."

"I hope so for your sake, or eventually you're going to end up sexually frustrated," I say.

"Maybe? I don't know. He's so sweet. He says all the right things."

"Don't they all?" I plop down on the edge of my bed and mess with the hem of my dress, smoothing out the ruffles. "I don't want to be negative—"

"Then don't be," Ellie interrupts.

I send her a look. "But just, be careful. Don't give too much of yourself to this guy. He could be all smoke and mirrors, with no actual substance."

"I've always loved illusionists," Ellie says with a laugh.

"Ha ha, funny." I roll my eyes and stand, going to my desk

so I can pick up my phone. "I'm going to go. I need to start getting ready. Thank you for helping me."

"Of course. Have fun. I'm sure it's going to go fabulously!" Ellie says.

We end the call and I go to the full-length mirror that's propped against my wall, resting my hands on my hips as I turn this way and that, checking out every angle of the dress. I absolutely love it. Not just because it's super cute, but also because every style of dress at this store has a name, and this one is called...

The Bennett Dress.

If that's not serendipitous, then I don't know what is.

I go to my closet and grab the cardigan that I think will match, shrugging it on as I make my way back to the mirror. It matches pretty well, but it's not perfect. The effect is like trying to throw a dark blanket over a bright and sunny painting. It's immediately dimmed. Boring. I make a face at my reflection, sticking out my tongue.

The sweater over the dress sucks.

I take it off and I'm immediately happy again. This is much prettier. I let one of the shoulders drop, my black bra strap exposed. There's no reason to wear a bra with this dress. I make quick work of it, slipping it off and tossing it on my bed.

There. That's even better. I curve my arm across my breasts and let both shoulders slip so they lie in the crook of my elbows. Oooh.

That's sexy.

Eli is going to die when he sees me in this.

I take my second shower for the day but don't wash my hair since I already did this morning. I shave everything I've got, plus use that expensive face scrub Mom bought me last Christmas. Once I'm out of the shower, I lotion up, slathering on my favorite body cream. I use that expensive cream on my face, also given to me by my mom at Christmas. I slip on a nude thong and then start curling my hair, doing my best to not curl it for too long. I don't want this hairstyle to look like I created it on purpose with a bunch of fully formed curls. I want it to look effortless. Casual.

As if I woke up looking like this.

Once I'm done with my hair, I go to my desk-slash-vanity table and start doing my makeup. I'm not one to wear a lot of it normally, but tonight seems to call for it. I use a little eyeshadow and mascara. Some tinted moisturizer and high-lighter. I even slick my lips with gloss, a subtle red that makes my mouth look like I just got kissed.

Leaning back, I stare at my reflection. Wow. I look… older. Definitely. I push my hair away from my face, tucking a few strands behind my ear. It's like I'm staring at my future self, I swear.

Mom and Dad aren't going to like this. At all.

I grab my phone and send Eli a quick text.

You still want me to get to your house at six-thirty?

He responds quickly.

Eli: **Yeah.**

Me: **But isn't your house about a half hour from the restaurant?**

Eli: **Give or take.**

He's not being very talkative. That's not a good sign.

Me: **We might end up being late for the reservation.**

Eli: **We don't have to be exactly on time.**

Me: **It's Saturday night though. It'll be busy.**

Eli: **You know what? Why don't I leave in a few minutes and come get you? That way we don't have to ride with any of my family to the restaurant.**

Me: **I don't mind.**

Eli: **Well I do. Let me come get you. The restaurant isn't too far from where you live anyway. I don't mind making** the extra drive. **Keeps me away from my brother a little while longer.**

I bite on the edge of my nail, worrying over that particular remark.

Me: **You're still mad at him?**

Eli: **Hell yeah. He's an asshole. I'll tell you about it when I get there.**

Me: **When will you get here?**

Eli: **Around sixish. See you soon. Love you.**

Me: **Love you too. Drive safe.**

I check the time. He'll be here in about forty minutes. I got ready way too soon. I'd love to take a nap since I didn't get much sleep last night, but no way am I going to ruin my hair for a twenty-minute snooze. Or wrinkle my dress.

Meaning I'm going to have to sit here in this chair for the next forty minutes or so and hardly move.

I scroll through my phone and check social media, almost immediately bored. On a whim, I decide to FaceTime my sister.

She answers on the second ring. I make sure and pose for her, ready for her expression when she sees me.

"What the—I almost didn't recognize you!" Autumn gushes.

I grin at her through the screen. "What do you think?"

"You're gorgeous. But I already knew that. Show me your entire outfit," Autumn demands.

This is why I called her. So I could talk about my date and my outfit, and get her approval. Our relationship has definitely changed these last couple of years. When she still lived at home, she'd always tell me I looked terrible or that I was trying too hard.

I'm so grateful we get along better now. I need her support. Now more than ever.

"Mom and Dad actually let you get that?" Autumn asks after I twirl in a circle.

"Are you shocked?"

"Beyond." Autumn laughs, making me laugh too. "It's a very—grown up dress."

"I know. That's why I wanted it. Plus, it's called the Bennett dress. Get it?" I say, raising my brows up and down like a weirdo.

"Yes, I get it," she says dryly. "You look beautiful. What's the special occasion?"

"I'm going to dinner with his family."

"In that dress? It's a tad scandalous."

"My boobs won't fall out. I promise." I lean forward to let her see how the dress really doesn't move. Thankfully neither of them accidentally slip out.

"You're a goof," Autumn says, shaking her head. "And this is a big deal, Ava. Going to dinner with the parents?"

"And his big brother, Ryan."

"Ryan Bennett?" Autumn frowns. "I remember him."

Her frown tells me her memories aren't the best, but I ignore that.

"Eli's parents are getting a divorce. It's pretty tense between them all right now, and Ryan hasn't been around for a while. This is the first weekend he's visited home in like… years," I admit.

"Well, that kind of sucks. And I've heard stories about their parents," Autumn says cryptically.

My mouth drops open. "You have? Eli used to act like no one knew."

"Everyone knew. The town is too small and his mom used to show up everywhere and drink a little too much. She's the one with the big mouth who would tell anyone who would listen what her husband did to her. How he cheated on her."

A sigh escapes me and I feel sad. For Eli. For his parents. Not so much for Ryan though. "That's so awful."

"It is," Autumn agrees. "You sure you want to get mixed up in that mess?"

"Eli didn't want me to come to the dinner. He didn't want to subject me to his parents and their antics," I say.

"What sort of antics?"

"I don't know. They probably involve too much alcohol, a lot of arguing and plenty of insults." That's the logical conclusion that I've come to.

Autumn makes a little face. "That sounds awful."

"I know," I say with a sigh. I've been trying to pretend the dread that's settled in my stomach didn't exist since it first showed up this morning, but here it comes, larger than life and difficult to ignore.

I'm scared to go to this dinner. Scared of what might happen, what might be said, how Eli will react. I don't want him upset, but I can almost guarantee he's going to show up already upset. Completely on edge. Tense and ready for a fight.

"Can I give you some advice?" Autumn asks, pulling me from my thoughts.

"Please. I need it," I say.

"Just—be quiet and listen to what everyone has to say. Don't say anything unless they ask you a question, or include you in the conversation. It might be best if you act like you're not even there. Be there for Eli, reassure him you're on his side, but let it all play out without getting yourself involved."

I nod, trying to absorb Autumn's words, my mind and spirit completely rebelling against them. That is so not who I am. Yes, I can be quiet. For most of my life, I've preferred to stay in the background. Let Jake get all the glory. Let Autumn be the oldest Callahan child and therefore act like she's the boss of me.

No way can I imagine myself sitting there and not saying a damn word the entire dinner. I agree it's not my place to speak up, but if any of them tear Eli down, I'm going to defend him.

I have to.

Unable to agree with what Autumn says, I change the subject and we talk about college. Ash. Santa Barbara. Football. The usual. By the time we're wrapping up our conversation, I hear the doorbell ring.

"He's here." The nerves jump in my stomach and I smile at Autumn. "I have to go. Wish me luck."

"Good luck! You've got this! Tell Eli he's got this too! Love you!"

We make kissy faces and I end the call, then grab my cardigan and tiny purse before I dash into the bathroom and check my reflection one more time.

I hope Mom doesn't make a big deal. Honestly, I hope Eli doesn't either.

I leave my bedroom and shut the door, then make my way downstairs. I can hear Mom complimenting Eli on how nice he looks and that gets my hopes up, excited to see him dressed up a little. I find them in the living room—Dad included—and when I make my appearance, I notice how my mom's eyes widen a little but otherwise, she says nothing.

"Ava. Hey." There is tension in Eli's face. His jaw is tight, but his eyes light up when they land on me, and I can't help but admire him in return.

He's wearing a white dress shirt and black trousers with a Gucci belt, no freaking joke. His hair is somewhat tamed and his face is clean shaven, and I've never seen Eli look as handsome as he does right now, at this very moment.

"You both look so wonderful. Can I take a photo?" Mom asks.

Eli slings his arm around my waist loosely as I roll my eyes. "Mom, you act like we're going to prom or something."

"Oh, I'll be worse when that happens. I'll want an hour-long photo session at least," she teases, glancing over at Dad. "What do you think, honey? Don't they look amazing?"

Dad crosses his arms, studying both of us. Making me the slightest bit uncomfortable. Thank God for the cardigan. It hides the worst and best parts of this dress. "The skirt is kind of short."

"Dad." I roll my eyes again.

"You look pretty," he says, his tone softening. He turns to Mom. "Take a couple of quick photos and let these kids go, Fable. They don't want to hang out with us."

"Fine, fine." She makes Eli and I pose and she snaps a few photos. Then I give her my phone and she takes even more photos. Eli smiles at all the right times, but I can tell it's slightly strained. And I can feel the tension in his body. He's very stiff.

I wish I could comfort him, but I'm not sure how.

"You two have fun tonight, okay?" Mom says as we make our way to the front door.

"Thanks, Mrs. C.," Eli says genuinely, giving her a quick hug before he grabs my hand.

Swear to God, my mother just blushed a little.

Once we're out of the house and approaching his car, I tell him, "Sorry about my parents."

"What about them? They're great. I love them," he says absently as he opens the passenger side door for me.

I slip inside the seat and close the door, shedding the cardigan immediately. Eli walks around the front of the car and opens the driver's door, climbing inside. "My mom can sometimes go overboard with all the photo taking," I say.

"It's cute. At least she wants to take photos. At least they both care about you."

His words hurt my heart.

He starts the car and glances in my direction, his gaze heated as it rakes over me. "Goddamn, princess. You look fuckin' hot in that dress."

Okay, there's my boyfriend. I was afraid I wouldn't even catch a glimpse of him tonight, considering how wound up he is over this dinner. "You really like it? You don't think it's too much?"

"Hell no. I think it's just right." He reaches out, brushing his fingers against the exposed, sensitive skin between my breasts. "I like this especially."

My entire body blooms with heat. "I knew you would. You know what's crazy? The salesperson told me it's called the Bennett Dress."

"No shit?" He slips his fingers beneath the dipping neckline, grazing the underside of my breast. "You don't have a bra on."

"I can't wear one with this dress. That would look terrible." My breath hitches when his thumb brushes my nipple. "Eli. We're in my driveway."

He removes his hand from my dress, growling with frustration and pounding his knee with his curled fist. "I'm so fuckin' tense, I feel like I'm going to explode."

I rest my hand across that fist, keeping it in place. "Bad day?"

Eli nods. "My brother's a smug dick. Mom is fawning all over him and that's irritating the shit out of me. I don't know, maybe I'm just jealous, but she acts like Ryan's the king while I'm the joker who's constantly trying to entertain her and she's oblivious to everything I do for her."

Removing my hand from his, I reach for his face, skim my fingers along his tense jaw. "I have an idea."

His pretty hazel eyes meet mine. "What is it?" he asks skeptically.

"Let's go somewhere real quick. We have time." I glance at the clock. It's barely six-fifteen. We definitely have enough time. "It's a secret spot not many people know of."

"I know all your secret spots," Eli cracks with a grin.

"Not this one." I shake my head and wave at the steering wheel. "Come on. Let's go."

He shifts the car into drive and presses his foot against the gas. "If you say so."

CHAPTER 30

ELI

I don't know what my girlfriend has up her sleeve, but from the sly smile that's curled her lips since we've left her house, I have a feeling it should be something good. Hopefully even mind-blowing.

Like a quickie blow job before we go to dinner?

Yeah, I couldn't be so lucky.

She directs me to a spot by the lake I've never been before. A tiny cove that isn't too far from where she lives. I pull into the dirt lot, grateful it's not raining because hey, I don't want to get mud all over my car, okay? I like to keep this baby as clean as possible.

I put the car in park and glance over at Ava to find she's already watching me.

That dress she's wearing is almost criminal, she looks so damn good in it. Her long legs are exposed, as well as her arms. Her chest—she makes one wrong move and a tit might fall out. Her hair is curled a little at the ends, and she's got all this makeup on her face. I could give a shit about her wearing makeup since she's beautiful no matter what, but she looks gorgeous tonight. Older. Like I can imagine this Ava two or three years from now.

"Is this it?" I ask her after a few seconds of silence. "Your secret spot?"

Hey, I never claimed to be patient.

"You're very tense," she says, her voice soft and almost seductive in the darkness of the car's interior. It's windy outside, and every few seconds it seems to rattle my car. Winter is coming, and it promises to be a real bitch when she arrives.

"When you have to deal with a bullshit family like mine, you'd be tense too," I tell her, hating how negative I sound. I clear my throat. Try my damnedest to clear my mind.

But it's no use. I've got a beautiful girl sitting next to me, and all I can focus on is the upcoming shitshow that'll be dinner with my parents and brother.

"I think I have a solution to your problem," she says.

"Oh yeah?" I glance over at her to find she's undoing her seatbelt. Anticipation rises within me, and I lick my lips, ready for what she's got in store next.

And fuck, she doesn't disappoint.

"Push back your chair," she says as she comes for me. I do as she asks, hitting the button that sends the driver's seat backwards, a grunt leaving me when she crawls over the center console and straddles me, her legs spread and knees bent as they press on either side of my hips. She rises above me, lifting her arm and running her fingers through her hair so it flips all to one side and I just stare at her like a stupid, wordless fuck, completely mesmerized. The satellite radio is still playing, and it's on some stupid classic rock station Ryan forced me to listen to when we went to lunch earlier, just the two of us.

We talked shit out and I guess I felt better after we ate, but he still annoyed me. I'm still not over what he did to me after he left for college. He can't fix his abandoning us for years with a weekend visit and a few conversations.

"Try to forget," Ava murmurs, her fingers slipping beneath my chin and tilting my face up. She leans in, pressing her lips to mine and a soft moan leaves her when I part her lips with my tongue. I do my best to concentrate on how good she feels, how delicious she tastes, but I'm still sitting here thinking about my brother, my mind sort of distracted by this stupid ass song that's almost over.

Thank Christ.

Ava takes my hand and slips it inside the front of her dress, and I touch her warm skin, my fingers brushing against her hard nipple. I circle my finger around it, making her gasp, and she plunges her hands in my hair, messing it up as she starts to slowly grind on my dick. All thoughts of my stupid family problems disappear, just like that.

I can get into this.

"We have to hurry," she whispers, her hands dropping to the front of my pants, shaky fingers undoing the snap and sliding down the zipper. "We don't want to be late to dinner."

I let her take charge, leaning back in the seat as she reaches inside my spread open pants and strokes her fingers along the front of my boxer briefs, my erection twitching every time she touches me. The dress slips off her shoulders, falling to the crooks of her elbows, her entire chest exposed and all I can do is stare at her.

She's so beautiful. And eager. And all mine.

A new song comes on. I don't recognize it, considering it is old as shit and is probably one of my grandma's favorites, but the music is soft. Pleasant. Just a piano at first. Ava's mouth returns to mine and I close my eyes, my heart starting to race when her tongue strokes and teases, her hands wandering, the lyrics filling my head.

I'm in you.

You're in me.

Accurate. Fucking accurate for what I feel about this girl. She's kissing my neck. Licking my throat. Nibbling my chin. Making me shiver. Making me impatient with wanting her. I slip my hands beneath her dress, touching her hips, playing with the thin waistband of her panties. She rubs her pelvis against my cock, an impatient sound escaping her and when I touch her between her legs, I discover her panties are wet.

My girl is gonna want to fuck. Right here.

Right now.

"Do you have a condom?" she asks breathlessly.

I fumble around, flipping open my center console and pulling out one of the condoms I stashed in there a few weeks ago. I figured I always want to be prepared.

I'm like a fucking boy scout.

"Here." I hold the condom in between us and Ava swipes it from my fingers, tearing open the wrapper and holding the ringed condom between her fingers as she stares at me.

"Hurry," she pants.

Impatient, bossy, horny Ava is a new version of my girl. I like her. A lot. I somehow yank my pants and boxers down so they're bunched past my knees. Ava's slipped one leg out of her panties so they're dangling from her thigh, a scrap of sheer nude fabric. She rolls the condom on my dick and a hiss of a breath escapes past my lips when her fingers brush against me. I want more. I'd like a hand job and I wouldn't mind getting her off with my fingers, but she's restless. Her movements urgent.

It's going to be a one and done type of night for us.

She rises above me once more, her fingers around the base of my cock as she settles herself on me. Slowly she glides down, engulfing me in nothing but wet, hot, tight heat and I briefly close my eyes, leaning my head against the seat as I try and catch my breath. Her hands gripping my shoulders, she starts to move, and again, I let her do all the work. It's fucking fascinating, watching Ava ride me. Strain against me. I keep my hands on her hips, guiding her, controlling the pace.

Tilting her head down, her eyes flutter open and she stares at me, whispering, "Faster, Eli. Please."

Well fuck.

Moving faster, I lift my hips, driving deep inside of her, desperate to give my girl what she wants. She tosses her head back, chanting, "Don't stop, don't stop," over and over again, and I do exactly that.

I don't stop. Until we're both coming so hard, I swear to God, I see fucking stars. And when it's over, and our breaths have evened out some and we're clinging to each other, she presses her lips to my cheek and whispers, "Are you still tense?"

A chuckle leaves me. "Not really."

I can feel her smile against my face. "Then my plan worked."

I'm full-blown laughing, surprised by Ava and everything she does for me. Though I don't know why I'm surprised. I should expect the unexpected when it comes to her.

Yeah, I sound like the fucking Big Brother motto on TV, but fuck it. I used to love watching that show when I was younger. With my family.

My messed-up family.

Pushing them out of my thoughts, I concentrate on Ava. My beautiful, sweet yet dirty Ava.

"I love you," I say, tangling my fingers in her hair, grasping the back of her neck and bringing her in for a long, deep kiss.

"I love you, too," she murmurs, pulling away to smile down at me. "But we need to get going or we're going to be late."

* * *

WE ARRIVE at the restaurant with two minutes to spare, both of us kind of a mess. Once we get out of the car, we set to work on ourselves so we're more presentable. She straightens her hair and readjusts her skirt, then slips the red sweater on over her shoulders, dimming the magic that is Ava in that fuckin' sexy dress. I tuck my shirt back into my pants as neatly as I can and pray there aren't any come stains on the front of them. I do as thorough a search as I possibly can, considering there's not much light out here.

From what I can tell, they're clean.

"Do I look all right?" She turns to face me as we stop in front of the entrance of the restaurant.

My gaze roams over her, taking her in. She looks freshly fucked, but no way can I tell her that. She might freak out.

Reaching toward her, I tuck a few hairs behind her ear. Touch the corner of her swollen lips with my thumb, making her smile. Her chest is still flushed from our earlier sex session in the car and I regret ever leaving that spot.

We should've stayed there all night.

"You look beautiful," I tell her with all the sincerity I can muster.

She smiles. Blushes. "So do you."

"You like me all dressed up?" I spread my arms out a little, as if I'm presenting myself to her. To the world.

"Yes." Her murmur is low and throaty, and she takes a step toward me, her hand going to my shoulder as she rises up and presses a soft kiss on my jaw. "Let's go inside and get this over with."

I take her hand and we enter the restaurant. It's packed, but that's not surprising, considering it's Saturday night and this is one of the finer restaurants in the area. I spot my mom sitting among strangers on a long bench in the waiting area.

My brother and father are nowhere to be found.

"There you are!" Mom rises to her feet—steadily I might add—and makes her way toward us, grabbing Ava's shoulders and dropping a kiss on her cheek. "Look at you! Ava, you're gorgeous." Before she turns her attention on me. "Have you seen your father or Ryan yet?"

I shake my head and hug my mom. "Nope. I thought you were all coming together."

"So did I, but then Ryan took off right before you left to pick up Ava, and he never came back. He eventually texted me and said he was coming to the restaurant with Dad."

Great. What if they don't show up? Mom will be devastated and drown her sorrows in too much wine, or maybe harder liquor if she's really down in the dumps.

That's the last thing I want Ava to witness.

"You look stunning in that dress, Ava," Mom says, and Ava smiles in response, her expression downright bashful. The complete opposite of the girl in my car who climbed on top of me and rode my dick not thirty minutes ago. "Isn't she beautiful tonight, Eli?" Mom turns to look at me.

"She's beautiful every single fuckin' day," I say, making Ava laugh.

Mom scowls. "You use that word much too freely."

"No one's paying any attention to us. Don't worry." I get annoyed when Mom makes a big deal out of me cursing. Everyone says bad words. I'm no exception.

We stand there and talk for a few minutes, Mom glancing nervously toward the entrance what feels like every thirty seconds. Maybe she's as worried about this dinner tonight as me. She might not want to deal with it—with Dad, with Ryan, with all of us together, either.

The giant wooden door swings open, bringing with it a gusty wind and...

Ryan and my father.

I stand up straighter, my muscles seizing, my shoulders tense. Ryan heads for Mom, wrapping her up in a big hug before he approaches me. "Little brother. Not so little anymore," he says, a lazy smile curling his lips as he holds out his hand for me to slap.

Oh shit. I hope he's not drunk.

"Were you two out drinking just now?" I ask, ignoring his offered hand.

Ryan gives me a dirty look, dropping his arm at his side. "What are you trying to imply? That you disapprove?" His attention switches to Ava, and he turns on the charm. "Hey there, pretty girl. You're looking extra beautiful tonight."

He hugs her—a little too close and a little too long—while I quietly seethe. The fuck? Would Ryan really try and make a move on my girlfriend?

Wouldn't put it past him.

Asshole.

"Hi." She disentangles herself from him as quickly as possible, then scoots closer to me, her shoulder brushing against mine. "It's nice to see you again."

She's so damn polite. Really, she should tell him to go suck a giant dick for what he just did.

I sling my arm around her shoulders and haul her in close, staking my claim so no one forgets it. That's aimed right at you, Ryan Bennett.

Ryan just grins and glances around the crowded waiting area. "Is there a bar in this place?"

Yeah. The night just keeps getting better. Has my big brother turned into an uncontrollable drunk like our mother? At least this evening she's acting relatively sober. She might've had a glass of wine to calm the agitated nerves before she left the house, but at the moment, she appears perfectly normal.

Actually, she looks really nice. Her hair is smooth and

neat, and I don't spot a single gray strand on her darkish blonde head. She must've just got it done. I think she's even wearing a new dress. And...yeah. She has makeup on. Mom put some extra effort into it to impress Dad maybe? I almost feel bad.

He's not even paying attention to her.

"Who's this?" Dad asks, indicating Ava with a wave of his fingers.

"My girlfriend," I say proudly. "This is Ava."

"Nice to meet you," she says when Dad shakes her hand.

"Nice to meet you too." Dad catches my gaze and winks. Code for he approves.

The horny bastard.

I tuck Ava closer, filled with the need to protect her. I should've known.

This night is going to be fucking brutal.

CHAPTER 31

AVA

The entire evening has been surreal.

Sex with Eli in his car had been…addicting. No other word for it. It all happened so fast and then we had to go. I was the one who rushed everything, and while I regret it a little, I also loved how quick it was. How exhilarated the entire experience made me feel.

Like I want to do that again.

And again and again and again.

Once we showed up at the restaurant and straightened ourselves up in the parking lot, I couldn't stop staring at my boyfriend. He practically looks like an adult in the black pants and the white button up shirt, the first couple of buttons undone so it's open at the collar. He has a sexy businessman vibe going on tonight, and I can't get over the fact that he's all mine. That I was just having sex with him in his car not even an hour ago.

I did that so he'd have a fond memory to cling to tonight, instead of what could potentially happen here and now at the restaurant. So far, his family has been somewhat fine. His mother looks really nice, like she took extra care when she

305

got ready. I love her dress. She definitely appears more youthful than she did the last time I saw her.

Ryan hugged me a little too close when we first saw each other, but he also smelled like alcohol so I blamed liquid courage on that. His dad seems perfectly polite. I have no idea what his parents' actual first names are.

Kind of weird, but I'm not asking either.

I do what Autumn suggested and remain quiet through the first part of the meal. I don't speak until spoken to. I listen to the conversations around me. I nod and smile when I think it's necessary. I keep my hand firmly on Eli's rock hard thigh between the appetizer and main entrée, digging my fingers in when he says something a little rude.

It only happened twice, and my gouging fingernails seemed to do the trick.

By the time we're halfway through our meal, that's when things start to get tense.

"Ryan says you played a hell of a game Friday night," his father says to Eli.

Eli's lips get tight. His entire body tenses visibly. "I suppose I did. You'd know for sure if you actually came to a game every once in a while."

His dad completely ignores Eli's snide remark. "You gonna try and do something with that in college then?" He saws into the rare steak he's eating, spilling red juice all over his plate.

It kind of turns my stomach.

Eli sets his fork down with a clatter, startling me. Startling his mother as well. "What exactly do you mean by that?"

"I mean exactly what I said," his father says. "Are you planning to play ball in college like your brother?"

"I hope to hell I don't end up like Ryan, benched my junior year because I'm on academic probation and basically fucking myself for the rest of my college football career," Eli says, his voice dripping with disdain.

Oh dear. That was kind of an awful thing to say.

"Eli," his mother scolds, her voice low, her gaze narrowed as she glares at him. "Please don't say that word."

"What word are you talking about huh, Mom? *Fuck?* Is that the word?" Eli's voice raises, and I can tell he's ready for a fight.

"Hey." I rest my hand on his thigh, wishing I could calm him. Wishing I could ease his anger and pain. "Play nice."

He sends me a scathing look, realizing a second too late what he just did. I see the immediate regret in his eyes, it's written all over his face and he places his hand over mine, squeezing gently.

I wish I could sooth him. And I know I can, but right now I think any soothing techniques I try on him will be impossible. His family riles him up too much, and I can see why. They're not a real support system. They don't have his back. Seeing it in action makes me feel...

Terrible. Heartbroken.

For Eli.

"Let's watch you get out in the real world next year and see how well you do," Ryan throws at him, his expression full of disgust. "It's not as easy as it looks."

Eli scoffs. "I'm sure I'll do ten times better than you. At least I won't run away and abandon my family. Though I probably should. Not a one of you gives a shit about me."

I wince. God, he's making things worse.

But then again, he has to get his feelings out.

"Eli," his mother sighs, shaking her head. "You know we care about you. I love you. It's just been a hard time."

"No shit, Mom. I've probably suffered the worst from all of this," my boyfriend says indignantly.

"Jesus. Stop acting like a baby," Ryan says, his words for

Eli. "Grow some balls and man up. No one *abandoned* you. I've had my own shit to deal with. Not that you cared."

"I'd care if you actually talked to me," Eli flings at him, the pain on his face obvious.

But it's like no one can see it. They're all so wrapped up in their own problems, they can't see how much Eli is suffering. Or maybe I'm so attuned to him, I hurt when he hurts. And right now, my chest aches. My limbs are stiff with tension. I wish I could magically take away Eli's pain.

"Why would I want to talk to you?" The scowl on Ryan's face is horrible. He looks so mean. "If you're looking for advice about college life, I've got one thing to say to you. Good luck to you, asshole."

"Ryan," their mom snaps, grabbing her wineglass and draining it before she continues. "Please stop."

"You should take your own advice," Eli's father says to his ex, nodding toward the now empty wineglass. "And quit while you're ahead."

"Please," she snaps. "You lost your right to tell me what to do the minute you served me with divorce papers."

Oh, this is spiraling out of control and quickly. I feel like I'm at a tennis match, my head turning left. Turning right. A battle of wills, a war of words. Tossed back and forth like precise bombs aimed to nail their targets right where it hurts.

"You were hitting the bottle long before I filed for divorce," Mr. Bennett says with a chuckle. Like he finds all of this amusing.

So heartless.

"Right. Just like you were sneaking your little sluts into your office before we got divorced too," she snips.

"Okay." Eli tosses his cloth napkin onto his half-eaten plate and jumps to his feet. "I'm out. I don't need to listen to this."

"Sit down," his father tells him firmly, not even looking at his face. He's still busy cutting into his bloody steak, sopping up the juice before he shoves his fork into his mouth and chews.

I glance up at Eli, who's still standing, his hands curled into fists at his sides, a muscle in his jaw flexing from clenching his teeth.

"I don't have to sit here and witness you two throw insults at each other. Ryan, I'm sorry. I probably shouldn't have said all that shit to you, but I was mad. I still am, but I'll get over it." He glances down at me, his expression pleading. "Let's go, Ava."

I grab my purse from the floor and stand, smiling at everyone at the table. They're all glaring at us in return, and I feel kind of terrible, but Eli's right.

This dinner turned toxic quick.

"Thank you for including me," I tell them, smiling but letting it fade quickly when none of them smile back. "And thank you for dinner. It was delicious."

Eli grabs my hand and practically drags me out of the restaurant. I hear his mother call his name, but he ignores her. Swear to God I hear his brother yell his name as well.

But we keep walking, never once hesitating or looking back.

"That was shit," Eli says once we're outside and he takes in a couple of deep breaths of cold, fresh air. He releases his grip on my hand and rests his hands on his hips, gazing up at the sky as if he's trying to collect himself.

"It wasn't bad until just now," I say, tugging my sweater closer around me. It's freaking freezing. My bare legs are going to turn to blocks of ice if we stand out here for too long. Then I'd have to admit to Ellie that she was right. I definitely got too cold.

"They would've kept going if we hadn't left, and it

would've gotten worse," Eli says, his expression full of annoyance. His eyes flashing with pain. "I can't be around them when they're like that. I just—I can't."

My heart breaks for him. Without thought I go to where he's standing and wrap him up in my arms, holding him close. He hugs me back, his arms tight, his chest warm, and I lean my cheek against the spot where his heart beats, steady and strong.

"Thank you for coming with me. You didn't have to do that," he murmurs against my hair.

"I wanted to. That's the difference." I pull away a little so I can meet his gaze. "I tried my best to distract you earlier. Maybe it wasn't enough."

He actually grins, and I'm sure he's remembering our moment in the car. "Babe, that was hot as hell. I'm down for another session if you are."

I smile in return, excitement fizzing in my veins despite what just happened in that restaurant. The promise in Eli's voice wiped out all my nerves, just like that. "Sounds good to me."

We start for his car when I hear Eli's brother call his name. We both glance over our shoulders to find Ryan headed straight for us.

"Maybe if we're fast enough we can outrun him?" Eli glances over at me.

I come to a stop. So does he. "Hear him out. You did apologize to him. Maybe he wants to do the same," I say. "I loved that you did that, by the way."

"I felt like shit for what I said to him," Eli admits, his gaze darkening as he watches Ryan approach. "I was just— mad."

Curling my arm around Eli's, I smile up at him, but he's too tense to smile back. His attention is solely for his brother.

"What you said in there was kind of fucked up," Ryan starts, and Eli glares at him.

"I don't want to get into this," he says firmly. "I already apologized. And I'm not in the mood to fight with you right now, especially in front of Ava."

I stand up a little straighter, proud of him for saying that.

"Listen to me." Ryan steps closer, staring Eli down. He's a little taller than his younger brother, but Eli doesn't back up. I keep my hold on him, feeling the slight tremble in his arm. "I was going to say it was fucked up, but only because the truth hurts. You're right. I messed up my chance with the football team and I blew it. Because I'd rather party and fuck around instead of studying for tests and actually passing my classes."

Eli blinks at him but otherwise doesn't say a word.

Ryan sighs and takes a step back, shaking his head. "I wanted to tell you that if you do go to a four-year university and you get on their football team, don't fuck it up like I did. Stay focused. Do what you're supposed to do. Keep up with your classes. Don't drown yourself in alcohol and drugs and think that's going to make your life better. Newsflash—it doesn't help. At all."

Eli exhales heavily, his entire body relaxing. "Okay. Yeah. Thanks for the advice." He hesitates for only a moment. "I'm really sorry I said what I said to you."

"I'm sorry too. For ignoring you the last few years. For pretending all of you didn't exist. I'm tired of running away from my past. I need to face it head on. I've made a lot of mistakes, and I pretty much regret every single one of them. The biggest one being how horribly I treated you. You're my little brother. I should've been there for you more." Ryan smiles faintly. "Wanna get breakfast tomorrow before I leave?"

"Just the two of us?" Eli asks hopefully.

"Mom wants to come too, if you don't mind. I never mentioned it to Dad. And really...he shouldn't be around Mom. He riles her up," Ryan says.

"He riles all of us up," Eli agrees. "But—yeah. Let's do breakfast before you fly out. That'll be cool."

"Awesome." He slaps Eli's back. "I'm going home with Mom."

"What about Dad?" Eli asks.

"Eh, what about him? He's headed back to his bachelor pad. Says he has a date with some woman that he met on a dating app at a bar later." Ryan rolls his eyes. "I think he might be getting too old for this shit."

"Whatever keeps him happy," Eli says, and they chuckle.

It's a nice sound, and it makes me smile, hopeful for Eli.

Maybe he and his brother can make amends after all.

Ryan turns to me. "I'm pretty sure you're the one who's keeping my brother happy. For that, thank you." He hugs me, and this time, he doesn't get too close and it doesn't last too long.

It feels genuine. I hug him back.

"I'm glad you came home for the weekend," I tell Ryan as we pull away from each other. "You should do it more often."

Ryan laughs and points at me. "I like her," he tells my boyfriend.

Eli smiles, his gaze soft as it connects with mine. "I do too."

CHAPTER 32

❦

ELI

*W*e pull up in front of Ava's house to find someone sitting outside on the front steps, waiting for us in the dark.

"Who is that?" Ava asks, sounding nervous.

My car lights cut across the person's face and irritation fills me.

It's Jake.

"What does he want?" I mutter, throwing the car into park and shutting off the engine. I'd really hoped to kiss Ava for a few minutes before she went inside.

Yet again, Jake ruins everything.

"I don't know," Ava says, her gaze meeting mine when I glance her way. She must see something in my eyes, my expression. "Don't start anything, okay?"

"Who says I'm going to start anything?" I climb out of the car, on the immediate defensive. Tonight is not the moment for Jake Callahan to pick a fight with me. I'm already on edge. Even though the dinner ended on a relatively good note, I'm still not over what happened between my family.

What a douche my dad was. How we can't even get together for a few hours and have a civil moment together without it getting ruined.

I approach the Callahan's front door, my gaze on Jake as he rises to his feet and dusts his hands off on the side of his jeans. I hear the passenger door slam, clicking heels following behind me and I wish Ava would've waited in the car.

But she lives here and that would just be weird.

"You guys are late," Jake says, his deep voice extra authoritative. As if he's in charge around here. In his fuckin' dreams.

"Gee, sorry Dad, didn't know—" I pull my phone out of my pocket to check the time before lifting my head so I can glare at him yet again. "Cinderella here turned orange if she got home before eleven."

"Besides, my curfew is at midnight," Ava says to her brother. "We're actually home early."

Only because we messed around some more after dinner and now we're beat. We didn't get much sleep last night after Jackson's party, and we woke up early this morning. Plus that dinner was emotionally exhausting. I'm tired. My girl is too.

And here's Jake acting like the macho man. The head of the Callahan fam. What the hell ever.

Deciding the best way to approach a problem is head on, I switch gears.

"What are you doing?" I ask Jake, walking right up to him, until I'm practically in his face. "When are you going to get over your hate toward me?"

"Eli—" Ava starts but I glance over my shoulder real quick, silencing her with a look, feeling like a complete asshole the moment it happens.

My girl deserves more respect than what I just showed her, but I have to get this dude off my ass once and for all. We need to come to terms with each other.

"Probably never," Jake retorts, his eyes flashing with annoyance.

Hey. At least he's honest.

"Listen. You have to understand. Me and Ava? This is happening." I take a step closer, until I pretty much am in his face. He's a couple inches taller than me. A little bit broader too. And I can give it to him—he's a better quarterback than I am. It's in his genes, in his blood, in all the encouragement and coaching and training he's received his entire life. He's a prodigy, and he's going to go on and do great things.

But he needs to back the fuck off. I'm in love with his sister, and nothing is ever going to change that. He can't chase me away with a few scowls and shitty comments. I'm sticking.

Whether he likes it or not.

"Not if I have any say in it," Jake says, beating that same dead horse.

I never really did understand that cliché saying until now.

"See, that's the thing. You don't have a choice," I say, my voice low, my gaze locked with his. "I'm not going anywhere. Ava and I are in love with each other."

"You're not good enough for her," Jake says, his voice downright menacing. "I have no idea what she sees in you."

"I agree," I say easily, noticing the surprise that flashes in Jake's eyes. "You're right. I'm definitely not good enough for her. I don't know what she sees in me either."

I can feel Ava's approach. Can even smell her sweet, intoxicating scent. I remain still, the tension easing from me when she gently rests her hand against the center of my back. She's not saying a word to either me or her brother, but that little touch is enough for me to know that she's got me.

This girl, she's always got me. And I've always got her.

"You don't deserve Ava," Jake continues, after he clears his throat. "My sister is a good person. She always wants to fix people. That's probably why she's drawn to you."

His words are like a kick in the gut, but I remain standing tall when all I really want to do is crumple and fold. He's more than likely right about that, too. Ava is good and strong and caring. She wants to help people. Is that why she's with me?

Maybe. But I refuse to let his words creep into my brain and make me feel insecure. I know how she feels about me.

"I might not be good enough for Ava, but I'm going to do my damnedest to prove to every one of you that I care about her with all I've got," I say, my voice dead serious. "I love her. More than anyone else in this world. She owns my heart. She owns *me*. I know I'm a complete fuck up, and I'm sure I'll make her mad or frustrate her, but I will always beg for her forgiveness. Because she's mine. And I am hers."

Jake says nothing for a while, though I note the obvious tightness in his jaw. The judgement clouding his eyes. His gaze shifts to Ava and she steps forward so she's by my side, her arm curling around mine, our fingers interlocking. We're a united front against her brother. Us against him.

"You break her heart, I'll break every bone in your body," Jake finally says before he turns and heads for the front door, wrenching it open. He enters the house, slamming the door so hard, the fall wreath hanging there rattles, nearly falling off its hook.

Exhaling with relief, I glance down at Ava to see her staring at the closed door with a giant smile on her face.

"Why are you smiling?" I ask.

She tilts her head back, still wearing that beautiful smile. "My brother loves me. And so do you."

I lean in, dropping a gentle kiss on her upturned lips. "Yeah I do."

"I love you too." Ava touches my cheek. Trails her fingers down my neck, making me shiver. "More than you'll ever know."

Yeah. I get it.

I know.

CHAPTER 33

AVA

*S*ix weeks later

LIFE IS WILD, you know? Sometimes it drags and you think certain dates or moments in time are never going to get here. I remember feeling that way about homecoming. Then every weekend, when I could actually see Eli again. Once I got kicked off the cheer team—I never did go back, I couldn't stand the thought of dealing with Cami again—I lived for every Friday night, so I could watch my boyfriend play football, my best friend by my side watching the boy she's still crushing on.

Yes, Ellie is still stuck on Jackson, while he's put her firmly in the friend zone. It's so frustrating.

As Halloween loomed, it couldn't come fast enough. There was a big costume party I was dying to go to and Eli and I went together. It was *so* much fun.

So. Much. Fun.

Can't share too many details though. Let's just say there

were some tricks played. And a lot of treats received. Some alcohol was consumed. We wore matching costumes and Eli suggested I keep the wig on when we had sex later that night because it made me seem mysterious.

He's kind of ridiculous, but I love him.

November began and with it, football playoffs. The Mustangs lasted three weeks before getting beat by a great team. I sat in the stands every single game, wearing the #1 jersey he gave me and cheering him on. Eli took the loss in stride. He's already sent in his application to Fresno State. Asher Davis has been encouraging him, giving him pointers on a weekly basis. They've somehow become friends and get together almost every weekend. Autumn and I think it's funny.

Jake doesn't find it funny at all, which is no surprise. But he's become used to Eli being at our house all the time. I think Hannah helps him with that. She's so good for my brother. Their relationship is solid, and I know they're serious. Maybe even the forever kind of serious. Hannah soothes Jake's frayed nerves. I feel like I do the same for Eli.

What's funny is I've realized more and more that my brother and my boyfriend actually share a lot of the same traits. If you tell Jake or Eli that they're similar in any way, they freak out. That is the last thing they want to hear.

Too bad, considering it's true.

The Badgers are still in the playoffs. Their next game is the Friday after Thanksgiving, and Dad and Jake are both excited yet nervous. I'm sure they'll be fine. Eli and I are going to the game together. It'll be strange to sit in the stands with my boyfriend, but I'm sure I'll love every second of it.

Currently, it's Thanksgiving Day. I've been looking forward to this day for what feels like forever, and it felt like it was never going to get here. I've been so anxious and even a little nervous as the date approached. Why?

Eli is coming to dinner. And so is Ash. And Hannah. Ellie will stop by for dessert like she has for the last couple of years.

Oh, and my Uncle Owen and Aunt Chelsea, and their three kids are here too. Yes, I have three cousins and I adore every single one of them. Especially Blair, who's a year younger than I am and the sweetest girl alive, like my aunt Chelsea. Knox is Jake's age, an excellent football player, and named for my uncle's best friend, Wade Knox, former pro football player who was on my father's team for a few years.

And then there's Ruby, who's fifteen and absolutely gorgeous. She's really shy and quiet, with dark hair and the Maguire green eyes. As she gets older, she's going to be absolutely stunning and I think my uncle has a serious problem with that.

Like...serious.

Anyway, we've all gathered at our house for the Thanksgiving holiday this year just like we always do, and my sister and I have been in the kitchen with my mom and aunt all day, helping them cook. Autumn and I were in charge of appetizers, and Blair and Ruby helped us. They're all gone already.

The men in this house pretty much gobbled them up.

Mom fixed the majority of the meal, including the turkey, and Chelsea made her beloved mashed potatoes. We cheated and bought homemade pumpkin and apple pies from a local market that sells them fresh.

"Where's Owen?" Mom asks Chelsea as they both putter around the kitchen.

"Outside with Drew and the boys," Chelsea answers, glancing toward the window that faces the spacious front yard.

"What boys?" I ask, glancing at my phone. It's three-thirty.

Eli said he'd be here at three. He's late. Hopefully everything is okay.

"The usual," Mom says as she makes her way to the window. "Your brothers. Knox. Oh look, there's Eli. And I think he brought a friend."

Relief flooding me, I rush to the window to see who she's talking about. There's Eli out on the lawn with everyone, and they're playing football. Another Thanksgiving tradition.

"How are you two doing?" Mom asks in a low murmur.

I turn to find she's standing right next to me, her gaze gentle when it meets mine. "We're doing great," I tell her truthfully. I'm a lot more open with Mom now, when it comes to discussing my relationship with her.

"I like Eli a lot. You balance each other out," Mom says. "Remember what I said to you at the Fresno State game?"

I nod, but don't respond. Of course, I remember. Her words got into my head and filled me with worry over my relationship. Eli loves me. He needs me. But I think he also needs what I can offer, thanks to my family.

Stability. Someone who cares.

"He loves you. It's clear. And since he's worked some things out with his mom and brother, I think he's a better person for it," Mom says. "Though he still has stars in his eyes when it comes to you."

A blush steals across my cheeks. I have stars in my eyes when it comes to Eli too.

"You two are cute together," Mom says, reaching out to give me a quick hug. "I'm glad he came today."

"Me too," I say into her hair before we pull away from each other.

"Hey, Ava."

I glance over my shoulder to find my cousin approaching us, stopping to peek out the window.

"That's your boyfriend?" Blair asks me. I smile at her and nod. "He's super cute."

She's gone completely boy crazy over the last year and thinks they're all super cute, but I take it as a compliment, because I know Eli is very cute.

More like gorgeous.

And he's all mine.

Lucky me.

We're still messing around in the kitchen thirty minutes later when Beck rushes in, out of breath and full of urgency. "Dad says you all need to come outside."

"Beck, we're preparing dinner," Mom reminds him. "It's almost done. Tell your father they should come in soon."

"Everything's done right? That's what Dad said. He told me to tell you to turn off the ovens and let the turkey rest on top of the stove. That way, you can all join us outside," Beck explains.

Mom rolls her eyes. "Your father knows my Thanksgiving preparations too well." She goes to the double oven and checks on the dishes inside before she turns the ovens off. She then glances over at the stove, where the turkey is already resting. "Let's go girls. I'm sure your fathers are wanting to put together a team."

We all follow her outside to the front yard. When we were little, Dad would make every single one of us play football before we ate dinner. We'd complain, especially us girls, but he refused to listen to us. He knew we would all have fun playing, and he was always right.

It's a family tradition he started because, as he confessed earlier today at breakfast, "I didn't have the best Thanksgivings when I was younger."

Mom got a sad look in her eyes, and she reached over to grab his hand, giving it a squeeze. I'm curious to know what he's referring to, but I have left it alone. Whenever they're ready to tell us, they will. I have faith in that.

I have always had faith in my parents.

Now I understand why Thanksgiving is such a big deal to my mom. She's admitted before she never had good holidays either, thanks to her mom who never seemed to care much about her or Uncle Owen. My parents care so much, it almost feels like overkill. But I love it. We all do.

And now I appreciate their Thanksgiving spirit even more.

Eli comes jogging over to me the minute he spots me, wearing that black Mustang sweatshirt with the horse up on his hind legs. I shake my head when he gives me a kiss and he starts laughing. "What?"

"You wore that on purpose." I point at his hoodie. "Wanting to rile up Jake and my dad with your Mustang gear, hmm?"

"Nah." He glances down at it and shrugs. "It's my favorite hoodie."

"I thought the one you stole from me was your favorite," I remind him. That seems so long ago. At the start of last summer, when we went to football camp and he terrorized me.

More like he seduced me. I had no idea at the time that he would become such an important part of my life, and when you think about it, it really wasn't that long ago.

Like I mentioned earlier, life is wild.

"Oh it definitely is, but I keep that one safe. Don't bring it out too much," Eli says with a grin. "Hey, you gonna be on my team or what?"

"Depends on whose team you're already on."

"Your uncle's." Eli takes a step closer, his voice lowering. "He's my fucking idol, babe. I can't believe I'm going to play football with him, even if it's on your lawn on Thanksgiving."

"That's the best time to play with my uncle. He's ruthless. He will do whatever it takes to beat my dad and Jake."

Eli grins. "Sounds good to me."

"Well, lucky you, I play on my uncle's team too." It's tradition. Autumn's the original daddy's girl, so she's always on his team. Which is fine by me, because last year, we got Ash, plus Knox and Uncle Owen.

We won. Barely.

Now that we have Eli, it's going to be even better. Beck is on Dad's team and he'll mow us all over without hesitation. He just keeps getting bigger and has zero qualms in taking one of us down.

Dad's counting on that.

We all split up and get into position. It's a clear afternoon, though the sun is already waning, and the air is crisp and cold, the gentle breeze rattling the last brittle leaves still clinging to the trees. We run back and forth across the cool grass, all of us hollering at each other and we cause such a commotion, some of our neighbors come over and watch us play. They know our tradition as well, and some of them enjoy watching us.

So many football greats on one yard. Two retired pros. One current college potential draft pick. Three high school players. One youth player. A bunch of girls who are all pretty athletic, plus their mamas.

We're having so much fun, we continue playing late into the afternoon, until the sun is beginning to set and the air becomes nippy. Mom starts rallying the troops, demanding we eat before the turkey dries out and all the food gets cold. Dad hauls her up in his arms and carries her into the house, feeling triumphant after beating my side in the family game.

It makes my heart happy to see that smile on my dad's face. My mom's smile too. I'll do everything I can to carry on their Thanksgiving tradition as I get older. It's important to them, which makes it important to me too.

Isn't that what family's all about?

"Don't let it get you down, kid," Uncle Owen tells Eli as they enter the house together. Giving him a pep talk, so cute. "We'll beat them next year. I figured out what their secret weapon is, and I'll have to come up with a work around for it."

"What's the secret weapon? Beck?" Eli asks.

"Yep," my uncle says, just before they both start laughing.

We help Mom put together all of the food, grabbing spoons and various other utensils, digging out every single pot holder we've got so we can handle the many hot dishes. The table was already set this morning by Autumn and Ruby, and we all serve ourselves buffet style in the kitchen, before we make our way to the dining room.

"I want to say something before we start eating," Dad announces above the din of constant chatter.

We all go silent, our focus on him.

"It's been a really good year. We've had some ups and downs, but nothing too terrible. Nothing I can complain about. My family is happy and healthy, including my brother-in-law and his wife and children, plus we have some new members to our family joining us this year. Eli and Hannah, welcome."

We all cheer. Hannah looks a tad embarrassed. Eli grins, like there's nowhere else he'd rather be.

"Thank you for coming to my home and sharing this meal with me and my family. This holiday is important to Fable and I," Dad says. "When we got married, we vowed to each other that our family would always come first. No matter what. We've stuck to that vow all these years, and now you're all practically grown up. It's—unbelievable." He hesitates and smiles at Mom, who's watching him with luminous eyes. "We are so proud of our children and what they've become. And our nephew and nieces. You are all going to do amazing things someday." He smiles.

Mom sniffs. So does Aunt Chelsea. I think they might be crying.

"I'm grateful for every single one of you," Dad says. "Now let's eat!"

We dig in, and it's so delicious, there's not much talking at first. Just the sound of utensils hitting plates and low murmurs of approval. Until finally Jake speaks.

To Eli.

"You applied to Fresno State, right?" he asks him.

Eli nods. "Sure did. Applied to a few other schools too. How about you?"

"Wait a minute," I say, interrupting their conversation. I point my fork at Jake. "Did you just ask Eli a question? On your own?"

Jake shrugs. "What's the big deal?"

"You *hate* him," I stress.

"Not anymore. I mean, he's here all the damn time. I had to get used to him eventually, right?" Jake asks, making everyone laugh.

"I'm not going anywhere," Eli says firmly.

"Oh, Jake," Hannah says with a sigh, which makes all the women laugh.

"A miracle has occurred," I announce. "My brother no longer hates my boyfriend. I never thought I'd see the day."

"You're being stupid," Jake tells me, which earns him a cross look from Mom. She's not a big fan of that word. "Sorry. You're being, uh, ridiculous."

"Whatever. I'm just happy the war is over," I say as I grab an olive off my plate and pop it in my mouth.

Why do we always eat olives on Thanksgiving anyway?

It's kind of weird. Something I've never really questioned before either.

Huh.

"Babe, the war is definitely not over," Eli says firmly, slowly shaking his head.

I look over at him with a frown. "What do you mean?"

"After that game today? We were straight up robbed. We need to get our revenge. And we're already making plans." Eli glances around the table, making eye contact with my uncle. Knox. Then me once more. "Next year we beat these losers, am I right? We'll have their asses in a sling!"

Beck roars his approval with a, "Get bent! We're definitely gonna kick your asses again!"

Mom yells at Beck, who appears contrite. Then she sends Eli a stern look. He offers up a quick sorry.

It's like he's become a regular part of the family.

"You are so right. You're not going anywhere," I tell Eli softly, settling my hand on his thigh as everyone starts chattering at once. "And I'm so glad you're here."

"I'm glad you invited me." His mom is spending Thanksgiving with a bunch of her friends on the coast. The only way she'd leave is if she knew Eli was with us, which I think was a comfort to her. Their relationship still isn't perfect, but they're trying with each other. They go out for breakfast every Sunday. His mom isn't drinking as much anymore either. Eli even takes Muffin on the occasional walk. Their relationship is slowly healing, and I'm so happy for them. I've been over to their house too, more than a few times. We've all gone out to dinner.

Though his relationship with his father isn't the best, he and Ryan have been talking more. Ryan came home earlier this month, and they spent the majority of the weekend together. They talk all the time. Eli doesn't feel resentful toward his brother any longer. And Ryan isn't so twisted up and in hiding all the time. Slowly but surely, they're healing too.

That's all they can ask for.

"I love you," I murmur, leaning in and pressing a lingering kiss to his cheek.

"Love you too." He turns his head and delivers a smacking kiss to my lips. "Think we can find a secret spot somewhere to hook up later?"

I laugh. He's always got sex on the brain. "Maybe we could go to that one spot I showed you."

"I love that spot." He jokingly leers at me, and I laugh all over again.

And can't help but think how much I love this boy.

* * *

Diego and Jocelyn's story is next in Fighting For You, available now! Keep reading for a sneak peek!

FIGHTING FOR YOU

JOCELYN

"Come on."

His voice is urgent, with a hint of demanding in it. That's how he's been operating lately, and most of the time I don't mind.

Like now.

I take his offered hand and he links our fingers together, whisking me out of Tony's house through the back door and into the still warm night.

"Where are we going?" We're wandering through Tony's large back yard, passing people we know. I nod and smile, but don't really say anything. I'm too keyed up, too excited. The football team won tonight, which means my boyfriend is in a great mood. His good moods are hard to come by lately, and I'd give anything to keep him happy tonight.

Anything.

"I think his back yard is as big as my entire neighborhood," Diego mutters, and I silently agree.

Tony Sorrento's house is a freaking mansion that sits directly on the lake. My father's a lawyer, so we're pretty well-to-do, but our house isn't nearly as opulent as this one.

There are so many rooms, I get lost every time I go in there. And it's only Tony and his mother who live there.

What's sad is, most of the time, Tony is completely alone. His parents divorced a few years ago, and his dad moved out. He lives in San Francisco now. Or Los Angeles—I can never remember. His mother is never around. She's constantly going out of town. I think that's why Tony has so many parties.

He's lonely.

"Let's check out Tony's guesthouse." The wicked grin Diego flashes at me from over his shoulder makes my stomach bottom out. And not in a bad way.

In a very, very good way.

"Diego." I come to a stop and so does he, a questioning look on his too handsome face. "Are you suggesting what I think you're suggesting?"

He nods, hope and expectation written all over him. "When do you have to be home?"

I grab my phone out of the back pocket of my denim shorts and check the time. "Midnight. We have maybe an hour before you need to take me there."

"Thank God you don't live too far from here. We can get a lot done in an hour." He waggles his dark brows at me, making me giggle, and then he smothers my laughter with a heated kiss.

We only come up for air when we hear voices nearby, and then Diego's leading me toward the lakeshore, where the tiny one-room cabin/guesthouse sits. It's owned by the Sorrento family, and it sits unoccupied most of the time.

"I called dibs on this place," Diego tells me when we stop in front of the closed door. He rises up on tiptoe and feels around the top of the doorframe, a triumphant "aha" leaving him when he shows me the key he discovered. "Someone else always gets it first. But tonight, it's ours."

I'm a little skeeved out that the guys call dibs on this cabin so they can mess around with girls privately, but I can't complain. Diego and I only recently started having sex. We've done plenty of other things, but mostly in a car. Or sometimes even outside. It's hard to find somewhere to be together, completely alone. Forget about getting comfortable, or even taking off all of our clothes. It's always hurried between us, with that nagging worry we might get caught.

His house is small and he lives in one of the older neighborhoods in the area. I think he might be ashamed of it, which is why we don't spend a lot of time there. I've only been there a handful of times, even though I get along great with his slightly overbearing mother.

And my house? It's never empty. Mom is always there. Or one of my siblings. I get no alone time.

None.

Excitement ripples over my skin when Diego opens the cabin door and we walk inside. There's a couch and a bed. That's it. Oh and there's an end table next to the couch with a lamp on it. Diego lets go of my hand and walks over to the table, switching on the lamp and illuminating the room in a pale-yellow glow.

"Not bad," he says as he glances around the space. He rests his hands on his hips, his gaze meeting mine. "What do you think?"

"It's small." But it looks clean. "Do you think they wash the sheets?"

"Probably. The asshole has servants at his every beck and call." Diego pulls me back into his arms, holding me close. So close, I can feel every inch of him. And he can feel every inch of me. "Who cares?"

"I kind of do," I say, just as he leans in and presses his full mouth against my neck, making me forget all my worries at the first touch of his lips. I close my eyes as he continues to kiss me, immediately lost in the path his mouth takes on my skin. "Don't—don't you care?"

"I only care about you," he murmurs against my throat, making me shiver. "If you're not comfortable with the bed, we can take this to the couch."

I open my eyes, gazing at the leather couch nearby. "Uh, no."

He laughs and pulls away from me, keeping my hand in his. "Then let's go to the bed."

I let him lead me there, and we both fall onto the mattress, reaching for each other, our mouths seeking. Finding.

Locking.

We kiss for what feels like forever, and again, I lose myself in him. His taste, the stroke of his tongue, the things he whispers to me. How good I make him feel. How much he misses me. How much he *needs* me.

His words are heady. Sometimes even overwhelming. He wants so much. *Needs* so much. Sometimes, like tonight, he calls me his angel. His savior.

I don't know if I can save him, but I want to try.

We've been arguing lately, but kissing seems to make us forget why we were mad at each other in the first place. His hands start to wander and I lean into his touch, too nervous still to ask for what I want. His fingers drift across my stomach and I imagine those fingers in other places. The throb starts low, steadily insistent and when he reaches for the snap of my shorts, I settle my hand over his, stopping him.

"Not yet," I whisper, afraid he might get ahead of himself and it'll be over before we even truly started.

He doesn't protest or act mad, which he does sometimes. Instead, he reaches for my shirt, and I help him pull it off of me. He gets on his knees, rising above me on the mattress, his gaze scorching as he drinks me in.

"Fucking beautiful," he breathes, the look on his face, the reverence in his voice making me ache.

He loves me. So much.

I reach between my breasts and undo the snap, the bra cups springing away from my skin. He leans in, gently pushing them away, his fingers brushing against my skin, making me gasp. Without warning his mouth is on me, his lips wrapped around a nipple, drawing it deep into his mouth. The ache intensifies, making me squirm, and when he moves to my other breast, I sink my fingers into his thick hair, holding him to me.

I wouldn't mind if he did this for the entire hour. Kissing me all over. He's pretty good at it. He's gone down on me a few times, and the first time was kind of awkward, but it's gotten better. To the point where I almost prefer it to actual sex.

He has a really talented tongue.

I watch as Diego whips his shirt off, ruffling his hair when he jerks the shirt over his head almost violently. His chest rises and falls at a rapid pace, as if he just ran clear across the football field. He rubs his hand across the front of his shorts, a wince on his face when he touches his erection.

It's fascinating, how he handles himself. Almost…roughly. He catches me watching, his lips forming into that arrogant smirk he wears so often. The one that masks all the insecurity and pain that he carries within him.

Diego is all bravado. Deep down, he's a scared little boy who's afraid he'll never measure up.

"You like watching?"

Maybe I should be embarrassed he asked that question, but I'm not. "Yes," I say truthfully.

"Want me to get naked so you can really see something?"

I nod, my heart rate speeding up. We have the time and I'm curious to see him in all his naked glory.

Without hesitation he hops off the bed, shedding the rest of his clothes in seconds. Until he's magnificently naked, crawling back onto the bed, rising on his knees once again. I spread my legs, accommodating him as he scoots closer, and his hand automatically goes to his erection, long fingers gripping the base.

"This is all for you," he says, his voice full of promise as he starts to stroke.

I have no other boy to compare him to, but I'm fairly certain he doesn't lack in the penis department. He's long. The first time we did it, it hurt. And he was sloppy. He pumped inside me maybe twice—or was it three times?—and then he came.

All in all, it was a complete disappointment. Not that I would ever tell him that.

It's gotten better between us lately. Sad that our actual relationship is suffering a little bit, but the sex is good. Maybe we're using it as a band-aid. I don't know. I love him. I want to show him that I love him, but sometimes, he makes it really difficult.

This time when he reaches for the snap on my denim shorts, I don't stop him. I help him get rid of them, though I leave my panties on. He strokes me there, over the thin fabric, touching me with purpose.

"Soaked," he murmurs, sounding pleased, his fingers sneaking beneath my panties, touching my bare flesh. "Fuck, Jos, I don't know how much longer I can wait."

I want to ask him to go down on me, but the words don't come. Instead, I arch into his hand, lifting my hips, a little whimper sounding when he touches me in a particular spot. I haven't orgasmed yet when we've had actual sex, and I want to so badly. I've realized quickly I need lots of foreplay, and sometimes Diego is patient.

And sometimes, he's not.

He continues stroking me, his thumb slipping over my clit, back and forth. Circling it. I push my panties down past my hips, and he helps me until I'm kicking them off, and now we're both completely naked. He returns his attention to my breasts, sucking my nipples, licking his way down my stomach.

Oh God. His mouth is getting closer to where I want him. My breath catches in my throat when his face is right there, and when he licks me, a ragged groan leaves me.

"You like that," he says, just before he licks me again.

"I love it," I say on a sigh, a wave of pleasure washing over me when he slips his finger inside my body. His mouth on me plus his fingers inside me? I'm already close to coming. It didn't take much time tonight, and I hope he keeps it up. If he stops now, I'm going to—

Diego stops, lifting his head to look at me. His lips are glossy with my juices and he runs his tongue across his upper lip, as if he's savoring the taste of me. "Want me to keep going?"

I want to kill him. Why would he stop now? I was so close. "Yes," I say through gritted teeth and he laughs.

Like he knows exactly what he's doing, though I don't know if he's that smart. I'm not insulting him. We're only seventeen. We still kind of don't know what we're doing in the sex department.

He experiments on me. Licking faster. Slower. Circling his tongue around my clit, pressing his tongue flat against my flesh. He adds another finger. Sucks my clit between his lips, and it feels so overwhelmingly good. I finally find the courage to give him direction, and he takes it.

"Faster," I whisper and he speeds up.

"Oh, right there," and he listens, staying at that one spot, lavishing all of his attention where I want it.

"Right—please. Oh *God.*" I'm overcome. As in, I'm coming. Sounds are leaving me, but they're not quite words. I'm not making any sense. And it's okay. I'm moaning. Thrashing about, and Diego grabs hold of my hips, keeping me in place as he continues to torture me with his mouth.

"Fuck," he breathes when he finally moves away from my body, his dark eyes hooded, his lips parted as he gazes at me as if I'm the prettiest girl he's ever seen. "You need to come like that more often."

I need to come more often in general, but I don't say that. Our satisfying sexual encounters lately have been a little one-sided. But not tonight.

Tonight I'm satiated. I feel downright lazy. Sleepy even. I watch as he positions himself in front of me, his erection in one hand as he leans over and props his other hand on the mattress beside my head. He brushes the tip against me, slowly dragging it between my folds and I tense up, my eyes going wide.

"Do you have a condom?"

His expression is pained. "Fuck. I forgot."

I reach out, resting my hands on his shoulders to push him away. "You need to get one."

"You need to get on the pill," he throws back at me, sounding the slightest bit irritated.

This is one of the things we argue about. He hates condoms. I don't know where to go to get on the pill. I can't ask my mom. She'll freak. Plus, our town is so small. If I show up at our doctor's office, I'm almost guaranteed to see someone I know. Or someone my mom or dad knows. And we don't have a Planned Parenthood around here.

I don't know what to do.

"I will get on the pill, but that doesn't mean we won't use condoms still," I remind him. I don't want to get pregnant.

That would ruin everything.

He thrusts against my core nice and slow, slipping inside my body only a little, and he groans. "Just—let me do this. Only for a few minutes. I'll pull out. Promise."

He pushes deeper, and I silently agree it does feel good. Diego inside of me with nothing between us. Just skin on skin. His flesh in mine. He starts to move, and I move with him. Surprisingly, we find our rhythm quickly, and I wrap my arms around his neck, pulling him down so he has no choice but to kiss me.

Our tongues tangle and our heated breaths mingle. He grunts with every thrust, pushing me farther up the mattress, a little bit at a time, and then he's suddenly moving in earnest.

Fast. Hard. He lifts his body away from mine, his hands shifting to my hips as he drives inside of me. Again and again.

"Oh shit, you feel so fucking good—" Diego's head hangs back, his eyes sliding closed just when mine pop open. He's coming.

"Diego!" My sharp voice snaps him back to reality and he reaches between us, pulling himself out of me, and I feel a little dribble on my skin. Not enough though.

Not nearly enough.

Without a word he flops over to lie beside me, both of us panting, trying to catch our breath. I stare at the ceiling, hating the fear that slowly creeps over me, like a low moving fog, until I'm completely engulfed and it's all I can think about.

He came inside of me. And I'm not on the pill. What if...

What if?

ACKNOWLEDGMENTS

Thank you, thank you, thank you for being patient with me while waiting for the conclusion to Ava and Eli's story. When I started out on this journey of writing about the Callahan family, I never expected to include a duet in the mix. Ava and Eli had lots to say, and I hope Meant To Be was everything you expected from these two. This book ended up being 90,000 words - meaning I've written a total of 210,000 words about this couple. That's a lot. I think that's the most I've devoted to any couple I've created. More than Drew and Fable. More than Tuttle and Amanda. Wow…

I want to thank all the reviewers, book bloggers and readers who supported me this year. Who've been supporting me throughout all the years - I appreciate all of you so much!

Thank you to my beta readers, specifically Brittany E., Brittany U., Serena, Jan C and Lindsey. Your input was so valuable, and it hopefully made the story even better.

As always, thank you to my publicist Nina for all your help, and for being there for me when I ramble, and when I need to plot and plan. To the entire team at Valentine PR - thank you. I can't do this without you.

It would mean everything to me if you could take a few moments and leave an honest review for **Meant To Be**. Thank you.

THE PLAYERS

Playing Hard to Get

Playing by The Rules

Playing to Win

WEDDED BLISS (LANCASTER)

The Reluctant Bride

The Ruthless Groom

The Reckless Union

The Arranged Marriage boxset

COLLEGE YEARS

The Freshman

The Sophomore

The Junior

The Senior

DATING SERIES

Save The Date

Fake Date

Holidate

Hate to Date You

Rate A Date

Wedding Date

Blind Date

THE CALLAHANS

Close to Me

Falling For Her

Addicted To Him

Meant To Be

Fighting For You

Making Her Mine

A Callahan Wedding

FOREVER YOURS SERIES

You Promised Me Forever

Thinking About You

Nothing Without You

DAMAGED HEARTS SERIES

Her Defiant Heart

His Wasted Heart

Damaged Hearts

FRIENDS SERIES

Just Friends

More Than Friends

Forever

THE NEVER DUET

Never Tear Us Apart

Never Let You Go

THE RULES SERIES

Fair Game

In The Dark

Slow Play

Safe Bet

THE FOWLER SISTERS SERIES

Owning Violet

Stealing Rose

Taming Lily

REVERIE SERIES

His Reverie

Her Destiny

BILLIONAIRE BACHELORS CLUB SERIES

Crave

Torn

Savor

Intoxicated

ONE WEEK GIRLFRIEND SERIES

One Week Girlfriend

Second Chance Boyfriend

Three Broken Promises

Drew + Fable Forever

Four Years Later

Five Days Until You

A Drew + Fable Christmas

STANDALONE YA TITLES

Daring The Bad Boy

Saving It

Pretty Dead Girls

ABOUT THE AUTHOR

Monica Murphy is a New York Times, USA Today and international bestselling author. Her books have been translated in almost a dozen languages and have sold millions of copies worldwide. Both a traditionally published and independently published author, she writes young adult and new adult romance, as well as contemporary romance and women's fiction. She's also known as USA Today bestselling author Karen Erickson.

- facebook.com/MonicaMurphyAuthor
- instagram.com/monicamurphyauthor
- bookbub.com/profile/monica-murphy
- goodreads.com/monicamurphyauthor
- amazon.com/Monica-Murphy/e/B00AVPYIGG
- pinterest.com/msmonicamurphy
- tiktok.com/@monicamurphyauthor

Printed in Great Britain
by Amazon